CHRONICLES
OF THE
LAST DAYS

I0663205

AMELIA SMITH

ISBN-13: 978-1-941334-18-8 (paperback)

ISBN-13: 978-1-941334-19-5 (ebook)

Published by Split Rock Books

Cover and book design by the author.

Cover illustration is a detail from "Landscape with the Fall of Icarus," circle of Pieter Bruegel the Elder, ca. 1590-1595.

The title font is Canto Brush Open, and the text is set in Starling Book, both by The Font Bureau.

Table of Contents

Theranis
land of the dragons

Seiganum

Teganum

Onarun

Naramun

Anamat

Lemirun

Slaradun

Galamun

Helanum

Getedun

Kiralun

Tiadun

ANAMAT CITY

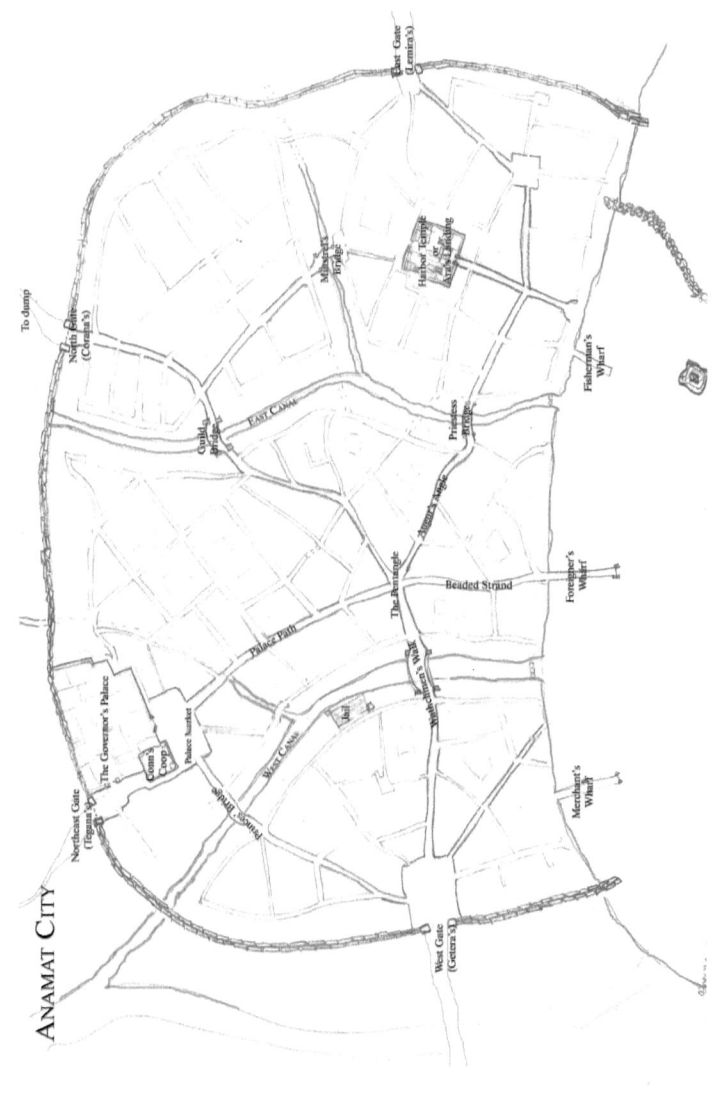

Character and Place Names

Core characters:
>Darna
>
>Thorat
>
>Iola
>
>Myril

Priestesses of Ara's Landing
>The Aralel, Nalani, head of the temple of Ara's Landing
>
>Lenasa, daughter of the prince of Galamun
>
>Savasa from the ruling family of Onarun
>
>Ganie, a former scrappling
>
>Sunna
>
>Taira, a librarian
>
>Jasela, ambassadress before Iola
>
>Irean, an older peresi
>
>Illaya, mistress of the old governor
>
>Geta, an elder in charge of the temple's baking

Defenders
>Eppie
>
>Sovara, the Enatel (heir of Enat)
>
>Garren, the West Gate baker
>
>Raina
>
>Ferrent
>
>Anot
>
>Varin
>
>Thorat
>
>Sunna (also a priestess)
>
>Harron
>
>Tennest
>
>Konnat (the former Enatel)
>
>Amigat

Bandits
> Larn
> Gran
> Forlan
> Kendet
> Vigda
> Gennie

Miscellaneous people in and around Anamat
> Parnet, the governor
> Tiagasa, his mistress, formerly a priestess of Ara's landing
> Giri/Girizit an officer of the Cerean king
> Squid, Eppie's former friend
> Lerat the Roper
> Pannen, head of East Market Boys, later a watchman.
> Chief Chronicler
> Tevan, a planners' guild member, later Darna's lover
> Nira, Darna's scrappling rival, abducted by Cereans
> Elna, was part of Darna's gang, went back to provinces.
> Luka, a weaver
> Venntental, a Cerean trading captain
> Raggy, a dog, guards the planners' guild hall.
> Tanest, candidate for Governor
> Orla, an innkeeper

People associated with Tiadun
> Terenet, prince of Tiadun
> Gallia, his mistress
> Calar, brother of Terenet, Darna's uncle
> Hedrin, son of Calar, Darna's cousin
> Renar, son of Calar, Darna's cousin
> Duke of the Southern Reaches

People associated with Slaradun
    Ivanat, the prince
    Kinner, page and keep steward-in-training
    Harzet, his Cerean advisor
    Ciffolga, a priestess
    Nolerin, an Enomaean horse handler

People from legend
    Ara
    Enat
    Conn, the first chieftain
    Morat, his son

Places and their dragons
    Anamat – Anara, Colors: red and gold
    Tiadun – dragon, Tiada, Colors, blue and orange
    Kiralun, Kirala, colors: Coral and white
    Slaradun/Salara, color dark green
    Helanum – Helana
    Teganum – Tegana
    Onarun – Onara
    Coradun, Corana" famous for apples"
    Galamun – Galara
    Getedun – Getera
    Naramun – Narama
    Seiganum – Seigana
    Lemirun – Lemira
    Na, Na's hills/peaks

Countries
    Theranis
    Cerea
    Ganat
    Enomae (main port, Calandria, principal god, Farseer)

Chapter 1

It was a perfect late spring day. Scrapplings made their way to Anamat on dusty feet, the wet prows of trading ships plowed into the harbor, and the markets stirred to life again after the long rainy winter. Only Iola, the ambassadress in her high-walled temple, felt a chill as the sun rose, or so she said later. She felt the earth tense beneath her back. Myril, despite her so-called gift of prophecy, felt nothing unusual that morning, though she knew that a change was coming.

The dragon Tiada had died, or gone to join the deepest stream, which is what a dragon does when they die to the world on the surface. Myril knew that Salara had changed and become a wild dragon. Those things would surely change human life on the surface of the dragons' land, as the dragons changed the faces they showed.

As the first rays of the sun touched the rooftops of Anamat that morning, golden with thatch and red with shining tiles, Myril did not think so much of the dragons. Soon, the gates would open and the farmers would come to the street where she lived, seeking healers and soothsayers. She was known for her herbs and simples. Bottled cures lined the back wall; the window looked out on the street, quiet in the early morning.

Up and down the street, some of the signs advertising cures or fortune-telling were missing, taken down as the trading season came in with more foreigners than ever. Many soothsayers and healers had grown wary, though they were not yet as frightened as the young priestesses in the lesser temples. Some of those were going to Ara's Landing, hoping to be safe there, safe from the foreign sailors who did not see their dignity. It didn't take a prophet to see that their refuge could not last.

One of the new soothsayers at the top of the hill had taken her sign down the past quarter-moon day, after a Cerean sailor demanded that she spread her skirts for him. She had never even been a priestess. The foreigner came in uninvited, when she was alone. She had a knife on hand and dissuaded him from raping her, but his intrusion left her shaken, as it would anyone. Some go on despite their fears, but that young woman left, gone into the villages or the hills, her freshly carved sign gathering dust in her vacant room. That was even before the change in the face of the earth.

Myril shook herself back to the present. The Chronicler had summoned her, and it was time to go, before the streets became too clamorous. Instead of dressing in her usual plain brown tunic, she put on the inky robes of her occasional guild. She latched the door behind her and bound it with a charm. On the street, she kept her head down and her hood up, but it wasn't enough to block out the clank and clatter, the chatter, the shouting from far away. She took the second-most-direct route to the Chroniclers' hall, up the hill to the Pentangle, then to the right, back down again along a quiet residential street, and across the canal to the northeast quarter and the guildhall.

She was crossing Guild Bridge when the stones faltered beneath her feet. For one glorious moment, there was total silence. The air was empty; she floated free. Myril's eyes – never as sharp as her second sight – saw a blurry shift in the skyline as she regained her balance. The smell came next, the smell of ash and fire and earth cutting over the familiar wet, green smell of the canal. Then the earth screamed.

The sound was far away and so quiet that no one else in Anamat would have heard it, but Myril thought that the earth screamed. Then again, maybe it was only the sound of the dragon Salara exacting revenge as his mountains sheared into the sea. Water came next. Waves crashed on the shore of the harbor, shook the breakwater, and rolled over it as the mountains far away shook like the pebbles. Still, the city stood. Myril could see it holding firm as the earth beneath it shuddered, but a huge wave rolled up from the sea, crashing foamy along the banks of the canal below.

Myril sprinted for the shore before it splashed past the bridge. She ran until her bones shook and the sound of the rushing water almost drowned out the shouts and screams around her. At a corner, she stopped, heart thundering, and leaned back against a building to gather her breath. Up above, the sky was still clear blue. Light, white clouds stretched over the mountains, but to the west, one cloud was gray, another fire. She couldn't see through the haze over Na's peaks with her ordinary sight, so she knew that whatever was happening sprang from the dragons. Despite Anara's absence in the sky, Myril had felt that already, but seeing those clouds made her sure.

The sound of the waves roared up again, and she felt as if the water was chasing her all the way to the guildhall door.

Inside, guild members and the green apprentices hurried in every direction, running to secure the scrolls that had rolled off their shelves. Folios slid across the slippery floor; ink had spilled. The guildhall was on high ground, so the water hadn't reached it, and the roof and walls still held. It was safe for the moment. Myril went straight to the master's study, where she found the master of the Chroniclers' Guild standing still as a statue in the midst of the building chaos, his white beard as unruffled as ever.

His eyes flicked to Myril as she entered, but he said nothing at first.

"You sent for me?" she said.

"Myril," he said. "Help me put these things back on the shelves."

The ground had quieted. When Myril stopped to listen, she heard only human voices and birdsong in the air and other ordinary sounds along the ground. The faraway earth had stopped screaming. She bent to pick up the fallen scrolls and set them back in their proper places. It didn't take long to put the study back in some semblance of order.

An apprentice appeared at the doorway as she set the last scroll back in its place. "Is there anything you require of us?" he asked the master.

The guildmaster shook his head, but his wave of dismissal stopped in midair. His hand trembled slightly.

"Secure the hall," he said. "Admit no one except our own guild members and apprentices. Set everything to rights, then go back to work on the catalog."

The apprentice bowed. "Will that be all?"

The guildmaster tipped his head, as if listening. "Tea for myself and my guest, if there's any to be had."

"Certainly." The apprentice bowed again and hurried away. The guildmaster sank into his leather-backed chair with a long sigh, like the sigh of the sea running back down the canals outside. There was a long silence before he spoke again.

"I will have to go to the palace," he said, looking down at his folded hands.

One of the elder guildsmen peeked in. "Pardon me," he said. "I thought you should know that the canal water has risen. It's halfway up the banks."

"Move all of the scrolls from the lower level to the attic, then," the guildmaster said without looking up.

Myril's guild-fellow nodded and went off, looking distressed.

"Will the waters rise higher?" the guildmaster asked.

It took Myril a moment to realize that the question was directed at her, in case her other sight had told her anything.

"I don't know," she said, after a moment's reflection. "The canals might spill over their banks, but not by much. They won't go much higher this season, I don't think. The earth feels quiet now. The waters will keep to their new bounds until the dragons shift the earth again."

"And when will that be?"

"I don't know. They have their own law; they're not like us, as anyone knows. Midsummer or Midwinter are the likeliest times, but I can't foresee anything."

"It's a wonder they've taken so long to shake us off," he mused.

"They haven't shaken us off yet, but –" She shook her head and shrugged. "There's so little we can do. Why did you call me here yesterday?"

"Well, I called you here when I thought that the foreign traders were the worst of our worries. Only earlier this morning, that was the most I was worried about." He let out a mirthless chuckle. "If the waters rise further and soon, then none of this will matter; the Chronicles of Anamat will be doomed by the dragons themselves."

"Maybe we can still save something?" Myril said.

Another head appeared in the doorway. "The lower level is still dry," a young man reported.

"Good," the guildmaster said. "Clear it anyway."

While the young man's footsteps padded away, the guildmaster motioned for Myril to close the door. After that, he spoke very quietly. She could hear him well enough, but it was hard to block out the worried voices from outside, both in the guildhall and on the streets.

"Are you aware of the emissary from the Cerean king?" he asked her.

"Of course. At least, I know of him. I haven't seen him."

"He's a fat young man, arrogant and grasping. Girizit, they call him."

The name sounded familiar, but Myril avoided the company of Cereans and of anyone except those who came to her door. She couldn't possibly know him, could she?

"He's about your age, or even a little younger, quite young to hold such authority to trade on the king's behalf, but he speaks our language well. Perhaps the king thought it would gain favor with our young governor to see someone even younger than himself, a peer of sorts."

The governor was only a few years older than Myril. His mistress Tiagasa had been initiated as a priestess the year before Myril had been. Tiagasa had never taken a petitioner other than the future governor, despite her ambition to become ambassadress. Life as the governor's mistress seemed a much better place for her to grasp the power she desired, but she still harbored a grudge against the temple and the Aralel for choosing Iola over her.

The guildmaster had fallen into a pensive silence. "Go on," Myril said.

"Apparently, part of Girizit's task here is to bleed us of what little wisdom we have left. The governor is collecting scrolls and histories, allegedly for the palace library. I believe they will be sent as tribute to Cerea."

The earth had just been shaking beneath their feet. The day before, when that quake had been only the faraway impulse of a provincial dragon, handing over Theranis's wisdom to Cerea would have been appalling. It still was, but the rising waters made it seem like a much smaller indignity. The whole record of Anamat's existence could be swallowed up at once if the earth and sea shifted again, and it would; the only question in Myril's mind was when it would happen. She felt the world sitting unsteady on the backs of the dragons.

"What do they want with our histories?" she asked. "Surely, the Cerean king can't read them."

The guildmaster leaned forward, resting his bearded chin on one hand. "I'm not entirely sure of that," he said. "The Cereans have a cold understanding of the world. They seem blind to the power of the dragons even as they grasp at it, and yet their rulers display more wisdom than our princes do, or at least more desire for knowledge."

"That wouldn't be difficult." Theranian noblemen aspired to a shallow image of manhood. They embraced swordsmanship and hunting, and eschewed the priestessly arts, leaving reading and writing to their secretaries.

"The Cereans value learning. They understand that it gives them power, more power than their clumsy swords do. If the Cerean king does not read our language, his scholars, including this Girizit, do."

A chill ran through her. "And what do they do with that knowledge?"

"Having killed their own dragons long ago, I believe they mean to chain ours by using the knowledge in our histories, coupled with the dragon stones they've already stolen. They want to enslave our dragons."

"As they enslave their women."

"Yes. Exactly." The guildmaster sat back. "I don't like to think that they *could* do it, but if it's possible – and I'm not saying it is – I don't want to help them."

"If they try, even if they fail, it will anger the dragons. This rising water, this morning's quake, will be like nothing," Myril said. There was a pattern to the change stirring beneath them. She didn't know quite what it was, but she could feel it gathering. "Meanwhile, they'll learn that they need priestesses to reach the dragons."

"Priestesses as slaves. After Tiadun's prince was killed last year and his brother's Cerean allies settled in, almost all of the province's priestesses disappeared from Tiadun. One hopes that they went to the hills, but one fears –"

Myril nodded. "Some of them have come to Ara's Landing," she said. "I think that most of them are safe, but I can't blame them for leaving." What would be the purpose, when there was no dragon to call up in the rite? The prince of Tiadun had been killed on a boar hunt. It had been an attempt to take the throne, and he might have succeeded except that his old brother's mistress had come to Anamat to state her case – that Calar, as a murderer, could not succeed his brother, and that the prince had sired a child, albeit a girl, one who happened to be a friend of Myril's. In the ordinary course of things, the old governor's mistress and her fellow priestesses would have ruled while the succession was decided, but instead, Calar and his allies had run them out of the province.

Outside, a tile slid off a roof and shattered on the paving stones below.

The guildmaster glanced over his shoulder, as if giving a nod to the outside world. "I worry for the priestesses, but I summoned you in hopes that they could help us. You say this morning's quake is the dragons' work?"

"Salara's. Salara has become male, like Na. I think the scream came from those hills."

"Most interesting!" The guildmaster seemed strangely delighted by the news.

"It sounded as if the mountains were falling there. I can't be sure, but someone is bound to come across the mountains to bring the news before long."

"Soon enough," the Chronicler agreed. "In any case, I called you here to help me keep the scrolls – our rarer and more secret ones – out of the governor's palace. I'd hoped that the Aralel would house them in the temple. It's on lower ground than we are, but the library tower is high. I believe they'll be safer there than here."

"A little bit safer," Myril said. Tiagasa still had eyes and ears in the temple, but not the unchecked power she and the governor had in the palace.

The guildmaster sighed. "We should wait to see if the waters go back down or rise further. That might change things. Meanwhile, ask the Aralel if she can help us, and look for any other safe place where we might keep our scrolls. I don't think the Cereans will cease their grasping if they see us floundering. If we are drowning, it will only bring them faster."

The Cereans would swoop in like vultures, joined by the Ganateans and maybe even Enomaeans. Myril shivered at the thought, glad that her room was on the second story and halfway up a hill. She could see the waters clearly in her mind's eye. They would not draw back. She wished she was blind to all of it and far from the city, but she would not go to the hills where Na, the wild dragon, reigned.

The guildmaster got to his feet and brushed himself off. "I leave you to it," he said. "Now I must see to our guildhall and to our Lord Governor."

§

The streets were disheveled but all in their places. Shopkeepers were sweeping their stoops and neighbors gathered, whispering and pointing to the roofs, discussing beams, cracks in the walls, and where any laborers or tradesmen might be found, whether it was worth paying their fees with the ground still unsteady beneath them.

A scrappling hurried through the square with a soggy satchel on her back, eyes wary, looking for a new place to hide. Myril paused as a half-dozen Cerean sailors sauntered up to the scrappling, speaking excitedly among themselves. They pushed one of their number forward as the others circled to block the girl's way.

"Little girl," the man said with a toothy smile.

"I'm not a little girl," the scrappling mumbled. She tried to back away but one of the other sailors pushed her forward again.

"Come with us, little girl. We go to a place where there is solid ground. You can have a nice bed, like priestesses." He chuckled as the girl looked for an opening. The circle of sailors closed tighter around her.

The scrappling girl spat on the ground and cursed them. The neighbors seemed too preoccupied with their own troubles to hear what was happening already. How could they not see? Myril's hands shook and her pulse quickened. She wanted to run away, but the scrappling needed help and fear froze her in her tracks. Maybe she could do something. The morning's quake had shaken the bonds that held the city together in more ways than one. She turned to face them, resolving to break in and at least distract the sailors.

One of the men – not the one who spoke Theranian – was grabbing the scrappling by her upper arm when a shout startled them all, a command in the Cereans' language. The sailors backed away from their prey and turned to face the newcomer. He was a Theranian, dressed in a strange combination of clothes – a Cerean tunic and a Ganatean scarf with Anamat-made sandals and belt, all of the finest workmanship. At his next command, the sailors bobbed their heads and hurried away in the direction of the harbor.

Myril knew him; she had touched him once, a long time ago. She shuddered at the memory of falling into the rite until the trance swallowed her whole and would not release her. The man had been naked then except for a petitioner's loose-wrapped cloth. Even the sight of him made Myril feel the old tug of trance. She turned away but it was too late – he'd seen her, recognized her.

"Is that you, Blessed One?" he asked. As he approached her, he lost all the air of command he'd had a moment before.

"I don't take that title anymore. I haven't for a long time." Myril focused on the small but solid things around her, like the details of the splatter of mud on the paving stones, the way the sunlight struck the rooftops.

"You should not be walking alone," he said.

Myril laughed at that. How else would she walk? "You sound like a Cerean, Lerat."

He smiled. "You do remember me, then. I've been a long time in their country, but as you can see, I've returned." A look of concern crossed his face. "They want what we have, and I don't want to see my homeland destroyed, not even the scrapplings. Especially not the scrapplings. I remember being one myself. No Theranian child should go with Cerean slavers like those."

"They followed your command."

He shrugged. "I can stop a few for now. They know a captain when they see one, but if more come –" He looked around and shook his head. "When word of this quake reaches Cerea, I fear that looters will take their chances with the governor and their king. Some of the merchants have been talking of raiding Anamat for years now. The governor's guardsmen and the city watch aren't strong or numerous enough hold them off. "

"They're only meant to dissuade pickpockets and keep the bandits to the hills," Myril said.

"Exactly. Our governor wouldn't be able to stop them even if he wanted to try."

Myril thought then of the Chronicles and what might happen to them if the waters continued to rise or if looters overran the city. She looked at Lerat again, more closely. The dragons might be out of sight, but perhaps they had sent him to cross her path for some purpose. She should not shrink away from the chance. Lerat was still handsome, but the sun had beaten many lines into his visage since the last time she'd seen him. She felt the distance in his eyes, the oceans he'd crossed more casually than she crossed the canal. He looked different. Years had passed, but he had pledged to help her if she ever had need. The texts were the guild's work, not her own, and he would not be obliged to help. Perhaps she shouldn't ask, after all.

"I have to be going. I'm sure you do, too."

He smiled at her, an open, friendly smile. "At the moment, I'm in no hurry," he said. "Let me walk with you."

Myril could think of no good reason to refuse his offer. It would be easy enough to find her if he wanted to – the place she lived was no secret. He held his hand out to take her arm, but she whisked it away before he could make contact.

"Don't touch me, please. You remember what it's like for me?"

"Still?" he asked. "That's a pity."

It wasn't a crossing time but she didn't want to risk being towed under in trance, with the world so unsteady around her and marauding Cereans waiting to take any priestess – or even scrapplings – away into slavery.

"I only touch others as I must, as a healer."

"You're a healer?" Lerat said. "That's a good trade."

"I'm also a Chronicler," she said, indicating her ink-black robes.

At that, he only nodded, indicating that she was to lead the way. They set off at a brisk pace over Guild Bridge, which held steady though it was still wet from the errant wave that had run up the canal. As they reached the top of the fortune-tellers' street, Myril decided to ask Lerat for that favor anyway.

"I know very little about the world beyond our shores," she said. "Are there libraries in other lands? Preferably out of reach of the Cerean king."

They stopped walking while Lerat considered the question. From where they stood, they had a good view down to the harbor. It was different from how it had been at dawn. The ships lay close to where they'd been, except for the ones that had been tied to the docks. Those had moved out to anchor. Sailors scurried over them, making repairs and bailing water out of their bilges.

"There must be libraries," he said after a while. "I've never traded much in texts, mostly in the crafts of Anamat, the gold of Cerea, spices from Enomae, and sometimes marble from Ganat. It depends on the season and the prices. I will make inquiries about libraries. I believe there are some in Enomae, away from the coast."

Myril spoke quietly. "We need some safe place to save the histories, and the texts which teach some of the priestesses' arts. The Cerean king – I believe he means to use them to try to control us. You would not have that, would you?"

Lerat shook his head. "No. I've lived in Cerea, and it's a good enough place in some ways, but they will grasp at everything and everyone that might give them a bit more power over other nations. They think only of military might in Cerea, to the detriment of their...well, of their relations with women."

Myril nodded. "They don't understand what we are."

"Not at all," he said. "It would be best for the wisdom of Anamat to remain here, safe from them."

"If the land lasts, yes, but if all of Theranis falls into the sea, as Slaradun did –"

Lerat placed his hand on her arm to stop her, and she felt a jolt like fire. She heard him apologize through the fog clouding her vision.

"What is this you say about Slaradun falling into the sea?" he was asking. Myril pulled herself back to the present, one breath at a time. "Is it worse than this rising of the seas in Anamat?"

"It is only visions now," Myril said, not looking at him. "I don't know exactly what happened. In a few days, I expect that we'll see people who have come from there, who can tell us what they saw."

"A few days?"

"It's three or four days' walk from here to the far side of the mountains."

"I can't stay that long," Lerat said with a frown. "I must sail to Ganat and back before Midsummer. I was going to leave this morning, but then this." He gestured to the harbor. "That's my ship, there." He pointed to one of the ones being bailed out. "I think we will sail on the next tide. When I return, seek me out. I'll be back in a moon-round."

"It will be nearly Midsummer then," Myril said.

"That's why I must sail today," Lerat said. His hands were thick; they looked strong, but he seemed like a kind man. Her memory of the fear of trance had obscured those other memories of him. "Let us go on," he said.

They started down the street. Many of Myril's neighbors were still outside, bedclothes wrapped around them, talking in tight knots, wary. Some turned to look at Lerat. Even Myril, who did not like to lie with men, could tell that he was uncommonly handsome.

"You've been in Cerea," she said. "Do you know anything of this Girizit who has the governor's ear?"

Lerat frowned and looked around. "Yes, everyone in Cerea does, but I won't speak of it today. I'll tell you some of what I know when we meet again, and if I can discover and of these libraries you seek."

It was a bribe, to make her seek him out when he returned, but a fair enough one. Myril nodded.

"I hope that you will accept my hospitality," he said. "I invite you to dine aboard my ship when I return at Midsummer, if you don't mind going on the water."

Myril had, as a young priestess, been especially prone to trance around water, whether it was a bath or a fountain. For a while, it had had such a strong pull on her that she couldn't even drink plain water. She was surprised that he'd remembered that.

"It doesn't matter if I mind the water; it's coming anyway," she said. She stiffened her thoughts against the tide of visions.

"Ask for me at Merchants' Wharf, if it's still there in a moon-round," Lerat said.

They had reached the entrance to Myril's place. "I'll come look for you," she promised.

"I would like to tell you more about your man at the palace," he said.

Standing beside him felt like balancing on a leaky raft with the waters of trance shimmering all around. Myril couldn't summon her voice again until he was gone halfway down to the bridge. There, he greeted an acquaintance in the Cerean manner, shaking his hand, then steering the man away from the street of frail former priestesses and healers, across newly placed planks to the still-dry arch of the bridge.

The clusters of gossiping neighbors began to break apart as frantic citizens arrived, seeking splints and bandages from minor injuries from the quake, but more than that, they sought to have their fortunes cast. Broken jars lay where they'd fallen along with roof tiles that had slid down from their perches. Myril went inside, hoping to shut it all out.

Her door was still latched, but the narrow stair up to it was crowded with people wanting to see her. One had a broken arm, another a case of fainting, and ten people sought prophecies. She set the broken arm and gave the fainting girl a bundle of herbs to brew, then sent the rest away and barred the door.

From her window, she could see that the water had risen just to the underside of the bridge's arch. The scrapplings who had always camped there were flooded out. Myril and her friends had sheltered there when they'd first come to Anamat. Since then, the bridge had sheltered one group of scrapplings after another. It was a way station, the way into the city, and it was gone. No one would ever find shelter there again. Myril felt sure that she would lose every dwelling she'd ever had in Anamat. She would be cast out on the sea, at the mercy of Lerat, or worse. She shuddered. Better Lerat than any of the others.

One of the ships in the harbor was setting sail; she could hear the sound of its going. Along with the sailors, some dozen or more Theranians crowded the decks, sitting on hastily packed trunks and bags.

"Where are we going?" one of them asked.

"Does it matter? I don't want to drown."

"We could drown as easily on a ship, more easily," complained a woman.

"We're going to Enomae," said another woman, her voice determined. "They say they have weavers there. I can be a weaver as easily as I can in Anamat, and no Cereans trying to take me slave."

"You're sure these aren't slavers?" one man asked.

"They've never been before," yet another person answered. "We have to take our chances with someone."

Myril turned her ears away from the harbor. She was not ready to say her farewells to Anamat yet.

§

Those were only the first to go. As the moon waned, more and more Theranians set sail on fishermen's boats and trading ships. Word came back that some of them had settled in Calandria, others in a large town in Ganat. If any went to Cerea, ancient enemy of the priestesses, no word came back from them. Rumors filled the streets as ships filled the harbor. Houses were abandoned and filled again, shops boarded up one day only to be opened again the next.

The first survivors from Slaradun reached the Anamat valley at the end of the third day after the quake, saying that the dragons' anger had come from those hills. People stood in long lines before the street-corner shrines and at the temples to leave offerings and to beg the dragons for peace – and protection – but the dragons did not listen, or at least did not deign to grant those requests. The merchants in the dockside markets and the apprentices of the Ropers' Guild sold passage across the sea to all who came with enough good Anamat beads or, better yet, Cerean gold. The temple's oracles said that the rising water would stop where it was, but not everyone believed them.

Myril avoided going to the temple, telling herself that she was not yet sure if the waters would rise or fall, or if the temple would be a safe place for the texts at all. The Aralel had troubles enough of her own. Petitioners crowded the temples, begging to know why the wrath of the dragons was upon them, as if it were a mystery. Myril didn't think that the Aralel could save the Chronicles even if she had the time to find a safe place for them. Anamat was shifting – how could there be any safe place in the city?

Across the seas, foreigners might try to steal the dragons' power, but if the dragons were gone, and the priestesses went another way, then at least some faraway library might be able to house the histories. Lerat's appearance had been a sign. Despite the threat of trance whenever he was near, Myril decided that she trusted him.

§

Chapter 2

Darna looked out over the Anamat valley from a border shrine tucked high in the mountains. She'd just glimpsed a dragonlet of Anara, or rather, she thought she might have, but she wasn't quite sure. With dragonlets, you could never be sure. The scene spread out ahead of her was a different matter. It had definitely changed since she'd last seen it, less than a moon-round before. The sea shone in the midday sun, just as it had then, but now it shone all the way up to its new, muddy banks, far inland from where they'd been before. The road into the city was mostly dry, but water encroached on it near the West Gate Market. An inlet ran up to one of the larger villages, where before there'd been only a stream. Boats moored on its banks in what had once been pasturelands, and a few tents stood nearby.

A quarter of the city was up to its ankles in water. "What have I done?" Darna thought aloud.

"*You* haven't done anything," Sunna scolded her. Darna hadn't meant to speak aloud. "It's the dragons, getting revenge on the Cereans. Look at them." She waved her hand at the tents and boats. "Crawling all over us."

"It looks more like revenge on us," Raina said. "But Sunna's right. This is Na's work, and he answers to no priestess, nor princes either. Maybe the other dragons are all going wild. Even if you moved some bits of stone out of place, you didn't shake the earth; only they can do that."

Darna couldn't explain to them why she'd felt her own hand in the shift of the land, even if it had been a dragon's force behind it. She'd known where the power ran through the earth and she'd helped to do something that she'd known was not quite right. Then she'd called up the dragon, or at least given Salara strength on that last day, the strength to do this. Salara had given her strength, too, but it had a price. She was pretty sure that the cramps in her gut were only the start of it.

The shift of the earth and the rising of the sea were echoes of what had happened when she and her lover had given strength to a wild dragon, strength to shake off the invaders – and to destroy themselves, it seemed.

"We'd better go on, if we want to get to Raina's place before dark," Sunna said.

It seemed absurd to worry about how far they had to walk that day when the city was ruined, or at least well on its way to ruin.

"We won't get there before dark, even if we could keep up a good pace," Raina said. They'd been traveling slowly so far because of Darna's cramps. "We could get in by midnight if we pushed through," Raina said. She was probably eager to get back to her house and her mostly fosterling children.

The three women set out again, Sunna and Raina flanking Darna, guarding her. The view of the city slid behind the trees for a while. The change in the land had been different in Slaradun. Terrifying there, too, except that she'd been beyond terror in Salara's embrace. Besides, the province had been so bleak and barren to begin with that it felt almost like a mercy to destroy it, like the death of her lover so soon after he had gone mad. He'd said that he didn't want to live that way, but she wondered if death was what he'd really wanted in the end.

The destruction of Anamat was more than she wanted to see, the end of its lush valley and the jewel of a city on the bay. It was home, as much as any place could be. Darna's thoughts stalled as the welts on her belly burned and her stomach cramped. She stumbled, unable to keep her eyes on the path as she watched the shining waters lapping at shores they'd never reached before.

By the time the sun was setting, they were barely halfway to the city and still a very long way from Raina's house, too.

"I'm hungry," Sunna said, giving voice to what they were all feeling. It had been a long day's walk, even though they hadn't traveled as far as they'd wanted to.

"We could stop to eat at South Turning," Raina suggested, indicating the small town not far ahead.

"What about all those Cereans camped around it?" Darna said. South Turning was the village they'd seen from the border, with the boats pulled up and the tents in its fields. It was a big place, considerably bigger than the town around Slaradun keep had been.

Raina shrugged. "If we're going to stop for the night, this is the best place, Cereans or no. Could you walk through to dawn?"

Another cramp shot around her guts. "No," Darna gasped. The pain was exhausting. "We'd better stop there."

They waited for Darna to recover – again – then went on. A short while later, they reached the town's dark and quiet streets and made their way to the temple on its central square. They heard no one walking near them, but Sunna kept one hand on the hilt of her sword, and Raina looked tense too. Darna wondered, briefiy, if there was any real difference between being a hunted woman and being a prisoner. Sunna was an old friend, and she and Raina had come to keep Darna safe, but they would not let her out of their sights, not even for a moment.

"Put your hood up," Sunna reminded her. It had fallen down again. Darna drew it up, though she wished she didn't have to. Covering her hair meant closing off her peripheral vision, and she felt half-blind as they crossed to the temple. She heard the hiss of the others' in-taken breath, then turned to look.

The temple's carved columns and gilded murals shone dimly in the moonlight. The gates, closed and barred, were dark. No lamp lighted the porch; no priestess waited in the gatehouse to take offerings. Something shone on the ground. Darna cast a wary glance over her shoulder. The men on the tavern porch across the square didn't seem to have seen them yet. She bent down to look.

"Phew," Sunna said, wrinkling her nose.

Sheep's entrails and blood lay across the temple threshold. Darna backed away.

"We'd better go to the tavern for supper, then," Raina said faintly.

"I'd like to know where the priestesses are," Sunna said.

"We can look for them after we eat, if the tavern keeper doesn't know what happened. I'll ask her," Raina said.

"Well, then, the tavern's the thing," Sunna said with grim resolution. "Do you know every tavern keeper in the valley?"

Raina shrugged. "No, just most of the ones along this road and a few others. It helps to keep up with what's happening."

Darna wondered how Raina managed to keep up with all of that along with her household and the Defenders, but there was no chance to ask; they'd already reached the tavern.

Unlike the temple, bright lamps lit the tavern porch, where a few village men lounged, holding jars of ale in both hands.

"What brings you out on such a night, guildswomen?" one of the men asked.

"Supper and a bed, same as anyone," Raina replied. "Is Orla here?"

The men looked at one another. "Can't say. You'll have to ask in the kitchen."

"I wouldn't go in there if I were you," another of the men said. Darna's hand was already on the curtain, pulling it aside, and Sunna and Raina were right behind her. She hesitated.

The scene within was not threatening, nor was it what Darna had expected. In ordinary times, the tavern would be full of travelers on their way to the city for Midsummer, a mix of men and women, some children, almost all Theranians. Instead, there were Cereans, Ganateans, and a lone Enomaean, all men of soldiering age or sailors with their various caps and headdresses, wearing pointed boots instead of sandals.

"My woman's at home; all of them are," said the first man on the porch.

"We're three together, and I know Orla," Raina said. She nudged Darna forward.

Some of the men inside looked up to see who was arriving, but most were preoccupied with discussions amongst themselves.

"I'll go ask for a private room," Raina said.

"No." Darna put a hand on her arm. "I want to stay here. Maybe we can learn something."

"I can't understand a word they're saying," Sunna complained.

"I don't speak their language well, but I can catch a word here and there," Darna said. Curiosity was getting the better of her. She spotted an empty table near the kitchen door and angled her way toward it, weaving between clusters of sailors leaning over their tables, arguing with one another and playing dice. Raina and Sunna followed close behind.

A barmaid darted out from the kitchen and nodded them to the empty table.

"Is Orla here?" Raina asked her.

The barmaid cast a nervous glance toward the kitchen. "She's gone out. She'll be back later. If you want to wait for her here?"

"We'd like a private room, to sleep."

"They're all taken. We're full up."

"When Orla gets back, tell her that Raina's here. Meanwhile, we'll have small ale and whatever's on the fire."

"Very well." The maid gave a quick bow and backed into the kitchen, returning moments later with their jars of ale. She set out across the room with a battle-weary expression on her face. Her elbows fended off reaching men. Darna noted that only a few of them made efforts to molest her, really only three of them, but they made up for the rest, who ignored their goings-on. There was one groper at a table by the winter fireplace, another next to the door, and the last one sitting in the middle of the room in a spot the barmaid had to pass often. His hair was especially oily under his silly Cerean cap.

Raina and Sunna sat in silence, and all three of them kept their backs to the wall. The maid returned with bowls of soup and a basket of bread. Sunna handed over a short string of beads, never taking her eyes off the room.

"Don't worry about them," the barmaid told her. "Their captain will be along soon to shoo them back to their camp. He says he doesn't want trouble, not yet."

"That's not very reassuring," Darna said.

"No, it isn't. We don't have any lodging, but if you don't mind the kitchen, there'll be others sleeping there too, and it's warm."

Raina and Sunna looked at each other, communicating something. "Thank you for the offer, and do send Orla to us when she gets back," Raina said.

The barmaid leaned in close and whispered. "She's seeing to the priestesses. I don't know when she'll be back."

Raina gave a knowing nod. So, the tavern keeper did know where they were gone, and if they weren't safe, then at least someone was working to get them to safety.

"Hey!" one of the Cereans shouted. He banged his empty jar on the table, sending the barmaid scurrying to refill it. She didn't stop to talk again as they sopped up their soup. At one point, a tall Ganatean glanced past the three women. He stopped, then doubled back to look again. Darna made a show of being intent on something in her bowl. When she looked up, the Ganatean was gone.

"Do you know that man?" she asked Sunna.

"The one that just left? No. It's possible that he recognized me from when I was watching the temple gate, but I doubt it."

"The Aralel isn't letting foreigners in now, is she?" Raina asked, alarmed.

Sunna shook her head. "No much, but you know the treasurers. If there's enough offering, they'll let almost anyone in." She turned to Darna. "Could he know you?"

It wasn't likely, but if he'd been one of the Ganateans who'd come to Slaradun, he could have seen her there. "I don't know. I hope not," she said. The Ganateans might not know her, but they might also have gotten wind that her uncle was still looking for a red-haired priestess who walked with a stick. She still had the hair, but she'd left the stick behind. No foreigner would recognize her as a priestess, dressed as she was in an old farm woman's tunic, and they were even less likely to connect her with the bounty offered by the usurper of Tiadun, but it was a big bounty, as these things went. She wished that she was still wearing the Enomaean turban to cover her hair better.

"Where in the ways is Orla?" Raina asked no one in particular as she tore her last piece of bread in two.

Darna's grasp on the Cerean language wasn't good, but she caught occasional words and snatches of conversation, including speculation about when they might raid another temple. That last was shushed as all the men at that table looked nervously to the kitchen door.

"We pay these wenches well enough," one of the Cereans said. "They oughta be glad for it. I'd just as soon come in and take it."

"Captain says to keep the peace until the others come."

"Others from home, or from that place... What was it called?"

"Terandun, something like that. They call all their places something-dun, lun, mun, bun,"

"Sun mun dun!" Another one echoed. "Women, all of them, and their puny little armies." Someone elbowed him, and he stopped.

"Captain."

The men in the room stood, blocking the view of their captain, who had just entered. Darna had glimpsed him only briefiy. He wore gold-woven cloth and had a thick belly. It wasn't as thick as the belly she'd seen on the captain who had duped her long ago, but fat enough. The face was familiar too. He was older now and wore a small beard, but she would have recognized Giri's darting eyes anywhere, still as nervous as they'd been the day she'd first seen him scurrying around the city dump, pretending to be a scrappling. Why would he return after what had happened that summer? Then again, who else in Cerea would know Anamat as he did? After all, she'd taught him.

She tipped up her jar to hide her face, though it was empty. Giri had betrayed her to the Cerean king. He'd planned it from before their first meeting and she'd been taken in, fool that she'd been. The Cerean king must have sent Giri to Anamat even then. Why would the king have done that if he didn't plan to make more use of him? Giri must have valued his power in the Cerean court more than he'd loved his season of freedom in Anamat, if he'd enjoyed it at all. Maybe he hadn't. He'd been terrified of the dragons, even of dragonlets. It seemed he'd preferred the threat of near-fatal beatings among his countrymen. He'd left no friends in the city that summer; that much was sure. She wondered if Pannen knew that Giri had returned, and that he was the one who'd sent Nira - Darna's old enemy and Pannen's old lover - into slavery.

The foreign sailors filed out, leaving an unsettled quiet in their wake. Darna looked up, thinking that the suddenly quiet room would be empty, but Giri was still there, crossing the room, headed straight for them. He saw her. He recognized her. She was sure of it. Or was she?

Sunna put a hand on her arm before she could say anything. Giri turned his gaze away from them and called into the kitchen. One of the barmaids came out and piled counting chips on a table. Giri counted out coins and beads from his pocket. When the account was settled, the barmaid hurried away. Giri tied his coin pouch carefully, then turned to go.

He was almost to the door when he stopped to look back. "Darnasa, they call you?" he said in Cerean.

Darna nodded.

"You still speak my language?"

She shrugged.

"Then hear this. If you make trouble for me or my men, you will pay as you should have paid before, and more. Stay away from the palace."

"I'll go where I please," Darna said. Her Cerean was embarrassingly bad.

Giri twitched his nose. "I have an army at my back now," he said.

"It's not your army. You're still a slave."

"Stay away from the palace. You've been warned." With that, he swept out.

"What was that about?" Sunna asked as soon as he was gone.

"Old, bad blood between us."

"Looked like it, but –"

Before any of them could say more, the barmaid hurried back in. "Orla's back," she announced. "My apologies, Raina of the Gone Duck Inn. She says you three may sleep in her rooms."

§

The three women were shown into a room where they found some of the tavern keeper's softest rugs. As they got ready to sleep, Darna told Sunna and Raina about how she'd run with Giri during her season on the streets of Anamat, when she'd settled under the bridge and scavenged in the scrap heaps. Long ago, she'd seen the scars from where his slave masters had lashed him. Despite that, he'd served the Cerean king all along. He'd duped her into stealing a dragon stone from the palace.

She'd stolen it back from the Cerean merchants, along with the statue Nira had stolen on Giri's behalf, and perhaps he'd paid a price for that, too. He'd meant to trick her into going with him to Cerea. She hadn't wanted to become a priestess, but it was a far better fate than life as a Cerean slave, from the evidence she'd seen on Giri's own back.

"So, he hasn't forgotten you or forgiven you," Sunna mused when Darna's whispered tale was told.

"It doesn't seem like it. I wonder why he's returned at all."

"Does he know about the tribunal?" Raina asked.

"Princes' successions don't get challenged often, so people are probably talking about it. Also, he called me Darnasa. He knows. Damn him to his own hells."

Orla came in then to see that they were well settled. She told Raina that they'd found a place for the priestesses to stay until they could be taken into the city in a few nights' time, to Ara's Landing, where half the priestesses in Theranis were seeking sanctuary.

They set out early. Darna's cramps were not as bad that day, so they reached Raina's house before midday. Her many children, most of them fosterlings, flooded out to greet her and dragged her inside. Sunna and Darna traveled the last stretch without her, entering the city just before the gates closed for the midday rest.

"We should go straight to the temple," Sunna said.

"I want to see Myril first. Her place is on the way, and you can go ahead to find out if the Aralel will have me and if the temple's safe enough."

"I doubt that it is, but it's the best we can do for now. All the priestesses are going there."

"That's half the trouble," Darna said. With so many newcomers, there were bound to be some she couldn't trust.

Sunna grumbled agreement.

A troop of guardsmen tromped up the road from the remains of Merchants' Wharf, escorting a well-dressed Ganatean to the palace. Sunna and Darna avoided them by ducking into a side alley, then made their way on down the street to Myril's place.

§

The waters stayed to their new bounds, and the women and men kept coming at all hours of the day and night, wanting to know what their futures held. They asked every healer and soothsayer on the street. Would their fortunes be better in Ganat? Should they sail to Calandria? Should they stay in their houses and villages? Their constant questions sailed through the walls and windows to Myril's hearing. She didn't know how to answer them and didn't want to know.

Her errand to the temple remained undone. It nagged at her, but the thought of asking the Aralel for help made her uneasy. She waited for some other solution, any other solution, to appear before her, at least one that would serve until Lerat found a place for the Chronicles far beyond the governor's reach. The half-moon came, and at last she felt that she could not delay any longer. She steeled herself for the fray and clamor of the streets and put on her plainest robe. She was about to set out when she heard a familiar voice at the top of the hill. It sounded like Darna. Yes, Darna and Sunna.

She waited but didn't hear Darna's footstep, the distinctive tip-tapping of her stick on the cobbles. Then she heard an unfamiliar step on the stair.

"I've closed," she said before the knock came at the door.

"It's me, Darna. Sunna's waiting below."

The voice was right even though the step was wrong. The footfalls on the stair had been steady and strong, not like

Darna's at all. Her gait had always been lopsided, even on days when her leg wasn't bothering her. Myril opened the door to let her in. Darna's face had been browned by the sun. She stood taller and wore a bulging pocket at her belt, but her tunic was as shabby as a scrappling's. None of that explained why she *seemed* so different.

"Where's your stick? What happened?" Myril asked.

Darna sank onto the seat by the window and leaned out to give Sunna a quick signal. "Why did you take down your sign?" she asked.

"I have other work to do, for the guild, and besides, it's not safe."

"You don't need to tell me that," Darna said. "I've never seen so many Cereans in my life."

Before Myril could reply, Sunna came in.

"I'm supposed to take Darna to the temple," she announced, "but I need to see if it's safe first, and I don't want to interrupt the Aralel at her supper. Besides, I'm hungry. I'll go get some soup from the lady down in the alley and bring it back."

Myril had been so nervous about her impending meeting with the Aralel that she hadn't felt like eating, but it was midday, and Darna brightened at the mention of food.

"Here." Myril handed Sunna her tray of bowls and a pitcher, along with some beads.

"Thanks," Sunna said. "I'll be back soon. Don't let anyone else in."

"Assassins?" Myril asked, as Sunna clattered away down the stair.

Darna nodded. "They haven't spotted me yet, but I doubt that Calar's called them off. And there's worse. I've seen Giri and he knows I'm here, knows who I am, too. He told me to stay away from the palace."

"Giri? Who's that?"

"You remember the Cerean scrappling who helped get Nira kidnapped? He's back."

"Oh." Myril put the pieces together. "Do they call him Girizit now? The king's emissary?"

"Yes, that was always his name, but –" Darna doubled over suddenly, shaking with pain. When she looked up, her face was pale beneath its tan.

"What is this?" Myril demanded.

Darna breathed a few times to steady herself. "I don't know. I thought maybe you could help."

Outside, the street was growing quieter as people gathered around their cookfires and went inside for the midday rest. "Did it happen in Slaradun?"

"I think so." Darna drew a shuddering breath. "It was at the gate, just before it all fell into the sea. You've heard about it?"

Myril nodded. "You can tell me how you think it happened after I look. What's that gold chain?"

"This?" Darna asked, as if she'd forgotten it. She fished a shining amulet out from between her breasts. It shone with its own light. "It was a gift from him, from the prince. It's one of Salara's stones."

"Would owning that have made you keep mistress there?"

Darna shook her head. "I don't think so, but anyway, there's no keep to be mistress of, and there's no prince anymore, so no, it doesn't. Salara's gone, too." Her face contorted again as another wave of pain washed through her.

"Come away from the window," Myril said. "I'll see if I can find where your pain is coming from. You'd better take off your tunic."

Sometimes, Myril felt as if she'd been trying to keep Darna alive since the moment they met long before on their

scrappling road to Anamat. In the space of a few days, she'd
gone from taking care of her slow-witted but sweet younger
sister to taking care of Darna, whose wits were as quick as
anyone's, and who was never sweet. Darna's recklessness
always threatened to carry her too far, except during their
years in the temple novitiate, which had only made her feel
miserable.

"The hermit priestesses gave me mint and chamomile, but
it didn't help much," Darna said as she unbuckled her belt.
She turned her back to Myril and stood in the darkest corner
of the room, facing the bed where patients sometimes slept if
their homes were a long walk away and they were weak from
the journey to the healers' street. Darna stripped off the tunic
and began to fold it, still facing away. "The pain comes at
random; I can't find a pattern in it," she said. "It doesn't last
for long. It's not like ordinary cramps, not even like I'm going
to be sick to my stomach. It's more like something sharp is
stabbing me from the inside, then like the blade is twisting
slowly 'til it stops just as suddenly as it came. I'm not sure
what triggers it. Some days, it doesn't bother me at all, like this
morning, when I was walking, though it did yesterday. Now,
though –"

Darna turned. She still had the long, silvery scar along her
right leg where her childhood injury had marked her skin, but
that was pale and faded. These wounds – if they were wounds
at all – were new and they glowed. They made a tracery over
her belly. They rippled with dragonfire.

"What is this? How did it happen?"

Darna sat and rested her face in her hands, curled around
herself, shutting out the world. She took a few deep,
shuddering breaths. "I suppose if I can tell anyone, I can tell
you," she said. "I had Salara inside me. He lifted me up, threw

me down on the rocks before his gate. He took Ivanat's mind away with him – Ivanat was my lover."

"The prince of Slaradun, I know."

"Salara took Ivanat's place in the rite with me. It was the first time Ivanat and I had ever knowingly gone in to the worship of the dragons together, and it fulfilled the prophecy his grandmother gave, which was that the dragon would destroy him. His friend took his life, though. The rite came too late; the Ganateans were already at the gate. Across the seas, Ivanat had learned to believe that the dragons didn't exist, or that if they did exist, they weren't important, even though he'd seen Salara." She stopped and swallowed.

"The scars?" Myril asked, when she seemed to have gathered her breath.

"Salara's belly against mine. The scales burned me, but it didn't hurt. That's not what hurts."

"May I touch them?" She needed to touch the dragon's mark to understand what had happened to Darna. It was dangerous, but –

"Don't go into trance," Darna said. "I don't think I can pull you out. I've almost forgotten how, and with this, I feel different, not like myself at all sometimes. I'm afraid I might fall right in after you, and then we'd both be lost. I'm not sure you should touch it, really, I mean, this might have something to do with it, but maybe it's just a worm in my guts from some bad water somewhere along the road."

"Shush, let me listen." Myril reached out and tentatively touched her belly. It was smooth between the ridges left by the scales, smooth like metal. Darna had always said that she was Tiada's child, a child of the dragons, and now she looked as if she was partially one in the flesh as well as in spirit. Myril could feel the heat coming from her belly.

"Don't go into trance," Darna repeated.

Myril let her hand drift down across the light ridges. They looked and felt just like dragon scales. She'd never touched dragon scales in the flesh, of course, unless her long-ago dream by the lake in the mountains had been real.

"She's marked you."

"Salara has, but Salara's male now," Darna said.

"I keep forgetting that. The only dragon I think of as male is Na. Do you think that's why Salara shook the province into the sea? Because he's male now?"

Darna shook her head. Something inside her shifted again, some energy. Myril's hand followed in its wake. It coursed around her belly as she spoke.

"I don't think it's because he's male," she said. "I think it was because he was strong enough, because we gave him the strength, Ivanat and I. I wish Tiada had done the same and saved herself, but she must have been so faded that she couldn't."

"Eppie saw Tiada a half-moon before she died. She hadn't faded all the way away."

"*Everyone* could see Salara at the end. Thorat said that even the Ganateans saw him. All of them did."

"Maybe that will persuade them to let us be," Myril mused.

Darna shook her head. "Lots of them are still here. I doubt they'll be driven off by something they pretend isn't real, no matter how much it should scare them."

Myril pressed at the points where the pain might be if Darna were carrying a baby in the wrong place, the baby of the prince of Slaradun and of a priestess who might be almost-heir to the throne of Tiadun. If Darna were carrying a baby, which still seemed the likeliest explanation for her pains, then it could be heir to both provinces. It would be a secret to guard closely until she was safe from her uncle's plots.

Darna did not cry out when those points were pressed, so Myril smoothed her hands across the belly again, hoping to find the strange pulse she'd sensed earlier. There it was, sharp and bright. Darna cringed, though Myril was not pushing down at all, but she relaxed again a moment later.

"It's in your womb, whatever it is, and it's alive and growing," Myril said as the thought formed in her mind.

"A baby?"

Myril had felt many women's middles early in their pregnancies when their bellies were still flat. She always felt the flicker of life inside them as a steady glow like a glowing coal from an old fire in the morning, but increasing. That energy didn't flash like this did; it wasn't hard.

"I should say that it's a baby, because I can't think of anything else it might be, but if it is, it's not an ordinary one. I don't know what it is. I've never seen or felt anything like it. You should go to the temple infirmary. Maybe Geta will know, if she's well enough to examine you." Geta, the elder priestess who oversaw the baking, had seemed impossibly old when Myril and Darna had first come to the temple, but it had been a dozen years since then and she was still in the thick of temple life, though she was growing frail, more so since the day that the waters had risen, or so the rumors said.

"I wish I didn't have to go to the temple. I know it's probably safer there, and I need the Aralel's allegiance, but I hate being trapped in there," Darna said. "There was a temple in the mountains. I didn't mind being there, but I was alone, so it was different. It was beautiful; I could have stayed there forever. I wonder if maybe I should have."

"More beautiful than Ara's Landing?" Myril asked. As much as she disliked being inside the temple, anyone could see that it was splendid.

Darna nodded.

"I have to go to speak with the Aralel today. That's where I was about to go when you arrived," Myril told her. "I could tell her that you're back in the city."

Darna shook her head. "I'd like to hear if Sunna thinks it's safe, first."

Just then, as if summoned by her name, Sunna appeared at the door with three cooling bowls of soup and a sack of bread balanced on the tray.

"I had to go halfway to the temple to find a pot that wasn't already empty," she complained. "It's as bad as Midsummer."

"Here's hoping it won't get worse," Darna said.

Myril shivered. The lines on Darna's belly writhed.

"Put that tunic back on," Myril said. Naked except for the worn amulet and the glowing pendant between her breasts, Darna looked immeasurably powerful. With the shabby tunic on, she'd looked just like a beggar. It had masked her power, and she needed that mask.

§

Over the soup and bread, they agreed that Myril should tell the Aralel that Darna had arrived in Anamat, unless she felt that she shouldn't. She left Sunna guarding Darna and set out for the temple just before the end of midday rest, determined to complete her long-delayed errand for the Chronicler at last. She felt too uneasy to try to block the clamor from her ears. Every footfall, voice, and drop of water falling assaulted her as she walked as quickly as she could to the side house.

The bells ending the midday rest rang out just as she reached the half-secret entrance to the temple. Myril paid the Grandmother her tribute, hoping that her visit wouldn't last long. The temple's atmosphere was still heavy but not as thick with trance and ritual as it had been when she'd first felt it so many years before. She wondered if Iola could ever be persuaded to leave that charmed sphere behind, to breathe ordinary air on the ordinary streets again.

With so many priestesses from the provinces seeking refuge, the elders' courtyard was far busier than usual. Myril nodded greetings to those she passed on her way to the Aralel's porch. The Aralel was not alone. A young priestess – not from Ara's landing – sat on the bench outside. She looked straight ahead, as if the colonnaded porch were not quite fine enough for her, wrinkling her nose at the view over the elders' garden with its perfectly laid-out beds of medicinal and ornamental plants.

"You can't go in," she said. "The governor said to make sure she isn't disturbed."

"I'll wait, then," Myril said. She looked away, not that the young priestess was probably going to engage her in conversation anyway.

The young priestess's robes showed that she was from Conn's Coop, the temple beside the palace that served the governor and his men, and maybe their foreign guests, too, men who didn't even pretend to come to worship the dragons. The young priestess seemed to think that Myril was beneath her notice, which suited Myril perfectly. She sat down and listened. Tiagasa was inside. Myril felt a brief flicker of pity for her young attendant priestess, but more than that, she was curious what the governor's mistress had come for that day.

§

Chapter 3

The Aralel and the governor's mistress were in the outer chamber, and they spoke as if they were alone and unobserved, unaware that Myril was listening. She wondered whether they would have changed anything they said if they'd known that she heard every word. She closed her eyes and pictured the scene within while the young priestess fidgeted, looking bored.

The Aralel was wearing some of her older robes. They made a soft, muffled sound when they moved. Myril heard her sit down, sigh, and brush back a loose strand of hair.

"Won't you send for tea?" Tiagasa asked the Aralel. Her voice was as crisp as the cloth of gold in her scarf, and bright as the crinkle of her hair dressings.

"I think we'd better have wine for this," the Aralel said. "It is yours to pour."

Tiagasa sniffed at the insult. The Aralel's rank eclipsed hers, but at the palace, Tiagasa was second only to the governor, and he was in her sway. The Aralel ruled all priestesses, including Tiagasa, and as such, she was the governor's equal, if not his superior. Tiagasa didn't argue about the pouring, but she made her show of deference a sloppy one. A drop fell out onto a page. Tiagasa was nervous, or at least not accustomed to pouring her own wine. Neither of the women drank at first.

"Please sit," the Aralel said. "I trust you have news of some importance, to come yourself?"

Tiagasa's clothing rustled and the Aralel *tsk*ed at the spill of wine on her worktable, then wiped it away, making Tiagasa wait for her attention.

"I do have news," Tiagasa said at last. "Perhaps you've noticed that we have more foreign traders than usual this year? They want the temple's treasures."

"That's no news. Foreigners have always wanted our treasures, but as any novice knows, they would misuse them, and they belong to the dragons and the dragons' loyal priestesses."

"Ships sailed out to Enomae, Ganat, and Cerea as soon as the seas rose. They'll carry news. All the world will all know that we're in peril. They will come and take what they want. They have armies and strong fleets. I say that it is better to trade for what we can while we still have possession of our land."

"The dragons own the land we call home," the Aralel said levelly. "The treasures are part of that. If the dragons want to take the land, they may take their treasures, too."

"You'd like to see them wasted at the bottom of the sea? That is careless of you, if I may say so."

"You may not," the Aralel said. "It is greedy as well as blasphemous for you to try to take the temple's riches to serve your own ends. It would upset the balance of power to see so much shift to your palace."

"It is not only in my interest; it's for the temple, too. I am sure you've noticed that the balance of power is shifting already, and there's nothing you can do to stop it. Some control goes to the governor's palace, but some goes further, out through the merchant docks. I pity Calar, not even crowned yet. He has an army of Cerean soldiers at his back, but they only obey his orders when it suits them. A shame, to see the land fall into their hands, even a miserable little province."

"Salara certainly seems to have thought so."

Tiagasa was silent for a moment, having nothing to say about Slaradun's fall into the sea. That had not been part of her plans. "The messengers say that Tiadun did not sink when we did. Its shoreline stands unchanged," she said.

"Interesting. That province has no ruler at present, as well as an absent dragon."

"The tribunal will be held as soon as Calar arrives, at most only another two or three days from now. Whether or not his challenger arrives is another question. It will all be decided then." Tiagasa's silks rustled as she poured more wine into her cup.

"And you think that Calar, the murderer, and his foreign army will prevail?"

"He's not proved a murderer, and in any case, it would be highly unusual for a princess to take a prince's throne, even if she bothers to come to the tribunal."

"It has been known to happen. There are two or three cases in our history."

"That was long ago. Besides, a dead woman cannot take a throne."

The Aralel stilled. "Do you have reason to think that Darnasa is dead?"

"No one has seen her," Tiagasa said, her voice rising into a bit of a lilt. "She may have been in Slaradun when that catastrophe came, besides which, as you no doubt have heard, Calar is offering a price for her head. She can hardly best him under those conditions. She's really just a scrappling still."

The Aralel moved some papers around. "Darnasa is a priestess and a guildswoman as well as a prince's daughter. Don't you think that offering such a large bounty suggests that Calar fears her?"

"Nonsense," Tiagasa said. "He's merely being thorough. He only needs to be confirmed as prince of his land to conclude his arrangements with his Cerean allies."

"Cerean masters, more likely," the Aralel muttered as she picked up a few disordered scrolls and tapped them on the table. "In any case, he has not come to the temple, asking us for aid. He seems to know better than that, at least."

"He may help the Cereans against you, if you offer him nothing. They offer more. You should let me speak to Calar's Cereans on your behalf when they arrive."

The Aralel's grunt suggested that she did not think much of that proposition. "Commerce with foreign lands is the palace's domain, not in the temple's sphere at all. So, that is the point of this, is it?"

"You may think that this temple is strong, but even a small force of armsmen could raze it in the time it takes to walk from here to the palace. I'm sure that you see the importance of protecting your priestesses from the assault of these sailors and soldiers."

"More than you do."

"I have as good an understanding as I need," Tiagasa huffed.

"I don't think that you do," the Aralel said. "Shall I tell you what happened to one young priestess in Getedun? She was scarcely out of the novitiate and ten men of Cerea broke down the gates of her temple. They raped her for days. Days. Without food, almost without water. They left her for dead."

Tiagasa's breath grew shallow.

"One of the girls in Tiadun died. Calar ignores this, or if he asks his so-called allies to go quietly, they see no need to follow his command. You must know they are not much under his control, and yet he's leading them to Anamat. You and your consort, our governor, are obliged by duty to drive them off."

"How did she live?" Tiagasa asked.

"The girl from Getedun? She is only the worst of a dozen cases like that. Some villagers came to the temple after the Cereans had left, to see what could be saved. The young priestess begged them to kill her, but they would not. They nursed her as well as they were able to and carried her here on a stretcher, all the way to Anamat. She arrived last night. You might go see her, if you wish."

Tiagasa shook her head.

"The priestesses in Galamun have fared better because their prince uses his guardsmen to ensure that the foreigners are not allowed to molest his people or his province. That prince, at least, still honors the dragons and the priestesses. You should have Parnet follow his example."

"The governor is not mine to command," Tiagasa said.

"Don't be a fool. Everyone knows that Parnet asks your counsel in all things, as he should. As his consort, you rule this city as much as he does."

Tiagasa gave a sniff of annoyance as a jewel came loose from her hair. She tucked it back in place before she stood. "I do not rule him. He rules me, as is good and proper."

The Aralel snorted. "How can you listen to those fools? There's nothing in the Cereans' philosophy which brings advantage to women."

"Not to women like you."

The Aralel drew herself up. "Women like me – and like you – are the root of all civilization, especially here in

Theranis. The dragons would never have let humankind settle these shores if Ara had not spoken to Anara when the first settlers landed, and they will not continue to tolerate our presence if we forget them."

"The dragons can be killed. They say that Tiada was."

"And what of Tiadun's harvest last year? Do their seeds still sprout?"

"I've heard only rumors," Tiagasa said. "They certainly had a harvest, but since your sources are so much better than mine, perhaps you should tell me."

The Aralel leaned over her table and picked up a piece of parchment. "Tiadun's temples are shuttered. The harvest came in, not much less than usual, and the villagers had adequate seed grain for the spring planting. The new season's grains have sprouted poorly, though, and if things continue as they are, this winter will bring famine."

"And all the priestesses from Tiadun are here now, for you to feed?" Tiagasa asked.

"We have enough here to provide for any who might come. Anara still lives, even if you no longer see her."

Myril could imagine Tiagasa's frown. The governor's mistress did not like to be reminded that she, too, used to be able to see the dragon. "You'll only have enough to eat if there are still farmers here to harvest it."

"The farmers will be true to their lands."

"Don't be so sure of it," Tiagasa said. "Where are those other priestesses who did not come here?"

"If I knew, I wouldn't tell you."

"I don't wish to betray my fellow priestesses," Tiagasa said, sounding like she was smiling a very thin smile.

"So, you admit that you are still one of us?"

"No. I *have been* one of you, but that was long ago. I've seen the error of our ways, but I still remember my sister priestesses here and would not like to see them come to such an end." The cloth of her robes rustled brightly again as she straightened.

"You have no sense of history, Tiagasa, but you were a priestess, and you are still one, even if you refused all but your favorite petitioner." The Aralel paused. "We all knew about that. You were foolish to even think that you could be ambassadress, but I supported your ambitions. I thought that seeing you go, seeing you destroyed, might have taught Iola better sense."

"You would have sacrificed *me* to teach that fool who –"

"Enough! Iola is not like the rest of us," the Aralel said.

"I couldn't agree more, but it's not a virtue in her. She's a madwoman, unhinged," Tiagasa said, as if she hadn't just been scolded.

"She is our ambassadress and an extremely gifted priestess, even if she is not as practically minded as you or I."

"You, practical? Then hear this: I say that it is easier to placate armed men than dragons. It's better, too. Parnet and I have been taking instruction from the best Cerean philosophers since we took charge of the palace. Their land is no larger than Theranis, and yet they rule half the world sea. They will rule us, too, if we don't drown first. We cannot drive them off, so we must take what advantage we can with them."

At least she knew that her small force of guardsmen was no match for the Cereans' armies.

"Even if you cannot conquer the Cereans in your own territory, the dragons can."

"They didn't in Tiadun."

"But they did in Slaradun," the Aralel said.

"Those were Ganateans," she muttered. "Listen, old woman! I came here to offer you safety, a proposition you cannot in conscience refuse. Will you at least hear it?"

The Aralel sipped her wine. Myril could smell it through the open casement window, a delicate, fruity wine, some of the temple's best. "Tell me," she said.

"The Cereans want to take your priestesses as bed slaves, because they think that's what we are already. I have tried to explain to them that we – that you, the priestesses of Theranis, the priestesses of the dragons – are also scholars and healers, that we have more to offer than mere sex."

"More to offer?" the Aralel's sneer came through in her voice. "How flattering that we can be so useful to them. So, did they hear you?"

"At first, they only laughed, but I have persuaded some of them to consider the women of Theranis as more than mere chattel," Tiagasa said, as if this was to her own credit. "We are not like their women, if what they tell me is true. They are kept indoors, always subjugated, and even their noblewomen do not learn to read. It has taken them some time to get used to the idea that here we are mistresses of our own fates, to a point. The leader of their trade delegation has said that he will persuade his men to stay away from the temples if you pay him tribute."

"Through you, of course. How much does he want? Is there any reason to believe he will honor his promise?"

"He has a reputation as an honest trader and is the most trusted emissary of the king of Cerea. He speaks our language better than any of the rest of his countrymen."

"Has he traded here long?" the Aralel asked.

"Girizit?" Tiagasa said his name slowly, pensively. "He cannot have traded here very long," she said, seeming to savor the thought of him. "He is young enough that his beard shows no white hairs, and his skin is scarcely wrinkled. He's a fine-looking man, well dressed."

"And I imagine that would sway you," the Aralel muttered under her breath.

"What was that?" Tiagasa asked.

"You did not answer my question. How much does he want?"

"He will send a chest to be filled every day until your treasuries are empty, and then he will take the contents of the library and the peresi's chambers. He will leave the elders' courtyard and the sanctuary for last."

"Until the treasury is empty?"

Tiagasa ought to have known that it was far too much to ask, but she asked anyway. This Girizit – or Giri – had some sway over her, as he'd once had over Darna. Was he a magician of their people? Neither Tiagasa nor Darna were fools, but he'd drawn them in.

"The offerings will buy you some time," Tiagasa said. "He will only take a little now, before Midsummer, only one chest a day, and there are not so many days remaining until your precious Iola flies to the dragons' realm again."

The Aralel drew in a sharp breath and was silent for a moment before letting it out slowly.

"We have ten days until Midsummer Eve. We can arrange for ten chests to be sent, but I want five guards from the palace to stand watch at the front gate, another five at the back. You can spare them."

"Only if you send us some of your treasure for safekeeping as well," Tiagasa said. "Scrolls will do nicely. They'll be safer from the waters up on the hill, and Parnet is collecting a library."

"Parnet cannot read."

"Ah, but I can. I can read to him."

"It would serve you well to do so, then," the Aralel said. "You read tolerably well when you were here among us. I trust that you have not forgotten how."

"Don't tell me my work," Tiagasa snapped. She poured herself yet another cup of wine and drank it in one gulp. "We don't need to send guards. Maybe the Cereans will keep their word."

"Maybe this Cerean emissary can control his men and the ones who are coming from Tiadun. Maybe he can't. Send us men. I will see about the scrolls."

"You'd better send them. I can't stand to think what would happen to you if I'm wrong about Girizit's influence with his people."

"You're a common viper, Tiagasa. You say that you would protect us, but only if it serves your own purposes."

"Am I any different from you in that?" Tiagasa asked. "I think that I am simply better at it than you are."

"Get out of my rooms!"

Tiagasa straightened the folds of her robe at a leisurely pace, one stiff pleat after another. "You have until morning to consider my offer."

"You will have my answer then," the Aralel replied.

Tiagasa was thoroughly wrapped up in her own thoughts as she swept out of the Aralel's chamber. She snapped her fingers for the young priestess to follow her, not noticing Myril until she reached the stair.

"You?" she said as she turned the corner. "Have you been listening again, you busybody?"

"Busybody" was a foreign word, one that had been introduced to common speech in Anamat only two or three years before. It had crept in when no one was looking, much like the Cerean tutors had crept into the keeps and palaces over the past few generations, bringing their way of thinking to Tiagasa and her ilk.

"Never mind," Tiagasa said. "It will go badly for you in the end."

Myril had a brief image of that poor young priestess bleeding in an abandoned temple, raped until she wished only for her own death. She felt faint with sympathy, but in the same heartbeat she knew that would not be her own fate. Prophecy is mostly a curse, but sometimes it can keep fear at bay in the face of empty-headed threats.

She heard a great rustle of documents from inside and a clatter as the Aralel swept her table bare, then banged the almost-empty carafe down on it. Myril stood in the open doorway and waited to be noticed.

"Chronicler," the Aralel said after a bit. She waved Myril in. "How much of that did you hear?"

"I arrived when you were asking her to pour the wine."

The Aralel smiled weakly and pulled out a box. "Sit, then, and write all that you can recall of that exchange while I consider what I need to do. You will leave –" She looked around the room and shook her head. "After that, you may relay whatever it is that you came to tell me. As you can see, I'm in no position to offer favors to the guilds, not even one as old and esteemed as the Chroniclers."

"Yes, Your Holiness," Myril said.

"Good," the Aralel said. With that, she went into her inner chamber, where she gave out a long sigh as she lay down to rest.

§

After a time, the Aralel sent for tea and food, and the young priestess who brought the tray set some before Myril, too. She ate without tasting as she concentrated on her writing.

A few of the newer peresi came to speak with the Aralel over the course of the afternoon. Sometimes, their words broke through Myril's concentration.

"No, he didn't strike me," one said, "but he said he'd heard that they do so in Cerea."

"He won't be admitted again. Give his description to the treasurers."

Another came in a while later, coolly composed. "We don't have many petitioners, not compared with last year," she complained.

"It will be easier when the foreigners leave after Midsummer. Don't worry; you'll be provided for."

Myril wrote on, picturing Tiagasa in her gold-threaded robe trying to outshine the Aralel. She hadn't succeeded, and she'd been a fool to think that she could. Myril had never liked Tiagasa, but she was a beauty and not unintelligent. She was greedy for power and bent all her best qualities to expanding her influence. No wonder she sought agreements with the Cereans. It was late afternoon by the time Myril finished the document to her satisfaction. She stood at the entrance to the Aralel's inner chamber, where she hesitated before calling out.

"Your Holiness?"

"Who? Ah, Myril. I didn't hear anyone at the outer door. Come in." She was lying on a couch with a cloth over her eyes, her pale gray hair spread on the pillows around her like a halo. She inhaled deeply before taking the cloth from her face and sitting up. Myril presented the parchments. The Aralel squinted at the writing, nodded, then took the work to a dark corner of her room.

"You should know where this box is," she said. "If anything were to happen to me, to the temple, I hope that the invaders will miss it." An invasion was coming, then; the Aralel was sure of it.

"Why me? Surely, some elder priestess would be better entrusted with this secret. I don't even live in the temple."

"Therefore, you have a better chance to survive," the Aralel said. "You have as much knowledge as some of our elders, yet you're still young and strong. Geta knows of this cache, but she's frail. She may not survive the winter; you will."

As she made that pronouncement, she rolled back the corner of a carpet to reveal a square paving stone, not obviously different from the ones around it. She pushed down on one end, which made the other end tilt up like the lid of a box. Myril held up the lid while the Aralel looked for a stick to prop it up with. It fit into the floor as closely as any of the other paving stones, matching their colors perfectly. The Aralel laid the new parchment pieces inside, on top of a bundle of scrolls and a few small packages containing dragon stones.

The Aralel looked up and away, as if she could see through the walls and across the city to where Tiagasa sat in the governor's palace, holding court for the Cerean emissary.

"I think I may know something more about that Girizit," Myril said.

The Aralel startled up. "You do? Tell me what you know, but let's close this up first."

Myril loosened the stick and tried to ease the stone down without dropping it, but it clanged noisily as it shut. Too many drops, or a drop at the wrong angle, and the stone would split. "Darna could probably devise some cushion for this," she thought aloud.

"Darna? I should say, Darnasa. She was in Slaradun. So many there were drowned. Is she alive?" the Aralel asked.

Myril nodded.

"I would like to see her," the Aralel said.

"She needs to take refuge in the temple, if it's safe here from her uncle and his assassins. Is it?"

"Mostly," the Aralel said slowly. "We'll need to make special arrangements. I'm sure that we can find a way somehow. Gallia, her father's old mistress, has been safe enough here since last Midsummer. Yes, we can offer her refuge. Is she well?"

Myril paused to listen for a moment. No one was in the outer chamber or on the porch to overhear them. "She's changed, but she's alive and mostly well. She survived the fall of Slaradun."

"It might be better for her if she looked sickly," the Aralel mused, as if she hadn't heard Myril at all. She looked away, abstractedly, then reached a moment of decision. "Have her come in the very early morning, before full light. I'll give you elders' robes, and in the dark, if you draw lines around her face with charcoal, she will look like an elder priestess."

"She doesn't hobble anymore."

"All the better," the Aralel said. "I look forward to her report of what happened in Slaradun." She smiled so that the wrinkles around her eyes spread out until they reached most of the way to her hairline, which was receding.

"Darna would like to speak with Gallia before the tribunal."

"Of course," the Aralel said. "I'll make all the arrangements, one way or another."

Myril worried that it might not be safe for Darna to stay with her even for one night. Midsummer meant drunken men in the streets, and even Theranians could make trouble. No one had broken down her door yet, but others hadn't been so lucky.

"Darna also knows more than I do about this Cerean Tiagasa mentioned, Girizit," she said as she prepared to leave.

"Really? How?"

"You'll have to let her tell that tale," Myril said, "and there's another matter, one that I should have come to you about half a moon ago."

"I am ill equipped to grant favors, and keeping Darnasa here is more than I should do, but she is one of ours, so I will make an exception and meddle in the affairs of princes," the Aralel said. "Go on, though. The parchment you wrote there is worth at least some repayment."

"It's not for myself; it's for the Chroniclers' guild," Myril explained. "We have to hide our histories, our scrolls, and as much of our library as we can. Parnet wants to take our texts to the palace, saying that it's for safekeeping. Tiagasa wanted the temple's texts too, I heard."

The Aralel shook her head. "So, as you heard, the Chroniclers' texts will be no safer here than they are at the guildhall. The only safe place for those secrets may be at the bottom of the sea."

"But they're our histories, our knowledge," Myril said. "The Chief Chronicler hopes that you can keep our most precious scrolls in the temple until the floods recede or until we can find another way of keeping them safe from the Cereans."

The Aralel laughed mirthlessly and shook her head. "I would guard them if I could, but you see I can't. The best I can do is to keep the girls safe, and I'm not even sure I can do that. If some of our peresi hoard their offerings and whatever else they can take from the temple, I can't fault them for it. Your Chronicles would be no safer here than they are in the guildhall, probably less so. More young women, ones I don't know, are coming in every day. You heard our precious Tiagasa. We must keep our treasure to buy them safety however we can, even if it means selling everything but their bodies to the Cereans. Some are leaving already for Ganat and Enomae, where they think it might be safer."

"Like the tradesmen from along the waterfront."

"You know that I can't save the Chronicles."

She was not lying, but Myril had to bring the Chronicler some solution. "Tiagasa asked for a box of scrolls for the palace, as part of your payment. Suppose I brought you some from the guild, to pay her with. We can choose some of the more common ones, ones well known even to provincial novices, ones we have many copies of."

"Tiagasa will notice," the Aralel said.

"She might if she takes the time to inspect them closely, but she won't be able to say that you cheated her. Meanwhile, she'll send guards. I know that Sunna was working on –"

"Sunna is doing as well as she can, but she is away much of the time, and the girls she tried to train this spring are young and none of them are as big or strong as armsmen. We have a dozen half-trained girls with weapons built for men, and Sunna will soon be called away by her other order, I fear."

"I heard you tell one of the young peresi that things would be better after Midsummer."

"I only hope so," the Aralel said. "I like to lend hope where I can, even if it's half wishful thinking. As I've said many times before, I'm no prophetess, but I believe we'll have half a year of quiet before those fools open the trading season again, if any of us lives that long." She steered Myril to the door. "I'm sorry; I can't even safeguard the scrolls we have already. You'll have to find some other way. If you do, come get what you can from our library before the Cereans take it. If you can bring those common scrolls for me, though, I'll find some other way to repay your guild."

"I'll tell the Chief Chronicler that," Myril said, "and I'll keep trying to find some other way."

"I expect to see Darna here tomorrow morning. I'd like for her to tell Iola about what happened in Slaradun, too. Perhaps she can dissuade our ambassadress from throwing her life away while the world is falling down around us."

Myril almost laughed at that. "Surely, you know Iola too. The fear of death won't keep her away."

"No, I suppose it won't, but I'd like for her to live. So many priestesses are afraid of the change in the dragons now that they're trying to leave Theranis like common tradespeople." The Aralel paused. "When you are looking for a place for your scrolls, are you looking beyond our shores?"

Myril shrugged. "I have thought of it. If the waters keep rising, they won't be safe here."

"I wonder where the rest of us will go when it ends," the Aralel said. "I know of nowhere that's safe for priestesses. If you hear of a place that's safe enough for the dragons' secrets, will you tell me? Perhaps the priestesses can go there too."

"I'll see what I can learn," Myril said.

"Do that, then," the Aralel replied, and then she sent Myril off with a threadbare robe for Darna's disguise.

§

Chapter 4

Sunna paced back and forth across the small room all afternoon while Darna lay on the dark bed with her arms around her belly and her face to the wall. The walk back to Anamat had tired her more than she'd thought it would, and she found herself taking deep breaths and falling in and out of a fitful sleep. She woke fully when Myril returned from the temple and the sun was sinking low in the sky.

"How was she?" Sunna asked as she paused in her pacing.

"The Aralel? Preoccupied. Tiagasa was there, demanding bribes and making threats. She seems to be doing the bidding of their Cerean advisor, or trade partner, or whatever he is." Myril turned to Darna. "She said that his name was Girizit, the king's emissary. Is he the one you saw on your way back here, the one you were worried about?"

Darna uncurled herself and sat up. She looked pale, even in the dim light. "It must be. I still don't know how he knew that I was called Darnasa. What does he want?"

"Tiagasa asked for chests of treasure on his behalf, to keep the temple safe, in return for which she would send guards to the temple, to keep the other Cereans away."

"Not much of a bargain," Sunna said. She sat like a man, legs splayed open, and rested her elbows on her knees. "Not one the Aralel could refuse, though."

"She promised to send chests only for the days leading up to Midsummer. After she'd had to go through all of that, I couldn't make much fuss about getting her to agree to keep you there too, but she will, of course," she told Darna. "She's expecting you at dawn. She says that there are too many people on the streets now, and that she needs to make arrangements."

Darna yawned. Whatever her ailment was, it seemed to be making her unnaturally tired.

"Quite right," Sunna agreed, strapping on her sword. "I'll go have a look around for myself and be back in time to see you to the temple, if it's safe enough."

"The Aralel thought she could find a place," Myril said.

"I'd rather know what you think, too," Darna told Sunna.

"Yes, Your Highness." Sunna smirked.

Darna threw a pillow at her, which she avoided by darting out of the door. The pillow fell flat at the threshold.

"I wish she hadn't called me that," Darna said as Sunna clattered away down the stair. "I just don't want to be one of them... I'm not a princess; I barely even wanted to be a keep mistress." Darna sighed. "I don't know why Giri knew who I was, how he figured it out, or how he even recognized me after all these years."

"You recognized him, too, and at least he didn't try to assassinate you outright," Myril pointed out. "He must have heard about you from his countrymen in Tiadun."

"I suppose," Darna mused. "There weren't any other scrapplings that year who would have matched the description they gave of me, little enough as it was."

"Maybe he was just testing the idea, to see how you would react."

"Possible," Darna said. "I may have given myself away. Most likely, he wouldn't want to be associated with that theft all those years ago, either."

Myril shook her head and went to fix herself a cup of tea. "It may not matter so much now. He seems to have Tiagasa in his sway, and as long as she favors him, no one else in the palace is likely to cross him either."

Darna snorted. "I'd like to see her – I don't know; maybe I wouldn't like to see her duped. Either way, I'll have to go to the palace for the tribunal, maybe even before. I wish I hadn't seen him."

They left the subject of Giri aside and had a light supper before resting again. Sunna returned near midnight.

"Unless Tiagasa's appeasers are against you – and I don't think they are yet – the temple itself seems safe enough for now," Sunna reported. "Gallia hasn't been bothered, anyway. She's in one of the old towers near the novices' quarters. I couldn't get much from her except she did say that Calar had always been vile."

"I didn't need her to tell me that," Darna said. "Anything else?"

"She says that they're not allowing Cerean armsmen into the palace at all, so for the tribunal itself, we only have Calar and his men to worry about, and they're no better than other common guardsmen, maybe worse." Sunna yawned. "I should go back to the training hall."

"Please, sleep here," Myril said. "I have another pallet, and I can wake you in the morning."

Sunna hesitated before accepting, but she did accept – after all, it was easier than walking up the hill to the Defenders' hidden hall. Soon, both she and Darna were snoring while

Myril sat vigil through the night. She roused them at cockcrow, sending them off into the still-dark morning.

§

The Aralel met Darna at the door of her chambers. "Ah, good," she said with a weary smile, face crinkled from sleep. "You do look rather old in this dim light, even without your limp."

"I'd like to see Gallia," Darna said.

The Aralel cast a wary eye across the elders' courtyard. "Later, maybe. Come inside. First, you must tell me about Slaradun. You know that my first duty to you is to your priessesshood, and don't tell me that you're not a priestess. I'll send for tea." As the Aralel shooed Darna in, she struck three quick notes on a bell. Across the elders' courtyard, someone shuffled off to the kitchens.

"Go in. Please, it would be best if you stayed out of sight," the Aralel urged her. She barred her outer door as they entered. The room inside was still dark as night; the only light was from a small brazier in the inner chamber, which smoked with a smell that brought elder priestesses to mind. Geta always smelled of one of those dusky herbs, as did most of the scryers, but the Aralel never had before. She shuffled across the carpeted room and sat heavily on her bed. She was getting old, Darna realized.

"You were the prince of Slaradun's lover, and he had no keep mistress," she began. "Given the fact that he is gone – or is he?"

"He's gone," Darna confirmed. "I saw him die, but his mind was gone before that. Just before that."

"I will regard you as his widow and the de facto ruler of Slaradun."

Darna laughed, which made her stomach ball up in agony. It took her some time to recover enough to speak.

"I am in no way – I mean I can't be. I was there for less than a year. I barely know the land, let alone the people, and besides, they're nearly all gone."

"Did the prince have any other heirs?"

"None that I know of, and I don't think any that he knew of. He would have said something, or Harzet might have."

"Harzet?"

"His Cerean advisor – more of a friend, really."

"So, the Cereans had a grip on Slaradun, as they do now on Tiadun? I was unaware of that."

Darna shook her head. "I don't think that Harzet has any power in Cerea. He was more like a steward to Ivanat than anything else, and a friend. He certainly didn't have his own army, not even a single guardsman. All the foreign armsmen I saw there were the ones who came with the Ganateans. In any case, Harzet's probably dead, too."

There was a clatter as someone set a tray down outside the door. The Aralel went to fetch it but handed it to Darna as she returned. Darna set it on a low table and began to pour. There were only a few pieces of bread.

"I don't eat much these days," the Aralel said. "You may have it all, increasing as you are."

Darna clenched her teeth against the cramp. "I don't know that it is that," she said. "I've never borne a baby before, but it doesn't feel right, and Myril thought there was something odd about it."

The Aralel let Darna drink her first cup of tea before she resumed her questions.

"When you came in the spring, you told us that Salara had become male. When the realm dragons begin to change, the land will not stay as it is. Only Na will remain; that's what the prophecies say."

"Will Anara change too?"

The Aralel shook her head. "I don't know. They are only prophecies, some of them secret from anyone except myself and the ambassadresses, but now the rumors on the streets of Anamat – what's left of them – outpace our prophecies. Rumor is a kind of prophecy in itself. It can shape the future, even the minds of the dragons, sometimes."

"I wouldn't have thought of it that way, but I suppose it makes sense," Darna said.

The Aralel cleared her throat. "In any case, you must tell me everything that happened that morning, when Slaradun fell into the sea."

Darna took a deep breath. "Nothing about that night and that early morning fit into the way I've always understood things to be. Dragons don't join with humans, not even priestesses. Not even Ara, or Iola."

The Aralel was still for a moment. "Not usually, but I'm not so sure about Iola, and there were always stories about Ara, how Enat was not her greatest love."

"Of course he wasn't; Anara was. Anyone can see that. It's like Iola with Thorat –" Darna stopped.

"The young man of Enat's order who was here after the attack on Tiada's gate?" the Aralel asked. "But then, he must be; it couldn't be otherwise. Do you know much about the Defenders?"

"Certainly more than I did a year ago, or even after I met the Enatel that day in the spring, but that's not my tale to tell."

"No, I suppose it's not. I'll ask Sunna later. Do go on. Dragons don't join with humans?"

"I didn't think it was possible, but that has to be what it was. I fainted, I suppose, but when I woke, everything was different, not just in the land but in me. My leg was healed. I could run. These pains didn't start right away, but there were the scars, the marks of Salara's scales on me."

"Let me see." The Aralel rose and drew back the heavy curtain from one window, letting in a gray light that seemed bright against the darkness of the chamber.

Reluctantly, Darna unbuckled her belt and drew up her tunic. The Aralel gasped and shut the curtain.

"It glows with its own light, like a dragon. Are you, could you be?"

"I am not a dragon; that much I'm sure of."

"And the thing in your belly?"

"I don't know; I don't think anyone can know. It's painful, though."

"It gives you power, power of a kind no prince of this land has ever had." The Aralel shook herself. "I'm no prophet. I hate it when words like that come to me."

Darna sat back down and took a piece of bread. "I don't think anyone likes prophecy much." She thought, though, that the Aralel should be able to handle prophecy better than anyone else. The fact that it discomfited her made Darna feel deeply uneasy.

"I still don't want Iola to go to the dragons," the Aralel said. "It's a senseless sacrifice. You must try to stop her from wanting to go, even though it's probably futile. Whatever is coming, her death won't stop it, and Anara will take her life when she goes under the earth, or Na will."

"I don't think that she'd want to die any other way."

The Aralel sighed, nodding. "True, but it serves no one. She must be made to see that. I'll have you go to her now. You'll stay in her quarters; it's the safest place in the temple for you. I'll see that a healer is sent over later to help you with the pain. Until then, please try to persuade our ambassadress that her reign is ending."

Darna could think of a dozen arguments for why Iola wouldn't believe that, but the Aralel already knew that it wouldn't be easy – otherwise, she would have done it herself.

"Yes, Your Holiness," Darna agreed.

§

She pulled her shabby gray veil over her head and made her way across the peresi's garden to the ambassadress's quarters, walking alone because she and the Aralel had agreed that that would be least conspicuous. She looked neither to the left nor to the right, locking her focus on her destination. The young peresi on guard at Iola's gate – who Darna did not recognize – let her in without question.

Inside the miniature temple that housed her, Iola was fuming. Not at being woken early but at the Aralel's orders to stay on the surface of the earth, which had been repeated to her again by the elder who brought her morning tea, now cooling on the table by her sleeping nook.

"I must fly!" she said as soon as she saw Darna. She paced around her gilded chamber like a flustered sparrow, robes flapping in her wake. "This decree of the Aralel is –" She stammered. "It's – I say it's blasphemous. How can she ignore the dragons? She's been there; she knows what it's like."

"Aren't you glad that I survived Slaradun?" Darna asked, not really surprised that all Iola could talk about was her own journey to the dragons' realm.

"Slaradun?" Iola said. "You were there?"

Darna nodded. "What have you heard about the last dawn there?" she asked.

Iola poured herself some tea, not bothering to offer any to Darna, who in any case had drunk her fill at the Aralel's rooms. She drank thirstily before answering. "You told me that Salara became male, like Na, and I heard a half-moon ago that he shifted his lands into the sea. I felt uneasy the morning that it happened, and I heard the stones shift as the city sank its heels into the sea. Some of the sea dragons drew closer, many of them. I could see them from the tower that morning. I haven't even told the Aralel, so I don't know why I'm telling you, after all..."

"I'm not surprised that the sea dragons came. They're wild too, aren't they?" Darna said. "Do you know if they're male or female?"

Iola tipped her head as she did when she wasn't sure of herself. As a girl and as a novice in the temple, she'd been perpetually uncertain, but life as a peresi and as the ambassadress had made her deeply self-assured, so long as she didn't stray from her practiced path. The sea dragons were just outside of her direct experience.

"Neither, I think," she answered at last. "They're shifting, like their element, the water."

"Maybe all of the dragons are," Darna said.

"I don't know if Salara lived or died – I don't mean that. Dragons can't die."

Darna's gut turned. "What about Tiada?"

"She went to join the deepest stream. I told you that. It's not death as we know it." She said it as if she were trying to explain something to a child or a particularly obtuse petitioner. "The dragon joins the deepest stream when she has wearied of the human world."

"So, she only dies to us, not to herself?" Darna asked.

"More or less," Iola said. She was being hopelessly vague.

"Did you see Tiada in the other realm?" Darna asked.

Iola looked over to the door. It was open but no one seemed to be it the garden outside, let alone on the stoop. She whispered anyway. "I'm not supposed to speak of the other realm, you know that."

"Did you see her or not?"

Iola glanced around again, this time at the statue of Anara. "A shadow, no more. I'm still human, even when I'm down there. She didn't show herself to me."

"What about Salara?"

"Only at a distance. He seemed to be in pain or sleeping. I wasn't sure, but he did fly up with the others at the crossing time."

Darna frowned. Iola knew that she'd been in Slaradun through the waning year and at the crossing time, but she didn't know the end of it, except whatever Myril or the Aralel might have told her, which couldn't be much.

"I don't mind the thought of dying, if only I can go to the dragons' realm again," Iola said.

"I know you don't mind, but other people do. The Aralel thinks it would be a senseless death."

"It wouldn't be. Maybe they could stop this change, bring Anara's city back above the waves."

"It's not under the waves yet, not even halfway," Darna said, "but it is sinking. Myril told me that people are leaving Anamat already, sailing to Ganat and Enomae, abandoning their places. They heard what happened in Slaradun, and they saw the waters rise here. You can hardly blame them for not wanting to drown."

"You were there," Iola said. "You didn't drown."

Darna looked to the door, wishing that she could just leave. "I didn't, but I was all the way up in the mountains, at Salara's gate, and he...he wouldn't have let me drown."

"No?" Iola sat down and looked up at Darna. "You don't have your cane," she observed.

"Salara is like Na," Darna said. "You'd have to be mad to worship him, or you'd go mad, I think."

"But you saw him?"

Darna closed her eyes and took a deep breath. "More than that," she said, looking Iola in the eye. "Much, much more than that." She wandered over to rest on the offering place, not at all surprised that it had taken Iola so long to notice the changes in her. Iola never paid much attention to the physical world beyond what she could touch with her body. Her jaw dropped as Darna lay back on the silken drapes and looked up at the statue of Anara rearing over her. The dragon's teeth were bright; her eyes shone. Darna felt the currents of the earth coursing up beneath her back. This offering place was a pillar of the world. Iola felt that power every day. For a moment, Darna was almost jealous of her. It was a holy place, as holy as any except maybe the rough gates joining one realm with the other. In the ambassadress's quarters, the realms joined in a different way, a more civilized, more human way. By temple law, only the ambassadress herself could lie there, but after Salara, Darna didn't care. It would hardly anger Anara any more than Salara had been angered by Ivanat, and she'd survived that.

It did, however, anger Iola.

"What are you doing?!"

"Lying on your offering place, or rather, the offering place of the ambassadress. I don't think I could do it here. I don't think I could kill a man. You've never met Calar, have you? I'd half like to sink a dagger in his back before he gets me."

She didn't want to think about Salara anymore. Even Calar was easier to face. She didn't really want to kill him with her bare hands so much as she wanted not to be killed herself.

"Calar didn't come last Midsummer, not to the temple. You can't take my place with him or with any of the others."

Darna sat up. Her belly didn't hurt when she lay on the offering place. "Well, that's just the thing," she said. "The Aralel almost asked me to when I was here in the spring. I never would have thought that I could, but now, I don't see why I couldn't, except that I don't really want to die. I'd rather you didn't either, not even in the dragons' realm."

"I don't know why they're so sure I would die. I didn't die last year. Tiada's shadowiness hurt, though. What does any of this have to do with Salara?"

As if in answer, a bolt of pain shot through Darna's belly, but it was brief and left a lightness in its wake rather than an ache. "Tiada's absence still hurts, doesn't it?"

Iola nodded. "Please, move. Get off of there. You don't belong there."

Darna wasn't so sure about that anymore. The offering place did seem to ease her pain. She moved, just not in any hurry. She sat and admired the drapes, looked carefully at the statue of Anara and the curve of the dome above her. Eventually, she got to her feet and went back to her cup of tea.

"I'm going to tell you about Slaradun, then maybe you'll see."

"I think the prince of Lemirun is supposed to be coming soon. You'd better go."

Darna shook her head. "The Aralel said that I would be staying here with you. It has to be the safest place in the temple. Besides, if anyone comes, they'll warn you; they always do, even for peresi in the outer courtyard."

Iola shook her head. "It's not like it used to be. Peresi are two to a chamber now. It's not the same at all."

"The ambassadress is a peresi too," Darna reminded Iola.

"Don't be ridiculous." Iola sighed and found a stool to sit on. She was thinner than she'd been a year before, but her hair was still darkly luminous and her fine bones had not lost their beauty. "If you must tell me, what happened in Slaradun?"

In answer, Darna began to take off her clothes. "You know that the prince and I were lovers," she began as she let her tattered gray robe fall onto the floor behind her. "At first, I was mostly not a priestess to him, but I was priestess-trained, and in the end, I couldn't help myself, even if it was against his wishes. Ivanat wanted to deny the existence of the dragons. He saw them, but foreigners were his only friends. They'd taught him most of what he knew, and he couldn't face their mockery, so he convinced himself that what he'd seen of the dragons wasn't real."

Darna took off her belt and threw it onto the bed, on top of her cloak. "Ivanat needed Theranian allies, too, though, so he called on Calar of Tiadun for help. When one of Calar's sons came, I fled."

"You told me all of this before."

"I did. I think I also told you about the temple in the mountains? It was old, as old as the hills. It was older, I think, than Anamat, but I could be wrong."

"You must be wrong. Ara and Enat were the first to worship the dragons. They came here."

"They also went into the hills. Maybe they built that place, or maybe they found it. I was inside it, in the baths, when Slaradun fell. I didn't even hear the earth move, let alone feel it."

"But what does that have to do with Salara?"

"I'm sorry; I skipped the most important part." Darna pulled her tunic off over her head, revealing the scale pattern burned onto her belly. "They are fiery creatures."

"What's inside you?" Iola asked, her voice far away. She'd jumped past how closely Salara had touched her, had changed her, as if it were almost a matter of course to lie with a dragon, though as far as Darna knew, Iola's skin was unmarked, unbroken.

"When Salara was done with me – and he is most definitely male – I was thrown to the earth, but rather than being broken, I was un-broken. I woke up on the rocky ground by the gate. Thorat had come to fight off the Ganateans, and I discovered that I could run. I left my stick there. I haven't needed it since. So, I can answer that one question."

Iola looked away.

"Ivanat had been lying with me when Salara came out of the gate. He – Ivanat – wasn't the same either. He'd been so clear in his mind –"

"– except for denying the dragons."

"He knew, though. Salara left him dragon-touched, literally. His madness was much worse than anything I saw among the bandits. His best friend killed him."

"The Cerean? Harzet?"

"You heard about him?" Darna asked, surprised.

Iola shrugged. "Tiagasa visited me. She said that there were other Cereans making arrangements with Slaradun and with Tiadun, as Girizit has been doing here. She was trying to tell me that there was no point in fighting them, that I should join her in adopting their ways."

"She should know you better than that."

"I said that I didn't need to welcome them, but she wants me to see Girizit, to give him audience."

Darna's laugh barked off the walls. "She's the one who's mad, even if it isn't from the dragons. She must be, or else Giri's changed more than anyone. Don't you remember how much he fears and hates the dragons? He'd never come to you."

"Don't I remember?" Iola asked, baffled.

"Girizit is Giri," Darna said. "He was that foreign boy who was pretending to be a scrappling, who tricked me into stealing that stone from the palace, who – I can't believe I believed him, but he had such scars on his back from being whipped. He was terrified of the dragons, always hiding his food from the birds in case they turned out to be dragonlets and clutching his little Cerean cap to his head. Surely, you remember him?"

Iola shook her head. "I was always looking for Anara, and I saw her, too, more than I do now." Her voice was so sad, it was almost heartbreaking, but at least she had seen the dragons and flown with them. So many had not.

Darna draped one of Iola's blankets around her shoulders and felt a strange heat stirring inside of her, a new sensation. Iola reached for Darna's belly, but she hesitated before touching it.

"Go ahead," Darna said.

Iola knelt on the bare marble floor and reached out her thin fingers to trace the lines Salara had left. As her fingers touched the scale-print, it glowed like a dragonlet. She leaned in closer and kissed Darna's belly, the heat of it rising to her lips.

"It belongs to the dragons. The Aralel's right; you should stay here to guard it. It's not safe outside, not even in the rest of the temple."

Darna slid away from Iola's covetous reach. "Do you think that I'm safe here, really?"

"You're not important. What's inside you is," Iola said. "I mean, it's not that you're not important at all; it's just that this is new, this is the seed of what's to come."

"It's probably just a baby," Darna said. "Villagers say that about babies all the time."

"You can stay here when I'm under the earth," Iola said.

"You're not going under the earth. Everyone agrees on that."

"I don't, and neither do the dragons. I don't think the elders have done a real divination. They can hardly tell me that the dragons don't want my sacrifice."

"With all of this, with the foreigners running across the land to steal everything they can, your death won't be enough," Darna said. "Surely, you must see that."

Iola shook her head. "My going down to the dragons might give them the strength they need to shake off the foreigners, to keep a little of their land without being overrun. Anara..." She looked up at the statue and shook her head. "I like to think that she would carry me down again."

"There's no purpose in it," Darna said.

"There is," Iola insisted.

In the silence after she spoke, they heard the clang of the gate opening outside.

"There's one more thing I should tell you: Thorat should be back in Anamat soon."

Iola brightened at that. "Oh!" Her cheer evaporated as quickly as it had come. "But it's no good. His usual way in is flooded."

"I'm sure he'll manage somehow." Darna wondered if maybe she could crouch behind the dais with a kitchen knife and dispatch Calar when he came to spill his power into Iola, if he came at all.

One of the treasurer priestesses hurried in, and Darna ducked out of sight of the doorway.

"The prince of Onarun is here. You will receive him now," the treasurer said.

Iola glanced in Darna's direction. "Tell him to come back tomorrow."

"The Aralel wishes us to keep the peace."

"All right, let him in, then," she said, resigned to this part of her fate, "but tell the Aralel I don't want to see any more today."

"As you wish, Most Blessed One." The treasurer priestess spat out the honorific, then left in a flurry of gold and green.

Iola sighed. "I'd better prepare myself. There's shelter in the garden; you can stay out there. I'll get rid of him as soon as I can."

"Be careful," Darna said.

"I will, I promise." Iola smiled. "And I'll see if I can't put that dragon-killer Calar off when he comes."

"If he comes," Darna said.

Iola followed her out into the garden and pointed the way to the hiding place, then ran back inside to prepare for her powerful but unwelcome petitioner. No, Darna did not envy her, not one bit.

§

Chapter 5

E ppie could have stayed in that mountain valley forever, even though its beds were rocky, the fare was rough, and its high cliffs cut out the soft slanting sunlight at the ends of the day. In that valley, surrounded by friends, she'd slept more deeply than she ever had before. She'd dreamed dreams that were not nightmares. There was no place in the world that felt more like home, even though she'd only been there a few days and knew that she would have to leave again soon. The village she'd been born in was so far away that it hardly mattered. Anamat felt more like her native place than the village did, but it was never entirely safe, always ready to cast an errant scrappling out.

She'd only just begun to feel at home in the Defenders' hidden hall when she'd been sent off to find Thorat in Tiadun, then back in the city, she still had to dodge the watch. The harbor was changing, becoming less welcoming, as new fleets of foreign ships came in and their dark warehouses multiplied. In the mountains, there were no foreigners or city watch, and there never would be. Some of the bandits were mad, true, but their madness came from the dragons, and she felt sure that none of them would harm her, especially not with Sovara at her back.

"You two go first," Sovara said the night after Darna had left. Eppie was sitting beside Thorat and the Enatel was looking right at them as she spoke. Sparks flew up from their campfire into the clear, still night air. They were running out of provisions, and more importantly, Midsummer was coming.

Eppie wanted to beg to stay until the end but she knew that they needed to leave in small groups. If they all went at once, it might draw attention to the place, and besides, the elders might want to council together without the younger Defenders. Eppie was little more than an apprentice, even though she'd been to the dragons' gates twice.

The bandits in their various groups and the Defenders had made the gathering something like the princes' Midsummer council. Together, they'd conferred about ways to keep foreigners and most lowlanders out of the hills. They'd also shared stories and fighting techniques. With the help of the dragons and a little luck, they hoped to help make Darna the de facto ruler of Tiadun, shaking the Cereans loose from their foothold in that one small, dragon-forsaken corner of Theranis.

Tiada wouldn't rise from below the deepest stream for a very long time, not until Anamat was long lost under the sea, its temples worn away to sand, Eppie realized.

"Eppie?" Garren said.

"Sorry, I wasn't listening."

"Sovara wants us to leave at first light," Thorat said. "She wants to make sure that I can find myself some position at the palace before this tribunal so we have ears there, even if mine aren't as good as some." He sighed. He didn't want to leave the valley any more than she did.

She looked around the circle. "I don't suppose I could –" Eppie began, but she stopped herself from wishing aloud. "All right, we'll go." They'd told her about the flooding in Anamat. She needed to see it for herself.

§

The next morning, Eppie found herself looking out at her once-familiar city and the changed face of the Anamat valley.

"We could have died in Slaradun," Thorat said.

"Or in Tiadun."

"Maybe that would have been better," he sighed.

She did wonder if it would have been better to die before seeing those changes. There was a ship on the horizon, heavy laden, bound away for some foreign port. She felt a weight in her heart like the weight of that ship's cargo as it dragged the city away in pieces. She swallowed and shook herself. "Does it make any difference what we do?" she wondered aloud.

Thorat shrugged. "I half-wish that we could just join the bandits, but I'm not ready to abandon Anamat to the Cereans just yet." Thorat's eyes rested on one spot, one particular golden roof. He was probably pining for the ambassadress again.

"We'd better go, then, if you're going to see the ambassadress before she flies again," Eppie said, and so they set off, taking it all in in silence.

As they walked down into the valley, two more ships appeared on the horizon, wending their way to Anamat harbor or, rather, the bay that had once contained the harbor. A long troop of soldiers was crossing the pass from Galamun, some of them bearing the orange-and-blue banners of Tiadun, others clad in drab Cerean gray cloth.

"That'll be Calar," Thorat said. "We'd better get to the city before he does."

They walked until after dark and slept in an orchard, then breakfasted at Raina's house. They set out again into the thick of the morning market crowds.

"I'd better go right up to the palace or I'll find some reason not to," Thorat said as they approached the gates. "I'll meet you at Myril's place later."

Eppie thought about going back to the hall, where there might be a bit of peace, but Myril would have news of Darna's arrival in the city, and she always had food, too. Eppie's stomach grumbled despite the bread she'd had at Raina's house.

A dense crowd stood in front of Garren's shop, waiting to get their sweets. Eppie checked her pocket. She had a few beads, so she joined the throng. At the counter, Garren's wife was looking harried but doing a brisk business.

"That'll be two small ones," she told the man in front of Eppie as she handed over a wrapped bundle.

She looked quickly at Eppie. "He's not here," she said.

"I know," Eppie replied. "He'll probably be back the day after tomorrow."

"Not soon enough. Here." Garren's wife handed her a nut pie. Eppie offered her a bead but Garren's wife waved it away. "Get going; I've got work to do. And keep away from the new dock. There's been trouble around there, slavers," she warned.

Eppie nodded, but of course, the first thing she did was to go down to the harbor. The route past Merchants' Wharf was the quickest, and right there at the shore, they were building a new dock haphazardly tacked on to the old one. There wasn't a Theranian in sight. Enomaean laborers worked on the dock while a Ganatean crew fitted out its vessel with ropes, which a Cerean appeared to be selling to them. A guardsman came along, swinging his staff, the only Theranian in sight, and not a

friendly one. Eppie backed into an alley just in time to get out
of the path of a noisy cart rattling down the road.

The alley led her to a spot just downhill from the
Pentangle, so she tucked her nut pie into her pouch and
crossed over to Myril's stair but found the door bolted shut, so
she thought she'd go see how far Calar and his army had
marched that morning. It was nearly midday, so she walked
back up the street, through the Pentangle, and down to the
West Canal to one of the old secret passageways. The way was
damper than it had been before – she had to wade at one point
and she stubbed her toe on a sharp rock – but it was still
passable.

She emerged into the hard light of the afternoon sun, on a
dusty embankment shaded only by a few thin bushes. Horses'
hooves beat like threshers on the ground, driving up the dust.

"To the palace gate!" Calar's order was relayed back
along the line.

"We'll camp there and pasture our horses," someone
said.

"I was hoping for better than a horse pasture," one of the
Cereans complained. "Anamat. After all these years, and I
can't even get in to have a look at a priestess."

"Shut it. We'll get in. Just have to have a word with the
governor."

Most of the grumbling voices made their complaints in
foreign languages. Dust dimmed the air, but the army was
splendid in its own way. The horses' flanks shone softly while
spears and spade weapons caught the light of the sun. They
looked ready to fight, or to despoil a dragon at the slightest
provocation, now that she knew that the spades they carried
were for fighting, more than for digging.

Eppie, darting from bush to bush, made for the head of
the army. There, Calar rode with his remaining son behind

him, their expressions blank and bored. They did look something like Darna in the hair and the shape of the nose, Eppie thought, but they had a different air about them, complacent where Darna always seemed fretful.

She stayed where she was as the rest of the army rode past. She counted fifty horsemen in all, most of them Cereans, and about a hundred foot soldiers and servants. Men whispered behind Calar's back, sending their own messages down the line and to their countrymen on the harbor. She watched until they reached the palace gates, then hurried back to safety.

§

Meanwhile, Myril listened. She'd heard Eppie come to the door but had been half-asleep, so she didn't recognize her until she was already most of the way back up the hill. She heard Calar's approach, too, the voices talking in strange languages, the clomp of horses' hooves, the cursing and muttering and an arrogant boast from Calar that no woman would unseat him, not even a whole pack of them, followed by muttered assurances from a soft-voiced Cerean, his voice dripping with cunning.

Myril blocked out the menace of Calar and his allies to turn her attention back to what was nearer at hand. On the street below, one of the women who told fortunes was attempting to have a conversation with a Ganatean man. They communicated mostly in hand gestures and anxious smiles. A young sailor came upon them and offered to translate, at which point the Ganatean gave him a small coin and the conversation moved forward.

"He wants to know when he will die," the young sailor translated.

The scryer hesitated. "Come inside," she said. Myril's sense was that neither man would threaten her neighbor, but she kept listening just in case. She could picture the scene by the sounds that came up through the floor. She'd been in that room many times; it was a familiar scene apart from the addition of the translator.

The Ganatean sat on a low cushion while the scryer prepared her bowl, swirling the water around it for a ritual cleansing. He said something and the translator interpreted it. "He says that he saw half of his shipmates drowned; he saw the dragon of Slaradun and thought that it would kill him."

"He saw the dragon?" The scryer startled, almost dropping her bowl. Water sloshed over its edge and a drop fell onto the carpet. She set the bowl down before her client with shaking hands. "He is very fortunate," she said to the translator. "Not all are so honored."

She lit the incense, and after several rounds of talk between the young sailor and the Ganatean, the sailor spoke in Theranian again.

"Can you tell him when he will die, he wants to know? Or if he can stop the dragon from killing him?"

"That dragon won't kill him, because she can't reach here; this isn't her realm," the scryer said, confident in that bit of traditional knowledge. "However, he should go to the temple or even to a street-corner shrine and make a free offering to Anara, not one just to seek a priestess's company. Then..." She trailed off. The water in her bowl had stilled. The scryer murmured a prayer over it. When she spoke again, it was in a faraway voice, as if she were in trance, though if it were at all genuine, it was a very light trance. Myril knew that the scryer was in full possession of herself, still cautious of the two men in her room. "Tell him that he should go home to his own country as soon as he can," she said. "The dragons cannot reach him there, and he is right to fear them, but the dragons of the sea will not trouble him."

The young sailor translated this, and the Ganatean grunted with satisfaction, even though she had not told him the time of his death as he'd asked. In all likelihood, he didn't really want to know. He opened his purse to the scryer and gave her the usual fee, a middling bead. She thanked him and he made his way out onto the street, but the translator stopped in the door before he left.

"Is that what you tell all of them?" he demanded. "To go home, to leave you alone? They won't do it, you know, not until they've got what they came for. They're a trading nation, haven't got much on their shores; they just get rich from bleeding other lands dry."

"And they would bleed us," the scryer said.

The translator shrugged. "Most of them aren't bad; it's just their rulers."

"He saw the dragon," the scryer mused. "Have you seen a dragon? Of course you haven't. It's not right that they should see them when we can't. I was born here in Anamat, and I've still only ever seen Anara at festivals, on crossing days."

"And you call yourself a scryer," the young sailor said. He spat on the ground, but he did not claim to have seen Anara himself. He trundled down toward what was left of the ropers' market, where his bead would buy him more weak ale than it would elsewhere.

A small band of drummers – farmers from just outside the city, about a dozen men and women – made their noisy way down the street, weaving from one doorway to the next, drunkenly urging the women of the street to join the song and dance. Myril retreated into her own thoughts as well as she was able.

She knew only pieces, secondhand tales of what had happened in the past year and a bit, but they were beginning to fit together into a tapestry of sorts. Two dragons had fallen after invaders came to their shores, but they'd fallen in very different ways, ways which made little sense in light of what she'd been taught as a young priestess. Which of the two places – Tiadun or Slaradun – was more like Anamat? How would Anamat fall, if it did? When it did.

Tiadun was a distant province, not well known for its piety or its wealth. It was a middling sort of a place, where harvests were generally good enough but not much happened. The priestesses who served there didn't complain of their lot, but they reported that the numbers and ardor of their petitioners had dwindled in the past generation, more so than elsewhere. The rulers there had turned their backs on the dragons. Darna's father, who had been the rightful prince, had worshiped Farseer, the Enomaeans' eagle-headed god, and stopped visiting the dragons' temples. His brother and murderer, Calar, continued to visit the temples, but Myril guessed that he and his sons treated the priestesses with contempt. She'd heard that they'd been seen in some of Anamat's lesser temples the past Midsummer.

All of it suggested that Tiada, once a mighty dragon, had dwindled and grown weary of humankind. When the miners came to rob her lifeblood from the land, their wayward arrows found their mark. She died, the soul of the land died, but the rock and soil of it went on, desolate.

Slaradun had been different. There, too, the dragon had been neglected and disappeared. The prince and his father had torn down their temples and driven out all but a few priestesses, most of whom had come to Anamat soon after Ivanat had taken charge of Slaradun keep. There hadn't been many, even then. From what Myril could piece together,

Salara had gone into the dragons' realm for a long time, and when he emerged, he was changed and stronger, perhaps ready to make war on humankind. He had drowned them, losing all of his land but the mountains.

And what did that mean for Anara? Anara had not faded, nor had she gone under the hills. Her temples were weakened, but they were still far stronger than Tiada's or Salara's had ever been, and yet the city played hostess to the men of Cerea, Ganat, Enomae, and other lands, all making war on the dragon by asking her priestesses to be other than they were, by presuming that Theranis's dragons were not real, while slavering after the stones, which anyone could touch, and believing in their magic despite their scorn of its source.

Myril's head ached. She closed her eyes as if that would shut out the too-high-pitched laughter of her fellow healers and scryers as they contended with the steady flow of people at their doorsteps who understood nothing. Now and again, she heard the familiar accents of valley farmers, the people who might have come to her if she'd only left her sign out, but she would not put it out again, at least not before Midsummer.

§

Despite the noise from below, Myril fell into an uneasy sleep. She woke when Eppie returned to try her door again, and they supped together. Eppie fell asleep in the late afternoon, and Thorat arrived around midnight, rapping loudly on the door frame. Myril got drowsily to her feet to let him in.

"Your sign is down," he said as she opened the door. "Is Eppie here?"

Myril put two fingers over her mouth to signal him to quiet. "She's sleeping. Come over by the window."

They sat down and looked out at the street. He didn't ask for tea and Myril was glad; she didn't feel like lighting a fire. He looked thin and a little paler than usual, but he didn't seem overly tired or feverish. Whatever wounds he'd taken were healing well.

"Things are dangerous these days, and I have other work to do," she said after a while. "Darna told me that you were wounded at the gate."

Thorat nodded. "Eppie tended me and took me to the bandit camp. It's mostly better now." He pulled his tunic back from the shoulder to show her. The wound was long and still red, but it was beginning to pucker together and someone had stitched it tolerably well. Though it wasn't festering, he did wince a bit when he flexed it, so as he talked, Myril prepared a poultice. Thorat spoke some about the fall of Salara's gate, then skipped over most of a moon-round to his return to Anamat.

"Eppie and I got back to the city this morning," he said. "The others will be back soon too. I went to the palace, just hoping to get some news, but they wanted to hire me on right away." He sighed. "I don't like Parnet, and surely one of these Midsummers, he's going to see that, but for now, I couldn't refuse. Someone has to be there to have ears on them all before the tribunal."

Myril nodded. "Darna was here yesterday. What happened to her in Slaradun?"

"At the gate?" Thorat said. "It's not mine to speak of."

"And no one understands it," Myril said. She wanted to know more, though, practical things if not the inner changes the dragon had wrought in Darna. "How many survivors do you think there were?"

"In Slaradun? I don't know," Thorat said. "Not many from the keep or the village around it, but I guess about half of the men who were at the camp lived – those were the ones who were going to mine Salara's stones. There were Ganateans and some Slaradun men, too. I'm not sure about the Cerean who came with them." He shook his head. "If I could have chosen who would survive..."

"You can't; none of us can." Myril didn't want to give him room to lapse into regret. Dark smudges under his eyes showed that the journey had tired him.

"Some survived, though. I saw a boy up at the palace who was a page for the prince of Slaradun. He was planning to take work in the palace scriptorium if they'd have him."

"He'd do better to apprentice to the Chroniclers' guild," Myril said.

"In any case, I was about to come back here when I crossed the path of our lord governor."

"And?" Myril prompted.

"He wanted me to join his personal guard again; Calar was marching up to the gate just then and he sent me to be outfitted right away, to shore up his showing of armsmen. I don't know that one more man in the guards makes much difference against so many, but there I was, back at his beck and call after all these years," Thorat said. "They don't seem to worry so much about the other Cereans, the ones that were already in Anamat and their own palace."

"Not as much as they should," Myril said. "So, what happened when Calar arrived?"

§

The governor, Parnet, went out to meet the arriving army, flanked by his mistress Tiagasa and his new advisor, Girizit, slave and emissary of the king of Cerea.

"You could have left them in your own province," Parnet said to Calar as soon as the formal greetings had been exchanged.

There were more Cerean soldiers and Theranian armsmen outside the palace gate than there were inside, certainly more than the palace could comfortably accommodate as guests. Thorat turned half away, not wanting to meet the gaze of any of the guardsmen he might have worked alongside in Tiadun. They would be sure to recognize him and might remember that he'd left shortly before the "hunting accident" that had taken the late prince's life. He kept his gaze on the governor, counting the arriving soldiers in his peripheral vision – two dozen, three dozen, maybe five dozen, though there were some around the bend in the wall, too.

"I wouldn't have them take advantage of my lands in my absence," Calar said. He neglected to mention that they were not yet confirmed as his own lands, and Parnet did not remind him of the fact just then.

"I'm sure you're happier that they run amok in neighboring provinces," Parnet said as they started toward the palace itself. He and Tiagasa flanked their visitor. "Galamun and Getedun are not happy. They might support your challenger at this tribunal."

Calar blanched for a moment. "I do not expect to see any challenger," he said.

"Word has come to us that she expects to see you, however."

"I see. Will Gallia come alone?"

"The Aralel says otherwise," Tiagasa put in. "I had a message from her this morning that Darnasa is in Anamat."

"I trust that the trading season is going well?" Calar said, as if he were ignoring Tiagasa.

Parnet gave a nod to Girizit, whose brocade waist wrap puffed ostentatiously. "It is going more than tolerably well, but we cannot accommodate your armsmen. You and your son will stay within the palace walls, of course. Will your other son be joining us, or is he remaining at your keep?"

"May my advisors enter?" Calar asked.

Girizit nodded to the governor, who frowned.

"They should make camp with their countrymen, but they may join us at the feast tonight. I'll ensure that they have tents suitable to their station."

Calar had no consort at his side, and one of his sons was also absent. Thorat wondered if Calar knew that he was probably dead in Slaradun. For all of the army at his back, Calar lacked the company of those who should have been his closest allies. Tiagasa patted Parnet's arm and made as if to say something, but Parnet waved her away. She cast her gaze downward. Girizit was observing her closely.

"Let us all go in now to the midday meal, my lords," she said sweetly as the inner gates shut behind them. Calar's son looked uneasily over his shoulder, though Calar himself did not turn around, affecting nonchalance.

Thorat ducked behind a pock-nosed guardsman as Tiagasa led her new guests to a moderately sized chamber where a generous meal was spread. The room faced one of the walled gardens, and though the food was plentiful and smelled delicious, the serving dishes were not quite as good as the ones that the governor would ordinarily have used when entertaining a prince. The governor would be an unlikely ally to Darna's case against her uncle. Then again, perhaps he only wanted to remind Calar that his position as ruler was not yet recognized in Anamat.

"You there," Parnet called to Thorat. "Check the wine."

Thorat took the glass, feeling every eye on him as he drank. "It is good."

Parnet watched him a moment longer, as did Calar. Calar's son looked too. A flicker of recognition crossed his face – they'd sparred often enough in training that of course he surely recognized Thorat, but still, all the Tiadun men really knew of him was that he'd been their champion at the Midwinter games. To them, he was only an ordinary guardsman, and it was not at all remarkable that he might have taken employment in the city at Midsummer. Few of them had been at Tiada's gate, where the Cereans had taken the lead. Thorat would try to avoid Calar's Cereans.

Tiagasa and Girizit were absent, as if they'd gone off to some private conference of their own.

A serving maid set platters in front of each guest, heaped with meat, greens, breads, and fruit, then filled their glasses with the excellent wine Thorat had just tasted.

"You have far too many Cereans in your company," Parnet said. "Our customs are clear. All trade is to be conducted through Anamat."

"Customs change, but that is not my purpose in bringing them here. The men who rode with me from Tiadun are not mere traders. They are my allies and advisors."

"They looked a great deal like common sailors to me, Lord Prince," Girizit said as he returned. He took a seat opposite Calar. He, at least, seemed eager to treat Calar as the legitimate ruler of Tiadun.

Parnet motioned for the serving maid, and a moment later, Girizit had a platter and a full cup of wine in front of him. Girizit looked curiously at Calar and his son.

"Girizit is the emissary of the king of Cerea. He is our honored guest," Parnet said by way of introduction.

Girizit bowed his head only slightly. He gave Calar a thin smile and turned his attention to his bread, which he tore into crumbs before eating it in tiny morsels, like a bird.

"I am sorry that we were not permitted to bring our own advisor here to dine with you," Calar said, frowning at the governor. "He is the steward of the Duke of the Southern Reaches of Cerea."

"I am aware of that," Girizit said. "Did you know that the duke was exiled?" He paused to watch Calar's face for a moment. "I see that you did not. Be advised."

"I have heard no such thing, and I do not believe it."

"I only heard the news this morning, when a new ship of ours arrived," Girizit said. "Word may not have reached you yet, but my sources are unimpeachable."

Tiagasa, too, had returned to the room. "What is this nonsense about the Cerean king exiling dukes? It's no concern of ours. Prince Calar, you are late to the councils. You may even be too late to take your turn with the ambassadress."

Calar was about to say something, but Parnet cut him off. "We will be able to arrange something, I'm sure. You will go to see the Most Blessed One as soon as this tribunal has confirmed your right as ruler."

If it does, Thorat thought. He made himself think of other things.

"As you wish, Your Excellency," Calar said. He turned to Girizit, who was leaning back as he picked at crumbs, squinting at Calar's son. "The duke of the Southern Reaches cannot possibly be in rebellion against his king," Calar said.

"It is more than possible," Girizit said as he dusted his crumbs onto the floor. "But I would not like to bore our lady with, as she says, affairs which are no concern of hers."

Calar seemed to take the hint. Talk turned to the condition of the roads across the Anamat valley, which Calar reported were good, and to the hunting in the hills, the only topic Calar's son seemed inclined to comment on. No one mentioned the ravaging of Getedun's temples again, not even obliquely. Tiagasa sat between Parnet and Girizit, keeping her eyes downcast. Girizit occasionally looked at Calar's son with a pensive expression, but then he would turn back to the mutilation of his meal, which he must have judged unsatisfactory, for he left most of it there, albeit in smaller pieces.

§

Later that afternoon, a box from the Chroniclers was delivered to the governor or, rather, to the Cerean emissary. Girizit opened it without ceremony and began scanning the scrolls and flinging them aside until he found one that was a little different from the others. He picked it up, inspected the writing along the edge, and sliced the wide ribbon that bound it together, then unfurled it on the table. He made to weigh down the ends, but being so lately bound, it lay flat of its own accord. Giri read it anyway, then he rolled it up again and slapped the table with it, as if he were swatting at a fly.

"The ink is scarcely dry," Girizit accused the governor. "This is a forgery. You are keeping the secrets of the dragons' magic from me."

"I am doing no such thing," Parnet protested. "I don't have the secrets you seek, and I'm not sure that the guild has them either, though if any of the guilds does, it would be the Chroniclers."

"The relevant texts must exist," Girizit hissed. He turned to Parnet. "These are your people. Are they not properly subjugated?"

"You know yourself that a governor, or even a king, must rule in concert with the merchant class," Parnet said. "You are a merchant, too; surely you must respect that."

Girizit threw the scrolls back into their box, called for his own servants, and left without ceremony.

"Will we see you for the feast tonight?" Parnet called after him.

"You may rely on it," Girizit said. "And make sure that Calar brings his Cerean friend, too. He and I have matters to discuss."

§

Chapter 6

Darna had always loved the ambassadress's garden, but it did not suit her mood. She paced the tiny quadrant of it that was out of sight of both the gate and the entrance to Iola's chamber, where the prince of Onarun was rutting away. Darna felt no stir in the energy of the dragons in the earth beneath her feet, despite the rite in progress. Maybe the magic of the ambassadress's realm was constant, unmoved by the rite no matter what the ambassadress did, or maybe the dragons had become indifferent to even the most alluring priestess in the land.

It was no good to be back in Anamat and then have to be shut up in the temple again, though she hoped that it would only be for a few days. She wondered – not for the first time – how Iola managed to live as she did, always trapped within those walls. Then again, she did get to go to the center of the earth, where no other living person could follow. Perhaps that compensated for her confinement. The princely petitioner lingered.

Darna itched to go out, to see what the rising waters had changed in all the quarters of the city, to find out which of her old secret ways were still passable. She even half-wanted to see Tevan, her never-quite-satisfactory former lover. She fidgeted.

The sun warmed the earth and the flagstone pathways. Some flowers reached for it while others shrank back into the shade. The cooling waterfall fountain burbled.

She needed to see Gallia. She wanted to talk to Myril, or even to Tiagasa, to find out what form the tribunal would take. Would Tiagasa take Calar's side, or hers, or would she hang back, the image of a meek Cerean woman? That would be the worst of all. It was foolish to confront Calar, who had any number of henchmen and an army at his back. She didn't want any throne, much less the throne of a barren land, a place where she had only ever loved the dragon, and the dragon was gone. Still, she could not let Tiada go unavenged. Letting Calar take the land and hand it to his Cerean troops would be the worst of insults to the dragons. Besides, the bandits in the hills and the Order of Enat thought she should take it back, and no one else could be expected to take her place. She could hardly let them down now.

At long last, when the sun was high in the sky, the prince of Onarun left. As he went out through the gates, a messenger arrived, a young priestess who must have been waiting for him to leave. Darna heard the murmur of their voices from inside, then the messenger hurried out again. She realized that she was hungry, but the cramps deeper in her belly hadn't troubled her all morning. As soon as the gate clanged shut behind the messenger, Darna darted back inside.

Iola was in the bath. "Who's there?" she called out.

"It's only me," Darna said.

"There's a message there for you – you're to go see someone. Sunna is coming to escort you. All of the princes have arrived, Calar too. They say he's at the palace gate now."

Darna's belly cramped briefly at the mention of her uncle's name.

"How many more do you have left to see?" she asked. As beautiful as the garden was, it was awkward to wait there while Iola saw her petitioners, not that it had ever bothered her much during her season in the peresi's courtyard. There, the young priestesses had often passed the doors of each others' chambers when there was a petitioner inside, just to be sure that all was going as it should. But that had been different: she hadn't been trapped and obliged to keep her presence a secret.

"Come in here, why don't you?" Iola said.

Darna realized that she'd been standing awkwardly in front of the offering place, which reeked of sex and perfume. Its power felt diminished, not as strong as it had been earlier when she'd lain there herself. At the door of the bath chamber, a wave of steam wrapped around her, like a tendril of the dragons' power reaching up.

"I think I'd better stay out here," Darna said.

Long ago, when they'd been young priestesses in the temple together, Myril had been sucked under in the baths, almost into the dragons' realm herself. The dragons had never wanted to claim Darna like that, but now, with whatever was in her belly, she was afraid to tempt them.

"I haven't seen all of them, I know that for sure," Iola said, drifting across the pool with languid strokes. "I think there have been eight so far, and Parnet."

"That should mean four more, including Calar," Darna calculated, "if he's going to come at all."

"That was the other part of the message! Their councils will begin tomorrow evening."

Anxiety gripped her by the throat. She wasn't ready. There was a cough at the outer doorway, and Darna turned to see Sunna standing there, dressed in priestess garb but with the unmistakable shape of a sword poking out the left side of her robes.

"Gallia's waiting," Sunna said. "Did you get any of that?" She pointed to a tray of food on a table beside the offering place, as far as possible from Iola's sleeping nook. It was piled high with some of the best delicacies Anamat had to offer, including juicy meat pies, a salad of early berries, the temple's bread, and a carafe of wine. One of the cakes had been bitten into, and there was a spoon in the bowl of olives, but otherwise it looked untouched. Darna salivated.

"Go on, eat quickly," Sunna urged her while taking one of the pies for herself. "I'll see if I can open the other passage." She disappeared into the garden while Iola continued to float in her bath, humming softly.

§

All too soon, Sunna hurried Darna across the garden and out through a hidden doorway behind a fall of ivy near the fountain. The door had an ingenious design. Darna noted the place where Sunna pushed against a bit of mosaic, all of her energy focused into her straining finger. The mechanism creaked, but it did open. Beyond it was a long, narrow tunnel lined with rough, ancient stone. The floor was slightly damp in places, but it had not flooded. The passage emerged into a storeroom near the old sanctuary. From there, they hurried across the back courtyard with their hoods up. Sunna shooed her into a meeting room on the elders' courtyard, then went off to fetch Gallia.

It took Darna a moment to realize where she was. The curtained room felt dusty in the dim light filtering around the edges of the curtains. When she'd first seen the place, as a novice, it had been sumptuous. There, she and the others had waited on the old governor and his guests on the day before their initiation. The room had been built to rival and surpass the governor's chambers in the palace. She wondered if its tapestries had been threadbare along the bottom hem then, or if they'd been worn ragged in the years since. Would the elders air the room before Parnet came to leer at whatever new girls, if any, were moving from the novices' halls to the peresi's garden?

Despite the dust, she could tell that everything in the room had been beautifully made. The tooled silver pot at the center of the table needed polishing, but it was old, probably from before the beginning of the decline of the guilds, some hundred years before. Darna was about to pick it up to examine it more closely when she heard one of the tapestries behind her move, and a slippered footfall on the stone floor at the room's hidden entrance.

Gallia paused to look around before she entered. When she saw that Darna was alone, she let the tapestry fall shut behind her.

At first, they said nothing to each other. Gallia looked older than she had the summer before, but then Darna smiled to realize that it was probably only her hair – she'd stopped dyeing it.

"I understand that Calar has arrived at the palace," Darna said.

Gallia nodded. "My girl there just brought me the news. They're to feast tonight, and the councils begin tomorrow night. Our part in it could come at any time, but Parnet will want to have it as soon as possible, to see whether or not to include Calar in the rest of the councils."

"Tomorrow?" Darna said. It was too soon. The bandits wouldn't have had a chance to come in from the hills in time.

"They will most likely have only their opening ceremonies tonight and drink a great deal of wine. That's what Terenet said they always did on the first night. He didn't enjoy that part of it. Maybe he was a little bit like you in that. Nalani tells me you're impatient."

Darna smirked. The Aralel would say that.

Gallia circled the heavy table that dominated the center of the room, to stand opposite Darna, resting her hands on the board. "What made you decide to help me in challenging Calar?"

Darna looked over her shoulder. She'd barred the door to the courtyard behind her, but she guessed that there might be more than one other entrance, too. She hadn't thought to look before Gallia had come in, which was foolish.

"A few things," she said, "one of which is that Hedrin tried to kill me, even though he wasn't really sure of who I was."

Gallia snorted. "He's a fool, that one, and always has been."

"The prince imprisoned him in the dungeon. If was still there when the waters rose, when Slaradun fell –"

"Then we need not worry about him anymore," Gallia said. "Sad, he was so young, but I doubt he would have improved much with age. His father certainly hasn't. That leaves only Renar, who was never even as good a swordsman as his brother. Neither of them had much else to recommend him. An excellent archer, though. It's lucky that the council chambers will be too crowded for a man to draw a bow in, to shoot you with, and that you have the prince of Slaradun as an ally."

Darna crossed quickly to the window. Someone was standing outside – probably just Sunna. "The prince of Slaradun is dead," Darna said. "I saw him die."

"So many young men. So, you have no one, apart from myself and perhaps the Aralel, to take your side?"

Darna shrugged. "I know some armsmen, some particularly skilled ones, who are upset at the death of Tiada, and who will guard me for the tribunal and maybe beyond."

"Good, you'll need them," Gallia said.

"I don't like Calar any more than you do."

"I doubt that," Gallia said with a low chuckle. "You've never had to live with him. I don't think anyone could hate him as I do."

"He killed Tiada, as much as a dragon can be killed."

"Let's sit."

As far as Darna knew, the room they stood in was reserved for the governor's visits alone. There was a chair for him on a low dais against the wall opposite the obvious door, flanked by chairs for his advisors arranged in a close semicircle. Darna had stood behind them once. She hadn't caught the governor's eye on that day, just before her initiation, and that had suited her well enough.

With a nervous laugh, Darna settled into Parnet's chair.

Gallia laughed too. "That's a thought. Maybe you could displace him, too." She took the chamberlain's seat, which was not quite as high-backed as the governor's chair but just as ornately carved. She sighed as she leaned back against its soft cushions.

"We should tell them when we'd like to have the tribunal. They don't need to take our suggestion, but Tiagasa can have things arranged."

"Tiagasa?" Darna had never liked the governor's mistress. "I don't think she likes me."

"She doesn't like Calar and his Cereans, either, for all that she keeps a Cerean of her own close at hand."

"Not Giri – Girizit, is it?"

Gallia waved her hand. "I don't know what his name is. Their names are only so much noise to me, no matter how I tried to please Terenet. He's the king's emissary."

"And his slave. He doesn't like me, either."

Gallia turned to her, eyes wrinkling at the corners. "He knows you? That may complicate things."

They lapsed into an awkward silence. After a while, Gallia straightened up and turned to Darna again.

"Never mind about the Cerean for now. Do tell me, heir of my prince: why did you run away all those years ago? Life on the streets of the Anamat can't have been easy."

"It was easier than working under the cook at Tiadun, and I wanted my freedom. I didn't have to answer to anyone for that one season," Darna said. "If the prince had acknowledged me, I would have been trapped at Tiadun keep forever. I never felt anything but caged when I was there, and the thought of never escaping it was unbearable, even if Calar wasn't trying to kill me then. I think he would have, if he'd known."

"He didn't know, nor did anyone else at the keep, as far as I know. I never learned about you until the end. No one really thought that it mattered, I suppose, as long as it was possible that that – that we could have had a son. I loved Tiadun keep, though, at least my rooms in it. They had a lovely view over the bay. But then, I helped rule the place for a time. It felt like the first place that was really mine."

"I used to feel that way about the city, Anamat, the whole city," Darna reflected.

"And now?"

Darna shook her head. "You know, I can't even show my face in the streets with this death threat, and with the waters rising, things are changing, ending. I need to set things right before the end, or at least see Calar condemned for sending

Tiada under the earth forever. Anamat may not be here much longer."

"I wonder if anything will be," Gallia said with a shiver.

"I don't know." A pain ricocheted through Darna's abdomen. She cringed, but Gallia didn't notice. She wondered what they would ask at the tribunal, and if she would even live that long.

"Tell me what you know, what you learned as ruler of Tiadun," Darna said.

"I was only the keep mistress, but that will take some time. Meanwhile, I'll send word to the palace that you are ready to challenge your usurping uncle. Are you?"

"I have no idea," Darna said, "but I suppose I'll try." Just at that moment, she did not feel ready. "I want to see their faces before I face them at the tribunal."

Gallia had begun to rise, but she paused.

"That's not a bad idea," she said, peering at Darna. "Come over here in the light." She rose and Darna went with her to the window. Gallia pulled the curtain aside just enough to let in some light. Someone was waiting outside: Sunna.

"It will be night, and the lamps will be dim. I see that someone has muted your hair with ash. That's good. A few more lines on your face, to make you seem even older, that would be advisable. I'll send for a servant's dress. Do you know your way around the palace?"

"I've been there," Darna said.

"Good, that's decided, then. I'll have my girl introduce you to the woman in charge of serving at these things. You know how to be a servant. Even that will serve you well."

With a bitter smile, Gallia let the curtain drop.

§

Myril heard a familiar step on the stair and Thorat was at the door a moment later.

"I just barely got away," he panted. "I'm supposed to be delivering an invitation to the temple; I can't stay." Carelessly, he picked up a piece of cheese and ate it while Myril poured him a cup of water. "I can't stand it; they're going to send him to her in the morning, before this tribunal even confirms him. The worst of it is, he's recognized me. I'm fairly sure of it. I don't want him to ask me anything."

"The tribunal can't confirm him," Myril said. "Tiagasa, well, maybe she's sending him to the temple to get some kind of revenge on Iola after all these years."

"I wish I could stop her, stop Tiagasa."

"It would be better if you could stop Iola from going down to the dragons. The Aralel doesn't want her to go. The dragons won't let her come back to us, if they even take her down at all. I'm not sure that they will."

Thorat took a gulp of water. "I have to see her. Can you help me?"

"I have a favor to ask of you in return," Myril said.

"Fine." Thorat walked over to Myril's shelves of dried herbs. "Do you have something in here that will make me sick to my stomach? Not too long-lasting?"

"I don't want to make you sick."

"It's only to persuade them to let me off duty for this cursed feast tonight. They're welcoming Calar along with the prince of Naramun. I can't bear not to see her before she goes down to the dragons for the last time."

"She already has gone for the last time, if you can persuade her to stay," Myril said. She took down a couple of jars, pinching a little from one, a bit more from the other, and mixing the pinches in a small leather pouch. She held it out to him but did not let go as his hand closed around it.

"Take this with water or ale a short time before you want to be sick. You'll feel ill. It would be good if you could have Sunna waiting, in guise of a healer priestess, to show you the way to the ambassadress's chambers."

Thorat nodded. "I think I can do that."

"Then, when you see Iola – I don't know what to say. She's more a creature of the dragons than any of us, except maybe Darna, now. If there's anyone who can convince her that human life is worth living, you can. Try to persuade her to stay on the earth, to stay alive."

"Is it that dire?"

"Anyone can see this rising water. The dragons are done with us, and I want Iola to stay as one of the living people on the surface of the earth."

Thorat nodded and swallowed. "I'll do that then," he said faintly.

Myril let go of the pouch and he took it.

"Should I try to poison Calar?" Thorat wondered aloud. "Could you do that?"

"I'd rather see him set down in the tribunal," Myril said. "Besides, he'll find his end soon enough. There's no need for you to bloody your own hands." She shuddered at the thought of it. Yes, Calar would meet his end soon enough.

§

Thorat was lucky to meet Sunna just outside of the secret way to the Defenders' training hall.

"Could you come up to the palace for me?" he asked.

"I'd rather not. What in... Na's balls, you did get a position there." She eyed his livery with distaste. "Better you than me. What all are they doing up there?"

Thorat looked over his shoulder at the busy street nearby. One of the neighbors was shaking a rug out her window. "I'll tell you another time. Walk with me?"

Sunna shook her head. "I have to get back to the Landing to look in on our other charge."

"So, she's there? Good." He was glad to know that Darna was safe.

"She's in with your favorite," Sunna said as they reached the main way up to the palace. A trio of armed Ganateans strolled by. One of them began to leer at Sunna, but Thorat froze him with a look.

"Wouldn't it be better for you to go about in a training tunic?" he asked her.

Sunna shrugged. "I'll survive. I always have. I'll see you later."

"Please, come up to the palace," Thorat said. "I'll be in the barracks. I'll need a healer priestess."

Sunna stopped. "Oh?"

"I want to go see her." He didn't need to tell Sunna who he meant. "Can I go to her tonight?"

"I don't know," Sunna said. "I'll see about it. I'll come to let you know, one way or the other."

It was late in the afternoon when he walked back into the barracks to find several of his fellow guardsmen helping themselves to the leftovers of the governor's midday meal.

"Mind if I have some of that?" Thorat said.

"Didn't see you in the mess hall," one of the men said.

"I looked in on a friend. Didn't think it would take so long. I didn't stop to eat." It was true that he was hungry. He surreptitiously slipped Myril's herbs into his ale and swirled it around.

"A friend, eh? I've seen you around other years. Priestess?"

Thorat shrugged noncommittally. "Former priestess."

"Ah, they're the best," one of the other men said. He launched into a long story about a young woman he'd met out in the provinces the year before, going into her charms in considerable detail. Thorat nodded along with the rest of them, starting to feel a bit worse for wear.

Just as they were marching across the front courtyard to resume their duties at one post or another, Thorat bent double. The contents of his stomach erupted onto the paving stones.

"Say, there."

"You all right?"

Thorat shook his head. "I'll be fine."

"You don't look so good."

"New fellow's sick," someone said.

A surly-looking serving woman arrived to escort him back to the barracks. "Now, you just rest easy, there. Which is your bunk?"

"I'm not sure. I just got here." He really did feel ill. "I'll just rest by the fire."

"Better for you to go to your bunk. I'll send for a healer."

Thorat shook his head. "No need. I'll be fine."

The serving woman looked skeptical but didn't linger to insist. Thorat sank onto the bench by the common fireplace, cold as it was, and wrapped a blanket around himself despite the heat beating down through the roof above.

He was wakened soon after by a hand on his shoulder.

"Get up, sleepyhead."

It was Sunna. "That was quick," he said.

"It wasn't," she said. "It's halfway into the night and you'd better hurry. If you can. You sure?"

"Of course I'm sure." He got to his feet with a great deal of effort and nearly lost his balance.

"You don't look so well."

"Myril says it'll wear off."

Sunna looked skeptical. "All right, then. Lend me your arm. Go on; you're supposed to be sick."

He took her arm, letting her support him a little while trying to maintain the look of being the one leading her. He needed to let his fellow guardsmen know that he was ill, but he didn't want to be seen as weak, either.

The walk down to the harbor temple seemed longer than usual. When they were nearly there, Sunna shooed him into a side alley and handed him a bundle of clothes.

"Give me your sword and put these on over your tunic," she said. They were the drab robes of an elder priestess. "I'll say that you're ill and that I'm taking you to the old sanctuary to wait for a bed in the infirmary. Whatever you do, don't talk. You couldn't even feign a woman's voice when you were pretending to be a minstrel."

"I could," Thorat protested.

"Not very well." She looked out of the alley to see that the street was clear. "Hurry up."

He started out, following her lead. She stopped. "That won't do."

"What?"

"Shush! You need to walk like an old woman, like this." Sunna demonstrated a shuffling step.

"That's the weakest gait I've ever seen."

"That's the idea. I don't know why I help you."

"Oh, yes, you do," Thorat whispered. "Myril told me. I'm supposed to convince Iola to stay on the surface of the earth."

§

The ambassadress's garden was peaceful in the moonlight. The scent of roses and jasmine filled the air. Sunna clutched the hilt of her sword more tightly and ushered Thorat forward.

"Is there something wrong?"

"It's too quiet."

Inside the ambassadress's marble-domed chamber, all was still. A single lamp burned on the altar, a lazy thread of smoke spiraling around its flame from a nearby incense burner. Slow, sleeping breaths sounded from one of the nooks in the side wall. Sunna went to a different nook.

"Where in the chambered world is Darna?" Sunna said, not bothering to try to be quiet.

Iola sat up, blankets falling down around her. "I think she went out." She yawned. "I don't really know."

"Out?! She can't go out. You know that."

Thorat laid a hand on Sunna's arm to try to calm her. "I'm here," he said.

"Thorat?" Iola swung her feet to the floor and started to hurry over to them, but then she staggered and had to hold on to the wall.

Sunna ground her teeth. "It's not safe for her to go out!"

"I was with a petitioner," Iola said. "She didn't ask me."

Thorat went to Iola and held her hand.

"I'll leave you two lovebirds and go look for her, then, since neither of you is any use," Sunna said. "Who did she go with?"

"She said something about Gallia," Iola said uncertainly.

"I'll go look for her first, then," Sunna said. "Thorat. Wait for me in the passage if I'm not here to show you out when you're done."

Thorat and Iola stood together, holding each other's hands gently until they couldn't hear Sunna's footsteps any more.

"It's all right," Thorat said. "Darna knows how to look after herself as long as there's no one trying to kill her."

"It's so strange to me that they would try to kill her. Oh, I understand that the threat is real, but why do they think she should stay here with me?"

"I can't think of a safer place," Thorat said. Iola glowed in it like a pearl in a perfect setting. "I'm glad to be here with only you, but -" He *was* worried about Darna. He dismissed his worry, or tried to. Sunna would find her, and then she would be all right. He had to cherish this one night with Iola. As always, it could be his last. "Come, let's light a lamp. I want to see you."

Iola went to her sleeping nook and took down a lamp, but her hand shook. "I'm not ready," she said. "If I should take anyone's offering, it should be the Defenders', but -"

"I didn't bring an offering," Thorat confessed. "I forgot. I only wanted to see you."

Iola set down the unlit lamp, her gray form moving hesitatingly away from him in the nearly dark chamber. Finally, she turned back to Thorat.

"Did the Enatel forget?"

Thorat hurried to her side and took her hand. "No, I'm sure she didn't; it's just that she's been away from Anamat and isn't back yet."

"You could bring the offering later, or send it with Sunna."

"Are you strong enough?"

Iola made an ambivalent gesture. "I can; it's only that I'm so tired. I've never been tired like this before. It's been worse since...after whatever happened in Slaradun."

The mostly healed wound on Thorat's shoulder itched at the mention of Slaradun. "You've seen what happened in Anamat, too?" he asked.

"I haven't." Iola swallowed. "They've told me, but I haven't been strong enough to climb the tower to see for myself. I haven't dared, either."

"I could help you," Thorat offered.

Iola didn't back away when he came to her. As their clothes brushed against each other, she took hold of his arm. "You're not a priestess. I'm the only one who's supposed to go up there."

"Well, maybe Darna can help you, when the sun is up."

"No, the moon is rising; let's go now," Iola said with sudden firmness. "I've been afraid, but with you, I'll go."

Thorat took Iola's arm, but she was the one to lead the way through the garden and to light the lamp. Her hands shook less. "I don't know if I can make the rite, since you haven't brought an offering," she said.

"Let me stay with you, at least." He didn't much like the idea that others had been lying with her, and pushed the thought away. She wasn't well. Sunna was right: she couldn't go to the other realm, not like this. Even being at its mouth was a strain. She should go to the hills. He couldn't help but think that the bandit women – or even Sovara – would know how to make her strong again.

Iola said nothing as they climbed the stairs. They had to stop several times for her to catch her breath. By the time they came to the top landing, the moon was high in the sky, its soft light shining on the seawater lapping the shore.

"Stay inside the tower," she said.

"Anara will know that I'm here. I don't want you to fall."

Iola chuckled. "There's more than one way to be a fallen priestess, I suppose." She let him follow her out onto the narrow ledge, but he regretted it almost immediately.

Below his feet, there was nothing. He could look straight down into the ambassadress's garden, but it made him dizzy.

"Look at the moon," Iola said. "It will steady you."

He had to clench his eyes shut to wrench his gaze away
from the drop. When he opened them again, he made sure to
look up. The sky looked just like it did from the ground, only
there was more of it, with no buildings, trees, or mountains in
the way. "You're right," Thorat said, but as he spoke, Iola
gasped.

"I had no idea," she said. "I mean, they told me there was
flooding, but it's as if half the city is gone."

"Less than a quarter of it," Thorat said. "At least, that's
what I'm told."

"Too much."

A distant, cloudy shape moved over the eastern hills and
spiraled down. Maybe it was only a bat, or an owl. "I don't
want Anara to –"

"She can hear you."

"I don't want her to steal you from me."

"And I don't want the rising seas to take you away. Look,
there's a ship under sail. What are they carrying, to go at night
like that?"

"It could be only a fisherman catching the tide," Thorat
said, but he knew that it wasn't true. No fishing boat hoisted so
many sails. "It's a Cerean merchant vessel. I hope they're not
carrying away any –"

"Priestesses. The Aralel told me. If I stay on the surface,
will that be my fate?"

"I won't let them take you."

The shape on the horizon circled again, crossing the edge
of the moon in a blur. It looked like an owl swooping.

"It's no use," Iola said. "I have to fly down, to see the
winged ones again."

"No," Thorat said. "We'll see them again somehow, before the end, but if you don't stay on the surface of the earth, you'll be lost to me forever."

From far away, they heard a distant rumble, almost like a bell-struck note reverberating through the crust of the earth.

"Wait for me here," Iola said. She squeezed his hand and left him standing by the small doorway as she slowly walked around the ledge, looking down at the city. When she returned, they descended together, hand in hand.

Iola wanted to go into the baths to warm herself, but the water was cooler than it had been. "It's like she's drawing away," Iola said.

Thorat nodded. "It was the same with Salara, or so Darna said."

"We don't neglect the dragons, here in Anamat," Iola said.

"You might not, but others do."

"We should make the rite. You might not be able to return."

"I brought no offering. It wouldn't be right."

Iola slid away from him. "I don't want to let you go, but I know you shouldn't stay."

"I have to stay until Sunna comes back, or another one of your petitioners comes. You should have retired and made someone else be ambassadress."

"You know there's no one to take my place, since Eppie won't." Iola's voice shook. She was angry or afraid. That wasn't like her.

"I'm sorry, but Eppie had to choose for herself. Maybe I should have tried harder, but I just can't see her as a priestess."

"Never mind." Iola got out of the bath. She was shivering.

"Let me warm you," Thorat said, following her.

"You can't," Iola protested, but when he led her back to the sleeping nook and lay down beside her, she welcomed him.

§

It was almost dawn when Sunna found them there, violating the protocol that governed the ambassadress and every other peresi. Not that she minded. No one was much of a stickler for the rules anymore, and many priestesses had lovers who only pretended to be petitioners when they had to. The birds were beginning to sing and a faint gray light was washing away the stars in the east.

"Two lovebirds?" she said, waking them.

Thorat sat up, and Iola pulled the blankets around herself. They felt guilty.

"You know you're not supposed to be in the sleeping nook."

"We only slept –" Iola began.

Sunna waved her away. "I haven't found Darna. She was at the palace, but she's gone now and no one knows where she is. Gallia said she'll send word to her 'girl' there to look for her, and to find out if there's any news."

"She's alive," Iola said.

"Oh?" Sunna looked skeptical, but Iola only shrugged.

"I just know," she said. "If anything had happened to her, I would know."

In the outer courtyard, an alarm bell rang. Sunna looked grim. Thorat looked for his sword. "I'd better go see what that's about," she said.

She nodded to Thorat. "You suit up. Get on those old priestess robes you wore last night. I'll see you out as soon as I've dealt with this."

"Another bad petitioner," Iola said, sadly.

"Do you have a bell of your own?" Thorat asked.

Iola shook her head. "I've been all right so far. The price is too high, but -"

"But that might not be enough," Thorat said. "I wish I could stay to guard you."

"You can't," Iola said firmly. "I'm going to send for tea. You'd better go."

§

Chapter 7

L ate in the afternoon, while Iola took another petitioner, Darna was waiting in the garden. The ambassadress's bell rang three times, a short gap, then two more rings. That was the signal she'd arranged with Gallia, who had told her a little more about the ruling of Tiadun while they waited for Gallia's "girl at the palace" to come for her instructions.

The elder priestess who was officially in charge of watching the gate jumped up to scold the messenger who'd tried to disturb the Most Blessed One while she was with a petitioner.

"I'm sorry," the young priestess said. "I didn't realize. I only brought a message."

"Come back with it later."

Darna heard no more as she closed the door of the secret passage behind her. She was plunged into total darkness. She'd forgotten to bring a lamp. She considered going back for it, but as her eyes adjusted, she could detect a faint glow far ahead. She made her way carefully along the length of the passage and stopped just inside the storeroom door. No one was there, but she could hear someone pacing outside the storeroom. She waited until the footsteps faded around the corner, then hurried through the storeroom, into the corridor, and to the old sanctuary. There, a young woman in priestess robes was waiting for her, carrying a bundle tied with a cord of blue- and orange-dyed leather. *Not a very subtle signal*, Darna thought.

She raised her eyebrows, at which the young woman stood to nervous attention. She was wearing robes, but she had the bearing of a servant, not a priestess.

"My mistress said we're to go out through the back gate," she whispered. "Would you change here?" she asked, thrusting the package toward Darna.

Darna shook her head. There were too many eyes and ears in the temple. There would be just as many in the palace, but surely she could find some hidden nook along the way. Without saying anything, she started out toward the back courtyard, the nervous servant trailing in her wake. She slowed down, remembering that she was supposed to be disguised as an elder priestess, not one who should be doing her part to fill the treasuries by lying on her back with petitioners. She shuddered at the thought. Never again. The thing in her belly struck, and she had to stop while the disguised serving girl stood by, looking uneasy.

She was glad when they were out of the temple, but the streets of Anamat felt less joyful than was usual for a night so close to Midsummer. The bones of the celebrations were still there: bonfires and drumming, dancing and pickpocketing. Somehow, it all felt more chaotic than usual. Darna led her messenger along a quiet street to a deep, unoccupied doorway off an alley. There, she changed into servant's garb. The dress fit her well enough, though it was a little long. She wished she still had her stick, to thwack her way through the crowds, but the assassins would be looking for a woman with a limp, so perhaps it was just as well that she didn't have it. She and Gallia's serving girl made do with their elbows when they crossed the market squares, and reached the kitchen gate just as the last glow of sunset was fading from the sky.

At the governor's palace, the usual familiar greetings among noblemen had been supplanted by wariness that made itself felt even among the kitchen staff. Gallia's girl led Darna directly to the room where the best serving dishes were kept. A maid was there, polishing silver goblets.

"This is my auntie," said the young woman who'd fetched Darna. "She's here to help serve tonight."

"Start with polishing those bowls," the maid told Darna, barely looking up. "We're to bring them out for the last course."

"I'll go ahead to see if they're ready," Gallia's girl said. That was the last Darna saw of her that night. There was too much to be done for the other servants to question where Darna had come from, or even to ask her name. She ghosted the maid she'd been introduced to through the kitchen, out to the hall, and back again. She positioned herself among the serving maids setting out for the chamber where Calar would be dining. Many of the servants knew one another, but some did not, having just come in from the countryside with one prince's retinue or another. As the moon was rising, they lit the lamps in their newly polished sconces and took their places in the relay to the kitchen.

Darna was not perfectly positioned, but at least she hadn't drawn attention to herself. Her legs, though stronger than they'd ever been before, felt tired already from her rush across the city and the unaccustomed running to and fro on stone floors. She stood in the shadow of the doorway as the governor and his guests entered, standing flat against the wall with the other servants.

Her cousin and uncle were already drowsy from drink. They lolled in their seats as soon as they took their places at the table. They would not be looking for her among the servants, even if that was where they'd last seen her, nor would Parnet take note of an old serving woman. Tiagasa and Giri, sitting side by side, were another matter.

"Go around with the wine," someone whispered to Darna.

She obeyed. They began with an ewer of aged Helanum wine, some of the best. It smelled so good that she almost wished she'd sampled a bit to steady her nerves, but there'd been no chance and a strong drink might have made her clumsy, too.

She circled the table, filling goblets as she went. She filled every goblet except Giri's. He held his hand over the cup as she passed, not looking at her, his gaze intent on Tiagasa. They spoke in low tones so as not to be overheard.

"I am not surprised that you don't go yourself. You are fastidious, like my lord governor."

"Perhaps more so," Giri said. He smiled at Tiagasa with a warmth that went beyond diplomacy. Darna wondered why Tiagasa didn't know that the governor *had* gone to Iola for a change.

"I will see that you find what you need to know, but it may take some time," she purred.

"I need some token to return to my king," Giri said. Darna had to move on, so she heard no more.

The princes of Getedun and Galamun were there, scowling across the wide board at Calar, whose armies and allies had ridden roughshod over their land and despoiled their temples.

"We will escort them on the return journey," the prince of Getedun was saying quietly to his neighbor. "We can take tribute from him in recompense, though I hope he will agree to pay it freely. I don't want to raise an army."

"We may have to. Did you see his forces?"

Darna heard nothing else of interest as she circled the table that first time. When the soup course was served, all of the talk seemed to turn to food and wine. When the minstrels came, the conversation ceased almost entirely. Darna was clearing away a platter of meat at the end of the table when she saw Girizit excuse himself, leaving Tiagasa with a kiss on the hand. Parnet observed that kiss with a frown, but his ear was taken by the prince of Lemirun, seated on his other side.

"I have no truck with these Cereans, not since my late father's mistake," the prince of Lemirun said, "but two of their ships sailed to my harbor a moon-round ago, wanting to trade. You should not blame Calar too much. It's not entirely his fault."

"He should know his obligations," Parnet said distractedly.

Girizit went around the table and leaned over to speak to the man seated beside Darna's cousins. The man – apparently Calar's Cerean advisor or supervisor – excused himself and followed Girizit to one side of the room.

"I've had a message; come," Girizit said to him in Cerean.

Darna hurried into the servants' corridor and handed her platter to a maid who was taking a moment's rest. "Can you take this to the kitchen for me?" Darna said. She was gone before the other woman could answer. The Cereans took the main corridor, toward the palace's front courtyard. There was no reason for a serving maid to go there, especially not one who'd been engaged to serve at the night's feast.

Darna untied her apron and tucked it under her arm as soon as she could, on a quiet stretch of corridor, but a maid carrying a pile of bed linens came along just then. "Kitchen's back that way," she said.

"Sorry, I lost my way," Darna said, trying to look more confused than she felt. She never lost her way. That was one thing her encounter with Salara hadn't changed.

She took a few steps toward the kitchen to avoid arousing suspicion as the other maid scurried away. By the time she felt safe enough to double back, she'd lost the trail of the Cereans. They'd been heading toward the front of the palace, so she did too, listening as she went. Just to one side of the main entry yard, the corridor passed a quiet and unremarkable garden, a perfect spot for a quiet conversation. She slowed as she approached it, going as quietly as she could, grateful that she was no longer needed a stick to walk. As handy as it had been, it was noisy.

"We have the men; we could do it now," one of the Cereans was saying in a whisper.

"We are not pleased," Girizit said.

"The duke has what he needs here. He will not wait on the king's permission."

"He should have waited for it," Girizit said. "This territory is for the king, as is that province you approached on the king's behalf. He will take this city."

"If it's left for him to take," said a third voice. Darna knew that voice. It sounded just like Harzet. Was he alive still? He might have seen her run from the gate. She stood stock still, her heart beating more loudly than it had before. She knew they couldn't possibly hear her, arguing as they were among themselves. She pressed herself against the wall and crept closer.

"You have men, I have men, but we are not together," Giri said quietly. "I tell you, the Duke is a traitor. What's more, we can't rely on your man in that province. I've learned that he hasn't even taken the throne."

From what Darna had seen, the Cerean armsmen who rode with Calar, plus his own forces, outnumbered the men at Giri's command – not by much, but if either Cerean force had the upper hand, it would be Calar's, an army through and through, rather than one wearing the false front of a merchant fleet.

"Forget that; we could make ourselves rich, rich and free," Calar's Cerean said.

Harzet chuckled mirthlessly.

"His taking the throne waits only for this formality, some trial."

"And when will that be?" Harzet asked.

"In two nights' time. A girl bastard of the old prince. It's unspeakable what these people think is a strong hand. Do you know they let their women rule between princes?"

Neither Giri nor Harzet answered that.

"We must go to the king," Giri said, before the agent of the Duke of the Southern Reaches could make more of a fool of himself. "This plunder will be of no use to us if His Highness condemns our souls."

If Giri was ever going to rebel against his king, he would have done it a long time ago. Darna wondered if she'd actually heard Harzet, or if it had been another man who only sounded like him.

"You think our king has that power?" the other man said after a while. "Soon, you'll be seeing the Theranians' dragons."

"You seek their magic too; don't condemn me for believing in its power," Giri said.

"I seek to profit by others' belief in it. Their lizards have no power over me," the other man said.

"The things I saw in Slaradun would cool your blood for this trade." That was definitely Harzet, then.

"We will take what we can," Girizit said tiredly, ignoring Harzet's warning. "We need not destroy the city."

"The city is as good as lost even without your help," Harzet said. "Ride your troops in or wait for the sea to take it, it's all one to me."

"But there is that little matter of the trial to come, to establish my princely ally on his throne." The man sounded exasperated. "The governor must uphold it. He cannot hand a province over to a whore."

"The Theranians don't see things that way," Harzet said, letting every word drop slowly but to no effect. "The ones you call their whores are surprisingly learned, better educated than some of even our courtiers, and certainly more learned than these Theranian princes. I was among the best students of my esteemed teacher; I know learning when I see it."

"Not that it's done you any good, without our king's blessing," Giri said.

Harzet muttered an oath and paced away from the other two.

"Tiadun stands. It is good farming land, if nothing else."

"The duke may be content with good farming land, but the king is not," Giri said. "He has farmland in plenty. He seeks what only this place can offer. Besides, Anamat is not the same as Slaradun, and you, Harzet, are a traitor and an exile." He shouted that last.

"A fate you might share some day, slave of the king." Harzet's voice was close to her, too close.

"I will never betray him as you did."

"I'll leave now, then, and save my own skin," Harzet said. "May you boil in the lava of the dragons' wrath."

The Cerean who'd come with Calar laughed. "The dragons have no wrath. They are nothing."

"Shush," Giri said. From his voice, Darna could imagine him clutching his cap to his head and looking fearfully at the sky, just as he had when they were scrapplings. "They can hear you, even if these fool Theranians cannot."

"You're superstitious like a woman, as slaves should be."

Darna heard Harzet's footsteps turn back toward the others, but before he could say anything more, a guardsman with a torch approached with quick steps.

"Are you gentlemen lost?" the guardsman said from the passageway. "I'll show you back."

Harzet, Giri, and the other Cerean said nothing.

"Come this way!" the guardsman shouted, as if speaking more loudly could make them understand.

"It's all right," Girizit said in Theranian. "I know the way."

"I'll show you along." The guardsman and his torch advanced, straight to where Darna stood.

Harzet was last among the trio, but he saw her first. "Darna?" her name was out of his mouth before he reached the corridor. "I thought you were dead. You look close to it. You are not well?"

By that time, Giri was looking at her, too. "Darna. If that's supposed to be a disguise, it's not a very good one," he said slowly in Theranian. "I told you to stay away from the palace, but you never did heed my warnings. I must say, I'm glad that you've come to hear this little play. It will be interesting."

"Your word is worthless," Darna said levelly, in Cerean. "I have to be going now."

"That's where you're wrong. I think I have an offer that might interest you. We wouldn't like to see your province ruled by our rebellious duke." The flash of a dagger glinted at his side. Darna wanted to run. She knew she should not hear Giri's offer, but she found herself nodding. Giri took a few steps away from the others and went on in a whisper: "Your unfortunate uncle could meet his brother's end," he whispered. "I could arrange it. All you must do is to pledge...cooperation."

"Never," Darna said.

"I'll see you at the tribunal, then. It would be so much easier if Calar were dead. Remember, I can arrange that. Easily." Giri stepped back but waited while the other two Cereans looked at her in full light of the torch and the risen moon. The palace guard stood uneasily beside them.

Calar's Cerean smiled a satisfied smile and gave her a nod, then started away, leaving the befuddled guardsman looking back and forth between Darna and Harzet.

"My apologies, sincere apologies," Harzet said. "I did think that you had died. I am glad at least that you escaped with your fee."

"That was worth less to me than he was," she said.

"I miss him too."

"Your fee?" Girizit chuckled. "Did you play the so-called priestesses of Anamat with our traitor, my scavenger friend?"

"I did not," Darna said. It was a ridiculous question. "Your country seems to be full of nothing but traitors, and from what I've heard of your king, I can't blame them. You should have been one of them. You could have stayed here and not gone back to your slavery. You understand nothing; you never did," Darna said. "I must go. Your countryman's so-called allies don't like me, and I like them even less, maybe even less than I like you. When you go home to your king, again, don't come back."

"Oh, I'll come back. And I'll take you with me." Giri leered.

"You have no power over me," Darna said. Calar's Cerean, the agent of the Duke of the Southern Reaches, had returned. He had his blade drawn. She saw it out of the corner of her eye and began to run for the palace's front gates. Behind her, the guardsman with the torch scuffled with the Cerean, slowing him but not stopping him. Darna slowed to a fast walk.

Harzet raced after her. "Lady Planner," he called to her as she crossed the yard. "I have wronged you, and for all your prying ways, I am glad to see that you still live."

"Don't lead them to me. Stop following me," Darna said, exasperated. "If you would do me any favors again, let it not be like the favor you did to your most beloved friend. I'd rather live, even if I am mad."

She reached the palace gates. The guards let her through, but they closed ranks behind her so that the foreigners could not follow. They would find a way to track her if they could, now that they'd seen her in Anamat. Harzet wouldn't be able to stop them even if he was willing to try. She walked as quickly as she could across the market square, and then she began to run again.

Cerean assassins would be on her trail, or Giri's slave traders. She slid into the hidden ways, weaving back and forth across the city. She turned down one street and then another and another again until she'd almost lost her bearings. She found a garden gate leading to a tunnel under a row of houses and emerged into a quiet, moonlit courtyard with a stair leading up to an attic door. There, she paused to catch her breath. She sat down on a stone beside the waterspout. She heard no sounds of pursuit. From beyond the courtyard came the sound of drumbeats and careful laughter, of bonfires crackling and of young people screeching with terror or delight. She closed her eyes and rested.

§

The sound of a footstep entering the courtyard startled Darna awake. She had fallen asleep with her head on a weathered wooden stair, as if some part of her had sensed that this place was safe from Calar and his agents. Dew soaked her dress. It was almost dawn. Someone was coming, stepping out of the passage and into the moonlight. She recognized him.

"Thorat? What are you doing here?"

"I should ask you that," he said, "but I'm glad you've found us. Sunna was worried sick over you. Where did you go?"

"To the palace. The Cereans saw me; they know I'm here now. The tribunal is in two days' time – the night after this, I think."

"Come upstairs. I'll explain to Sovara when she's back, and send someone with a message to Sunna, who's been looking for you all night."

"Is this the place where –"

"Shh," Thorat said. "What were you thinking, going to the palace like that?"

Darna picked herself up off the step and rearranged her crumpled dress. "I wanted to see them. I went to the palace dressed as a serving maid, as you can see, and overheard a bit of the Cereans' chatter," she said as Thorat led her up the rickety-looking stair. "Giri recognized me, and so did Harzet, the Cerean who was in Slaradun. Giri called him a traitor. There must be a lot of traitors in Cerea."

"I should have been there," Thorat said.

Darna shook her head. "You went to see Iola, didn't you? Did you convince her to stay?"

"Not yet," Thorat said. "Sunna wasn't a bit happy that you'd left."

Darna sighed. "Maybe I should have told her. It would have been safer."

They paused on the landing. Thorat smelled of temple incense, and his stomach was making noises that sounded not at all pleasant.

"Wait here," he said.

Darna nodded and perched on the railing. From the shape of the rooftops around her, she could tell that she was about halfway between the palace and the harbor, somewhere between the Pentangle and the East Canal, but beyond that, the exact location seemed somehow to not line up with what she expected. She'd never felt so disoriented in the city before.

"She found the courtyard on her own," Thorat was saying from inside.

The Enatel let out a long, ragged breath and coughed. "Let her in, then."

Darna didn't wait for Thorat to come back up and get her. She went inside and down the stairs into an open and strangely familiar-feeling room as long as three houses put together. Most of the hall was pitch dark except for a thin glow around the gaps under the eaves, flooded with dawn light. The Enatel held a dim lamp, but the others were snoring in bedding on the floor. They still smelled slightly of the mountain valley.

"I thank you for your hospitality, Lady Enatel," Darna said.

"No titles," the Enatel said. "How did you find this place?"

"I've always been able to find places, but I'd never found this one before."

"The Cereans and Calar know she's in the city now," Thorat explained. "She went up to the palace."

"The temple won't be safe enough, not if they know you're there," the Enatel said. She peered at Darna. "Normally, if a young scrappling finds this place, I take it as a sign that he or she is to become one of us, but you're too old, and a priestess already, but at least you know who we are already. You must keep our secrets if we're to safeguard you."

"I will," Darna promised.

"Don't even tell Myril," Thorat said. "She knows that we exist, but not where we are in the city. Not even Iola can know."

"Iola wouldn't be able to find her way from the temple to the East Market," Darna said. "Even when she was out in the city, she couldn't go anywhere without someone to show her the way."

"Now, now, no maligning the Most Blessed One," Sunna said as she hurried into the room. "I certainly didn't expect to find you *here*. You led the palace guard on a merry chase."

"I'm sorry that I worried you," Darna said.

"Was it worth it?" Sunna demanded, sounding annoyed.

Darna considered that for a moment before answering. "I'd have to say yes, it was, especially since I survived. I learned a few things."

"Such as?" the Enatel prompted.

"The Cereans don't get along with each other. One of them wants to be my ally – two of them do, actually, but I won't be played by the king's slave again."

"Stay away from those Cereans," came a gravelly voice from one of the bedrolls at the far end of the room. It was Vigda, sitting up and straightening her ragged clothes.

"I'm sure you know better than to trust those cap-headed enemies of the dragons," the Enatel said. "Now it's time we got these sleepyheads up. You might as well see if you can do anything with a sword, while you're here. It will pass the time."

"Well, I was pretty handy with a cane when I was a scrappling," Darna said, but she was skeptical, and so was Thorat. Sunna ushered Darna over to the rack of swords and thrust one into her hands.

"There. You won't learn much in a day, or even in two days, but there's no harm in it. After all, it's a princely pursuit." Sunna paused, looking worried.

"What about Iola?" Darna asked.

"I'd rather send you to her than Calar," Sunna said, "but the treasurers have other ideas. She might have to see him today."

Darna shuddered at the thought of joining Iola in the rite herself. The image of Calar was distasteful too, but in a more common way. "I hope she makes his manhood wither like an old raisin."

Sunna grunted as she adjusted her sword belt.

The morning light was streaming in under the eaves now that the sun had risen. It lit the rafters and the walls more brightly than Darna would have expected. In fact, it was rather like – "Sunna. Did you ever notice that this place is built exactly like the old sanctuary at the temple?"

"Exactly?" Sunna said. "It's the same general kind of room, but I don't know about exactly."

"No, it's the same," Darna said. "The dimensions and the spacing between the beams and the orientation of the roof. It must be hundreds of years old – no one builds to this kind of symmetry anymore."

"It's not that old. It's a copy," the Enatel said.

"Of the old sanctuary at Ara's Landing?" Sunna asked.

The Enatel shrugged noncommittally. "As far as I know, it's a copy of our old hall, the one from before the Darkest Night – that's when we ceased to exist, officially at least," she explained to Darna. "That's been gone a hundred years or more. This is only a copy, but don't malign it by saying it's like a priestess temple."

Darna frowned. It was exactly like a priestess temple. The master planner would be overjoyed to find such a place. She wondered how it had been built, and if there was anything about it in the guild records. She wished that she could go see for herself, but she couldn't go back to the guild now, not with Calar in the city and the tribunal coming.

While they'd been talking, all of the sleeping figures had gotten up and packed their bedrolls away in a pile at the back of the room. Garren arrived, carrying a big basket of bread, and Eppie made two runs down to the waterspout in the courtyard below. Sunna showed Darna how to hold her sword, and the Enatel came by and nodded approvingly.

"If you're going to have someone stabbing you in the back, the least you can do is make it more painful for them," she said. "Come on, we'll show you how."

§

Chapter 8

"Calar of Tiadun," the treasurer announced.

Iola crossed her arms over her chest. "Did the Aralel approve this?"

The treasurer shrugged. "The Aralel is busy, and surely you must take offering from Tiada's realm."

The treasurer was either unaware of or indifferent to the fact that Tiada had been sent to the deepest stream by a Cerean mining expedition that Calar himself had led into the dragons' hills. No one much probably talked about it outside of the inner circles of those who knew the dragons, those few who could see the winged ones. The treasurer priestess might not have ever seen a dragon herself, outside of festival times, so the fact that Iola could no longer see Tiada would mean very little to her, if anything.

"Tell him to come back if he succeeds at this tribunal," Iola said.

The treasurer shook her head. "He's given his offering." She turned on her heel and bustled away before Iola could reiterate her objection. She sighed and went inside to make ready to bring the murderer himself into the dragon's presence. It would be better if Darna were there, and Sunna. Iola didn't think that she could kill a man, but she did half hope that the statue of Anara would come to life and fry Calar like a pig's tail over a cookfire. Chances were better that Sunna would return. Anara had never entered that offering chamber in the flesh, and her dragonlets passed through petitioners as if they were nothing more than a trick of the light.

It was almost midday and Iola's breakfast sat like a lump in her belly. She did not feel ready to make the rite, especially not with a man who'd had his realm dragon destroyed. Especially not when she'd lain beside Thorat so recently and only slept in his arms. Of course, the treasurer couldn't know about that. She hadn't felt strong enough to risk common lovemaking this time, though she had done it before with him, once or twice, even though it was forbidden. She knew that nearly everyone else did it, but as she was ambassadress, they would, rightly, expect her to uphold the traditions better than a common peresi.

The rite was her work, she told herself sternly. She could always take a petitioner to the dragons, even if he was unwilling and Calar would be there at any moment. She had to at least put on the robes of her office. He would be walking across the peresi's garden, loincloth loose around his hips, probably leering at her fellow priestesses. Iola put on her plainest tunic and went to the door. She stood at the top of the steps up to her own inner temple and watched him come, guided along by the treasurer who had an even heavier-than-usual purse in her hand.

As Calar came closer, she could see little that she liked about him. He was a tallish man – not as tall as some, but taller than most – and well built, with only a little paunch at his middle, and he walked with a swagger that seemed borrowed from someone else. Maybe he'd taken on the Cerean custom of wearing high-heeled boots and felt uncomfortable in his bare feet. His skin was pale, except for his sunburned face and hands. He had the same complexion as Darna, only in male form and worn down by more years. She could see some family resemblance. Darna wasn't a beauty in the classical sense, but she had a kind of magnetism that her uncle clearly lacked. Iola resolved not to give Calar any strength. She would deal with the treasurer's displeasure later if she had to. She probably didn't care as long as she got the petitioner's gold.

The treasurer made Calar wait at the garden gate and hurried in to Iola. "What are you about? You're not prepared."

"I'm as prepared as I need to be, Honored One," Iola said.

The treasurer frowned. "I'll return with his tray, your tray, set for the midday meal."

"That won't be necessary," Iola said. "Send only tea."

The treasurer clearly did not want to follow that order, but Iola stood firm. "Very well, Most Blessed One." She paused on her way out to mutter something to Calar.

Calar sauntered up the path as if nothing at all were amiss, as if he shouldn't be boiled in dragons' blood. Iola shuddered to look at him, but he smiled as he reached her. He bent down to touch her feet with his clammy hands.

"Pretty," he said. "I had heard that you were a beauty, and I see that it's true. A bit thin for my tastes, but I won't let that trouble me."

"No, you wouldn't," Iola said.

"Pardon? Aren't you supposed to say, 'Welcome to the rite,' or some more ornate form of that?"

"I need not take you to the rite. I won't."

"Don't be silly." Calar pushed past her and into her sanctuary. He sat down on the offering place as if he were lounging on a common tavern bench.

"Get off of the altar." Iola wished that the treasurer would return, even though she'd be no help. Why was Sunna off chasing after Darna? Where was Darna, for that matter?

Calar got up lazily. "I expected better reception," he said. "Or do you want to wait until I am officially crowned, as I must be?"

"You are not the prince of Tiadun."

"Technically, no, not yet, but I'm the closest thing there is, or will be for a long time."

"I'd rather take Darnasa," Iola said. "She at least honors the dragons."

"You priestesses pleasure each other?" Calar said. His eyes gleamed beadily as his lip curled. "You're a hypocrite, too. Look at all this around you! This doesn't come from the dragons or even from your fellow priestesses; this is the work of men."

"And of women. It's also the work of the dragons, whether you can see that or not." Iola remained standing in the doorway, where the passing peresi in the outer garden and the one standing guard at the gate could see her. She didn't want to be alone with Calar. She wasn't particularly afraid that he would abuse her, but without witnesses, she might lose the strength of her conviction and let him in after all, or else that he would lie about it later and say that she *had* accepted him into the rite, even when she hadn't.

"I'll bow down to you if you like," he said, as if that were making some great concession. He walked back toward her. "You do like your dragons, they say."

"They're not my dragons. I'm theirs, and so are you."

"This is a temple," Calar said, "but I'll have you know that I'm freed from them. Come on, you're supposed to take all the rulers. You haven't had a prince of Tiadun in years."

Iola couldn't deny that, unless Darna counted, but she had only kissed Darna when perhaps she should not have. Still, that small touch had made the dragons' power flow better than the rite did with most of the princes.

"My brother never came to you?" Calar asked, twisting his loincloth around his finger. "I wasn't sure of that. I thank you for confirming it. I wondered if he might have, despite his devotions to Farseer. A pity. He should have enjoyed women other than his mistress more often, or we would not have come to this impasse."

"An impasse. Is that what you call murder?"

Calar waved the accusation away. "He would have despoiled our land with his Enomaean allies. It was the same, with me taking it. At least I could sire a boy child."

"If that's all you have to your credit, I don't think that's enough."

The gate rattled – the treasurer, returning with the tray of tea. She'd brought meat pies and cakes too, though Iola had asked her not to.

"Most Blessed One?" she said as she came up the steps.

"Put it down inside. I will stand here," Iola said.

Calar stood awkwardly just inside the door. "You will leave now with the lady treasurer," Iola told him. "You may take a pie if you are hungry. I will not take you to the rite."

The treasurer's neck muscles tensed but she said nothing. She knew as well as any of them that any priestess could refuse a petitioner, and that the ambassadress was a priestess more than she was anything else.

"What about the offering from Tiadun?" the treasurer said at last.

"Calar and his allies sent their dragon to the deepest stream, the closest thing to killing a dragon. I cannot take

Tiada anything; she is beyond my reach," Iola said. "This, in any case, is no prince."

Calar had untied his loincloth when he'd first crossed her threshold, exposing his flaccid member. Now he tied the cloth back on, yanking the knot tight. "You'll pay for this," he said. "You'll pay for this when I'm prince."

"And that, say the dragons, will never be."

The stones went cold beneath Iola's bare feet as she spoke. Calar, oblivious to the shift in the dragons' power, scowled at her once more before the treasurer led him away, his gold secure in her pouch, with or without the rite. Iola shivered and hoped that Darna would be back soon.

§

Darna spent all day at the Defenders' secret training hall. It was a little bit like being back in the mountain valley, except that she could sense the reassuring presence of the city all around her. It comforted her to be back in Anamat, even if the city was sinking and full of knives and arrows aimed at her back. Her belly didn't trouble her much while she was in the hall, but after all the drills Sunna and Sovara ran her through, every other muscle in her body shook with exhaustion.

Thorat had to hurry off to the palace as soon as the early-morning training session was done and said that he wasn't sure if he'd be able to return that night. Sunna left to attend Iola just before the midday training session. Darna stood at the back of the room to watch the others practice their art, lifting their swords in salutation when the shrine doors slid open. It was as ceremonial as anything in the temple and as reverent, if not more so. The symmetry of their movements was astounding at times, ragged tunics and all. It was not quite like watching a dance, but here in their hall, she could see parallels with the priestesses' dances that had been invisible to her in the mountain valley. She would have to ask Sunna about it sometime.

Around sunset, Eppie and one of the bandit men fetched an evening meal from a nearby tavern. They set it on the rough table at the back of the hall, and the bandits and Defenders lined up to fill their battered bowls and take their rounds of bread. Darna sniffed. It was better than what they'd eaten in the mountains, but not very good by Anamat standards, but she was hungry enough to eat almost anything. She was looking for a place to eat when Vigda waved her over.

"Come sit over here by me," she said. As Darna followed her, she noticed the Enatel coming to join them too.

"So, what will we do about this tribunal?" Vigda asked Sovara.

Sovara looked to Darna. "You were at the palace last night. What's the best way to get in and out without getting killed these days?"

Darna considered the question. "I wouldn't worry about getting killed there, ordinarily, and if all goes well, lots of people will be watching Calar, but he must have some allies, and I don't know who they all are. I've never been to the council chamber myself, but I know more or less where it is. It's about half the size of this hall and faces on a courtyard. The corridors leading up to it are narrow, easy to get caught in."

"Easy to defend, too," the Enatel said.

Vigda nodded. "I don't like closed-in spaces, but they have some advantages."

"Thorat would know more about it than I do," Darna said. "With any luck, he'll have a good idea of who's on Calar's side, too."

"That old mistress of Terenet's would know better than anyone," Vigda said. "You should ask her about it."

Sovara shook her head. "I won't go to the temple. There's enough treachery in there to make an Enomaean blush."

Darna frowned. She counted at least one Enomaean as a friend, and their horses weren't even that bad, for all that they were terrified of dragonlets. At least they weren't dragon-blind. She wondered what Nolerin was doing, if he was still in Theranis or if he'd gone back to Calandria. Either way, he probably couldn't help much.

"I could send a message to Gallia," Darna offered. "There must be some place we can meet, and I'll have to get up to the tribunal somehow, and so will she."

Sovara nodded and signaled to Eppie. "We need you to carry a message down to the temple and bring one back if you can," she told Eppie. "What's your message?" she asked Darna.

"I was going to write it, but –"

"Keep it simple," Vigda advised. "She'll know who it's from and we don't want it intercepted."

They were all looking to her. "There's a place just east of Guild Bridge where there's a blind alley that we can probably wait in and talk without being overheard. If she comes in a palanquin, she'd be hidden."

"Or you could be. You're the one with a price on your life," Vigda said.

Sovara looked around the room. "Some of us can act as bearers. Will she trust who we send?"

"I don't know," Darna said. "She might. If she has her own guardsmen, I haven't heard of it."

"I'll talk to her," Eppie said. "I can get into the temple without much trouble. Sunna's brought me there a few times, says I'm from another temple."

Vigda tipped her head at Eppie. "You don't look like much of a priestess, girl."

Eppie smiled. "I'm not, but I can get past the gates."

"Do that, then," Vigda said as she shooed Eppie away. Sovara, the Enatel, slunk off to her private corner, where a dim flicker of lamplight filtered out through the curtain as her hammer tapped on metal. Darna found a bedroll and fell into a deep sleep.

§

The next thing Darna knew, it was almost dawn and Eppie was shaking her awake.

"I found that place you were talking about," Eppie said. "Ferrent and Forlan have gone down to carry the palanquin up from the temple with Vigda. Sunna's got it in the Landing's back courtyard, and we'll meet her at the alley."

Darna rolled up to a sitting position. Her stomach hurt. "Where are we going?" She was too sleepy to piece it together.

"Up to the palace. The governor's mistress is giving you one of her rooms to use until the tribunal tonight."

Darna shook herself awake a little more. "Tiagasa? What's she thinking?"

"I don't know, but Gallia said it would be all right."

"I hope she knows what we're getting into. I know I don't."

There was no tea to be had and Eppie was in a great rush, so they hurried out of the hall in only the time it took for Darna to strap on her sandals. They rattled down the stairs and out through the dark passage in the gray light of early morning, landing on a narrow side street that Darna had passed from time to time. Looking behind her, she could see no trace of the passage to the hidden courtyard.

Eppie hurried her on, so she couldn't poke around to figure out how the Defenders' passage was hidden. They slipped through another hidden way and over to the blind alley by Guild Bridge just as the palanquin was coming into view on the far side of the canal. Ferrent was carrying the front set of poles and Forlan took the rear. Four women in priestess robes walked alongside, veils hiding their faces.

Ferrent paused at the mouth of the alley and set the palanquin down.

"In you go," Sunna said from behind one of the veils.

Darna looked at the other three veiled priestesses. One of them was Gallia; the other might have been her girl at the palace who'd helped Darna get her temporary maidservant position. Vigda was the other one – she still smelled a bit like a bandit despite her borrowed robes. Vigda and Sunna both wore swords, as did the two men. It was as strong a phalanx of guards as most princes had.

"Could I walk?" Darna asked.

"No," Sunna said. "Get in."

"Safer that way," Vigda said, "and more suited to your station."

"Are you coming?" Sunna asked Eppie.

"Not now; I'll see you back at the hall," Eppie said.

"Wait, Eppie?" Darna said. "Would you go tell Myril where I am? Ask her to come, if it's not too hard for her."

Eppie agreed to that, then she slipped away down what was left of the canal bank as Darna climbed into the palanquin. She had carried a palanquin pole before, when Iola went down to the harbor to fly to the other realm, but she'd never ridden in one before. This one was a bit smaller that the ambassadress's ceremonial chair, but it was also filigreed around the arches and draped with brocade curtains, altogether too ornate for a guildswoman.

"I'm supposed to be the one who's in there," Gallia whispered as they started up the street. "I told that upstart

Tiagasa that I didn't know where you'd gone. She said she hoped you'd turn up alive."

"I hope we can manage that, for her sake," Darna grumbled. It was strange to think of Tiagasa as an ally, but they hadn't spoken to each other in a very long time. Maybe the governor's mistress had changed, but Darna doubted it.

"Stop chattering," Vigda scolded. "Let's go on."

The palanquin rocked like a small boat on a harbor's stormy waves. Despite the warmth and lack of damp, Darna thought of Slaradun and how different things had been a year earlier. It felt like years had passed, not just a moon-round and a half, since Hedrin had attacked her in that lonely keep on Theranis's western shore. It was stupid to think that she would step willingly into the affairs of princes, but there she was, riding in a palanquin. She'd rather measure a harbor's depth and choose stones for a foundation.

As they approached the palace, Darna heard Gallia complain. "Where did that old woman go?"

Sunna shushed her. A few steps farther along, the sound of Vigda's labored breathing let Darna know that the old bandit woman was back.

"What happened?" she whispered.

"Archer. Sitting in a tavern window. Gone now," Vigda said.

Darna mumbled her thanks. She tried to sit back so as not to show her profile when they entered the palace market square, brightly lit by the rising sun. At the palace gates, Gallia's girl at the palace presented a letter to the guard and said something about "Her Ladyship," meaning Tiagasa. From there, Darna was carried into the central part of the palace and the area of the governor's private rooms, which adjoined the main council chamber. At long last, Ferrent and Forlan set down the palanquin at a chamber door

"May I get out now?" Darna asked.

"Hold a moment," Sunna said. Darna could hear her walking away down the corridor, probably checking to see if anyone was lurking nearby. She came back and declared the way clear.

Gallia squeezed past the palanquin, through the door.

"Her Ladyship isn't awake," said a young woman's sleepy voice. "She's not receiving visitors."

"She's given me the use of her lily chamber for the day, to prepare for tonight's tribunal," Gallia said. "She would be most displeased if I were kept waiting."

"Oh. She said it was for the Tiadun ladies. Are there more of you?" The young priestess looked out. "All priestesses?"

"And our guardsmen," Gallia said.

"I'm afraid they'll have to stay outside. We don't want to play favorites, so only the palace guardsmen are allowed in."

"Very well. I'll send them back to the temple with the chair, and I'll speak to Tiagasa about that when she wakes. Show us in."

Darna slipped out through the palanquin's curtains into a gap between Sunna and Vigda, who hastily threw a veil over her head. Tiagasa's attendant did not look pleased to have been woken so early, or to be seen with the mark of bedsheets still on her face. She curled her lip at the sight of Darna.

"I'd heard that Tiadun had fallen on hard times, but one must wear better robes at the palace," she said.

"That will all be taken care of, as you will see," Gallia said smoothly. "Now show us to the lily chamber and have our breakfast brought."

"As you wish, Honored One," the young woman said. She scurried ahead of them and down another short, narrow corridor to a high-ceilinged room with frescoes of enormous lilies painted on the walls, reaching up taller than any of them in a sort of forest of flowers. The effect was...soothing, Darna decided. The room had only two small, high windows. If she guessed right, they were at one side of the garden that faced onto the main council chamber. There would be a tile roof outside those windows that covered the walkway around the garden. It was not perfectly safe – someone might be able to look in on them from above if they climbed onto that roof – but it would do.

Tiagasa's attendant didn't linger. As soon as she'd gone out, Darna asked if a watch could be kept on the roof outside.

"I'll ask Thorat what he thinks as soon as I can find him," Sunna said. She yawned and looked around. Apart from the paintings and a mosaic at the center of the floor, depicting more ordinary-sized lilies, it was a plain room, furnished only with cushioned benches along the walls and a couple of small, low tables. Sunna lay down on one of the benches and closed her eyes. Gallia gestured to Darna to sit in the far corner with her, away from Sunna. Vigda removed her veil and took a seat beside the door. She let her sword hang out of the gap in her priestess robes.

"And who would you be?" Gallia asked her.

"I have an interest in this matter," Vigda said. "Also a good sword arm, which no one suspects of an old woman."

Gallia raised her eyebrows. "For all your white hair, you're not so very old, are you?"

"Older than you are by five years and a half, more or less."

"I see," Gallia said. "I'll have to get better robes for you, too." She looked pointedly at her girl at the palace, who had shed her priestess robes and looked like an ordinary serving girl again. "See to getting robes for these two appropriate to their station."

The girl at the palace gave a little bow to her mistress. "I'm sorry," she said hesitatingly, "but what station would that be?"

"Heir to the prince of Tiadun and... What would you call yourself?"

Vigda tipped her head to one side, considering. "You may dress me as a village chief or his wife. I've been something like that."

"That will do," Gallia said. "Off with you, and see to it that they send their best breakfast. Terenet's heir must get used to her position."

Darna wasn't so sure about that, but she saw no need to argue with Gallia. She, at least, knew her way around the palace, which was more than Darna could say for herself. Over breakfast, her father's old mistress had filled her head with names and places, bits of geography and intrigue, everything she thought was most essential to the management of Tiadun.

"You know the keep itself," Gallia said, "and of course I'll go back with you for a little while, but after that, I'd like to visit my home province again."

"Which province is that?" Sunna asked from her bench.

"Helanum, young lady, and I'll have you know it's unacceptable to lie down like that when a prince is keeping court."

"I'm not keeping court," Darna said. "And really, I don't mind."

"You'll have to learn a thing or two about keeping up appearances, then," Gallia said.

Vigda sprang to her feet, sword drawn, as someone appeared at the door. It was Tiagasa.

"Do put that down," the governor's mistress said testily. She gave Gallia a nod and looked skeptically at Darna. "Your father's mistress is absolutely correct. You will have to learn something about appearances. I'm shocked that you never did, for all your years as a novice priestess." She shook her head at the state of Darna's dress, which was her serving-woman garb from two nights before.

Vigda let her sword drop but did not re-sheathe it, and Sunna stopped pretending to rest. She got up to greet Tiagasa with a low bow.

"I see you've left the temple," Tiagasa said to Sunna. "You must think that your protégée here has a chance."

"I'm only here until the tribunal," Sunna said. "And yes, I think Darna will prevail. If you thought that she wouldn't, then we wouldn't be here, would we?"

Tiagasa smiled. "No, you would not. Now, Darna, or Darnasa, let us see what we can do to make you look like less of a disgrace to your bloodline."

§

While the day at the Defenders' hall had been physically exhausting, it had also been companionable and interesting, with quiet moments here and there. The day in Tiagasa's borrowed chamber was an unrelenting barrage of exactly the kind of things Darna had always disliked about Tiagasa and her kind, namely their obsessive attention to fashion and constant social maneuvering. She bore with it, though. She was coming to like Gallia, and Vigda seemed to have taken a strangely strong interest in the trial, for a bandit chief who despised the lowlands.

In the late afternoon, Tiagasa accompanied the delivery of a pile of excessively embroidered robes, but no jewels. Darna still had her stone from Slaradun and wondered if she should wear it outside her robes or inside. She was contemplating that question as Tiagasa discussed the robes with Gallia.

"Now, Darna," Tiagasa said suddenly. "I'd like to see you prevail. If you don't, we may have to turn you over to your uncle's care, and there's no telling what he might do." Her voice was chilly.

Darna immediately thought of Hedrin, his boot on her neck on the cold floor of Slaradun keep in the darkest hour of the night. If Calar found out that she and Ivanat had left Hedrin imprisoned there, he would want revenge for his son's life. If she'd let him kill her, he might have walked free and escaped the flooding and ruin of Slaradun. But then, she would be dead. She shuddered to think what would happen if Calar had charge over her. She would not live long, or if she did, he would make her wish she was dead.

"You'd better do well," Tiagasa said. "You and I may have some work to do." There was menace in that, too, but not as much as there had been in the earlier threat. Darna forced a tense smile onto her face.

"Now," Tiagasa said lightly, "you ladies will want to rest before the evening. I'll see you in the council chambers." With that, she made her exit, smiling coldly.

The brief rest did revive Darna's energy. As she walked across the garden to the council chamber, she tried to convince herself that Calar could not prevail. Her head was packed full of Gallia's lessons about Tiadun, which village chiefs were loyal to Calar, which had been her father's most ardent supporters, and what she should do to secure their loyalties if she was successful in unseating Calar. Gallia did not discuss what would happen if she failed. She had a little more delicacy about that than Tiagasa did, but there was a grim set to her jaw.

"It's no use pretending that there's any doubt," Gallia had said at last. "Even if you're not his daughter – and I believe you are – you're our best chance of defeating Calar."

"I'm not even sure that I want to go back to Tiadun," Darna mused.

"Anamat is sinking, Tiadun isn't," Gallia pointed out, "and someone has to put Calar off the throne."

Darna could agree with that much. Gallia led on. Sunna had gone back to the temple but Vigda had stayed with her, and Forlan and Ferrent had rejoined them. The guardsmen were only allowed to watch from outside, in the garden, along with the guardsmen of the other princes.

For someone who was supposed to be seizing the throne of a province, Darna felt rather like a bundle of goods. She'd never wanted to be a princess, always being bundled around on some political errand or other, and it felt like that already, even though the tribunal hadn't yet begun. She tried to imagine Calar groveling but couldn't get a firm image of him in her mind, despite having seen him only two nights before. What was her remaining cousin's name? Renar, that was it. Gallia said that he wasn't quite as vile as Hedrin had been, but only because he was more dull-witted. She was glad that she hadn't grown up among them. It had been far better to run free on the streets of Anamat, however briefly. Even when the other princesses had sneered at her in the temple, she'd had more friends than she would have in Tiadun. She wondered where Myril was.

Darna wore blue-and-orange robes, Tiada's color. She looked the part of a noble challenger, thanks to everyone but herself. There would be no more scurrying around trying to find her freedom in the hidden ways. She missed her old life.

§

Chapter 9

Hot, sweaty air wafted out of the council chamber. Most of the princes and guild chiefs were already assembled.

"We'd better go in," Vigda said, which made Darna realize that she'd stopped at the door. A hill bandit was advising her on how to behave in court.

She was smiling at the absurdity of it when she stepped into the council chamber. Her uncle and cousin were seated directly across from her, and she had a clear view of their faces for the first time. They'd been placed a few seats away from Parnet and Tiagasa, separated from the governor by a phalanx of dark-robed men and women with sheaves of parchment and writing implements. Myril was there, standing just behind the Chief Chronicler. The palace scribes stood in front. All around the rest of the room stood the princes of the provinces with their consorts and heirs.

Darna turned to make her obeisance to the governor and his consort, keeping her gaze away from her usurping uncle. Tiagasa looked down on her, stony-faced. Had her help that day been some kind of complicated ruse? Tiagasa could be simply hedging her bets. Darna decided that the later possibility was most likely.

"Darnasa it is, then," Tiagasa said, adding the honorific to Darna's name for possibly the first time ever. "Welcome to our court. You come to present your case?"

Darna stood straight and turned slightly so that she could keep half an eye on Calar and Renar. The two older women, bandit and keep mistress, stood behind her. Vigda would be keeping watch. "I come to challenge my uncle" Darna said. "He has unjustly murdered my father. He and his allies drove the dragon of Tiadun to the deepest stream. He is a murderer and despoils the heart of the land he claims to want to rule. He is unfit."

"It is ridiculous to say that about the dragon, who may not even exist," Calar said.

"Nonetheless, it is part of your challenger's accusation," Parnet said.

"Also, you know nothing of me," Calar said to Darna.

"I know enough."

"Please," Parnet said. "Take your places."

He waved Darna to a place opposite Calar's, a bench with a narrow table before it. Vigda and Gallia flanked her. Darna was fairly sure that Vigda had at least three blades hidden under her robes. That was reassuring.

She focused on Calar as Tiagasa and Parnet took their seats. Girizit stood behind them, regarding her through narrowed eyes and with a slight sneer on his lips. She resisted the urge to sneer back at him. There were some advantages to priestess training – she was able to keep her face blank when she had to.

Calar wore Tiadun's colors too, a bright blue tunic and an orange cape embroidered more thickly than Darna's borrowed robes. He was tall, but his son Renar towered over him. It took Darna a moment to realize that although they were both tall,

Renar was wearing Cerean boots. Calar had had just enough sense not to come to the tribunal dressed like a foreigner.

Various palace dignitaries and gossips had crammed into the room, leaving a central spot open for whoever was speaking. Darna had to look twice before she spotted Thorat standing in the shadows behind Parnet and Giri. One of the maids she'd worked alongside was leaning in at the doorway. Near her, she saw Kinner standing behind the prince of Galamun and Harzet the Cerean. Harzet smiled at her ruefully.

Some of the onlookers were clearly ranged on Calar's side, including the princes of Kiralun, Naramun, and Seiganum. Most stood a bit apart, undecided.

The governor thudded his table for attention.

"I open this evening's tribunal in the name of Anara and all the dragons. We come here tonight at the behest of Gallia, once keep mistress of Tiadun. She alleges that Calar, brother of the late prince Terenct, is unfit to rule, and that Terenet's daughter should serve as regent in his stead until she bears a son and raises him to adulthood."

Darna blanched at the thought of conceiving an heir, let alone birthing and raising one, but it was better than seeing Calar on the throne.

"First, we will hear challenges to Calar's right to the throne. Gallia brought this suit. Please come forward."

Gallia stepped into the center of the room. She was doing her best to maintain the calm air of command she'd used when they'd arrived at Tiagasa's rooms that morning, but her shaking voice betrayed her.

"Your Excellency, Blessed One." She bowed to the Parnet and Tiagasa. "I thank you for hearing my case. In the springtime of the past year, my most beloved prince set out on a hunting expedition with his brother and a group of Cereans, who, as we know, have plentiful boar in their own country but no dragons or dragon stones. That is what they were hunting, though my beloved Terenet went with them in order to try to keep them to their stated goal of hunting boar and other wild game in our hills.

"They brought him back to me pierced with an arrow and dying. On his deathbed, he told me of his daughter, sired not long after I first met him. As you can see, she is now a woman grown and a respected member of her guild."

Across the room, someone coughed to cover a laugh. Darna - and many others - turned to see who it was. Standing opposite the chief of the planner's guild, Tevan stood near Calar and Renar, looking odious. She'd thought he liked her better than this. He had always been greedy and selfish. She should never have tolerated him so long.

"Unfortunately," Gallia continued, "Calar overheard us. After Terenet died, he broke with custom and blocked the priestesses from their right to rule until a new prince was confirmed. There was some unrest in the villages, but the Cereans who had come to steal the dragons' stones - those who had not died in the attempt - helped him to put the protests down."

At the mention of the death of the Cereans, Calar's Cerean advisor shuddered a little. Perhaps he did not like to lose his armsmen to creatures he did not quite believe in, or to shadowy warriors from the hills, dressed in rags.

"And then," Parnet put in, "Calar is said to have put a price on Darnasa's life. Can any confirm this?"

There was a long silence.

"No? Then perhaps that rumor is false?"

Thorat stepped out of the shadows. "Pardon me, Your Excellency, may I speak?"

Parnet glanced at Tiagasa who gave him an almost-imperceptible nod as she frowned. The governor directed his guardsman to step forward.

Thorat was playing a part, Darna realized as he walked out to the center of the room. His shoulders were more hunched than usual, and he glanced at the courtiers around him out of the corners of his eyes, as if he were intimidated by them. He'd faced dragons, and he must know that he could match and surpass anyone in the room in a contest of arms. He was not intimidated, but he wanted to look the part of an obedient servant.

He cleared his throat. "I served as a guardsman at Tiadun keep starting the Midsummer before last. I was not there when this hunting party went out, having been called back to the family farm." He might be thinking of Raina's place, but he was coloring the truth quite liberally. "When I arrived, it seemed I'd be better off back at my old work, so I returned to Anamat to take up guarding again. I met another Tiadun guardsman in the tavern out there on the square, and he told me about the price on Darnasa's head." He glanced up at Darna quickly, then stared at the floor in front of his feet.

"Then what was the price?" the governor prompted.

"The price? He offered a land grant and Cerean slave girls, I think."

"You didn't pursue this?"

Darna felt Vigda tense beside her, but Thorat answered in character.

"No, Your Excellency. I don't like the thought of killing women who've done me no harm, and Calar hadn't shown himself to honor his word before." He looked up, as if he were warming to the topic.

"Thank you; that will be all," Tiagasa said. She whispered something in Parnet's ear. She must know or suspect that Thorat knew Darna as a friend.

Thorat bowed and returned to his place in the shadows.

"Who else speaks for Darnasa, allegedly of Tiadun, or against Calar?"

The princes of Getedun and Galamun stepped forward. "Calar rode roughshod over our lands, letting his foreign allies abuse our people. Anyone who can unseat him would be better."

Calar sneered. "Even a girl?" he said.

Parnet picked up a heavy dagger with a jewel-encrusted hilt and raised it for attention. Calar was out of turn. Parnet gestured to Darna.

"Darnasa. Have you any other allies?"

Darna could not name her bandit allies from the hills and the governor wouldn't accept their testimony, anyway. "I do not know what other allies I have," she said, "but I submit to the governor that I am not a girl but a grown woman, an initiated priestess of Ara's Landing and a full member of the Planners' Guild."

Two men stepped out of the crowd – the planner's guild chief and the chief of the swordsmiths' guild. Three more joined them, which meant that most of the chiefs of the higher guilds of Anamat stood for her side. The Chronicler stayed beside the governor, hand poised over a piece of parchment, recording the proceedings.

"The guilds, then," Parnet said. He sounded slightly nervous at that. "Do any of the guilds stand for Calar?"

No one stepped forward.

"That is irrelevant!" Calar said. "I have my village chiefs. What should the guildmasters of Anamat care for a faraway province like mine?"

The guildsmen grumbled among themselves. "We care that we haven't been paid our due in two years!" someone shouted from the back of the room.

"Order!" Parnet pounded his jewel-hilted dagger on the table, crushing the wood beneath it. "Calar's point is taken. Guildsmen, stand down."

Tiagasa looked nervous.

Parnet gestured for Darna to come forward. "Do you have any more to say about the basis of your claim?"

Darna felt her racing heart calm as she stepped into what felt like a role in a play. She did not feel at all like her own self. "I am said to be Terenet's daughter," she said, "though I have never quite believed it. Seeing my cousin there, I don't doubt that we're related somehow."

She could see people nodding and felt them looking at her. Renar rested his hand on his sword hilt. She was grateful that she had guards. Myril's presence among the Chroniclers was reassuring, too.

"I know that I was born in a village in Tiadun. I was raised a fosterling and sent to the keep to be a servant after my foster parents had a child of their own and I was – I was damaged. I had a limp for many years. It's cured now, thanks to the winged ones." Let them think it was ordinary piety. She didn't need to tell them about Salara. They wouldn't believe her, anyway.

Tiagasa nodded slowly. "Your cure came after many years," she remarked.

"It did," Darna said. "But I stand here, most likely Terenet's daughter, now that it seems to matter. I am not accused of murder."

"That is not the object of our inquiry at present," the governor said. "You may return to your place, Lady Darnasa. Who speaks in favor of Calar?"

"I do," said Renar, not waiting to be acknowledged. He teetered forward on his high heels. "I would take a challenger to establish my father's right to rule, by right of arms."

Parnet nodded. "That would have been acceptable last year, had your challenger brought a champion of her own. Have you a champion?"

Darna nodded. She didn't know who would stand to fight Renar, but Thorat might, or one of the others. Gallia had said that Renar was handy with a sword, and an excellent archer, but she thought any of the men in the Defenders' hall could probably match him.

"At this juncture, however, there are complications," the governor said. "Let us hear from another." He gave a nod to the prince of Naramun, who stepped forward.

"You cannot give rule to a woman and a priestess," said the prince. "It would upset the balance."

"She would rule as regent only, with her consort. She would need to choose a consort," Tiagasa said, "but we will take that into consideration."

Darna felt acid rise in her gorge at the thought of choosing a consort. She wasn't ready for that. Most likely, she never would be.

The princes of Seiganum and Kiralun presented themselves as Calar's backers, too.

"Are there any others?" Parnet asked.

Calar's Cerean advisor stepped forward. "As the emissary of the Duke of the Southern Reaches –"

Parnet slapped his hand down on the table. "No," he said. "We thank your countrymen for the gifts they have brought and for their allegiance –" Girizit leaned forward to whisper in the governor's ear, but Parnet brushed him away like one of the errant flies buzzing around the remnants of a feast. "We thank you and your countrymen for your interest in our affairs, but this must be decided by our own laws."

Girizit smiled at Darna and shrugged. She looked away. She did not want his allegiance, useful as it might be. She hoped that she wouldn't need it.

"Any others? Men – or women – of Theranis?"

Someone stepped out from behind Calar. It took Darna a long moment to recognize her.

"I was a priestess of Salara," she said. "I say that this woman is no true priestess of the dragons, that she is an impostor in this, too." Ciffolga was not the weeping, ragged-robed figure from a cottage hearthside in a village anymore. She'd been transformed into an Anamat priestess, albeit one from Conn's Coop, not Ara's landing. She wore robes nearly as rich as Darna's borrowed ones and was wreathed in a heady perfume.

"I present my consort, Ciffolga," Renar said. "I propose that if my father is deemed unfit to rule, that I take his place in Tiadun keep, with this consort, a true priestess, by my side." His eyes flicked over to Darna but he looked away before his gaze could settle. They did look alike. Darna avoided looking at Ciffolga. She was alive – Darna would have rejoiced at that, but she'd betrayed the dragons after all those years of working in secret. Calar's son must have promised her wealth, power, and security. Those were prizes Ciffolga had never been offered before, so it seemed that she had turned.

The governor nodded. A young man with a consort and skill at arms fit the part of a candidate for a princedom in dispute. Darna could feel the sense of the room turning against her.

"Others?" Parnet said.

Tevan stepped forward. *Curse him!* Darna thought. He sauntered to the center of the floor as Ciffolga dropped back. He looked up at his old lover.

"Darna's just a guildswoman," he said. "I've known her well for many years. She never said anything about being a princess, and she doesn't act like one."

There were titters of amusement from around the room. Anyone could see that Darna, despite her fine robes, was not like the other noblewomen.

"And how many princesses have you known, young man?" Vigda shouted.

The laughter stopped. Everyone turned to look at her. "Would you speak, lady... What is your name and title?" Parnet asked.

"That doesn't matter," Vigda said as she shouldered past Darna and stood in the center of the room. Her voice carried better than Renar's had – priestess training. She held her head high.

"I was a priestess at a village temple in Tiadun," she began. "When the prince made his rounds, he visited me, my only petitioner that moon-round. I was already growing weary of temple life and considering going to my hermitage in the hills. I am pleased to have met my daughter again at last, and if there are any of you who say that she is not a true priestess, ask Tiada, if you can find her, or Salara, or Anara. All three of these dragons know this young woman for who she is, the rightful ruler of Tiadun. I gave birth to her, and I stand with her."

Darna barely heard the voices around her. It was like a distant wind, like a storm, roaring in her ears like so much meaningless noise.

"Are you?"

Vigda nodded. "I knew it the moment I saw you, up in the mountains. I used to have a mirror to gaze in before I went into the hills, and of course I knew your father when he was a younger man too, even before he chose Gallia for his consort. Better her than me. I prefer the hills. You must take the keep."

Parnet banged his dagger again. Tiagasa looked like she might faint and took a long drink from the goblet in front of her. The servant standing behind her refilled it.

Tiagasa stepped up. "I have one further piece of evidence," she said.

"Speak, then," Parnet said, but he was unhappy with the prospect, as was Girizit. Giri even reached out as if to hold Tiagasa back, but, seeing that the rest of the room waited on Tiagasa's word, he tucked his many-ringed fingers back into the folds of his tunic.

"When Darna first came to Ara's Landing, she was called Darnasa. I was a novice priestess there at the time, only a year ahead of Darnasa. She was as ragged as any foul-footed scrappling I ever saw, and lame, too. I did not think that she was a fit priestess. All of us – the well-born girls who once went to the priestesses to learn their arts – all of us thought that she was only a peasant until she left the temple only a single season after her initiation, clear of debt and without scandal. It seemed odd that she was not bound to the temple, as scrappling novices must be. I learned that the prince of Tiadun had paid her fees from the beginning and had in fact compelled the priestesses to bring her in for training despite her deformities." Tiagasa shook her head. "So, you see that for all her peasant-like ways, she must be a princess by birth. Much as I hate to say it, it's true."

Giri looked uncomfortable. Darna smiled.

"Thank you, my sister," she said to Tiagasa.

Tiagasa nodded, as if to say, *Remember it; I'll collect my payment later.*

"Where is the Aralel, then, to confirm or deny all this?" Parnet demanded.

"Wise to keep her nose out of this farce. We'll take our due!" The voice came from Calar's side, but Darna wasn't sure who had spoken.

The Chronicler rested his writing hand and looked in that general direction. "It is unseemly to threaten the ladies of the dragons, and unwise," he said.

"Keep to your work, man," Parnet said.

The Chronicler did not react except to pick up his pen again.

"We will retire to consult on this matter," Parnet said. "Council!"

The chiefs of the greater guilds and those princes who had not taken sides in the dispute followed the governor into a neighboring chamber. Girizit leaned over to whisper in Tiagasa's ear. She shook her head and followed the council into their chamber, leaving Girizit alone beside the governor's chair, flanked by half of his guardsmen. Darna was glad to see Thorat among them. She hoped that Myril would be able to hear what was said in that council, to tell her later. She glanced across at Myril, who gave her a quick smile before turning back to her work.

Something else was happening. Girizit met the gaze of Calar's Cerean advisor. The two foreigners approached each other, meeting in the neutral center of the room.

"Your Duke is in disgrace," Giri said in Cerean.

"It does not matter. We have an army here." He glanced up at Darna, who looked away. "A woman and a cripple," he said. "Shameful."

"Shameful, yes," Girizit said. "A thief, too, but she understands what you say, you know."

Then Giri turned to Darna and smiled, a broad smile that melded a triumphant grin with a sneer of derision.

"You can take your army and sail it home," Darna said in Cerean. "I advise you to."

"Boldly spoken," Giri said. "But it is I, and the king, who will bring our own down. I leave your so-called uncle to you, whore's spawn."

"Slave," Darna countered. She turned away.

"What was that?" Vigda asked her.

"He insulted you, and all priestesses, in the way they usually do. Also, the duke's man there, Calar's Cerean, threatens me with his army, but he has his own countrymen ranged against him, so maybe they'll hold him back."

"His own countrymen will take his side if it comes to losing Tiadun," Gallia said. "We must be on guard."

Before Darna could reply, Tiagasa returned to the council chamber. All hushed as the councilors filed in behind her. Parnet took his place behind the table with his dagger in his hand.

"It is decided," he said. "Calar and his sons – if Hedrin can be found – will be given over to the princes of Galamun and Getedun, who between them may demand such penance as they see fit. Their guardsmen are released from their contracts. Should they wish to remain in their posts, they may negotiate that with Darnasa as regent of Tiadun. She will take that place in the return journey, beginning on Midsummer morning, until such time as she produces a fitting heir."

Darna's belly clenched and cramped. The edges of her vision grew dark but she took a deep breath and did not faint. She bowed, and barely heard as the governor dismissed the meeting.

Tiagasa and Parnet cut through the throng that was gathering around her as Calar and Renar were ushered out roughly by the prince of Getedun and his armsmen.

"I'll have Calar's things moved out of the Tiadun prince's apartments. You and your retinue may move in now," Tiagasa said.

"My retinue?" Darna said.

Tiagasa waved her hand vaguely. "Oh, you know. Princesses are born knowing these things. You need a chamberlain, a secretary, a captain of the guard, and perhaps a Cerean tutor. You must arrange all of that."

"I don't need a Cerean tutor." People were crowding around her, princes and their consorts who Darna recognized only by the colors of their robes, which corresponded to the realm colors she'd learned as a priestess. She didn't know any of them. None of them knew her. That would all have to change.

"You may find that you do need one," Tiagasa said. "And you can't have mine."

"I wouldn't want him, as he knows." There were other men she didn't need. She could still see Tevan arguing with their guildmaster. Their words were inaudible through the din, but she could see the color rising in Tevan's face. Would he be dismissed from the guild? She felt faint.

"We'll see to it that our regent is properly attended," Gallia said, taking command. "Thank you, Your Ladyship, for your gracious hospitality."

"You have been most generous," Darna added as an afterthought.

Vigda gave the slightest of bows. "Let's go out into the courtyard," she said to Darna as Tiagasa turned away.

"Yes, let's," Darna said. She looked over her shoulder for Myril and gestured for her to come join them, then escaped the crowded council chamber as quickly as she could.

The courtyard was only slightly less crowded, but at least there was a cool breeze.

"You must assemble your people quickly," Gallia said. "Are there any here?"

Darna looked behind her to see that Myril was approaching. Thorat had gone off with the governor already. Forlan and Ferrent stood on either side of her, visibly watchful and intimidating. Calar's Cerean saw them, frowned, and walked away.

"Those two should stay with you," Gallia said, gesturing to the brothers.

Vigda nodded. "They'll guard you well. That girl Eppie might help too."

"You know her?" Gallia asked.

Vigda shrugged. "May the winged ones go with you, daughter. I'll see you in Tiadun."

"But –" Darna protested. Myril caught up with her just then and wrapped her in a warm embrace.

"I'm so glad you're safe," Myril said. "I lost the sound of you the night before last. I was worried."

Darna pulled away, looking for Vigda. "My mother," she said. "She just left."

"I'm sorry," Myril said. "What happened the other night?"

"I was all right. Didn't Thorat tell you?"

Myril shook her head. "I haven't seen him since."

After one more look for Vigda, Darna reached for Myril's hand. "Would you join my...would you be my secretary, or chamberlain, now that I'm a regent?"

Myril looked down and shook her head. "I'm sorry; I have other work to do, and the palace here..."

Darna understood, but she wished that Myril would have faced it for her.

"I'll help you however I can, but I have to go now. I'll visit you every day while you're here."

Darna thanked her. Myril hurried off as the prince of Helanum and his mistress came to greet her.

"I knew as soon as we met at Midwinter that you were no ordinary guildswoman," the prince said. "I am most pleased to see that you have prevailed. Would you breakfast with us tomorrow?"

Darna agreed, but then the Getedun prince's mistress asked her to breakfast, too, and she had to demur. Another invitation followed, and another.

"Don't accept them all," Gallia coached her. "Remember you'll have the councils in the evenings."

Darna took a deep breath. "How long do they last?"

"Until the night before Midsummer Eve," a man to her left said. He turned out to be the prince of Coradun, a man somewhat past his prime but kindly-looking. "I am most pleased to make your acquaintance."

Darna returned his bow, and as she was rising, she finally recognized the young man who'd been lingering nearby. "Kinner!" she called to him. "Would you be my secretary?"

Kinner blushed. "I don't know that I'm ready, but I'll try."

"I feel the same way," she told him. As more and more of the nobles and guild chiefs came to greet her, Kinner stayed by her side. By the time Tiagasa returned to say that their rooms were ready, Darna's head was in a whirl, trying to remember all of the names and faces. Myril returned then too.

"I'm sorry I had to go," she said. "I spoke with Thorat."

"Will you walk with me to my new chambers?" Darna asked. "Wait, though. Can you hear Vigda?"

Myril paused to listen, then shook her head. "She's gone. She went out the kitchen gate while I was talking to Thorat."

Darna's heart sank. She'd spent her whole life trying not to imagine her mother, but she liked Vigda, and Vigda seemed to like her. It was too soon to say goodbye.

§

Chapter 10

At the end of the Tribunal, Thorat accompanied Parnet back to his quarters. Dismissed for the night, he staggered toward the barracks, too exhausted to celebrate the fact that Darna had become the next thing to a prince. It was strange to think that his scrappling friend was a ruler of a province as well as being a priestess. He shook his head at the thought. She still seemed like a scrappling to him. Perhaps he should ask Parnet to let him go to attend her in Tiadun, but he wasn't sure if he really wanted to be Darna's man-at-arms.

The hour was late, so the courtyard was quiet, but a few straggling revelers and messengers drifted past – the palace was never entirely asleep. He was almost to the door of the barracks when a cloaked figure accosted him. He had his hand on the hilt of his sword before he recognized her.

"Myril? Why are you still here?"

Myril looked over her shoulder and spoke in a low voice. "I have a duty to my guild. I came back to speak to you. Some of these Cereans are trying to take the secrets hidden in our histories. We need to hide them."

"I can't help," Thorat said. "I'm here attending the governor. I have no time, and besides –"

"You know of a place that they can't find. Even I can't find it. Would you take some scrolls there? They include some histories that might interest the others there."

The Defenders' hall was indeed secret, but they'd never hidden anything but themselves and their shrine there. It didn't seem like the sort or thing that the Enatel would agree to. Still, keeping the dragons' secrets was half the work of defending them. "I'll ask," he said. "She might agree."

Another person was coming toward them.

"Let me know," Myril said, "or talk to the Chief Chronicler if you see him first. He's the one who asked me to help. I have to go to the temple now with the news." She scurried away. Myril and Iola were no longer lovers, but he still envied the ease with which Myril could go to see Iola in the temple.

A few days later, he was able to return to the training hall. Half of the bandits had disappeared after the tribunal, but the others were lingering around temples and street-corner shrines in between training sessions, making sure that no one was trying to steal anything from the altars there. Tiagasa had sent guards down to Ara's Landing, so that place was safe, but elsewhere, the priestesses were mostly left to fend for themselves. Raina looked grim when she talked about it.

"Most of them are safe enough," she said, "but they're all afraid."

"Those men had better all go back to their own lands after Midsummer," Sovara added.

"Why wouldn't they?" Thorat said, realizing how stupid the question was as soon as the words were spoken. "Never mind," he said. The world was out of order.

"Your Grace?" he said. "I have a request to ask of you. It's –" He hesitated.

"Out with it," Raina prompted.

He'd meant to ask Sovara alone, but if she agreed, then all of them would know, and if she didn't, then it wouldn't matter. "It's a request from Myril, from her guild. The Cereans are trying to take their scrolls and folios. I don't know what they think they'll discover there, but Myril says that they have the dragons' secrets in them. She wants us to hide them here."

"Here in the hall?" Sovara said. "Have you told her where it is?"

"No, she only knows that we have some hidden place," Thorat said.

"It's foolish to keep secrets in a form that can be picked up and carried away," Sovara said. "I don't like it. Why don't they just destroy them?"

Thorat tried to imagine Myril destroying an old text. He shook his head.

"They wouldn't do that," Raina said, saving him from answering. "There's a lot of knowledge in those texts, and people are forgetful. Besides, sometimes students don't learn all their lessons."

Sovara nodded to that but still didn't look convinced. "I still say it's better to lose them to fire than to the dragons' enemies." She frowned and looked out in the general direction of the guild halls. "Does this Chronicler know that we exist?" she asked.

Thorat shook his head. "I'm not sure, but he probably knows that we *did* exist. I don't think Myril would have asked me if it weren't important."

§

Thorat saw the Chief Chronicler the very next day. That afternoon, he was standing to one side in Parnet's chamber, the image of a silent, forgettable guardsman. Girizit said something to Parnet in Cerean, and Parnet nodded.

"You two," the governor said, pointing at Thorat and another guard. "Go down to the Chroniclers' guild and bring back another box of their scrolls for our friend here."

Thorat bowed and went out. His fellow guardsman was a thickset country man, new to the city, with a pockmarked nose. He grumbled about being made to march through the streets in the hot sun so near midday, but Thorat was glad to be out from under Parnet's glare and cheerfully ignored his fellow guardsman.

At the guildhall, they were shown in with reluctant courtesy. The Chronicler was not pleased to see them.

"Box of scrolls for His Excellency," the pock-nosed guardsman barked.

The Chronicler sat down behind his table and made himself comfortable before answering. "You may go outside to wait. I will have them delivered in my own time."

"He wants 'em now." Thorat's fellow guardsman rested his hand on the hilt of his sword and nodded meaningfully. Thorat kept his expression blank.

"You will wait outside."

"That's not our orders," the guardsman said.

"Begging your pardon, Lord Chronicler, but His Excellency has expressed some urgency," Thorat said.

The Chronicler squinted at him.

"I can make it worth your while," Thorat said.

"What are you saying that for? That's not in our orders."

"I just want to hurry things along," Thorat said.

"Well, I'm sticking to orders."

"Wait outside the hall. I will have a box for you to carry to 'His Excellency' in short order. I'll even send for tea for you if you clear out of here," the Chronicler said.

"I prefer ale, myself," Thorat's fellow guardsman said.

"Come on," Thorat urged, practically dragging the man away. He led the way back out to the guild hall's steps, where they settled down on a shady bench. After a little while, an apprentice scribe came out to say that their tea was ready if one of them would fetch it.

"Fetching our own tea!" the other guardsman said, huffing as if that wasn't just what he did every morning in the barracks.

"I'll get it," Thorat said. The apprentice led him in, but Thorat walked behind him and, at the turning of a corner, slipped off back to the Chief Chronicler's study, his absence unnoticed for a moment.

"Lord Chronicler," he said.

The Chronicler looked up, startled.

"Myril tells me that you have a need," he said quietly. "Her Grace says that she will meet with you."

"Her Grace?" the Chronicler looked puzzled, then a smile spread across his face, wrinkling the corners of his eyes. "I thought that it would be a 'His Grace.' Very well, then. You'd best go get your tea now."

Thorat turned to see the distraught apprentice coming up behind him.

"You were to follow me!" the apprentice said.

"And you should be more careful with our visitors from the palace," the Chronicler told the apprentice. "Go now. I'll see you later." He said it as if he were speaking to the young apprentice, but Thorat felt that he'd meant the words for both of them.

Thorat got the tea, and it wasn't long after when two apprentice chroniclers emerged with a box and dropped it onto the bench between the guardsmen. Thorat and his fellow guard took the box by its handles and walked back up to the palace, leaving their unfinished cups of tea behind.

"Don't know what he wants with these old things. If it was me, I'd go to the goldsmiths or the bead makers more."

Thorat grunted noncommittally. The other man finally took the hint and dropped the conversation.

The midday gongs were sounding by the time they returned to the palace, and the governor was still conferring with Girizit. Thorat wished he'd been able to send a message to Sovara. Maybe he would be able to find Eppie on her way to or from delivering some message to Darna in her princely apartment.

"What's this we have here, the same again?" Girizit said.

The box had been lifted up onto the conference table and opened while Thorat was woolgathering.

"You did ask for scrolls," Parnet said, looking down into the box and shaking his head. "Those are scrolls."

"But look," Girizit said, rapidly unfurling one of the ones on top. "This is just another copy of those children's stories, a copy book."

Parnet gestured helplessly at his guards. "You can hardly ask these men to tell the difference," he said. He himself wouldn't know the difference either. Besides, no one had asked them to inspect the scrolls.

Girizit plucked the texts out of the box one by one, tossing most of them aside and tucking a select few into his own satchel. He signaled for his page to take the satchel away.

"I don't even know that the Chroniclers' guild has what you're seeking," Parnet said.

"Then go into the temples for it," Girizit said. "Or shall I ask your lady wife where those secrets are hid."

"I will speak with the Chronicler again," Parnet said. "I will be more explicit this time."

"Do that," Girizit said. "We will see you tomorrow."

"Rest assured, I will wait on your honorable presence."

"And I on yours, Your Excellency," Girizit said. He then performed an obeisance of such groveling complexity that Parnet seemed to forget the sneering tone of Girizit's orders.

§

Thorat spotted Eppie on his way to a late midday meal at the kitchen and she promised to carry word to Sovara. She returned late in the afternoon to say that he should go to the training hall as soon as he could get away that night. It was still well before midnight when the evening's council concluded, but he didn't dare stop in the barracks to give notice that he was going out. He walked straight out of the gate and down to the Defenders' hall in his guardsman's livery.

At the top of the outside stair into the training hall, he stopped short. Garren was there, lying on a mat and looking up at the sky.

"Still in that guardsman's rig?" he said. "I don't know how you stand it up there at the palace."

"What are you doing out here?" Thorat asked. It was unusual to see Garren lounging anywhere, and he was usually at the hall only for training sessions and vigils. It was late in the night.

"Looking at the stars. No trace of the dragons tonight, though I don't doubt they're coming. The sailors say that the tides have changed again." Garren sat up. "I must be off on my errand, now that you're here. I'll see you at Ink Pounders."

"Ink Pounders?" The tavern was not a place Thorat had expected to go that night. He regretted not changing out of his livery.

Garren got to his feet. "That's what she said. You're going to walk there with her if she decides to go. I'm off to fetch the guildmaster." Garren bounded away before Thorat could ask him anymore. He took one look at the peaceful, starry sky then went inside.

The hall was quiet, with a few sleeping forms snoring softly along the wall. A clink of metal on metal sounded from inside Sovara's curtained nook.

"Your Grace?" Thorat ventured.

"Don't call me that," Sovara said.

Thorat looked in. The Enatel worked by the light of a single bright lamp, squinting over a pile of small metal pieces, mostly copper and silver. She had a copper pin clenched between her teeth. She set her small hammer down and removed the pin to glare at Thorat, but then she beckoned for him to come in.

It was a small room, with only the stool and workbench and a raised pallet for sleeping. The lamp dimmed as Sovara turned away from her workbench, as if the flame were sentient.

"I don't know about all of this," Sovara said. "I wouldn't want the Chronicler to go writing anything down about us to send the governor hunting us down again. I don't know that we can help with these histories. They're no use to us. We have our teachings handed down from one to another."

"But then the Cereans will get the texts and whatever's in them. The Cerean king's emissary seems to think the scrolls will teach them to use the dragons' magic."

"If the knowledge of how to use the dragons' stones could be had so easily, they'd have had it long ago," Sovara said. "Any knowledge worth having can't be had from reading scrolls."

"They seem to think it can," Thorat said.

"Did you learn to wield a sword by reading scrolls? Does a priestess learn to channel the dragons' power by hearing stories? No, it's practice. They don't have the first idea of what to do, and they never will."

She picked up her hammer and began tapping again. The lamp brightened in response. The piece she was working on looked like a broad pin for a sash, big enough to offer some protection from an errant dagger to the heart. A moment later, she sighed and pushed her work aside.

"I sent word that I'd talk to him, though," she said. "We'd better be going."

§

The Ink Pounders tavern lay on the upper banks of the East Canal, about midway between the sword hall and the Chroniclers' guildhall.

"Are you sure this is the right place to meet?" Thorat asked Sovara. The taproom was crowded with men and women from the guilds, merchants from the harbor front, and even more from beyond the city walls. There were provincial tradesmen and foreign sailors, who used to be unwelcome in the guilds' favorite watering spots. The din was deafening.

Sovara ignored Thorat's question and wove across the room, meandering like any other white-haired old lady, looking frail among the mostly young drunkards. Thorat wondered whether or not she'd really recovered from her illness the year before. Was her strength an illusion, or was this frailty the camouflage?

The barmaid hurried over to them, looking apologetic.

"Ma'am," she began.

"The attic room, please," Sovara said. She opened her hand and showed the barmaid a token that glimmered briefly before it disappeared into Sovara's pocket. As far as Thorat knew, Ink Pounders had no private rooms.

The barmaid looked carefully at Sovara, then shrugged. "I don't know you, but you have the token, so I suppose," she said. "Go on in."

"The Chief Chronicler will be coming to meet us, along with another guardsman," Sovara said. "Show them upstairs as well."

"As you wish, ma'am. Will you be wanting food and drink?"

Sovara shook her head, but Thorat said, "Please do," and the barmaid called a young kitchen helper over. She whispered instructions to the boy, then hurried back out to the taproom. Sovara made her way across the kitchen as if she knew the place well, going into the small pantry beside the hearth. On its bare back wall, she found a latch and pushed. Half of the wall swung aside, revealing a narrow stair up to a low-ceilinged attic full of barrels and sacks of grain. The young kitchen servant followed, carrying a lamp. At the far end of the attic, he opened a door and went in before them. He lit half a dozen lamps, which brightened a room hung with tapestries woven with ancient and erotic scenes. It was the kind of thing found in a priestess's chamber or in the bedrooms of the palace. The floor was laid with furs around a low table of polished bronze.

Thorat let out a whistle as the serving boy left. "I never knew this was here."

"Of course you didn't; there's been no need for you to know," Sovara said. "The noise from below covers most conversation, so the guildmasters like to use it sometimes."

Thorat sat back on the cushions and let his eyelids close. The thick floor muffled the sound of conversation from below so well that he couldn't even make out snatches. The soft roar had almost lulled him to sleep by the time the young servant returned with ale and a pot of even-better-than-usual stew, plus a basket of bread that smelled good enough to have come from Ara's Landing itself. Sovara took a piece of the bread and sniffed it. She shook her head.

"They're selling the bread. That doesn't bode well."

"Who are, the priestesses?" Thorat asked. "I thought this was just very good bread, not temple bread itself."

There was a clatter on the stair. A moment later, Garren opened the door to let in the sleepy-eyed Chief Chronicler.

"My Lady Enatel?" the Chronicler said. "Or should I say, Your Grace?"

"I dislike titles, Lord Chronicler. Let's sit."

Sovara did not reach for the ale, but Thorat poured for the rest of them. The Chronicler pushed it away. "Have them send water," he said. "But is this temple bread?"

"It seems so," Sovara said. "Either the dragons' ladies are selling it or the scrapplings are."

The Chronicler turned it over in his hand. "Curious. It's been a long time since I've enjoyed this bread."

Garren inspected his piece closely. "It has the mark of the temple on it. I don't know what price it fetches down by the harbor, but I'd imagine that a half-moon's worth would be enough to buy a scrappling passage to Calandria or Ganat."

The Chronicler nodded soberly. "I can't blame people for fleeing the rising water, but still, I hate to see them go. The city feels emptier every day, despite Midsummer coming."

"Not empty enough, with all these foreigners," Sovara said.

The Chronicler tipped his head. "There is that, as well. Have we met, Lady Enatel? I think that I've seen you at the palace from time to time."

"I haven't been there for many years," Sovara said. "But yes, we met before that. You're as old as I am. Sometimes, ten years passes like a season."

"So it does, though not this season. It's worn me more than most, and I'm not the only one." He leaned back and pulled on his beard, looking at Sovara. "I was surprised to learn that your order still exists."

"We have kept ourselves to ourselves," Sovara said. "I'd like to keep it that way, but with the waters rising everything seems to be in flux. I'll hear what you have to say. Why should we hide your scrolls, from the governor?"

"Mostly to keep them from the foreigners," the Chronicler said with a shrug. "They would use our secrets against the dragons you swear to protect. Also, we kept the histories of Enat's followers before your order was publicly dissolved. You might like to know what's in them."

"I would," Sovara admitted. "There are gaps in our knowledge, but still, I doubt that the Cereans could make any use of these scrolls, not without direct training and experience of the dragons."

"That's not a chance I'm willing to take, even if they are all dragon-blind," the Chronicler said.

"They're not," Thorat said. "There was one Cerean at Tiada's gate who saw her, who walked right in. Many of the Ganateans in Slaradun saw Salara at the end, too. I don't think many of them survived."

"Some did," the Chronicler said. He looked at Thorat with renewed interest. "You were in both places?"

"I was."

"I'd like to know what you saw there."

Sovara raised a hand to cut him off. "Not tonight."

"Very well," the Chronicler said. "Do you have news of the palace, then, guardsman of our governor?"

"I overhear some," Thorat said. "After we brought your scrolls to Parnet, Girizit looked through them and was angry not to find what we was looking for. Parnet said that you might not have what he wants, that it might be in the temples. Girizit said he would ask Tiagasa where they were hidden."

"I hear that Tiagasa has already gone to the Aralel, looking for them. I would much rather that they not be found."

Sovara was leaning on the table and resting her chin on her fingertips. They all turned to look at her.

"I still doubt that any worthwhile magic can be unlocked merely by reciting some words in a text," she said.

"A reasonable doubt," the Chronicler said, "but did you know that some of the old texts also include physical instructions, even for fighting techniques?"

"I didn't know that, but could most men could learn fighting techniques from marks on parchment?"

Garren nodded at that, and Thorat might have agreed too, but the Chronicler's grave expression gave him pause.

"It only needs one man who can learn from the parchment to teach the rest," the Chronicler said. "The priestesses do it. I see no reason why a foreigner might not be able to learn, if he were intelligent and receptive to the power of the land. They overcome their terror of the dragons enough to raid the gates. I used to wonder why it took them so long for them to find those gates, but I can see now that your order must have done something to keep them away."

"There were bandits who played a part too," Sovara said. "There haven't been enough in our sword hall to hold them all back for many years now. When I was an apprentice, we had twice a dozen members of the order, enough that one of us could keep watch on each dragon's gate, every year, while half of us stayed in Anamat to train with the Enatel. Now we are fewer, many fewer, and we have only one apprentice. She's likely to be our last."

"I'm sorry to hear that. Some guilds have given up even looking for apprentices. Some of our journeymen are starting to leave for worlds beyond the dragons' shores. Does your spoken lore have anything to say about these rising waters?" the Chronicler asked Sovara.

She shook her head. "I don't like it, though. Our shrine and the taproom here haven't fiooded yet, but the waters are pushing in on them since Slaradun fell."

"I see," the Chronicler said. "Then let me tell you about one old prophecy. A priestess some three hundred years ago dreamed that Slaradun would fall into the sea. Then she saw all of the dragons rise, leaving nothing but open sea where the land had been."

"How?" Thorat asked.

"No one knows. It's only a prophecy, but I share it to say that this favor I ask of you is only for one season at most. Some of our guild members are searching for some safe place to go,

away from the rising waters and the Cereans, and away from
Theranis. The king of Cerea has offered our governor and
some princes gold and a position of power in his court; the
alleged rebellion of this Duke of the Southern Reaches is very
conveniently timed for him. There are already Theranians in
the Cerean court who can interpret these texts."

"And what about Ganat?" Thorat said. "The men who
raided Slaradun were from Ganat, not Cerea."

"They've been slower to come to our shores than the
Cereans, but the two nations are similar, from what I've
learned of them."

"So, you think that we, with our knowledge of dragons
and the art of defending them, are also suitable to defend these
texts until we are all drowned?" Sovara said.

"You are so secretive that I, standing watch over the
histories of our land, did not even know that you existed," the
Chronicler said. "I'm still not entirely convinced that you're
really who you say you are, but if anyone can keep these
secrets, you're better suited to it than the priestesses are,
especially with Tiagasa circling their treasuries."

"That much, I can agree with," Sovara said.

"You may not think much of the priestesses, but they
have considerable power, even wisdom. The foreigners want
their power, as well as their bodies, and it's only a matter of
time before they raid our guildhall for the texts they're looking
for. They may even come during the waning year."

Sovara nodded grimly. "They would do something like
that." She pushed away from the table. "All right, we'll keep
any texts that concern our order, and a few more besides, but
you will be limited to what Garren here can carry in a satchel
every day."

"I've seen you, too," the Chronicler said to Garren.

"I keep a sweet shop in the West Gate market."

The Chronicler smiled. "Then I will send my apprentices there for bread in the coming days. They will bring the packages. I thank you all. Just think of the threat to the dragons if the foreigners try to chain them."

"The foreigners would be destroyed, but of course, the dragons can be wounded, too. If they couldn't, there would be no need for us," Sovara said. "I must also think of my students and successors, if any of them survive, and how to keep our order alive a little longer."

The Chronicler smiled. "In that, you are just like the Aralel."

"Don't remind me of it."

They all rose from the table then, and Thorat gulped down the last of his ale. The Chronicler settled the bill with the serving boy, then went out alone, through the back way. Sovara slipped out after him, shaking off Thorat and Garren's offers of help.

Thorat felt thirsty for another ale, so he made his way to a small, unoccupied table in the corner by the hearth of the taproom below. Another patron was sidling up by the time he reached it – one of Thorat's old fellow pickpockets, Pannen, who'd become a captain of the city watch.

"Is that you?" Pannen said. "I've hardly seen you for years." He thumped Thorat on the back. "Wearing the governor's colors now? That's too bad. We could use you in the city watch."

"Is that so?" Thorat was just as glad he'd never joined the watch. He still thought of them as the enemy, an old prejudice left over from his season as a scrappling.

The barmaid arrived and they raised their cups to each other.

"It's nice to be back in my old quarter again," Pannen said. He'd become watch chief for the city's southeast quarter, the area around the harbor temple. "I thought I knew all its tricks when I was young, but things are different now. You'd hardly believe the trouble we've been having down by Fishermen's Wharf."

"Oh? I always thought that was a peaceful enough place."

"It was, before this season. Now the cursed Cereans and the Enomaeans are trying to drive the fishermen off. They want more places on the wharves, and I say this is for the fishermen, that's why it's called Fishermen's Wharf, but they just carry on as if they can't understand a thing, and half the time they can't." He paused for a drink. "And then there's the priestesses. We could probably work something out with the Enomaeans, they're reasonable enough, but the priestesses won't have it, say they need that way clear for Midsummer Eve, which is days away still. I'm counting every quarter-day until I can get a full night's rest again. Any way you look at it, they're all making trouble, and the traders have hired away half the decent swordsmen in the city, with the governor taking the rest, not that I wouldn't do the same if I were him, but we're shorthanded."

"I'm sorry to hear it," Thorat said. "I would help, but the governor has me in his clutches."

"I can't take you, then. It would be like old times, having you in the gang," Pannen said with a faraway smile. "And then I'll be away. If not now, then after Midwinter."

"Will you? Where are you going?"

"I don't know," Pannen said. "Maybe to Cerea first."

"Looking for Nira?"

Pannen nodded. "If she's still alive, I'll find her. I never should have let her go." With that, he downed the rest of his ale, and they bid each other farewell.

§

Chapter 11

Every day, Myril went to the palace to visit with Darna but she never stayed long. It was strange to see her old friend as regent of Tiadun, and it meant that Darna would have to go back to Tiadun, which would mean only seeing her at Midsummer, if the land held. If it didn't, there was no telling if they would even survive, let alone be able to see each other.

On the day before Midsummer Eve, Myril set out for the palace in the late morning. During the midday rest, the palace's clamor was a little less intense, so she tried to go then. The streets were another matter. Everyone seemed to be in a hurry, going to the market or the harbor, shouting to neighbors or scurrying past, wary of pickpockets, slavers, or both.

She was crossing the Pentangle when a man hailed her: Lerat again.

"My Lady," he said, bending down to kiss Myril's hand. "I would walk with you, but business calls me to my ship."

"That's all right. I'm accustomed to walking on my own."

His smile faded. "Is it safe?"

"I don't hear any threats to myself, or you, right now," she said. "I haven't heard of any outright kidnappings, though there've been attempts."

Lerat looked over his shoulder, back toward the harbor. "I just arrived this morning, later than I hoped to, and I must set sail on the morning of Midsummer. Would you come to dine with me this midday?"

"I'm on my way to spend my midday at the palace," Myril said. "I have a friend there." She paused to listen. "Walk with me a little way. No one here is listening, but they might grow curious if we stand too long."

Lerat nodded and fell into step beside her.

"I have a friend from my scrappling days who is at the palace now," she said as they walked. "I don't advise her in any official capacity, but I don't want to lose her company any sooner than I have to. That's who I plan to spend my midday with."

"You may bring her to my ship then, to dine, if you like, and if you don't mind her hearing about this man at the palace you were asking about before."

Myril had almost forgotten that she'd mentioned Giri to Lerat. "My friend would be rather interested in that." She paused. "Be warned, though, she does bring guardsmen with her, as a precaution."

"Most interesting," Lerat said. "I hope to see you both soon, then."

He made his bow and hurried back to his ship, while Myril walked the rest of the way to the palace alone, wondering if he'd guessed that her friend was the new regent of Tiadun.

She found Darna in her apartment with only her young secretary, Kinner, attending her.

"Where is Gallia?" Myril asked as she went to embrace her friend. The older woman rarely left Darna's side.

"Sleeping." Darna said. "The nights have been late for her, and she rises early."

Myril squeezed Darna's hand as she turned pale. "Are the cramps worse?" she asked in a whisper.

"A bit," Darna said. "But just now, I think that half of it is hunger. I woke too late to breakfast."

"I will go to the kitchens for you, if you like, Your Highness?" Kinner said, getting up.

"I'd rather you not call me that," Darna said.

Kinner looked nervously toward the room where Gallia was sleeping. "She insists," Darna said, wearily.

"Go on, then. Come back and tell me if it's ready yet," she said, waving Kinner on his way.

As soon as Kinner had gone, Myril told Darna about Lerat's invitation.

"I don't know if I should go," Darna said. "Ferrent's sleeping and Forlan has gone out."

"I'm not asleep," came a gravelly voice from one of the inner chambers. There were creaking and clattering as Ferrent emerged, buckling on his sword. "What's the trouble?" he asked.

Darna explained that she wanted to go down to the harbor, to dine on a ship. Myril clarified that she trusted the captain, and that it was a Theranian ship.

"Still, not the safest place," Ferrent commented. "We'll stop to get Forlan on the way."

Myril didn't ask where, and she didn't find out except that it was somewhere between the palace and the Pentangle. She and Darna waited on a nondescript side street while Ferrent disappeared for a very short amount of time, returning with his brother. The two of them together conveyed more strength than the governor's guard force of half a dozen men. Darna wore the plainest tunic she'd been able to find, but she still looked more princely than the average guildswoman, especially with the two guardsmen flanking her. Voices hushed and people turned to stare as they passed the taverns and corner food stalls. After they'd gone by, excited whispers rose up.

"I heard that the prince of Tiadun is a woman now. D'you suppose that's her?"

"Not a prince, a regent, but probably not. Not enough guards. Everyone has guardsmen these days, if they have the beads for it."

Myril tried to block out the voices, but she couldn't do it without also blocking out the sound of approaching threats, so she let herself listen a little more.

"Heard she was a priestess. Cereans won't like that."

"Or they will, when they capture her."

Perhaps they should have stayed at the palace after all, but Darna was hurrying on, oblivious to the dangers around her as she savored the chance to walk the streets of Anamat again.

"The palace isn't as bad as the temple," she'd said, "but it's stifling in its own way. I'm glad I won't be there long."

They soon reached the new edge of the harbor, right up against the merchants' warehouses. In winter, the harbor was quiet, troubled only by noisy gulls swooping down to steal from the fishermen's nets. Midsummer had always been busier, but now the enlarged harbor was so crowded with foreign ships that Myril could only spot one lone fishing boat hauled up on the banks of the East Canal. Its crew carried their baskets toward the market – now almost submerged at its lower end – while the gulls wheeled overhead, ignoring the foreign merchants who thronged the shore like vultures, their caps and turbans almost more numerous than the bare heads of the Theranians.

They'd rebuilt Merchants' Wharf in only a few days after the waters rose. Sailors and merchantmen, with the help of a few laborers, had bolted and lashed new pilings on top of the old, and moved the wharf's submerged planks up into the dry air. It was shoddy workmanship, but it would last the rest of the short trading season, and no one really expected the waters to stay where they were for another year. A pair of city watchmen stood at the end of the newly rebuilt wharf to keep scrapplings and any other casual marauders away. Lerat was waiting there for them and ushered them past the watchmen.

"My ladies," Lerat said with a bow. "Gentlemen," he nodded to the two guardsmen and looked them over quickly. "You may come onto my ship, but do not go belowdecks unless these ladies call for you. Is that agreed?"

Forlan and Ferrent waited for Darna's nod before agreeing. Lerat squinted at Darna as they walked out toward the end of the dock, but did not ask her to introduce herself.

Lerat's ship was second in size only to the Cerean king's ship – or, rather, the ship of his merchant emissary. It was the very same ship that Darna had boarded so many years before, when she was a scrappling bent on stealing back the dragon's stone she'd taken from the palace, hardly knowing what she was doing. Darna averted her eyes from it.

Lerat offered Myril a hand for balance as she stepped from the dock to the boat.

"I'll be fine," Myril said, shaking off his help as soon as she was aboard. The rocking of the boat was easier to manage than the self-consciousness she felt when Lerat looked at her. "My friend might need help, though."

Before Lerat could offer his hand, Darna crossed onto the ship with a spring in her step. She looked up admiringly at the rigging above, her balance perfect. Myril still hadn't gotten used to the change in her yet. She was herself, but she sounded and looked so different from before that she might have been almost unrecognizable, apart from her face, which was the same as ever.

"Would you like a tour of the rigging?" Lerat asked Darna.

"I would," Darna said. "I've never been aboard such a big ship by daylight, and I'm fascinated, but..." Her gaze strayed to the Cerean ship with its bright-painted figurehead.

"It would be conspicuous, especially as you are wearing your realm's colors, Regent. It's subtle, but they could be looking for it," Lerat said. Though Darna's tunic was mostly plain, it had a bright trim of blue-and-orange ribbon, and her guards wore bright blue capes.

"Come into my cabin," Lerat said. "I've sent for victuals from the Thirst of Conn, so the meal will be hot." The Thirst of Conn was a tavern frequented by the city watch. It was not one Myril would have chosen, but only because she felt uneasy going there alone. Their cooking was among the best of the city's taverns, or so she'd heard.

Near the center of the boat, Lerat lifted a hatch, revealing a ladder-like stair into the belly of the ship. "After you, ladies," he said.

Myril might have hesitated, but the guards were right behind them and would come to their rescue at any sign of trouble, which she truly didn't expect. Darna was already on the stair down. Lerat told one of the sailors to prop up another hatch a little farther toward the bow of the ship. As the hatch was opened, Darna gasped with delight.

"It's marvelous," she said as Myril climbed down after her. To Myril's eye, it was only a small, dark room, cramped but clean and well enough appointed. It would be almost airless when the hatches were closed.

Lerat waited while she made her way down. "I'm glad that at least one of you likes it," he said. "Your Highness?" he ventured, addressing Darna.

"I believe that the correct form of address is 'Your Ladyship,'" Darna said, "though everyone seems to find 'Your Highness' easier to remember. That, or they're just trying to curry my favor."

"Be that as it may, Your Ladyship, Regent of Tiadun. I am pleased to make your acquaintance so soon. Welcome to my ship."

"It really is beautiful," Darna said, "So many drawers and nooks. The craftsmanship is exquisite, but it doesn't look like Anamat work, at least not all of it."

Myril wished that she could borrow some of Darna's sudden ease in the cramped space. Above, on the deck, she could hear Forlan and Ferrent chatting companionably with the sailors and refusing an offered jar of ale.

"I had the bones of the boat made here, but some of this is from Calandria," Lerat said, indicating the cabinets. "The most successful merchants from Cerea and Ganat have their ships outfitted there."

Darna nodded. "I hear it's the largest city in the world."

"It's the largest I've seen, but there are rumors of even larger cities, deep in the continent. Enomae is part of a broad land, far bigger that anything we Theranians can imagine." Lerat turned to Myril, who was still standing awkwardly at the foot of the ladder-stair. "Please sit, make yourself comfortable. My steward will bring the wine."

Myril shook her head. "Tea for me, if anything," she said. She was dizzy enough already from the motion of the ship on the harbor's small swells.

"I'll send for that, too, then." Lerat went back to the hatch and signaled to one of his men. There were two bunks on either side of the room, and he reached up to let down a narrow table between them as he took his seat.

The steward soon arrived with a fruity, heady wine. Myril could almost feel its effects from the smell alone. It had a little juniper scenting it, and apricots. Darna accepted a small cup and Lerat took one for himself, regarding her carefully.

"I've never been aboard such a ship in daylight," she said.

"Not in daylight?" Lerat asked, amused. "They say that this new regent of Tiadun was a guildswoman and a priestess, but in those days, the ladies of Ara's Landing never went visiting sailors on their ships, as far as I knew."

Darna laughed. "Nothing like that. It was before those days." She paused before she went on. "It was a long time ago. I had to recover something which should not have been sold."

Lerat was silent in thought for a moment. "That? Some ten years ago, or is it eleven or twelve?"

"Eleven, I think," Darna said. "This cabin is as intricate as the one on that Cerean ship was, maybe even more so. I only saw it by snatches of moonlight."

"I haven't been belowdecks over there, so I wouldn't know," Lerat said. "They're as wary of us as we are of them; most of them are, at least. Now I see why you wanted to know more about Girizit. I'd be curious what information you have to add, Your Ladyship."

"You may ask anything," Darna said, "and I'll consider whether or not to answer it." She was blushing. It took Myril a moment to realize that Lerat had been flirting with her, though very subtly and without serious intent. They seemed to be enjoying each other's company.

The steward returned, carrying a covered platter, which he set on the table. He laid out dishes and cutlery, then removed the lid before going out again to bring Myril her pot of tea. After that was delivered, he bowed and left.

The food on the platter was not at all what Myril had expected. The usual tavern fare was stew and bread, with few variations. Here, Lerat presented a roasted duck carved into bite-sized morsels and served on a bed of steamed greens, with a rich purple sauce made of mountain berries to one side and a loaf of white bread. Without asking what anyone wanted, he apportioned some to each of his guests, then took a sip of wine and leaned back, looking at Myril.

"It is always pleasure to see you," he said. Myril blushed. "You are always as beautiful as I remember, but of course, beauty is too fragile to trade on for long. Texts are fragile, too."

"This is delicious," Darna said, in a belated effort to turn the conversation. "Better than what they have at the palace, though not quite as good as what the temple kitchens can do at their best."

"You've said that you would help me in any way that you could. I've been charged with finding a way to save the Chronicles of Anamat, in case our city falls into the sea as Slaradun did. It is more than I can do by my usual means," Myril explained, worried that Darna might spend the whole time talking of food and old times.

"If we fall as Slaradun did, I don't think there will be much saved at all, only what we can carry," Darna said. "Even that may not survive." She took another drink, closing her eyes to savor the wine.

"Texts are too fragile to carry on the sea unless they are very well boxed, while gold and gems travel well and are always eagerly sought in the markets of Calandria," Lerat said. "I have learned that there are some libraries in Ganat and Enomae, but they are small and remote, and may not welcome texts in a language they cannot understand. Your histories are, I am sorry to say, useless without those who can interpret them."

"Would you really send the Chronicles across the sea?" Darna asked Myril.

"It's better than having them lost forever, but Lerat's right; they're useless without someone who understands them." Myril toyed with the greens at the edge of her plate as the other two ate and drank in silence.

"People have been leaving," she said after a little while. "A few priestesses have been among them. Can you think of any safe haven for both the texts and the priestesses?"

Lerat frowned and scratched his chin. "Not immediately. The Cereans don't travel far inland, so those cities deep in the continent might provide some safe haven. There are other possibilities, farther away. If I were to seek such a place, I would need a priestess to go with me to see if it would be suitable for the others, and perhaps to negotiate with the people there. Our priestesses are skilled healers, and no land ever has enough of those."

"I can't go," Myril said.

Lerat sighed. "I know, but it need not be you. I would rather you came, but..." He turned to Darna.

"I have to return to Tiadun," Darna said. Then she took a piece of bread and began to eat it with obvious enjoyment.

"The priestesses would be safest staying here, as long as anything is safe here," Lerat said. "There's no other place like this, not that I've heard of. Do you also think that Anamat will fall into the sea?" he asked Darna. "Will it be worse than it is now?"

Darna put down the morsel she'd been about to eat and licked her fingers. Lerat poured her another cup of wine.

"I was there when Salara shook his land into the sea," she said. "Salara was angry, and not as weak as Tiada had become. Anara isn't weak either. She may choose to drown her city. In Slaradun, the Ganateans were trying to take the jewels and take over the province for themselves. They –" Darna stopped and shook her head. "It was far too easy for them to overwhelm the prince. I don't think that the other princes are much stronger, at least not in their force of guardsmen. Theranis is precious, but we have no armies of any size."

Lerat nodded. "The armies of Cerea and Ganat are formidable."

"This rising water is only the beginning," Darna said. "I'm not a priestess anymore, though, and I haven't heard Anara say so or had any prophecies, so it's only a thought."

Myril kicked her under the table. "Only the ambassadress speaks to Anara like that. You are a priestess."

Lerat frowned. "Never mind about the ambassadress for now," he said. "What happened to those Ganateans in Slaradun?"

Darna shrugged. "Some of them died by the swords of...of the bandits. Others must have drowned or been taken down by landslides in the mountains. The earth shook for some time, and when it had stilled, most of Slaradun keep was under the waves. I could see it from the mountains. Some people could have reached the high ground, especially the fishermen with their boats, and the Ganateans had boats, too."

Lerat nodded. "Rumor suggests that some did escape and sail home. In Ganat now, it's said that the land of Theranis is gone, or disappearing in a storm of earth. I don't know whether the people who hear those rumors will come to steal what they can or whether they'll stay away out of fear for their lives, as so many here seem to be doing."

"Anamat is well built, but much of it rests on Anara's power and the powers of her dragonlets. If she withdraws those..." Darna spread her hands and shrugged.

"Were you also a planner, then? I had heard that you were a guildswoman, but not which guild. Well, Your Ladyship or my Lady Planner, if you say that Anara can destroy this city, I believe you, but I see also that the men of Cerea or Ganat could ransack it in a day, or in a few days' time at the most. We are besieged on all sides. We need not believe in Anara's power to see that our fair city might come to its end."

Myril shuddered. Better for Anara to take it, she thought. Lerat reached toward her but stopped short. "I can see why you think that the priestesses need to be saved," he said. "I'll go to the Aralel to find out what she can offer me for their safe passage if I can find some land where they will not be treated as they would be in Cerea."

"Whatever happened to Nira?" Darna asked suddenly.

"Nira?" Lerat echoed.

"She was a scrappling of Anamat, a scavenger. She'd been on the streets for more than a season, which wasn't so common in those days. Giri made a bad bargain with her and sent her to Cerea after she stole a statue from the temple courtyard for him."

"One with a dragon stone in it?"

Darna nodded. "We got it back, though."

"As for your friend, and Girizit, I was not in Cerea that season. I did hear that the king had a concubine from Anamat, but I never met her. She was sent to a castle he had in the mountains, a sort of a hunting lodge. She must have disappointed him."

"But Giri did not?" Darna said.

"No, not at all. Girizit was a clever boy, as you seem to know, and his command of the Theranian language was good, or at least better than anyone else's in the court there. He gained the king's trust, and now here he is, insinuating his way into the governor's palace, too. What involvement did he have in that theft which... Well, I heard of it at the time and have always been impressed that you managed to regain the stone."

Darna shook her head. "It was foolish of me to steal it for him in the first place. I should have suspected something or at least wondered how he knew so exactly where to find it. No scrappling would ordinarily know so much about the palace, especially not a foreign one."

"Foolish as the theft itself might have been, I don't flatter you when I say that it would have been very difficult to get anything off that ship. Cerean merchants guard their cargo well. The king was disappointed at losing his prize, but I suppose that girl's company might have slaked his anger at Girizit, even when he discovered that she wasn't a priestess and that she had no special powers." Lerat paused. "How is it that you recognize Girizit and the governor does not?"

"The governor didn't spend a season scavenging with him," Darna said. "I'd be surprised if he even saw Giri when he was here that season. But surely, he must have returned to Theranis since, if he still speaks so well?"

"I'm not sure about that," Lerat said. "He may have had tutors in Cerea – there have been Theranians there over the years, besides myself." Lerat looked at Darna again. "You do bear a family resemblance to Calar's sons, though you are obviously far more intelligent than they are."

"Were," Darna said. "One of them may have died in Slaradun."

"Oh?" Lerat said. He raised his eyebrows but didn't pursue the question further. Instead, he turned to Myril. "If you do learn anything more about what's happening with this rising water, I would most appreciate the knowledge, to help me forecast the tides."

"I don't mind doing that, but I hope that you can find a place for the Chroniclers' texts," she said.

"Where are those texts now?"

"I don't know. The Chronicler said he'd found a place where they'll be safe until Midwinter, provided the seas don't rise over the whole city."

Lerat reached to pour more wine but Darna turned her cup over, signaling that she was done.

"This is a fine meal but unusual," Myril said. "You say it came from the Thirst of Conn?"

Lerat nodded. "It's an imitation of what they serve to guests in Cerea. I developed a taste for their food when I was there. The woman who cooks at Conn's is adept at serving meals to different tastes when you know what to ask for. I thought you might appreciate something you wouldn't find elsewhere."

"I do," Myril said. "I'm surprised to find that there's something to like about Cerea."

"Not much, but they do cook well," Lerat said.

"The sauce is delicious. I appreciate your concern, but..."

"I do enjoy your company. You remind me that there are mysteries in the world which I will never plumb."

"That's more flattery than praising me for a beauty."

Lerat shrugged. "Tell me, then: how many priestesses do you think will flee Anamat?"

"You'd get a better answer by asking the Aralel, if you plan to go see her," Myril said, but Darna was already calculating.

"There are three dozen in the peresi's court, maybe half that many novices now, between the hill temple and the Landing. There are twice as many elders of one kind or another. If more come in from the provinces, that could double their numbers, maybe more."

"A hundred will fill my ships, but if the Aralel makes it worth my while, I'm sure I can find a way to carry more," Lerat said.

"You won't do it for the love of the dragons?" Myril asked.

"Not if Anara ruins her own city," he said. He rose from his seat and gestured to his guests to rise too, ushering Darna out first.

"I had hoped to speak with you more," he said quietly to Myril as Darna climbed up onto the deck. "I hope that we all live until Midwinter and meet again."

"I hope so too," Myril said, and was surprised at herself for feeling that she did want to see Lerat again. He still reminded her too much of that near-deadly trance on her initiation night, but he also promised that there was hope in the lands beyond Theranis. For the moment, that promise seemed more real than the oblivion of the dragons. The world stayed steady and solid around her as he helped her up the ladder. When they reached the shore, she looked back, hoping to catch one more glimpse of him before he sailed away with another priestess by his side.

§

Myril walked partway up the hill with Darna and her guardsmen, but the clamor drove her back, and she made her excuses, taking a side alley toward the eastern part of the town. Although the temple didn't usually feel like a refuge, she went there next, grateful that the high, white walls blocked out so much of the noise from outside, foreigners and Theranians alike. She skirted past the elders' courtyard to the peresi's garden. She knew that she ought to look in on Iola, but she hadn't taken the tea to block trance, and the ambassadress's quarters dragged her down more than anywhere. It was bad enough with only the scent of roses and the bubbling fountain of the peresi's courtyard.

Lenasa's chamber was next to the passage to the kitchens, where the tea urn was kept on festival days. She was sitting on the bench beside it, her brow wrinkled as she studied a scroll. She was the younger daughter of the brother of the prince of Getedun and had been raised in the keep there. She'd arrived at the temple the image of a young princess, with curling coppery hair and a soft, shy gaze. She was still beautiful, but her hair no longer curled and her mien had grown sharper over the years. Once, her father had tried to match her with a village chieftain, but she'd chosen to remain in the peresi's court. There, she had her own chamber and needed not to rely on any one man.

"What brings you here?" she asked as Myril approached. "Visiting Iola?"

Myril shook her head. "I've come looking for you, actually."

"You have?" Lenasa scooted away from Myril, making room for her to sit. Once she sat and quieted herself, Myril could hear the priestesses and their petitioners in the chambers around the courtyard, chanting and arguing mixing with sounds of feigned ecstasy and pouring tea while wisps of perfume and incense floated out of the doorways.

Lenasa stared at her. Myril gathered her thoughts.

"The Aralel is afraid that we're sinking."

"She does a good job of hiding it, if she is. She tells us all not to worry, that it's impossible, even though anyone can see it if they bother to walk out on the streets," Lenasa said. "What does she think is happening?"

"She doesn't know; no one does, not for sure."

"So, the all-powerful Aralel is as ignorant as anyone? That's reassuring," Lenasa said bitterly.

"I'm trying to discover if there's any place where we can go," Myril said.

"Oh, there are places. Petitioners tell me about them all the time. First, there's Cerea, where you can be bought and sold like a nanny goat and given about as much respect. Then there's Ganat. A better place, if you don't mind seeking one man's protection, and only one man's, for the rest of your life or as long as he's willing to keep you. Then you're on your own, and it's no better than Cerea after that, maybe worse. If you're lucky, they let women there scrub the floors when their skin begins to sag. So generous. That leaves Enomae." She sighed and shook her head. "Some women there stay together, and any of our offering chests could buy a place to live in Calandria, walls and a roof, but no way of making a life for those of us who aren't guild trained. I don't know what to do."

"If Anamat falls as Slaradun did, anyone who stays here will die."

"Do you really think that Slaradun fell?" Lenasa asked.

"Yes. I know people who saw it. Does anyone doubt it?"

Lenasa nodded. "Since the sea has stayed where it was after that day, some say that the rumors are only travelers' tales, a ploy to keep us away while Ganateans ransack it or what's left of it."

Myril shook her head. "It's not a ploy. Darna was there, in the mountains. She saw it for herself."

"Darna saw it herself? Well, I've never known her to lie about anything important. Now she's regent of Tiadun, they say, so maybe she'll have to learn. How does that suit her?"

Myril laughed. "Not at all. She'd still rather cobble scrap together."

"Better her than Calar. Now, what did you come here for? I have a petitioner coming as soon as this one's done." She indicated her doorway. "We're two to a chamber now. It's... busy."

"I wouldn't like it either," Myril said. "I didn't like it here even before all of this, but this is what I came to say. I'll be sending you a petitioner later, my only petitioner, Lerat the Roper."

"I won't be able to surpass you, I don't think," Lenasa said. Lerat had praised Myril so much that she still hadn't stopped hearing about it, even all these years later.

"I've asked him to try to find a place for us in case we need to leave Theranis," she said. "I want you to go with him."

"Me? Why don't you go yourself?" She looked at Myril. "Do you have another lover here?"

"No, not for years," Myril said. "But I have other things to do, and I thought that you might like to go, that you would be better able to understand what's happening in other places than most of the rest of you. Besides, you're not deceptive."

"I won't lie to you, but I don't know anything about the world beyond these shores."

"Lerat does, though, and you know what we need as priestesses. Together, maybe you can find a place."

§

Myril saw Lenasa again the next morning. The gong rang, its sound a bright shiver through the soft morning air. The procession to the harbor was led by a priestess veiled in diaphanous red to match the fire of the dragons, but there was something different about the woman in the ambassadress's robes. Her attendants crowded more closely around her. They, too, were veiled. Myril was fairly sure that one of the attendants was Darna and that another was Iola. That meant that someone else was taking the ambassadress's place. She didn't want to listen closely enough to be sure, or to know who was in Iola's robes.

Myril felt the other world pressing in on her as she always did at crossing times, but not quite as much as she had in other years. She took Lenasa's hand to steady herself and Lenasa squeezed it, as if to reassure her that she hadn't misplaced her trust. Myril clung to that hand as they walked, dropping in and out of the chant. Chanting kept the world at bay, but that morning, Myril also wanted to hear what the people were saying around her, especially whether or not any of them saw the dragon or pretended to. She hadn't seen Anara since early spring, herself, and then she'd been pale in the distance.

At the temple gates, a group of masked armsmen took the palanquin's poles to carry it down to the shore. Every window and balcony was decked with garlands of flowers, just like any other Midsummer morning. The shore was closer, though, the walk shorter, and the tide rising. The long night's vigil and carousing had been the same as any other year, and the people lining the streets and along the shore looked no more tired than usual. Myril could smell and hear the foreigners among them, and that was not the same as it always had been. Usually, they would have sailed away before the ambassadress flew.

As they rounded a bend in the processional way, the harbor came into sight.

"His ship is already cast off," Myril said to Lenasa.

"One of the fishermen will carry me out to it," she said. They resumed the chant and walked on. Girizit's ship with its gilded prow was already on the horizon, with a fleet of smaller Cerean ships behind it, though Girizit was not on it. The Enomaeans were all aboard their ships but rested on their oars, hoping to catch a glimpse of the dragon. Sailors were drawing up anchors and setting the rigging on the handful of Ganatean ships still in the harbor. A horse stamped aboard one of the Enomaean ships, making a dissonant drumbeat of its fear.

Lerat's ship sat just beyond the submerged breakwater, waiting with its sails at the ready.

Lenasa let go of Myril's hand and stepped into an alley, where a gentle-looking young man waited for her with a plain brown cloak.

"Anara's blessing go with you," Myril said.

"If it can," Lenasa said. "If she can."

§

Chapter 12

Life in the palace left Darna feeling off-balance. Gallia waited at her elbow, always helpful even while she tried to bend every interaction to her accustomed way of doing things, as she must have done with Darna's father. It was still strange to think of him as her father. She'd always doubted it, but she believed Vigda. There'd been no word of Vigda since the tribunal. Darna more than half-wished she could go to the hills with the bandits, herself, but life in the palace wasn't all bad.

Even the princes who'd sided with Calar in the tribunal were polite to her. Tiagasa was downright solicitous, which amused Darna. She'd never seen Tiagasa grovel before. Now, between council meetings, she passed by Darna's rooms from time to time with little gifts – a jewel, some fine wine – sometimes from herself and sometimes from Girizit.

"Girizit says that you simply must allow him to help you see these Cereans on their way. They're out of favor with their king," Tiagasa reminded her.

Darna told Tiagasa that she would consider the offer. Surely, there must be better ways of getting rid of Calar's Cereans, ones that didn't involve putting herself in debt to Giri or the Cerean king. Harzet agreed. He'd come along to stand

in as her Cerean advisor. Despite the fact that she still didn't
entirely like Harzet, she'd begun to rely on him. He and Kinner
were the only link she had to her year of exile in Slaradun, the
only ones who'd seen something of what had happened to her
cousin Hedrin after he'd tried to murder her. They hadn't
passed the news of his likely death on to Calar until after the
tribunal, when she'd told them to do so – most of Calar's
Cereans were ranged outside the walls of Anamat city, and
some of them had deserted to join Girizit's forces.

Kinner acted as her secretary, standing below and behind
her in the councils. Gallia took the place set for the keep
mistress, to act as Darna's advisor. Most nights' business in the
councils did not concern them much. On the first night, there
was another question of succession, between two nephews of a
village chief in Coradun. That was to be decided by a contest
of arms on Midsummer Eve. Next there was some minor
business concerning requisitions for the Midsummer feast. On
the following night, the supplies for the following summer's
feast were argued again, and the prince of Naramun asked the
council's approval to build up his harbor for trading ships.
Darna felt obliged to say something about that, and Parnet
recognized her. She stepped to the center of the room.

"Ivanat of Slaradun embarked on a similar project," she
said. "I was with him there until the opening of the trading
season, in my former work as a guildswoman. Although the
harbor would have accommodated trading ships well, he put
himself in debt to Ganat to build it."

"Better Ganat than Cerea," someone said, and was
quickly shushed.

"Do you think that the harbor building caused the
catastrophe?" Tiagasa asked, batting her eyelashes.

"I don't know," Darna said. She returned to her place.

"You must say more if you go forward again," Gallia whispered in her ear. "And don't mention that you were in the guilds! It makes your fellow princes uneasy."

Darna nodded and ignored her. The council requested that Naramun not go forward with its harbor-improvement plans, shaking their heads over the tragic fall of Slaradun and worrying that the same fate might await them all. Then again, they still hoped that it might not.

The visit to Lerat's ship had been a welcome change of place before the final night of the princes' councils.

On that last night before Midsummer Eve, the prince of Helanum again brought forward the question of what had happened to cause the province of Slaradun to fall into the sea. Darna glanced back at Kinner. He shook his head. Harzet the Cerean was called as witness. His eyes flicked to Darna once, at the beginning, but they'd agreed earlier that she would distance herself from the troubles in Slaradun, having said too much already. None of the princes needed to know that she'd been there at the end.

"Your Highnesses, Ladies," Harzet began. In the council chamber, his Theranian sounded stiffer and more heavily accented. "I served as advisor to Ivanat of Slaradun from the time he returned to this land until his death. I do not believe much in the power of your dragons, not even as many of my countrymen do."

On the dais behind the governor, Girizit sneered briefly.

"I am only a scholar, not a merchant or a ruler. I had little interest in the wealth that the stones might bring, or in their alleged powers." He hesitated and glanced to the courtyard door. "The Ganateans who traded with Ivanat went into the hills to mine for the dragons' stones. The earth shook and fell as they arrived at the – at the place where they thought they would mine. I find it – I think it would not have happened if they had not mined."

"Had they begun?" Girizit asked.

Harzet shook his head. "Hardly, but they were ready."

"Thank you; that will be all," Parnet said quickly.

Harzet looked as if he had more to say, but stepped aside. He sat down on one of the low benches near where Darna stood, and she could see him fiexing his jaw with impatience as the prince of Helanum took the fioor.

"I did not realize the depth of Ivanat's treachery," the prince of Helanum said. "Had I known, I might have gone across the border –"

"Which you may not do without an invitation or an injunction from the governor," the prince of Naramun cut in.

"Order," Parnet said. He waved the prince of Helanum to the side. Darna felt that she ought to say something. Parnet turned to her. "Tiadun did not fall when these Cereans Calar brought went to mine, did it?"

Darna turned to Gallia, who stepped forward.

"Tiadun did not fall, but our harvests this year were poor," she said.

Girizit nudged Parnet and whispered something in his ear. Parnet motioned for Gallia to step back. "I understand that the Cereans have other ways of improving harvests that do not involve appealing to the gods," Parnet said.

The prince of Lemirun came forward next. "It seems to me," he began, "that as wise as our Cerean advisors might be, their merchantmen bring nothing but trouble and strife to the villages. We should limit our trading season to the traditional three moons before Midsummer again."

"You've been heard," Parnet said.

The prince of Naramun came forward again. "Trade with the Cereans, even without an improved harbor, has expanded our keep town and brought much good to our province. I would not want to lose that advantage."

"Even if it means that your lands fall to the sea?" the prince of Helanum demanded.

Everyone began to speak at once, shouting at each other. Parnet shouted for order until he was red in the face. Tiagasa looked flustered and grasped Girizit's hand. Darna looked to Harzet.

"Don't let them worry you," he said. "They know less than we do."

"Enough!" Parnet shouted again. This time, the noise calmed and everyone settled back to their places. He turned to Darna. "Tell us what the situation was in Slaradun before its catastrophe."

"The temples of Slaradun were closed, many of them destroyed," Darna said. Looking around the room, she wondered what had happened in the other provinces, how many of them still had all of their temples or their priestesses. Myril and Sunna had said that many had come to Ara's Landing, and she'd seen a few of them herself, even when she was just passing through. "I was priestess trained, as you know. I believe that the neglect of the dragons may have caused the fall, but also it seemed that the Ganateans had taken control of the prince, more than merely influencing him. My uncle, too, was letting his Cerean allies force his actions."

Parnet frowned. "So, as long as we retain our lawful control of the land and appease the dragons, we should survive?"

It was the most directly that anyone in the council had spoken of the much-whispered fear that they would all be sunk into the sea as Slaradun had been.

Darna shook her head. "I'm not sure that would be enough, but giving over control to the foreigners seems a sure way to doom us all."

She looked up to see Girizit shaking his head. She suppressed the urge to shoot him a rude gesture.

Another spate of out-of-turn conversation surged up as she retreated to her place. Parnet banged his gavel. "You will all return to your provinces on Midsummer morning. Send messengers back to Anamat if there is any change in your lands during the waning year. This council is –"

"Wait!" Harzet stepped out into the center of the room. "There's another matter," he said. "Darnasa, Regent of Tiadun, bears the prince of Slaradun's child."

Darna opened her mouth to object, then shut it. The hubbub rose around them once more.

"Order!" Parnet hammered the table as Tiagasa reached for a mallet to strike the gong. "Is that so?" he asked Darna.

"The prince Ivanat was my lover this past half-year," Darna admitted, "and a healer said that I was –" Myril had said there was something odd about it, but pregnancy was a logical conclusion.

"As I understand it, she may be about to produce an heir to two realms," Harzet said, not letting her go on to explain how she wasn't so sure about things. "I submit that Tiadun will not be a safe-enough haven for her in her current condition until it is cleared of her uncle's henchmen."

Tiagasa whispered something to Parnet, who nodded.

"Darnasa may send her agents to oversee the keep until she is deemed fit to travel after her delivery, and we find whether or not this is a son she bears," Parnet said. "Meanwhile, I trust that the temple of Ara's Landing will take her in and give her into the care of their best healers."

"I don't want to go to the temple," Darna thought aloud.

Gallia placed a hand on her arm. "It's not a bad idea. You'll be safe there. I'll take a few guardsmen back to Tiadun and see that the keep is put in order. We'll return for you after Midwinter."

Darna nodded. Safe. As if that was what she wanted, what she'd ever wanted. She could feel the walls of the temple closing in on her again, but it was true that the temple could keep her alive. She wanted to curse Harzet.

None of the noblemen had any idea what was happening to the earth beneath their feet, except that it was sinking and parts of it had fallen. They were probably all looking for a way to escape their disappearing realms, even if it meant giving themselves over to Ganat and Cerea. The prophecies from the elders of Ara's landing may have reached them, but they did not feel any faith in those reassurances, however slim they were. Darna didn't trust the prophecies either. She felt more sympathy for the noblemen, her fellow princes, than she ever would have thought possible.

§

Early the next morning, Darna woke with a pain in her gut like a pair of cats fighting over a rotten fish. It was Midsummer Eve, and Harzet had condemned her to confinement in the temple. Her head hurt. She could smell Harzet in the next room, his cloying Cerean oils even more pungent than usual. He'd left the moment he'd said his piece the night before, so she hadn't had a chance to tell him what she thought of him then. It didn't help that Gallia was delighted with the development. No doubt she was just happy to get full rule over Tiadun for a season, though she said that she was only overjoyed at the prospect of seeing Terenet's grandchild born and raised.

Darna swung her feet to the floor and yanked on her still-too-fine tunic, then stomped into the apartment's main room, where Harzet was waiting, looking only slightly sheepish. Kinner, beside him, had borne most of Darna's foul temper the night before. It had taken her until halfway to dawn to fall asleep, and her dreams had not been pleasant.

"What did you say that for?" she demanded without preamble.

Harzet cleared his throat and looked down. "I knew that you were unhappy with what I said, but please, hear me out."

Darna flopped down on one of the couches.

"You can't deny that you're, ah, expecting."

"I could deny it. The best healer in Anamat said that it didn't look like any pregnancy she'd ever seen."

Kinner was blushing. Harzet was not. "Do you have a better explanation?"

"Not really," Darna admitted.

"I've come to respect you more than I did, but whatever my feelings about you, I would be most happy to learn that my dear friend was not entirely gone from this world, that he left a little of himself behind."

"He left the destruction of Slaradun behind," Darna said. She could hear Forlan and Ferrent clattering around in their chamber, hurrying to put on their clothes.

Harzet looked over his shoulder at the door, then approached Darna's couch. He stood awkwardly over her, but she didn't move to make room for him to sit.

"I didn't say that because of whatever it is that's making you clutch your belly," Harzet said.

"Then why?"

He crouched down beside her. "It's only a rumor, but I've heard that the Duke of the Southern Reaches is planning to sail for Tiadun with the rest of his army as soon as your ambassadress has done whatever it is she does at Midsummer. You would be walking into the teeth of a seasoned army, and whatever you are, you're not a general yet."

Darna shifted to let him sit. "Where did you hear that? Is it true?"

"It is only a rumor, but it fits his way of doing things. I would be surprised if he didn't do something like that."

"All the more reason for me to go back," Darna said. "If he establishes himself in Tiadun, he would be hard to dislodge. Shouldn't you have warned Gallia instead?"

Harzet shook his head. "Someone needs to go to secure the place for you, and I've told her as much as I've just told you. She knows the land well enough to hide if she needs to, and the guardsmen and village chiefs will be sympathetic to her. They know her much better than they know you."

"That's true," Darna admitted. "Do you want me to thank you?"

"No need; I only wish for whatever's in your belly to be safe." He stood to go.

"Are you leaving?" Darna asked.

"I've heard there's a ship sailing to Calandria on the noon tide. I plan to be on it."

"So, you won't go with Gallia to keep watch over Tiadun for me? Someone has to parlay with the duke and his forces."

"I'm not staying in Theranis," Harzet said. "I have other places in the world to go." Forlan and Ferrent emerged from their room, but Darna waved them away. Harzet went on in a whisper. "I've been in exile for five years now, and the king will have a price on my head if I return, but if the Duke of the Southern Reaches is in rebellion, there's a chance my own town is trying to shake off the king too. I would like to see that."

Darna thought that she should be glad to be rid of him, but she wasn't. "I wish you luck, then, and I thank you for keeping your ears open for me. I only hope that the people I have left here will be as quick to hear and understand."

Harzet gave Kinner a nod. "His Cerean is not as good as mine, but he's quick enough. You'll have ears here still unless you send him with Gallia."

Darna looked at Kinner. No, she wouldn't send him to Tiadun. The boy needed to see more of Anamat, and perhaps she could get him apprenticed with the Chroniclers or see him settled in the palace scriptorium to gather rumors for her.

She clasped Harzet's hands in farewell and sent him off to his ship. He left the noxious scent of hair-oil in his wake. She really ought to be glad to see the last of him. She sent Kinner to fetch tea and bread from the kitchen and prepared to leave the palace behind, but for the temple, not Tiadun. Either way, she would be shut up behind old walls, but she would have rather gone back to Tiadun.

She and Gallia were just finishing their breakfast when the palanquin from the temple arrived. Sunna was there, along with a trio of strong young priestesses to hold the poles while the guards trotted alongside. Gallia ordered more tea, but before long, they were on their way.

"I'd rather walk," Darna told Sunna.

"It's not about what you'd rather do; it's about what makes the right impression," Gallia cut in. Sunna shrugged in a way that implied she agreed with Gallia.

"It's the Aralel's orders," Sunna said.

"And quite right of her," Gallia said. "The guardsmen can bring your things down later, and your boy can see it's done right. It's a pity you won't let him come to Tiadun with me. He would be useful there. I'll walk with you to the temple, and we can discuss that as we go."

"I don't think there's anything to discuss. He'll serve a half-year apprenticeship with the Chroniclers, if they'll have him, and I think they will."

"Well, you are the regent," Gallia said.

"Yes, and you're my agent in Tiadun," Darna said, which did appease Gallia somewhat.

The old keep mistress had plans to turn the temple back the way it had been and to see if baths could be built anywhere in or near the keep. She paid so little attention to Forlan and Ferrent that Darna worried about her ability to manage the guardsmen at Tiadun keep. Still, there was nothing she could do about it until she went back herself. She was about to let herself be bundled into the palanquin when Tiagasa arrived, smiling from one ear to the other, her eyes quick and calculating.

"I'm so sorry that you're going back to the temple," Tiagasa said. "It's been a pleasure having you here, and I hope we'll have a chance to get further acquainted. Girizit wished to send you a little gift, but he says that he hasn't been able to find anything suitable."

"Perhaps after Midwinter," Darna said, thinking, *Better yet, never.*

"Oh, no, didn't you hear? He'll be staying with us for the waning year."

"I see. Send him my regards, and tell him that really, there's no need for gifts."

Tiagasa looked confused for a moment before her stiff smile reasserted itself. "Do send the Aralel my regards," she said. "And remind her of our agreement."

Behind Tiagasa's back, Sunna was making a ridiculous face. Darna couldn't speak for fear of laughing, so she just nodded and ducked into the palanquin, grateful that the curtains hid her face. It was a very short moment of gratitude.

The motion of the palanquin was unpleasant, something she'd scarcely noticed on her short trip to the palace a few days before, and it made her stomach cramp horribly.

"I'd like to walk," Darna said, leaning out.

Ferrent shook his head.

"Dear, you're much safer in there," Gallia said.

"I'll puke," Darna promised.

"It's not much further," Forlan said.

Darna sat back on her satiny cushions. It wasn't fair. She *had* had more freedom as a scrappling. This was exactly the kind of thing she'd come to Anamat to escape, all this being bundled around like a parcel of fine cloth and ordered by everyone all the time. She didn't *want* to be shut into the temple. Then again, she didn't want to die. She *could* endure half a year of complete idleness, she supposed. She'd heard that the Cereans believed that a pregnant woman should do as little as possible. She didn't even know that she was pregnant; it just hurt. It wasn't supposed to be like that; even Myril had said so.

They arrived at the back gate of the temple, and at last Darna was able to get out of the wretched moving chair. The Aralel was waiting for her, arms held wide.

Darna, rather stiffly, let the Aralel her fold her into a warm embrace. After all, she was the leader of all the priestesses in Theranis, the heir of Ara, and one of the wisest women she knew.

"You are not happy to be joining us again?"

Darna couldn't *say* that she wasn't, so she just shrugged. "You'll hardly let me join in the peresi's work again, will you?"

Gallia overheard that, and out of the corner of her eye Darna could see her appalled expression. Darna didn't want to spend the whole waning year on her back, but it would pass the time and maybe it would help ease the cramps.

"No," the Aralel said slowly, "but we'll try to find something to keep you occupied."

She wasn't entirely unaware of Darna's restlessness, at least.

"Let me say farewell to my armsmen," Darna said.

The Aralel turned her attention to Forlan and Ferrent. "Are they?"

Darna nodded.

The Aralel lifted her hand, and one of the young priestesses came hurrying over, then scurried away again as Darna made a small bow to Forlan and Ferrent.

"Will you go with Gallia back to Tiadun?" she asked.

Forlan nodded. "And keep an eye on her."

"Especially going through Getedun," Ferrent said. "In case your murderous uncle gets loose."

Darna nodded. It wasn't likely that the prince of Getedun would let his prisoners free, but then, the princes did have a foolish habit of forgiving the bad debts of their fellow noblemen. Maybe that forgiveness would extend to fratricide and letting foreign rapists run rampant.

"Please do, and return with her at Midwinter, if you would," she said, knowing that although they were acting as her guardsmen, they answered first to the Enatel.

"We intend to," Ferrent said, "but we may have other obligations."

"I see," Darna said. "Send my regards to Vigda and to the others if you see them."

Behind her, Gallia cleared her throat. Darna looked up the street to see Kinner running toward them.

"The Chronicler says I may stay at the guild hall," he said breathlessly. "Will I be able to visit you here?"

The Aralel appeared by Darna's side and answered for her. "The regent of Tiadun will not be accepting visitors or petitioners."

Kinner blushed beet red.

"I'm sure that's not what he had in mind," Darna muttered under her breath. Kinner blushed even more.

"We will be able to exchange letters," Darna said. "I'm sure that someone will carry them."

Kinner nodded. "I'll ask Eppie."

"Is she staying in Anamat?" Forlan asked.

Ferrent gave him a quelling look.

The Aralel placed her hand on Darna's shoulder. "We really must be going inside now, Your Highness."

"Isn't the correct form of address 'Your Ladyship'?" Darna asked as she let the Aralel lead her inside the gates, but the Aralel only shook her head.

The young priestesses had already carried the palanquin to its storage closet. The temple walls rose high and white around her. Stifling as they were, they were beautiful, and at least the back courtyard had always been lively. That morning, it was livelier than ever. Visiting priestesses and quarreling scrapplings were all trying to turn their double shares of festival bread into quadruple shares, while the kitchen priestesses tried to ensure that there was enough for everyone.

As they crossed into the relative quiet of the long passage across the temple, the Aralel spoke again. "I must say, I'm glad that you've come to us. It's quite convenient."

"I wouldn't think it would be," Darna said.

"You'll stay in the ambassadress's chamber while she's beneath the earth."

"I see."

"It's really the only place suitable for a prince, or a regent, and no petitioner will trouble you there."

The Aralel did not need to say that she had no intention of letting the ambassadress fly. Darna would be the official, acknowledged occupant of the chamber, of the temple-within-the-temple. It would not go fallow, as it was supposed to, and it would be much more acceptable for trays of food and bundles of laundry to come and go than it would be if they had to pretend that no one at all was there.

"Of course, you won't be able to come out much, if at all. It's troubling, this whole situation, and I think it best if you don't mix too much with the...peresi. So many of them have been leaving, and I can't trust all of them."

Darna nodded. Myril had said that she'd heard some young women going down to the ships, carrying the temple's treasure with them. "Haven't they heard what it's like in Cerea, even in Ganat?"

The Aralel nodded. "Most likely, but with the crowding here, the absence of the dragons, and the sinking earth, I can't stop them from going, not in good conscience. You don't need to worry about them, though. You have your own troubles."

"I have to worry about something," Darna said. She wished, again, that they'd let her walk from the palace, to see the streets of Anamat again, and because walking did ease her cramps.

"Worrying about yourself should be plenty," the Aralel said. They were in a deserted small garden, but she spoke very softly anyway. "And about Iola. She will need company."

"I'm not good at that," Darna said.

"Well, then, you'll have to learn. And there's always needlework."

§

Chapter 13

Iola was not at all resigned to staying on the surface of the earth. She was still thin, but she was filled with angry vigor, as if she gathered energy from the crossing day itself and the dragons were reaching up to animate her, half-mad already. The promise of a half-year of needlework and keeping Iola partly sane did nothing to improve Darna's mood.

"I can't stay," Iola said. "I'm the ambassadress. We've cheated the dragons of too much already. Let me go. It will help."

"It won't be enough, and besides, it's not up to me. The Aralel said you can't go," Darna said.

"They can't stop me."

Darna wondered how far Iola would go to get her way, and how far the Aralel was willing to go to prevent her. With the earth shifting so much, Darna was convinced that Iola needed to stay among humankind. She might even die before she reached the dragons' realm.

That evening, Darna put on the ceremonial garb of the ambassadress's attendants. They would all be veiled for the long ceremony leading up to dawn, but she knew that Sunna, Eppie, and her old fellow novice Ganie were Iola's other attendants. Eppie was about the same height and build as Iola, though she was more muscular underneath her robes.

Night fell and the sanctuary filled with priestesses, more of them than Darna had ever seen together before, as if all of the priestesses remaining in Theranis had crowded into the temple. Their chants rose high into the night air, filling the domed sanctuary, overflowing it, rising to the sky and falling to the earth, even down to the dragons' realm, where Anara waited, listening. The edge of Darna's veil rippled, and she saw something flicker in the corner of her vision. Was that a dragonlet? She'd never seen dragonlets in the temple before, but so much was changing, and it was a crossing time. If they were ever going to be seen in the temple, then this would be the night.

She didn't see it again, and at long last, the light of dawn began to filter in through the clerestories. Most of the priestesses filed out to the peresi's courtyard to drink a fortifying cup of tea before the procession down to the harbor's edge, but Iola and her attendants went into the ambassadress's chamber, where the Aralel was waiting for them.

"Eppie, Iola, change clothes."

"I won't do it," Iola said.

"You are far too frail. You know that," the Aralel said.

"If anyone is going to die in the dragon's realm, let it be me."

"You did want this girl to replace you," the Aralel pointed out.

"I'm not replacing her," Eppie said. "I'm just walking down to the harbor as if I'm her."

"And then what?" Iola said.

"We have a plan," Sunna said. "I think it's best if we don't send anyone to certain death."

"And how do you know that it would be certain death?" Iola complained.

"Enough arguing. Do as I say. You'll see," the Aralel said.

Iola obeyed the order, though she made it clear that she wasn't happy about it. Darna took the place beside her, with Sunna behind Iola to keep an eye on her. Eppie stood at the center of the group, dressed as the ambassadress. The Aralel led them all out into the peresi's courtyard together, veiled.

In the temple's forecourt, Eppie climbed into the ambassadress's palanquin while the others took the poles. Iola had a hard time managing hers, but it was only a short distance to the front gate, where four of the masked oarsmen took up the palanquin. The priestesses walked beside them. Darna saw Myril in the procession behind them, talking to someone who disappeared into an alley. There were still too many ships on the harbor, but the Cerean king's ship was well underway. She hoped that Giri was on it, and wondered if Tiagasa had been telling her the truth about his plans to stay. Maybe she was lying or mistaken. Sunna had said that she was planning to go away for the waning year, to walk the paths of the mountains and see all of the dragons' gates.

Darna took deep breaths as her belly threatened to cramp again. After the morning, she would be shut into the temple with its stifling air until this belly of hers finished whatever it was going to do. In a shadowed corner of her mind, it occurred to her that she might not survive whatever it was. Women did die in childbirth, and if this was no ordinary pregnancy, then it would be all the more likely to kill her. She hoped that she would die where she could see the sky, and not within temple walls, but she knew well enough that it was beyond her control.

The Aralel, Sunna, and Eppie stepped onto the waiting raft. Darna, Iola, and Ganie were supposed to stay on the shore. The raft looked out of place, bobbing between the buildings halfway up the processional way. The houses around them stood, but their ground floors were full of seawater.

Eppie turned to face the crowded shore and raised her hands in blessing, looking up for the dragon. The sky was empty.

Darna's veil rippled, creating tricks of light that she might have thought were dragons if she'd never seen one so close before. Eppie settled into her seat at the center of the raft, but just as the oarsmen were about to shove off from the shore, Iola leaped onto the stern.

"Get back," the Aralel hissed.

"I won't. I must go," Iola hissed.

The Aralel gave a signal for Ganie to stay behind, but Darna leaped aboard after Iola. As the oarsmen pushed away from the shore, she wondered what was going to happen out on Anara's island. The sunrise colors faded as the oarsmen propelled them across the long stretch of water.

One attendant and the Aralel were supposed to accompany the ambassadress onto the island to wait for Anara with her, outside the tower. Iola stepped over the side of the raft and sat beside Eppie, almost but not quite pushing her aside and claiming the place for herself. Darna and Sunna grabbed the offering chest and hurried after them.

"I will not have Anara's choice taken from her," Iola said.

"The princes' offerings are not sufficient, and that's the least of it," the Aralel said.

Iola tugged the decoy ambassadress over to the tower that hid Anara's gate. Strangely, the low-lying island was still above the waves. It didn't make sense, or at least didn't fit with what had happened along the shore. Darna was pretty sure that it was no smaller than it had been before the water rose. It must have risen. There were cracks in the tower walls, but she couldn't tell how old they were or how the ground could have moved.

"You can't go." Eppie's voice, from behind the ambassadress's veil, was sharp and not priestessly at all.

"Neither can you. You don't have any of the offerings. I at least have some," Iola argued.

"The attendants stay outside of the tower, Iola," the Aralel sharply.

"Not this year," Iola said. Nearly everyone in Anamat was watching them from the shore, ranged along the sand and rooftops, craning their necks to see the ambassadress or the dragon, searching the empty sky above. The priestesses they'd left behind chanted and ululated, calling up the sun, calling up the dragon, and sending the ambassadress on her way. A fishing boat launched out onto the water with a cloaked figure in its stern. Darna wanted to pull her veil aside to see better, but the Aralel pushed her into the tower after Iola along with the offering chest.

It was like being at the bottom of a well or, rather, halfway down it, perched on a ledge. Darna looked down, then wished she hadn't. It looked as if the pit went straight down into the center of the earth while the tower shot up to the sky. Something rumbled below them. It reminded Darna of the gate of Salara, except that it was turned on its side. The only way through it was to fall, unless you could fly.

Iola looked ready to leap. "I can go to them; I can go to them myself," she was saying, as if talking to herself and not caring whether or not anyone else was listening.

"Since you're here, you'd better hold on to the ambassadress," said a voice from the shadows. It was Sovara, the Enatel.

"I can't move in this cursed veil," Eppie said.

"You take my robes," Iola said. "You can go out with Darna."

"We've already changed robes; I'm not doing it again," Eppie said. She edged away from Iola as she pulled the top layer of veils off and threw them to Darna.

The sound of chanting and drumbeats outside shifted. The sun's first rays were cresting over the eastern hills. The pit at their feet was silent.

Darna felt a rumbling in her belly, not the usual sharp pain but a slow, smooth rolling feeling, really quite pleasant. "Anara's coming," she said.

She ventured a look down again. The pit churned darkly, with flickers of blue light here and there sparking in and out in threads. Next, it glowed a dark, luminous green. It passed through a range of other colors, the light growing closer and closer until the red and gold of Anara lapped at their feet like lava, hot if you touched it but cool from an arm's length away. Darna's belly moved as if in answer to the ripples of light as they turned into scales and wings, eyes and teeth: Anara in dragon form.

Take that away from this place to another land, the dragon said to Darna.

Then she turned to Iola and opened her mouth. Iola reached out to Anara. Her feet lifted off the ground as if drawn physically up by Anara's bright eyes.

Something flashed in the pit below, not dragonlight but plain, ordinary steel, reflecting the distant light of the sky above.

"Hold her back!" the Enatel said.

Hold who back? Darna wondered. She stood, mesmerized by Anara's eyes, which were swirling with so much power behind them. Iola's thin arm crossed her line of sight. The dragon would devour her; Darna was sure of it. Anara touched

Iola with a tongue of flame, then both shrieked, a dragon's call and a noise from Iola that was as inhuman as Anara's voice.

Darna felt sick again, looking down into the gyre of the dragons' realm. "Let's go," she said, more to herself than to Iola. She lunged and caught hold of Iola's robe, then her arm. She pulled, dragging Iola back to the door of the tower and pushing her out through it. They stumbled back onto the ordinary cold stone shore of the island.

Iola was bleeding, as if from a miscarriage but faster. She lay limp in Darna's arms, but she was still trying to reach toward the tower with all of her vanishing strength.

"Take her to the raft," the Aralel said. "Is the... Is the other one safe?"

"I don't know," Darna said. She only knew for sure that she was outside, with the sky above and the ground below, not in that tower gate with the dragon's passageway turning colors and roiling with powers that were too much to survive. How any ambassadress ever flew there and lived, she didn't know.

In a burst of light, Anara rose from the tower's top, like flame from a too-short chimney. The dragon was stronger, fiercer than she'd been the year before, but not as drastically changed as Salara had been. Anara raced low over the city, touching down here and there leaving fire in her wake. It took some time for people to see what was happening and to race back to their guild halls and houses to stop the flames from spreading over the city's scattering of thatched roofs and into the wooden beams that supported the tile roofs of most buildings. The taverns and the market stalls began to burn, matching the red rising light of the sun.

The sun's light shone a darker red through the smoke as Anara wheeled back to her tower. Faster than the spiraling ash from all the scattered fires, thunderheads massed over the city, letting loose a rain as sudden and fierce as Iola's blood.

"Get back to the temple!" the Aralel said over the roar of rain.

"What about Eppie and the Enatel?"

"Don't worry about them."

Darna could see that there was nothing she could do for them. It was going to be hard enough to get Iola back to shore safely, but she didn't think that anyone could survive inside the tower.

"She's bleeding!" Darna said.

"Thank goodness for the rain, then," Sunna said.

They looked up just in time to see Anara plunge back into the tower, a volcano in reverse. The dragon ripped down through the rain cloud. Blue sky shone through the gap, which closed as she burned down through the pouring rain and into her tower.

The world hung suspended in Anara's wake. Even the raindrops seemed to pause in midair. The wind stilled. Then a raindrop fell on Darna's head, stirring her back to life. Everything around her still seemed cold and still, the tower a frozen, dead thing in the warm wet summer rain. Eppie and the Enatel were still in there. She started back for the tower, but Iola's weight slowed her. She leaned forward to listen and thought she heard a voice over the thunder and the pounding rain, saying, "Come this way!" If that was the Enatel talking, then they were alive.

"Bring her to the boat!" the Aralel said.

Iola was limp. Darna tried to wrest her to her feet, but it was as if her thin frame had no power in it at all. The Aralel came back and took Iola's legs while Darna held her up by the shoulders. When the wind began, the oarsmen had pushed off from the shore to save the raft from being battered on the rocks, and the Aralel did not beckon them back. Instead, she, Sunna, and Darna waded out up to their waists, dragging Iola between them. They loaded her into the boat like a sack of grain and clustered around her. Not a scrap of cloth on the raft was dry; they had no cloak to warm her with.

"Is she all right?" Ganie asked.

"She's breathing," the Aralel said.

The oarsmen leaned on their poles and moved them across the water, making a slow, wet trail back to the rain-drenched shore. As the raft crossed the harbor, the downpour slackened into an ordinary soaking rain. By the time they nosed up onto the cobblestone street, the water had risen so that the shore was two buildings closer to the temple than it had been when they set out. The clouds had begun to let through a bit more light. All but the most ardent spectators had dispersed. Even most of the priestesses had run back to the temple or had taken shelter in doorways and under awnings. Perhaps a few more had climbed into the tenders and fishing boats that were now taking their passengers out to the seagoing craft beyond the breakwater.

Iola was awake by the time they landed, but lethargic. Darna and Sunna propped her up between them to climb out of the raft. They stumbled on their cold, numb feet. Their fine gauze veils spilled red dye as the rain washed them down, dripping on the paving stones like the blood splattering from Iola's wounds.

The Aralel stood on the high seat at the stern of the raft and announced that the ambassadress had flown, a lie no one heard.

§

Myril took shelter from the rain in a house half-drowned on the ground floor but still dry upstairs, in a loft with a balcony looking out over the harbor. The balcony had been crowded when the ambassadress's raft set out, but when the rain came, the people on it had retreated. They parted to let Myril through – her priestess robes gave her their respect that morning – and one of them recognized her as a healer. They let her take a place just inside the balcony door, and from there she watched. There was a scrap of red cloth on Anara's back as she rose through the sky, but it was gone again when she plunged, or was it? It was impossible to see through the smoke and rain, and she couldn't quite pick out the noises, either, not with the pounding of the rain. She thought that she heard the cloth ripping. What she didn't hear was the heartbeat of the ambassadress or her quickened breath as the dragon rose. Iola had been on the raft, despite the Aralel's plans to keep her away from the dragon's gate. The rain ran down Myril's face, dripping onto her chest as she leaned up to watch the lightning streak through the dark clouds. Anara appeared again, arcing up once more, then plunging into her tower, into her gate, into the other world.

Was Iola still on the surface of the earth? Myril wasn't sure. She'd heard a scream, then nothing. She could make out several heartbeats on the island, several pairs of feet, but she didn't know whose they were. Two disappeared, going down into the tower. She saw the Aralel and one of the attendants haul another of the attendants out onto the raft.

As the raft moved closer again, she thanked the keeper of the house for letting her take shelter there and rejoined the few of her fellow priestesses on the shore. Someone started to chant. After the raft landed, they all fell into place behind the Aralel. The ambassadress's attendants limped up the processional way. Yes, the one who'd fainted was Iola. Myril recognized the air about her, but her presence was diminished, like it had been at Midwinter, only worse. Darna and Sunna held her up on either side.

The Aralel stopped at the temple gates and watched each of them file through, like a mother hen counting her chicks. Myril stopped before she passed.

"You may go, Myril, but return later," the Aralel told her. "You must visit with the regent."

"Yes, Your Holiness." She watched the ambassadress's attendants limp toward the peresi's garden until they turned a corner, out of sight, then she made her way to the small bathhouse near her street. There, she washed off the running red dye of her ceremonial robes and rinsed them in cool water. She soaked in the hot bath – which did not seem as hot as usual – then put on a plain tunic before going back to her room to hang her wet things up.

Back out on the street, the air was heavy with the pull of the other realm, as it always was at Midsummer, even outside of the temple. The ambassadress hadn't gone to the dragons, but it was still a crossing time. Myril went back inside and took a handful of grounding, trance-blocking herbs. She chewed them whole. If she stayed to make tea, she would never leave her room again before the end of the day, and she needed to see Darna and Iola before she found some excuse not to. She walked back down to the new shore. It was only a little farther up the street than it had been before, but the waters had risen. They would rise again at Midwinter, but they might rise even before then. The dragons were uneasy. She could feel them, sense the gaps in the walls.

She took another pinch of herbs and chewed. They tasted awful, dry and astringent. She knew that she should go to the temple, but first she looked out onto the bay, beyond the breakwater. Ships lumbered toward the horizon. Some of them were still bailing rainwater over their sides, others were driven by oarsmen as their sails hung wet and heavy, but they were all moving away, fleeing Anamat, abandoning it, or preparing to return to steal its treasures before it fell again.

The ships slipped over the horizon, one after another. The Cereans were almost out of sight by the time the rainclouds had cleared. The Enomaeans had lingered longer and their sails were heavy from the rain of Anara's passing. Lerat's ship, with a few smaller vessels around him, was almost last to go, but he'd left his sails furled and under loose oilcloths. As the sun shone out again, he raised them, and they dried quickly as they filled with clean, fresh air.

Myril watched him sail away. She was seized with the sudden worry that she should have gone with him after all, despite the fact that it meant leaving Iola behind. Iola would have left her to go to the dragons. Perhaps she shouldn't have stayed to fuss over the frustrated ambassadress. She should have gone to find a place to take the texts. Lerat's ship carried her hopes away. She didn't long for Lerat, but she dreamed of a safe haven on a foreign shore. They would find it; they must find it.

She wondered if the water had reached the guildhalls yet, and went to see.

The Chief Chronicler was closing his study door when she arrived.

"Myril," he said. "Surely, you have no work to do here this morning. It's a holy day."

"Not as holy as it used to be," Myril said. "I came to tell you that one of the priestesses has sailed with a merchantman in search of a safe haven for both the chronicles and the priestesses. I thought you would like to know."

"It seems a fool's errand," the Chronicler said with a sigh. "If the tides swallow our city before the ships return at Midwinter, there's no saving any of it."

"You asked me to try. I've done that."

The Chronicler looked away, as if he'd thought better of it but hadn't bothered to tell her so.

"There are more histories to save, aren't there?" Myril asked.

"You need not continue with this. I've heard word of a place in Enomae, but my friend there... Well, it is good of you to have tried. I suppose you won't be going to the temple much, will you?"

"I will, actually. The regent is staying there, and I promised her that I would visit her."

"Since you'll be there anyway, it would be good of you to see that the texts there are secure for now, whatever the coming trading season brings." He yawned. "Pardon me. These last nights have been long. It would be interesting to have the regent of Tiadun's story in our library, don't you think? A scrappling prince, or at least a princess. I'm sure such a thing has never happened before."

"It's unlikely to happen again," Myril said. "I'll write down what I know."

"Good. I should thank you also for sending that guardsman to me. This so-called Enatel is an interesting phenomenon. I am not quite convinced that they are what they claim to be, but the young man said that you sent him, so I let them take the texts. Also, that baker in the West Market is known to be trustworthy. Do you know if their hiding place is higher than our hall?"

"I've never been there. I hope it is. Did you see that the waters rose a little more this morning?"

The Chronicler nodded. "It's more than just the rain," he said. "I've read of these swordsmen in the old stories. Even if they still exist, they can't have their old power or their legendary skill. They're in disgrace, and their totemic stone is gone."

"It was the priestesses' totemic stone, too," Myril said, "and we still honor the Aralel."

"Ah, but the Aralel has many things to offer the princes. Armsmen can be had anywhere, for a price, and not so high a price as the Aralel's finest. In any case, you've done enough for this moon-round. You may go back to your other work, I think, while you write the history of the regent of Tiadun. Quite an unusual story."

The Chronicler was not meeting her gaze. He was avoiding looking at her. She had the sense that he wanted her to leave. He was acting uncomfortable where he had always seemed so self-assured. She inhaled. He'd been drinking, and more than just Anamat ale. She smelled a whiff of a foreigner's perfume, too.

She looked at him more closely as she spoke. "I may do that," she said. "There are always farmers looking for charms in the harvest season. Are you quite sure?"

"Yes, yes. Take what you need with you today. I'll see you when you've completed it."

It would take her more than a moon-round. He *was* trying to send her away.

The Chronicler looked over his shoulder. In the shadows in the corridor behind him, Myril glimpsed someone – a foreigner with a turban around his head, a slight man who smelled of horses and perfume. The Chronicler was dealing with foreigners too, like almost everyone else.

"I leave you to your rest, then, guildmaster."

"And I trust you will go to yours, too," he smiled at her, looking more like his usual self again. Myril was not put at ease.

§

They had to swim the last stretch through the Defenders' secret passage between Anara's island and one of the secret ways that riddled the underbelly of Ara's Landing. The secret way had been carved by the dragons themselves, then shored up by the temple launderers and the first of Enat's heirs.

At the base of Anara's tower, out on the island, there were two ledges on which to perch over the vertical gate into the dragons' world. The upper one was where the ambassadress stood to meet Anara. The lower one was where the Defenders had stood guard at every crossing time. That morning, Eppie had swung down from the upper ledge to the lower.

"Get into the passage now!" Sovara told her over the roar of the approaching dragon.

Eppie waited for the Enatel to follow. Sovara edged closer to the passage entry but waited on the ledge until Anara surged up. Her tail swished, sweeping the ledge as if she wanted to be rid of them. Anara glared at Eppie, garbed as she was as a false ambassadress. It was a fragment of a moment, but she saw into the dragon's eyes and was terrified. She didn't know what Sovara saw. As soon as they heard the priestesses stumble out of the tower, they turned and ran, down into the hollow pipe beneath the harbor burned out by Anara, long ago, when the Defenders spoke to her and she to them.

Eppie and Sovara ran. Eppie felt half-naked in the ambassadress's fine robes which were draped to suggest breasts and thighs and passion. She hiked up the fine silk, as seawater covered the slick floors at the passage's lowest point. They went on at a run, splashing through the invading seawater while Anara raged in the sky above. The walls shook around them as if they might break and the seawater come rushing in, crushing them before they could draw breath. Somehow, the old walls held, but the water grew deeper. It rose up to their waists, and at the last stretch, they had to swim.

They emerged, sodden, somewhere under the peresi's baths.

"You go that way; I'll see you back at the hall," Sovara said. Eppie had no time to respond before the Enatel ducked into a connecting tunnel that led out to the East Canal. It was a wonder the dragons' enemies had never found the passages, there were so many of them, but if the water kept rising, soon only a fish would be able to get through.

The launderers never spoke except in silent hand-signals and unintelligible whispers. One of the women met Eppie, as if she'd been expecting her visit. The laundress's face was impassive as she handed Eppie an ordinary priestess robe and took the ambassadress's showy ceremonial robe and veil from her. She only frowned a little as she turned away and led Eppie to the landing where the temple priestesses brought their laundry.

From there, she went up to the main part of the temple. The peresi were in disarray, their robes rain-soaked, their elaborate hairdos falling down in every direction. They whispered to one another, their fearful speculation filling the air. No one noticed her. They must have thought that she was one of them, in her fine red robes, even though she didn't feel like she fit the part.

Sunna met her at the ambassadress's gate.

"I was worried," she said.

"We made it out all right," Eppie said. There was no one visible nearby to listen. "It's getting wet, though. The water came into the...you know."

Sunna nodded. "It's risen on the streets, too. I'm going to see what it's done elsewhere."

"What do you mean?"

"Didn't you hear? I'm done with this place, this charade of being a priestess."

"I don't want to do it!"

"You have to. I'm going to visit Vigda's band and then some other places. I'll meet you at the border shrine at the second full moon to give you the news of Tiadun, which you can bring back here to the regent."

"Can I go wandering, then?"

Sunna shook her head and Eppie knew that it was hopeless. "Sovara wants you to stay. You'll have another full season of training and then you'll be able to best any swordsman in the world."

A gong sounded from the back of the temple.

"It'll be midday soon; I have to go now," Sunna said, and she darted away before Eppie could say anything more.

Geta was keeping watch at the gate to the ambassadress's chambers, but she was too infirm to go back to work in the kitchens. She peered at Eppie.

"Did the Aralel send you?" she asked.

"No, the Enatel," Eppie mumbled.

"The who?" Geta croaked.

"Eppie, is that you?" Darna called from inside.

Geta took another look at Eppie, nodded, and gave her permission to pass before she closed and locked the gate.

"Where's Myril? We need her." Darna was more agitated than Eppie had ever seen her before.

"I don't know. I just came through. I haven't seen her. Aren't you happy I'm alive?"

Darna stilled. "Yes, I'm delighted that you survived, but we need a healer."

Geta came to a creaky-kneed stand. "I'm a healer," she said. "I can do more than bake bread. Now, what seems to be the trouble?"

"It's her," Darna said, jerking her thumb toward the ambassadress's chamber.

"In we go. Quiet now." Geta groaned as she walked, but as they got closer to the ambassadress's doorway, Eppie could hear that not all of the groans were coming from the elder priestess.

Inside, Iola lay on the floor. Someone had stuck a pillow under her head, and there was another near her feet. She was shaking.

"I couldn't lift her by myself," Darna said. She was keeping her distance from Iola, as if she didn't want to touch her, but together, the two of them moved Iola to her sleeping nook. There, Geta fussed over her for a moment before she bustled off to the kitchens. For the rest of the morning, Eppie fetched and carried herbs and cloths as Geta tended Iola's wounds, visible and invisible. She wanted to go back to the training hall and sleep, but Darna fretted, Geta made demands, and Iola stayed in a stupor. Late in the midday rest, the Aralel herself came to look in on, purportedly, the regent of Tiadun.

"She's only in a sulk," Geta told the Aralel as they looked down at Iola.

"I can see that," the Aralel concurred. "Well, she's got nothing to do for the next half-year but to get herself out of it, if that's all it is. We'll see that she's fed when she wakes up and hope the farmers harvest enough to feed all the rest of them." She looked harried.

"It's going to be a good harvest. They will," Geta said.

"I hope you're right." The Aralel turned to Eppie. "I understand you're taking the Blessed Sunna's place?"

"I don't think of it that way," Eppie said.

"Can you train the young priestesses and our three novices in sword work?"

"I don't know that much myself," Eppie said, shaking her head.

"Well, they'll just have to make do with what they've learned so far. I'll try to get more blades," the Aralel mused. She let out a long sigh and looked toward the peresi's courtyard. "Carry your messages, then. Come to me if there's trouble no one else here can manage."

"Yes, Your Holiness," Eppie said.

Behind the Aralel's back, Darna was smirking, a smirk that disappeared when the Aralel turned to her. "And you, regent, have only to help your old friend stay here among the living, in mind as well as in body." She didn't give Darna time to respond. "No excuses. You're the only one we can keep in here with her. She needs you."

Darna looked down at Iola lying pale and weak in her sleeping nook. She nodded.

It was going to be a long half-year for all of them.

§

Chapter 14

Myril took her bundle of parchment and bottles of ink back to her room and set them down on a small table by the window. It should not be difficult for her to write the history of the regent of Tiadun. She knew most of the shape of Darna's life. Some parts were missing, but Darna had never been reticent. Myril wondered what Darna would think of recording her story for the guild's histories. She might not like it, just to be contrary – she wouldn't be in the best of tempers, locked up all through the waning year in the temple's heart of hearts.

She looked out her window, wrote a few lines, and looked out again. She listened. There were very few Cereans left in the harborside warehouses and taverns, now that the ambassadress had flown. Girizit remained at the palace, keeping mostly to his own chambers. He was also listening, as if he could also hear more than others did.

The days passed, the moon waned, and still she did not go to the temple, though she knew that she should. She'd gone once, on Midsummer morning, to tend to Iola, but she'd left as soon as she could. Her sketch of Darna's story was in fragments. Why not write of the last ambassadress to the dragons instead? She worried about Iola. That was what finally drove her to leave her quiet haven again.

Anamat was a ghost of itself that season. Many had fled, and those who remained were uneasy. The city wore the facade of its usual autumnal rhythm, with the gathering-in of the harvest that filled the markets with the winter's provisions, and the clearing-away of the detritus of the summer migrations and festival. Floodwaters eased back from the riverbanks as late summer brought dry skies until they were almost at their before-Midsummer levels, and the ripening crops drew up the few light showers of rain. The valley closed in on itself, but it was not the old peace of the waning year. It was anxious in its quiet, waiting for the next turning of the year. The scrappling who crouched on the corner by the temple's side house was skinny and ragged and looking toward the harbor, not the temple, for a way forward.

Myril slipped into the side house. After the eerie quiet of the streets, the temple's usual oppressive air seemed almost comforting. The Grandmother let her pass without comment. There were two open doors in the room above ground level, as if priestesses were staying there, where they never had before. Had all the life of the city gone into the temple, then? Myril put on her temple robes in the attic and stepped out into the narrow passage above the elders' court. Crossing it, she slowed to listen to the voices coming from inside the Aralel's study.

"I told him that it would be imprudent to send his own men to collect the texts in this season."

"It is imprudent of him to be in our city in this season," the Aralel said. "Even his fellow Cerean merchants know that much."

"I've told you before: Girizit is no mere merchant," Tiagasa said.

"And I suppose that means you're not merely a merchant's bed slave."

Tiagasa's breath hissed in.

"Don't slap me," the Aralel said.

"You should not call me such things, Your Holiness."

"This is my domain, and you would do well to remember it. You are part of it too."

"No, I belong to the governor's palace. I merely visit you out of respect."

"Respect? Is that what you call it? Even now, I think that your girl is taking treasures from the peresi, taking bribes for passage across to slavery."

"It's not slavery. Besides, I hear that you only plan to let them drown."

"If you ever had any wisdom, it seems you've lost it. I ask that you keep your girl from coming here again."

"Would you drive me away, too?"

"If you come only to steal and not to take counsel from your elders," the Aralel said. "I have other matters to attend to now."

Myril had stopped halfway across the garden to listen, and people had noticed her standing there. The elders didn't seem to mind, but Tiagasa or her handmaid would be another matter. She hurried on through the peresi's garden.

Old Geta sat in the little gatehouse at the entrance to Iola's realm. Her eyelids sagged and her chin nodded down onto her chest. She looked very old, but she looked up as Myril approached, and brightened visibly when she recognized her.

"You're a sight for old eyes," Geta said. "I'm sure the regent will want to see you." She winked or blinked something out of her eye as she opened the gate and let Myril in, closing it swiftly behind her.

Myril had never been in the ambassadress's garden during the waning year before, but she'd glimpsed it through the gate many times. When the ambassadress was under the earth, it was usually untended and in disarray, brown in the summer droughts with weeds running over the walkways. This year was different. She could see fresh scratches in the dirt, and some of the too-lush growth was bound up with twine. Geta looked too old and frail to have done the work herself.

She found Darna in a corner, pruning fading blossoms from a rosebush.

"Gardening. That's a princely occupation," Myril said. Darna had never liked gardening very much before.

"It's that or needlework," Darna grumbled, "or talking to Iola. This way, I don't have to listen to her."

Myril felt a shiver. She'd heard enough to reassure herself that Iola was inside, but hadn't focused on her.

"I should go in to see her."

"Better you than me," Darna said.

Myril left Darna with her pruning knife, snapping twigs and muttering to herself as she made the garden even more beautiful than it had been before. Strange that there were roses there that only bloomed when the ambassadress was supposed to be under the earth.

Iola was sitting up, but her sleeping nook had the air of a sickbed about it and her skin was deathly pale.

"Myril? I'm so glad you came. Come sit by me." Her voice was as distant and hollow as her eyes. The sense of the dragons' power still hung around her like the lingering smoke around a cookfire after it had been put out. Myril didn't think that Iola would put her into trance in her sickly condition, but she was cautious anyway. She found a stool and pulled it up opposite Iola. The table at her bedside was littered with empty cups and crumbled cloths. Myril tidied them as she spoke.

"I'm glad that you survived Midsummer," she began. "Did the girl who went in your robes survive too?"

"It was Eppie," Iola said resentfully. "She comes here every day."

"I'm sure she doesn't come to gloat."

"You'll see for yourself. She usually comes at midday with the excuse that she's carrying messages for the regent, but she doesn't leave me alone."

"Have you been eating?"

Iola rolled her eyes, as if tired of the question. "Of course I eat." She frowned and looked away, as if simply too tired to bother saying anything more.

"You wish that you were down there," Myril said.

Iola nodded mutely and her frown turned into a scowl. She trembled as she looked up. "Of course! Where else would I be? I'm not supposed to be here. I'd rather be dead."

Outside, she could hear Darna wiping off the blade of her pruning knife. There was a disturbance at the gate to the garden, too.

"I would speak with the regent of Tiadun," someone said. It was Tiagasa again.

"You may send her a message," Geta said. "She is indisposed today."

"I am sorry to hear she's not well. I must speak to her on matters of state."

"She will send word when she wishes to see you," Geta said.

"I am the mistress of the governor's palace."

"Yes, young one, I've heard that. Still, the regent is indisposed today." Geta did not unlock the gate.

Myril reached out to lay a soothing hand on Iola's thin arm, but the air around it felt so cold that she pulled back. She wondered if Iola would care that Tiagasa was outside. She probably wouldn't. She didn't seem to care about much of anything.

"You should take a bath," Myril said. "It would warm you."

Iola shook her head. "No. It's no good anymore. They're not in it anymore. It's cold."

Darna came in, brushing dirt off of her hands. "It's true," she said. "It was warm enough on Midsummer morning, but by the time we woke up the next day, it was as cold as the canal."

Myril looked between the two of them. They did smell less washed than usual. "The baths out in the city are the same as ever," she said. "I haven't heard of anything different in the other baths. Could I see?"

"Why not?" Darna said. "I'll show you."

"Do you mind?"

Iola shook her head. "But I won't go with you," she said. "I'm going back to sleep." She lay down and pulled a blanket over her head to feign sleep, but Myril could hear by her breathing that she was still awake, and angry. Well, better anger than lethargy.

Darna was tense and restless, but at least she wasn't fading away as Iola seemed to be. "I usually sit in here when I'm not in the garden," she said as she led Myril through the arched doorway into the baths. "It's cold, but I never have a cramp when my feet are in the water." She sat down on the tiles, pulled up her robe, and dropped her feet into the bath. It was not steaming. It smelled a little moldy. Myril crouched beside Darna but decided not to touch the water.

"I think it might do this every year," Darna said. "Why would the dragons heat the baths if their ambassadress isn't here?"

"I suppose," Myril said. "You don't think it's odd?"

"No more than it ever has been. Nothing else has changed in here."

"Except for the garden, now that you're tending it."

Darna shrugged. On the whole, she was in much better condition than Iola. Her cramps continued and her belly was starting to look more rounded. It looked as if Darna was simply pregnant, but Myril couldn't shake off the sense that it wasn't right, that it wasn't ordinary. The only movement she'd felt in it was a distant sense of heat, but it was too early to feel anything more than that, yet. Soon, though, they would be feeling movement, if it was what it looked like.

When Myril returned to her room, she took her assignment from the guildmaster, the pieces of Darna's story, and put them in a box underneath the bed. She would return to it only if Darna survived Midwinter and whatever was in her belly.

§

Through the whole waning year, Thorat remained on guard duty in the palace. He observed the governor, his mistress, and their remaining foreign guests. In addition to Girizit, there were the usual Enomaean horse-handlers and a few Cerean armsmen and scholars. Those mostly kept to themselves except when they visited the scriptorium to take texts or went down to the harborside brothel or to visit the merchants there. Girizit stayed to his chamber and visited Tiagasa. Together, they puzzled over the texts that the temple had sent up before Midsummer, trying in vain to unravel the secrets Tiagasa had never bothered to learn before.

Minstrels still carried news and rumors from the provinces beyond Anamat. The guardsmen of Galamun and Getedun combined their forces to escort the common armsmen who'd come from Tiadun back to their home province, and also drove the remaining Cereans Calar had brought back to their ships there. They set sail to rejoin the duke of the Southern Reaches and perhaps to shore up his rebellion against the Cerean king, but the autumn storms came early. Rumors flew across the seas.

Fishermen said the storm had swamped the Cerean ships, and that one of them was lost outright, with all the men aboard, while the other two were badly damaged. It was dangerous to sail on the dragons' waters out of season.

At the second full moon after Midsummer, Eppie went out to meet Sunna at the border shrine. She returned to the training hall with the news that, apart from Tiadun and Slaradun, the dragon gates in the southern provinces were all where they'd been before. She would go on to make the longer circuit of the northern provinces. Eppie said wistfully that Sunna looked happier than she'd ever been.

One day not long after that, Thorat went to visit Myril. He arrived late in the afternoon, just as she was returning from the temple.

"It's dustier than usual in here," Thorat commented.

Myril looked around. "I suppose it is. I've been distracted."

"Your sign's still down. Are people still coming for your cures?"

Myril shook her head and sighed. "I have too much to do for Darna, and Iola, too. I can't do anything for all of this." She made a sweeping motion, indicating the world beyond her walls.

"What of Iola?"

Myril froze. "Did you know that she didn't fly?"

Thorat shook his head. "I knew that people were trying to stop her. No one told me they'd succeeded."

"I shouldn't have said anything. I thought that Eppie or the Enatel might have told you. Well, you know now."

"Is she well?"

"She's alive. There's that much. You'd better not try to see her, not before Midwinter."

"What about your guild, then? The governor isn't sending us down there for texts anymore. Giri's only studying the ones we brought before Midsummer, and maybe a few that Tiagasa got from the temple."

"I don't know anything about the guild these days," Myril said, still looking out the window. "I was supposed to write a history of Darna, the Scrappling Prince, but I can't. She might die."

"She won't die," Thorat said. "She hasn't yet."

"He said to bring it back when I'd written for him. I've gone, but he won't see me. He's keeping something from me."

Myril had always been both secretive and trustworthy, as far as Thorat could tell. The Chief Chronicler seemed to have a high opinion of her. "What would he hide from you?"

"Maybe it's a who, not a what," Myril said, as if an idea had suddenly occurred to her. She turned back to face him. "There's an Enomaean at the guild. I could smell his perfume and horses. Somehow, the Chronicler has gotten mixed up with him. I don't like it. He's never been so secretive before."

"An Enomaean?" Thorat thought aloud. "Could it be Nolerin?"

"Who's that?"

"He's the one who brought Darna over the mountains from Slaradun," Thorat said. "I liked him, after I got used to him, and Darna trusted him. He prayed every day at sunrise to their eagle god, but I never saw him make sacrifices, and he never said anything against the dragons."

"Darna trusted him? Well, then maybe it's all right, but it just seems wrong. Everything seems wrong. The temple is feeding three times as many as it ever has before. The kitchens stink and clatter day and night. There aren't so many scrapplings, but I see grown villagers camping in the streets some nights. Everything is out of season."

Thorat couldn't disagree with that. He left Myril's room a short while later with a message for Raina, asking her to go to help Myril look at Darna's belly. Walking up the street back to the training hall, he felt less sanguine than before the visit, despite the news that Iola was safe on the surface of the earth. Why had no one told him?

§

That waning year was the longest season of Iola's life. She felt the wrongness of it with every breath, until her absence from the dragons had poisoned her as much as it could and every bone in her body was weak with it, and the only thing left to do was to breathe the ordinary air of the surface of the earth again, to eat the common food of the temple, and to sit up a little more.

She settled into a loose rhythm. She slept nearly as much as Darna did, but she didn't bathe, didn't want to be reminded that the dragons had withdrawn even from her baths. The other baths were still warm, she heard. She spent long hours contemplating the cold, dusty statue of Anara over her old offering place. She vowed never to lie on that altar again. She'd failed it. She could scarcely stand to look at it.

After the second full moon after Midsummer had come and gone, when Eppie had come to tell them that the dragons' gates still glowed in most of the southern provinces, she stirred herself to do a little more. Late in the night, well after dark and when Darna was asleep, she climbed the tower to look out over the city. She could see a long way from up there, even if she couldn't see Anara. Soon, she would have to leave the protective circle of her high white walls. She didn't want to be lost when she did. She circled the narrow ledge around the tower, looking down at the city streets, trying to memorize the ways they turned and twisted, then looking beyond them to the roads leading out of the city, into the valley, into the mountains, and beyond. Perhaps she would ask Thorat to come with her, if he came to her again, but she wouldn't meet him as a priestess, not anymore.

As the nights grew noticeably longer than the days, she began to eat more of the food they brought from the kitchens, where before she'd only picked at the dry crumbs. She asked for wine instead of tea sometimes and went out into the garden more and more. After all, it was no colder there than in the indoor part of her prison. For the first time, her quarters felt like a cage, which they never had before. She wished that she had wings to fly again, or even just scales. Darna had scales. Darna had never loved the dragons as she had. Or had she? Darna hadn't been to that other realm, hadn't lived there, and yet the dragons had touched her more deeply than Iola had thought possible, more deeply than she would have been able to withstand. She'd never realized before how far from the dragons she really was.

There had been times that the dragons had touched her, face to face. In the early days, Anara had almost drained the life out of her one night on the tower. Darna, of all people, had rescued her. She'd healed quickly, just as she'd always healed after her journeys to that other realm, those journeys where she'd lived in a different kind of prison, a gilded alcove at the edge of the dragons' realm, a place from which she could see them but never really be among them. They would come one at a time to lay their heads in her lap, to receive their offerings and to warm her better than any man ever could. Yes, she'd touched the dragons, but they didn't live inside her, not as they lived inside Darna.

Darna and Iola spent as much time as they could apart, but they still had to share a table when Eppie or Geta brought their meals. They gave each other common courtesy, at least. What else could they do? Time would pass and the temple would fall. After that lay nothing but the windblown wilderness beyond her impossibly perfect walls, the temple's future ruins.

§

Eppie carried the tray to Darna and Iola for the hundredth time – no, it had been more times than that. She'd lost count moons before. It was Midwinter Eve, late in the day, and she didn't like the temple any more than she had at Midsummer. She would be glad when this farce of playing a provincial priestess was over. Being one of the dragons' ladies, even for a small part of the day, made her feel caged in. She didn't know how Darna could stand it. Iola and the other priestesses were different, far better suited to their walled-in life.

No one in the temple ever asked who she was or where she was going. They accepted her as one of their own without question. After all, she was young and female, so it didn't seem to occur to them that she could be anything other than a priestess, unless she were just seeking refuge, and that amounted to nearly the same thing.

The farmers brought a portion of their harvests to the back gates, and whatever came in went straight to the kitchens to feed the throngs of priestesses, with none set aside for the waxing year, despite the usual seasonal bounty. Eppie heard that there were petitioners, too, but she avoided learning anything more about them by skirting through the peresi's courtyard as quickly as possible.

There were so many priestesses in the temple that it seemed they'd given up keeping track of who was there. She wondered if even the treasurers knew who came and went. The librarian didn't seem to notice that some priestesses never returned the scrolls they borrowed. The Chronicler had stopped sending scrolls to Garren's shop for the Defenders to guard, but Myril had begun to bring Darna and Iola a few texts from the temple library, obscure ones, valuable ones, ones that apparently would not be missed and would be safe in Iola's realm for a while. Most of the time, neither Darna nor Iola bothered to read them, too far gone in whatever agonies their bodies were suffering. After the texts had sat there for a few days, Eppie would take them out on the empty food tray and carry them up to the training hall, where she piled them next to the others. It wasn't a big pile, but secrets didn't take up much space.

At least Iola was looking better, Eppie reflected as Geta let her in that day. Darna was pacing in the garden, as she often did. When she wasn't in the garden, she just sat in the baths, letting the water dampen whatever fire was inside her. Except for her belly, she looked the same as she had at Midsummer, but her efforts to be polite were strained and short, when she bothered at all. She ate as if it were an onerous chore, even when old Geta sent over cakes that were so light and sweet that Eppie salivated just thinking of them.

"Food's here," Eppie announced. She set it down on a garden bench near Darna. "How's the Most Blessed One?"

"Don't know," Darna grumbled. She walked past the tray and lifted the plate cover, took out a piece of bread, and kept pacing.

"Why aren't you in the bath?"

"Don't know," Darna said. She looked up at the sky. "Too empty in there."

The garden felt neglected again. "Is Iola awake?" Eppie asked.

Darna gestured to the tower. "She went up there a while ago. I'm not waiting for her."

Eppie sighed. "The Aralel told me to make sure that she eats."

Darna shrugged. "Well, I'm hungry now, and all of this is supposed to be for me and you, isn't it?"

Eppie wondered if she should wait for Iola, but when Iola went up to the tower, there was no telling when she would come down. She moved the tray to a table out of sight of the gate, closer to the base of the tower, where Iola might see it. She poured out two small cups of wine and drank one herself, handing the other to Darna.

"Thanks," Darna grunted. She took the cup and raised it to her lips, then suddenly her whole body convulsed. Wine and cup went flying. Darna clutched her belly and began to fall to the ground.

Eppie dropped her own wine just in time to catch Darna before she hit the flagstones. "Sit," she commanded as she dragged Darna to the bench. She pushed the tray aside. Darna collapsed into a sitting position.

"Worse?"

Darna nodded. She convulsed, then arched her back and screamed.

By the fourth time Darna cried out, her agony didn't even sound human. A trio of elder priestesses stormed the gate. They circled around Darna, holding her arms, stopping her from falling or hitting her head against the stone table. Geta was there. Good. The Aralel. Maybe not so good. Another kitchen priestess.

Darna said that she was going to faint. They lifted her up and carried her inside.

"Where's Iola?" The Aralel whispered.

"In the tower," Eppie said. It was the wine that had set it off, maybe, or else it was simply the fact that the Midwinter Eve sun was setting.

"Go get Myril. Raina. Get Raina," Darna said between convulsions. "Bring them!"

§

Chapter 15

Eppie hesitated a moment before she left. The elders looked frail and tired as they witnessed Darna's agony. She wondered if Myril wouldn't just come on her own – surely she would have heard Darna's cries – but Raina would not have heard, and Darna had asked for her. She wondered how many of the elders knew that Iola had stayed on the surface of the earth, and if all the helpers streaming in for Darna would be able to keep up the deception, or if Iola would simply stay out of sight until after the sun rose. Midwinter dawn was close. Eppie swallowed hard and set out.

Myril was probably on her way already, Eppie told herself, but her place was on the way to the West Gate and Raina's farm. Halfway across the peresi's courtyard, Eppie paused to strip off her priestess robes and bundle them under her arm. She would go out through the front courtyard – it would be faster than going the other way.

Over the course of the waning year, she felt like she'd worn grooves in the paving stones between the temple, the fortune-tellers' street, the palace, and the training hall. She'd run in all those places as a scrappling, but not with the frenetic energy of her role as a messenger. Sometimes at night, after training, she met Kinner at Ink Pounders to hear what was happening at the guild, as well as to get his letters for Darna. Sometimes, they met for no reason at all. Despite his scrawny boyishness, he was nearly her own age, and sometimes he surprised her with some bit of elderly-sounding wisdom. She refrained from picking his pockets and even taught him how to avoid falling victim to the last desperate remains of the scrapplings of Anamat.

There was a gang of them outside the front gates of the temple that evening, waiting to pick petitioners' pockets, or maybe to beg for refuge when the ambassadress "returned." The treasurers at the gate ignored Eppie as she ran out, making her wonder how many priestesses had left while the gatekeepers turned the other way. A dark mass of foreign ships stood on the horizon, or maybe it was only the dark of a gathering storm.

She felt a tug. One of the scrapplings had crept up behind her and gotten a grip on the priestess robe under her arm. The youth – maybe a girl, maybe a boy – yanked it free of her grip. Eppie saw the scrappling's look of exultation.

"Hey! Give that back!"

The scrappling only shook her head and ran, as fast as the crowds would let her through.

Eppie wondered what price a priestess robe would fetch as she chased the scrappling down toward the harbor. She was fast, and she would be able to catch the scrappling eventually if she gave chase, but she didn't need that robe. What she needed was to get Myril and Raina for Darna. Some of the other scrapplings were closing in to block her pursuit. She knew this game, she could dodge them, but it would take time.

"Fine! Take it, then!" she shouted after the fleeing thief. She turned and ran the other way, shouldering past the surprised scrappling boy who'd been just behind her, ready to push or trip her up.

A group of petitioners, smelling of sandalwood and gold, blocked her way, but these were clumsier than the scrapplings and she passed them easily, breaking through onto the relatively empty street down to the East Canal bridge and Myril's place.

The underside of the bridge was still fiooded out, no longer providing any shelter or refuge. She jumped over the risen water at either end rather than balancing across the slippery planks. Her feet got wet, but she didn't have far to go.

She found Myril waiting in her doorway, a satchel held tight against her chest.

"It's a crossing time. I might trance if I go to the temple," Myril said as Eppie approached.

"Darna needs you."

"I know," Myril said. "It's only that I'm –"

"She's screaming with pain. It doesn't seem like her to do that." At Tiada's gate, when everything had been thrown into chaos, Darna had seemed quite calm, for all that had happened to her. Myril nodded. She had none of her usual placid air. She was shaking as she stood at the foot of her stair, as if she were being pushed back inside.

"Don't you have herbs to steady you?" Eppie asked.

"I used them all."

"I'm sure Geta has more. Darna asked me to come for you."

"I know," Myril said. "I'll go to her, but..."

Down the street, a huge clay jar shattered and someone screamed. Men's ribald laughter followed, and more screams. Of course Myril was afraid, anyone would be, but it would only get worse as the night went on.

"We have to go quickly. I'm supposed to get Raina, too. I have to go all the way out to her farm."

Myril shook her head. "She's in the city. I heard her come in. I think she must have gone to your training hall. I can't hear her anymore."

Eppie nodded and took Myril by the arm, propelling her out into the street. She wished she had a sword with her instead of just the long knife she kept in her belt. Myril marched stiffly down the street and across the bridge, where the water churned underneath them with the rising tide.

They paused at the mouth of the alley to the side house. Myril leaned against the wall as if she could sink into it, as Darna had once been able to do, but then she shook herself and went in to see the Grandmother. Once she was inside, she would be safe enough, Eppie told herself.

From there, she set out for the training hall. A year ago, there had been several ways to go between the side entrance of the temple and the training hall, but since the waters had risen at Midsummer, the back alleys around the canal were flooded out. She had to go by the main roads, but she didn't mind the crowds that were gathering, most of the time. Normally, she enjoyed the press of the crowds, but that morning, there was an undertone of worry to the usual celebrations. The fires were smaller and fewer but the crowds were larger. Perhaps people were remembering how the roofs had caught fire at Midsummer and didn't want to destroy their own city when even its own dragon seemed to have turned against it.

Myril's sense of dread had infected her, Eppie reflected. Women often died, in childbed or after, and there was nothing she could do to help. She'd carried food to the women in the ambassadress's quarters all through the waning year, but now all she could do was to fetch Raina.

Based on the wet stench of the fires, people seemed to be raiding the midden heaps more than usual. As Eppie passed through the last square before the entrance to the training hall, someone threw a wet sack of something foul onto the bonfire there, sending up a cloud of damp, putrid smoke. The people in the square shouted, but the miscreant fled faster than they could follow, back to the harbor.

The underground passage into the courtyard was still dry, unlike the hidden passages around the temple. As Eppie ran up the stairs, taking them two at a time, she wondered whether the waters had reached the shrine below her feet yet. She burst into the hall just as Midwinter practice was about to begin.

"Darna's in labor. She asked for Raina to come," she announced breathlessly.

Raina looked back and forth between Eppie and the shrine.

"Must she go now?" Sovara asked.

Raina frowned pensively. "I don't think I need to go yet. It's her first. It won't come before dawn, and she's not alone, is she?"

Eppie shook her head. "Geta and the Aralel were there when I left, and Myril's on her way, but she seemed to be in a lot of pain. It didn't seem normal."

"Have you ever seen a woman in labor before?" Raina asked. Eppie had not. "It can wait for practice and –" She didn't name the shrine below but only looked anxiously at the trapdoor. Eppie could tell from Raina's voice that she was just as afraid as any of the rest of them about what lay below. No one had been down there since midsummer. Apart from Raina and Sunna, only Garren, Thorat, and Anot were at the hall. Forlan, Ferrent, and Sunna were all still off in the provinces or with the bandits. They were expected to return soon, though, maybe even that night.

Eppie shook off her sandals and took her practice sword down from the wall, though half of her thoughts were with Darna, back in the temple. The Defenders stretched out in a long row before the upper shrine, the one that was part of the everyday training hall. Sovara sounded the gong and they bowed together, beginning their silent practice. The Midwinter practice felt weightier than the one at Midsummer. Eppie faced her comrades one at a time. The rest of them were still far more skilled than she was, but in the last two rounds, when she worked her sword against Thorat and Sovara, she at least managed not to fumble. Sovara gave her a nod – as close to a blessing as anything she would give.

Finally, they rested their swords and gathered before the shrine. Sovara opened the hatch and they walked down. Eppie went last. She could hear what was happening up ahead, though. Sovara's feet splashed into water at the bottom steps, and one by one, the others followed, gasping with the cold. When it hit her own toes, she almost shrank back, but the others had gone on, even though the water must have made their ankles ache, too. The cave of the world-tree was knee deep in water, strangely bright water.

The tree was a sign and map of the dragons' world. Its branches reflected the paths of the dragons and burned with their fire, which flickered on the water's surface. The tree gave just enough light to see by. The moment Eppie stepped into the room, the water around her feet turned warm.

Sovara said words which Eppie still did not understand, and the tree flared to life.

It roared.

It screamed.

Its fire filled the cave, driving them back to the rough walls, which had once been smooth and dry but were now slick and rough with the sea's reaching weeds and barnacles. Eppie clung to those stones, seeking anchorage. Then she looked up.

Each branch of the tree was a white-hot cord firing up through the cracks in the surface of the earth, yellow and red layers of heat around it, no cool threads to mark any one dragon's place.

"We go now," Sovara said.

Underneath them, under the water, the bedrock shook.

Eppie reached the stairs first. The moment her feet were out of the water, everything seemed quite ordinary again, and that was strangest thing of all.

There were whispers as they climbed, hurriedly hushed. No one really spoke until Sovara had secured the bit of flooring over the stair at the top. The training hall and the shrine were just as they'd left them a short while before. Sovara stopped to light more incense, but instead of putting on a few pieces into the brazier, she emptied a whole box of it in, filling the hall with smoke.

"I've never seen it like that before," Sovara said, breaking the silence at last.

"The waters rising," Garren said. "We're caught between fire and water."

Raina nodded. Her eyes were red.

"What will we do?" Anot asked.

Sovara looked slowly at each of them in turn. "For tonight, we will keep vigil as always. I don't think that we should go to the island. The ambassadress is not returning, and we don't know if Anara will come at all. If she does, it will not be in peace. Whatever happens, it will not be as it has been; we shouldn't pretend otherwise, even if the priestesses choose to keep up a facade."

"What about the oarsmen?" Garren asked. He and several of the others were among the oarsmen who took the ambassadress's raft out to the island gate. Eppie had suspected it, but no one had told her about it explicitly.

"I suppose the oarsmen should go," Sovara said. "We are pledged to protect the priestesses. It's a lesser pledge than our oath to the dragons, but this morning, we can fulfill it for the last time."

"For the last time?" Thorat said.

Sovara nodded. "Yes, for the last time. Make what efforts you can to convince the city watch – or even the palace guardsmen – to watch over the ladies of the temples, but after the sun rises, we will devote ourselves wholly to the defense of the dragons' gates. We cannot be everywhere, and for myself, I choose the dragons."

"I'm going to stay right where I have been," Raina said.

"Then you can keep the shrine... or what's left of it," Sovara said.

"Where will you go?" Garren asked Sovara.

She looked toward the door. "First, to the hills, and then probably to the northern provinces, which have not sunk so much. You can go to the near provinces, or do what you can here, I suppose."

"I'll go with you," Anot volunteered. He glanced at Eppie, but she shook her head. She didn't want to leave, but she thought that maybe she could go see to one more dragon's gate, maybe back in Coradun, where she'd been born. Thorat was looking away, as if he could see through the walls all the way down to the temple and into the ambassadress's chamber. If he'd seen as much of it as she had, he wouldn't be looking at it so longingly.

"Is that all?" Raina said after a long silence. "I'd better go see about the regent of Tiadun and her labor pains."

Eppie considered following her, but she wasn't ready to face the temple again. She settled down in front of the shrine, choking on the clouds of incense, to keep her final vigil with the Enatel.

§

Up above, in the tower, Iola heard the screams, but she heard so much more that she was reluctant to come down. Maybe this was what it was like for Myril, she thought, hearing and seeing everything in a never-ending cacophony. The sun was sinking toward the horizon. It was the first time she'd seen the Midwinter sunset from the tower, Iola thought, the first time she'd seen it at all since she became ambassadress. It would probably be the last, too, because whatever the waxing year brought, her perch in the temple would not survive it. She might not survive it herself, but she was going to try.

Below her, the women of the temple were making their way to the sanctuary for the night's vigil, the vigil that was supposed to be for her safety. Too many of them were gathered in the garden and in her quarters below, but the sanctuary would be even more crowded. She counted the priestesses as they left the peresi's garden after the last of their petitioners left. They carried small lamps and walked in pairs and trios. They were three and four to a room now, even more than there had been at Midsummer. Even the priestesses had ignored the ban on travel, or maybe these had just come from the village temples around the valley.

The sun set into a bank of clouds, which were on fire with the colors of all the dragons but most especially red and golden, like Anara. Iola leaned back against the wall and gazed out at the sunset. Yes, it would be possible to console herself with this world if the dragons turned their backs on her and made themselves invisible. The clouds washed over the sky as the chants rose up from the sanctuary. The dew fell, chilling her, as city folk and villagers danced around bonfires in squares and on greens. She thought about going down, but what would she do? Darna's screams had eased. She heard someone say that the baths were warm again.

Around midnight, the clouds began to blow away. In the last watch of the night, the Midwinter sky was as clear and sharp as diamonds. A deep stillness lay over the valley, muting the sounds of the chanting priestesses below. As the first wash of gray brightened the sky beyond Lemira's hills, Darna cried out again. No one could pretend that was an ordinary cry. With one more longing prayer to Anara, Iola began her descent. It was time for her to rejoin the world.

§

At times, it seemed to Darna that she floated free of her body. Hundreds of priestesses gathered in the sanctuary that night: those who'd lived most of their lives in the temple and those who'd come only in the past half a year, those who had been under the earth, and many, many more who had never even felt the tug of trance. They gathered and they barred the outer gates. The Aralel was late in coming to the sanctuary, but Darna knew where she was, standing over her labor pains, even though her soul hovered over her fellow priestesses in the sanctuary.

The Aralel arrived in the sanctuary at last, so Darna knew that someone must have taken her place in the ambassadress's chambers. The priestesses could still hear her cries from time to time over the beat of the drums and the hum of the chant, through the shuffle of dancing feet and the blurring cloud of incense. Darna felt as if she were chanting, just as she had through so many vigils before. She opened her eyes and saw the concerned lined faces bending over her. They seemed too far away to reach. Every ounce of her breath went to screaming and refilling her lungs. She could not spare or slow it for speech, or hold it in except to gasp for it again.

The heat grew unbearable. She tried to slow her breathing, and this time she succeeded. "Baths," she managed to say. Myril had arrived, but Raina had not. Between Myril, Geta, and her own efforts, Darna managed to get moved into the bath. The skin on her belly felt like it was on fire. "Water," she said.

Some time later, Raina arrived, looking worried. She and Geta muttered in the background, then someone went out, whispering about telling the Aralel. Darna wanted to say that nothing had changed about her belly, but maybe that wasn't what they were talking about.

The bath helped, but she felt like she was a world away, with the dragons. It wasn't cold any longer. She melted into it, the boundary of her skin feeling no more significant than a whisper in the air, a change in the current.

It was dark outside. She was fairly sure that it was dark outside. Iola was still in the tower. Time passed. They brought her some kind of tea. Sweat rolled off her brow.

"The water!" Raina said. "It's too hot. Help me get her out."

"I can't," Myril said weakly.

"Come on; I'll hold you, too," Raina said brusquely.

Darna managed to open her eyes enough to see Geta slip something into Myril's hand, which Myril put into her mouth to chew.

"That'll hold you," Geta said.

They pulled Darna out of the bath. She was red, like Anara, the scales on her belly the dark green of the dragon who'd last marked her. The second dragon who'd marked her.

Time passed more slowly once she was out of the water. They moved her to one of the sleeping nooks. Someone else arrived, and though she could hear people talking, she couldn't make out their words.

"Put her on the altar," Raina said.

"You can't do that!" It was Gallia. That must have been who had come in.

"I can go on the altar," Darna croaked out. It could hardly be worse than being out in the naked air. The dragon currents there might warm her, as they had in the bath, or ease the pain as they had before.

After a moment of indecision, they helped move her to the altar. Geta began to arrange linens for the birth. Darna began to scream again. She fainted, then the pain woke her once more. Hands pressed down on her. She felt like shaking them off, like Salara had shaken her off.

"Something's not right," Raina said. "I can't feel feet. It's too big, too hard."

Darna tried to reach for her belly, but it was as if her arms had decided not to obey her. With an effort, she pulled herself back into her body, trying to block out the pain.

"It won't come out like that," Darna said. "Cut it."

She'd seen it done once before, with a nanny goat back in Tiadun. The nanny goat had struggled all day, and she'd been losing strength. They brought the midwife, and between them, she and the farmer managed it. Darna had missed the details, but there was more blood than usual. The kids, two of them, had lived, and the nanny goat survived that next year but never recovered her strength. She didn't care if she never recovered her strength. She couldn't go on with the pain.

"I don't know if it's come to that," Raina said, though Darna could tell that she was considering it.

Myril said, "I'll be back," and then she was gone.

Gallia paced as anxiously as a young father.

"Here, drink this," Geta said, thrusting a bitter liquid at Darna. It was hard to swallow, but she could feel her toes growing numb, then her hands and her legs. Everything was very distant, pleasantly so. The pain was still there, but it was far away.

"More?" she asked.

"That should be enough," someone said. It sounded like Vigda's voice, but that was impossible; her mother was a bandit in the hills. She could not be in Anamat on Midwinter night, could she?

Myril came back, carrying a bundle.

The pain came again. "I need it out. I can't birth it."

Darna felt Raina's hands on her again. "It's not moving the way it should. Your skin, though. It's also hard and different."

"These are the best knives," Myril said.

"They've gone down to the harbor," Geta reported. "They're going to say that the ambassadress died."

Everything felt numb. Darna didn't need to drift so far away. She wondered where Iola was.

"They can't. I'm right here," said Iola's voice, but Darna couldn't see her, her eyes were clouding. She fell into welcoming darkness, feeling only a comforting hand in her own, callused and wrinkled.

§

Everyone paused as Iola announced her presence. She looked serene and impossibly distant from the sweat-stained sheets on her altar where Darna lay unconscious, her pulse flickering madly.

"You'd better go tell her that you're alive, then," Myril said. "The rest of us are busy." She had the knife in her hand, but she wasn't sure where to begin.

"It's all right; I'll go," Gallia said.

Myril was glad to see the last of Gallia. Vigda seemed less nervous. She smelled of the mountains and a little bit of dragonfire, and she did look a bit like a much-older version of Darna.

"There was an old priestess who used to do this; we would call her in when the mother couldn't push anymore," Geta said. "I remember seeing it, but you must use the knife; my nerves are too old."

"Me?" Myril said. They were all looking at her. "Can't you, Raina?"

Raina shook her head.

"That thing will kill her," Vigda said. "I'll help. I saw it done on a goat one time, and another time they cut a woman in the village. I think I can help. You two, get clean cloths," she ordered Geta and Iola.

Iola hesitated only a moment before running to a chest at the far side of the chamber. She took the cloths and laid them on the altar beside Darna. "Let her live," she said, gazing up at the dragon's statue rearing above them.

Myril felt Geta's hand on hers, covering and guiding her grip on the knife. Iola moved around to hold Darna still, in case she should wake with the pain.

"We must move quickly," Vigda said. "Is there thread and needle?"

Iola nodded and ran to get them, then returned to hold Darna's limp hand. Myril couldn't look at her.

"Start here. Slice as neatly as you can."

Myril cut. She did not faint. She had only ever fainted at the threat of trance, and this was nothing like that. It was blood, human and grounded and falling, not ethereal, not mind-numbing. It sharpened her wits. Vigda and Geta guided her and cleaned the way as she cut through skin, muscle, so much blood and something thick and hard then finally something completely unyielding, like stiffened leather.

"What is it?" Iola said.

Geta shushed her. Blood and water poured out. Myril ignored the flicker of flame, dragonfire reaching up from inside Darna's belly, and pulled the round, hard, luminous thing into the air. Geta's hands were under hers, very steady.

"Take it to the baths," Vigda said.

Iola reached for it, but Geta was already there.

"You stay. Hold the girl still while they stitch."

Iola handed Myril a needle and thread and Raina took another one. They made stitches to close the cuts, which still bled and bled and bled.

Geta returned, looking grim.

"Is it alive, the baby?" Myril asked stupidly.

"Is Darna?" Geta asked.

Vigda felt Darna's wrist for a pulse and nodded. "She's breathing."

"Keep her that way," Geta said. "I'll go fetch the Aralel."

Myril looked up. The sun's first rays were coming through the clerestories. "I think that the Aralel is gone," she said.

§

Darna woke to the sound of Iola's voice.

"Oh," Iola was saying. "Oh, oh."

"What?" Darna managed to croak.

"You're alive!" It was Vigda. Myril and Raina crowded around her too.

"What is it?" Darna asked.

"It's an egg," Iola said. "Geta showed me."

"It's what?" Darna tried to sit up but it felt like she was ripping herself in two. The dragon scale marks on her belly burned with fresh ferocity. Someone was holding her down. "I can't get up," she said. She looked up at the beard of Anara. She'd never really thought about the way the dragon's chin dripped before, even in the statue. The real Anara was out there somewhere, all too close and getting closer.

"That's no kind of heir," Gallia said from the doorway.

"That's not for you to say," Darna gasped out. "Let me see."

"Hold still; I'm still stitching you up," Myril said. "We're almost done." Raina's hands were holding her down at the hips. She could feel the earth in them, their intimacy with the valley soil, with the growing things. They made her feel better. Iola and Vigda held her arms.

"It's a lot of blood," Raina said.

"She'll live," Geta decreed. "She'll live. I'm going to have a little nap."

"Wait 'til they hear this." Gallia again, her voice grating.

She might have been a priestess once, but this was not her mystery. Fortunately, Darna didn't have to say anything.

"They won't hear it," Iola said. She'd never been so glad to hear Iola's voice before. Also, she'd never heard Iola snarl before, not for a long time, anyway. "Don't you tell anyone. This is a mystery, our mystery. It's not for the palace."

Darna managed to smile faintly as she met Iola's gaze.

"You do what you're told," Vigda said to Gallia. "There are others of us loyal to Darnasa, even in Tiadun. We'll make sure you know it."

"It's no kind of heir," Gallia repeated. That was the last Darna heard of her.

Vigda handed a packet of salve to Raina, who plastered it over Darna's split and mended belly. Darna felt every stab and tug of Myril's needle and thread, pulling her back together into yet another new shape. Her breasts were sore. Other than that, she felt rather like herself, only very, very weak. The pain was everywhere and not just in her hip or on her skin. Still, she felt more ordinary than she had since she'd gone to Slaradun, maybe even longer than that. As Myril tied off the last of the stitches, she realized that she could wiggle her fingers again. She pushed herself up just a little, and Iola thrust a pillow under her back.

The egg was right beside her, glowing, but its glow was already fading and hardening. She reached out to touch it, but it burned her fingers. It was cooling, though.

Suddenly, she started laughing, so hard that she almost cried. "It's an egg. Well. They're always calling us hens, like Conn's Coop. Well, I laid an egg."

"It's not a hen's egg," Iola pointed out.

"No, it's not," Raina agreed. "Nothing like a hen's egg."

Then everything began to shake and they scrambled for safe cover, egg and all.

§

Chapter 16

The city gates stood open through Midwinter night so the people of the valley could come in to watch the ambassadress's return. The open gates also allowed the Defenders who'd been wandering the land in the waning year to return to the training hall in time to take part in the morning's crossings. Thorat heard them come in and take their places beside him – first Sunna, then Forlan and Ferrent. As the first birds of morning began to sing, Sovara sounded the ceremonial gong to break the silence. They bowed to Anara together, then turned to greet one another.

Sunna reported that the gates of the dragons were all more or less where they'd last been, as far as she could tell, but that the roads had been rough in the north and that the villages were less friendly than usual, which was saying something. Many roadside shrines looked neglected or even abandoned, but that was nothing new. The waters had risen most in the northwest provinces and hardly at all in the far south, in Tiadun, Kiralun, and Getedun.

"Maybe they've suffered as much as they're going to," Ferrent said. "The keep at Tiadun seems secure enough, and the village chieftains seemed glad not to have Calar and the Cereans ruling over them."

"Someone should go tell Darna," Thorat said.

Sunna nodded. "Gallia and Vigda went straight to the temple. I'll go later."

"I hope they're not too late," Eppie said, and then had to explain again that Darna seemed to be in labor. After a while, Sovara looked around the room in a way that made them all fall silent.

I'll continue my vigil here," she said. "The rest of you may go down to the harbor, if you wish."

Garren, Anot, Forlan, and Ferrent took masks from their hiding place and set off to help row the raft out to the island, to pretend to carry the ambassadress back to the shore, or whatever the priestesses were planning. Not even the Defenders knew for sure who the other masked oarsmen were. They were strange, masked figures who spoke in a language that Thorat couldn't place, no matter how many times he heard it.

Thorat didn't feel like going back to the palace, nor did he want to stay in the training hall with the shrine beneath their feet opening up to floodwaters.

"I'll walk you down to the temple, if that's where you're going," he said to Sunna.

Sunna nodded. "I should let the Aralel know that I'm back, and look in on Darna."

"She looked pretty bad last night," Eppie said.

"All the more reason to go," Sunna said. "How about the other one?"

Eppie looked at Thorat. "Iola's all right, as far as I know. She doesn't talk to me much."

At least Eppie got to see her and talk to her, Thorat thought. Maybe she would be out on the island. He knew how to get there through the secret passage. He'd only stood guard there once, and Iola hadn't seen him, but he'd been able to see her, and that had made him feel better about her going to the dragons. Even though she'd been on the surface this past season, hidden only behind a few thin marble walls instead of under the crust of the earth, she might as well have been much farther away, for all that he'd seen of her.

The three of them walked across the city together. Despite the floodwaters in the shrine, the canal hadn't risen in the night, but with every step, Thorat felt as if the ground were softening beneath his feet. Anara's island tower came into view as they crossed the Pentangle and they stopped to look at it.

"Will there be anyone on the island?" he wondered aloud.

Eppie and Sunna frowned at him. "The raft will be going out. I imagine that the Aralel and the Most Blessed One's attendants will be on it," Eppie said.

Thorat realized belatedly that there were people all around them, listening. He didn't think that he'd revealed any secrets.

"We shouldn't talk about it," Thorat said, but an idea began to form in his mind. He missed Iola. He missed her terribly. It was almost worse, knowing that she was so close. When she was with the dragons, he didn't feel such frustration. When she was under the earth, she wasn't quite human, but being on the surface for the season should have brought her closer, even if she was trapped inside the temple. He needed to see her.

He left Sunna and Eppie at the alley into the temple side house, then wandered down to see the raft at the end of the East Canal. Garren spotted him and shooed him away. The raft, which usually shone with polished wood and gilt, was dark and slick with rot, showing brush marks where the worst of the slime had been scrubbed away. It smelled as if it had been submerged all through the waning year. Perhaps it had been.

Thorat headed back toward the shore. There was not quite enough time to get out to the island, certainly not enough if the secret passage to it had been flooded, but he couldn't stand idly, knowing that there was no one there to guard the dragon's passage, or guard Iola if the Aralel brought her there.

He soon reached the hidden opening to the passage on the canal. He tucked his sandals into his belt and felt his way down the bank, hoping that there would be a place where he could slip through and that, once in, there would be air to breathe. The entrance wasn't even fully submerged. He waded into the chilly water and slipped through a crack between the rocks. He had to wade for the first stretch. Where the floor dipped to go under the harbor, the water rose, but the dragons' currents warmed the passage and the water in it, and it came only up to his knees at the deepest point.

He waded through the interminable darkness, all the way to the dragon's tower in the harbor. When he reached the opening, he paused. Sovara had said that she wouldn't go, and she'd as good as told the rest of them not to go either. She wouldn't be there to see him disobey her orders, but she wasn't one to stand aside out of fear, and he was sure that she hadn't turned her back on the dragons. Perhaps she sensed some current in the earth that Thorat had missed. More likely, though, she was only leaving the priestesses to fend for themselves, angry at the deception they were playing out. Sovara couldn't have approved of their pretense of sending the ambassadress on her way when they'd done nothing of the sort.

Ignoring the knot in his gut, Thorat opened the door and stepped onto the lower ledge inside the tower.

He immediately wished that he'd left the door closed. Where there had been water at his ankles, tongues of flame snapped at him like hungry dogs leaping up to devour dripping meat. He pushed the door closed, but the frame had already warped. It would not shut. It was too late. The passage behind him shuddered and a single stone fell with a splash into the knee-high saltwater. Another followed it. The capstones were falling like hail.

It didn't take an engineer to see that the vaulted way would crumble. A spout of water gushed in.

This was folly. He should have paid attention to the worry in his gut, or at least heard Sovara's implied warning, not to mention Sunna's. Death by water behind him – the passage was far too long to cross under water, even if it held, which looked increasingly impossible – or death by fiame on the other side of the door, but if he went into the fiames, he would have a chance of seeing Iola.

He sprang through, seizing the ledge above and scrambling for toeholds on the wall, the ones that had always been there. They were too hot, and few and far between. He fell back onto the cool, solid rock of the ledge he'd just been standing on. It was still wet from the harbor waters coming in through the door behind him. A rock fell from the tower above and he dodged it, but it landed on the ledge beside him. Though it rocked and threatened to tumble off the edge, he managed to use it to clamber up onto the ledge above.

Distracted by the roar of blood in his own veins, he'd hardly noticed how silent the fire was, though the falling stones must have made a noise. He perched on the priestesses' ledge over the gateway to the other realm, full of silent fire and lava, white-hot at its core, too bright to look at. Overhead, the sky was deep blue, despite the coming dawn. He'd forgotten how that window on the sky was indifferent to the morning light.

As soon as he turned his attention to the outside world, he heard the raft coming, the swish of the oarsmen's poles punctuating the reckless beat of the waves on the shore. The priestesses would come into the tower. They would come in to get the ambassadress, even knowing that she wasn't there.

The entrance to the tower faced out to sea, away from the town. Only the Aralel held the key to that tightly shut door. He had to warn her, had to stop her before the flames surged up. He looked down again. Perhaps a dragon could pass through that. They were creatures of fire more than of flesh. Anara might come, but if she did...

The stones shivered around him, like a man flexing his muscles before a fight. Thorat leaped over the gap left by the falling rock and reached the inside of the door just as the Aralel fitted her key to its lock.

Pain seared his back and he flew out, knocking the old woman to the ground. Beside him, a younger woman screamed. Another blast of heat and the ground beneath him bucked, throwing him into the water. Just before he lost consciousness, he thought he saw Anara rising into the sky, all flame. He joined the water, joined the fishes. He'd been born to be a fisherman, once upon a time. The light faded.

§

The morning air was ominously still. Eppie thought she heard a scream as she skirted around the east side of the temple, but she wasn't sure. The scream could have been anything, especially these days when even Ara's Landing wasn't safe from the outside world. She'd left Sunna at the side house, even though she knew that she should go see if Darna was all right, but she was no healer, and she wasn't ready to see Darna dead. After the dragon flew, she would go in. She went around the back of the temple and down through the alleys of city's southeast quarter, wading along the path by the wall until she reached the shore. She knew of a little boat hidden there that she borrowed sometimes. It was right where she'd left it last. She found a bit of wood to use as a pole and a broader piece to paddle with. She pushed it out between partly flooded buildings until she reached what had been the shore, at the near end of the old jetty. Its rocks lay mostly under water, as they had since summer, but they peeked out at low tide, reminding everyone that it was there. Anara's island still stood.

The ambassadress's raft was just setting out with a tent pitched across the stern to hide the ambassadress's condition – or absence – when they returned. Eppie wondered if Iola had managed to sneak aboard, but she didn't think that the Aralel would have allowed it, not after Midsummer. Eppie and her boat stayed in the shadow of the buildings as the raft moved out into the open water. The Aralel sat beside the tent, her embroidered robes shining richly in the thin morning light. Her veil parted just enough to show a little of her pale gray hair. Some other priestesses sat around her, young ones, Eppie guessed, but no one she recognized. Sovara said that she had warned the Aralel to stay away, but the Aralel didn't answer to her, and at least there would be someone there to greet the dragon.

It felt strange, knowing that there had always been Defenders there to mark the dragon's crossing at the ambassadress's return, and knowing now that the Enatel had turned her back on them. It was wrong. Someone should be there.

The raft had almost reached the island. The tower shone in the light of the rising sun, like a beacon of fire, brighter than it ever had been. Fragments of quartz in its stone walls like diamonds in a trick of the light, it was brighter than a reflection.

The oarsmen poled on. Eppie pushed out, hurrying to join them as fast as she could with her makeshift paddle.

The raft reached the island's shore as the sun rose. The Aralel stood, going through the tent on her way to the prow of the raft. One of the oarsmen handed her out. From where Eppie was, out on the water, she could just see a young, thin priestess shadowing the Aralel. Whoever she was, Eppie was pretty sure it wasn't Iola. The ambassadress was taller and would never scuttle along like that.

The men and women on the boat rested their oars. *Now* the sun was rising. Eppie realized belatedly that the tower had been shining from within. It had not done that before, not that she'd seen. The light hadn't been the light of the sun at all. It was the dragon's own light.

Then everything exploded. The tower blasted open, scattering rocks as big as grown men like scattered pebbles into the harbor. The earth rocked, the waves rose, and screams cried out. Then there was a pause.

For a moment, silence reigned. Eppie heard the moans of an injured man, or maybe a woman, but apart from that, there was nothing. Even the birds were silent. The waves seemed to freeze, to gather themselves. And then the tower exploded yet again, throwing molten lava into the sky, and brimstone.

Anara was made of fire and lava, shedding pieces of herself as she fiew up into the sky, raining her body down over the city. The burning rocks hissed into the canals, mostly, raising a mist so thick that it blotted out the shore.

From her little boat rocking on the wild waves, Eppie saw a few fires fiare up before the mist closed in. Anara's fire slid off the tile roofs, but here and there it found ready tinder in one of the remaining thatched roofs or on the shingled roof of a shed. Fires sparked, then smoked, and only added to the fog that had begun to hide the city from her.

"You there!" One of the always-silent oarsmen was shouting to her. It wasn't one of the Defenders. "Come help!"

Eppie poled over to them. The island was erupting, leaving no trace of the quiet place it had been moments before.

"I have her." One of the oarsmen had his arms under the shoulders of a burned and mangled body in red robes.

"She's lucky that man fell on top of her."

"Not lucky enough."

"What happened to him?"

"Thrown into the water, I think."

There'd been a man on the island? How? Eppie thought.

"I don't think she's going to make it." Another of the oarsmen was carrying a thinner, younger-looking red-robed body back to the raft.

"Put them inside the tent."

One of the oarsmen looked up at Eppie and waved her away.

"I can help," Eppie offered.

"Too late for that." It sounded like Garren's voice, and it was definitely a dismissal.

Eppie looked back as the oarsmen got the two priestesses – or what was left of them – under cover of the tent. A few of the oarsmen were bleeding too, and two seemed unable to sit up. The rest took up their oars to push the raft back to shore, far more slowly than they'd come.

Eppie turned her little rowboat back in the general direction of its hiding place. She couldn't see the shore very well except for a few slender towers rising up above the fog, but she could see the choppy shallow waters over the breakwater and follow the line of it back. It wasn't until she was looking at the mostly submerged breakwater that she noticed the body caught on a jagged bit of rock as it floated out to sea. The familiar curl of the brown hair on its head was singed and sodden. *Curse him to Na!* Eppie paddled to him. His back was burned mottled red and blackened, raw, with the white of bone showing through in one place. He was face down. Drowned? Most likely. She leaned over to reach toward him, and he moved, a reflexive jerk bringing his face up. He gasped for air and his eyes blinked open, not long enough to focus before they shut again. He was not dead. A wave rolled him over, but the rocks kept him from drifting farther away, at least for the moment. Eppie grabbed him.

She set one foot on the barely submerged breakwater and hooked the body with her paddle, then pulled it up into the boat.

"Breathe, damn you!" She wrestled him up over the half-sunken gunwale, pushing the water out of his lungs and into the bottom of the boat along with the harbor water that was gushing over the side. She got him in and righted the boat as well as she could.

She couldn't see the shore and she doubted that anyone there could see her. Out on the bay, a single merchant ship raised its sails and put out oars, making way for the open sea again as fast as its prow could push through the rising foaming waves as panicked deckhands threw water onto a fire on its deck.

Eppie thumped Thorat on an intact bit of his back. He groaned. "Good, you're not dead yet," she said, and by the incoherent noise he made, she thought that maybe he might have heard and understood her, but she wasn't sure. She needed to get him to a healer. "Probably should be dead, though. What were you thinking?" She didn't really need to ask, just wanted to keep him half-awake if he was still conscious, still listening. Maybe he wasn't, but he was breathing, so at least there was that. She hoped he'd keep breathing, but she couldn't spare him much attention. The waves were rising, making for hard paddling.

There was a wooden scoop in the boat and Eppie used it to bail out the water she'd taken on. More waves washed over the edge, threatening to swamp them again. She got enough out that she could get the boat to creep toward shore, hoping that they would get to a healer before it was too late.

§

Myril pulled out the corners of the blanket that Darna had been lying on for the birth. It was bloody and gory. Darna needed to be moved to a fresh bed, one that was better protected. She couldn't stay where she was, not with the roof shaking like that. The dome above was strong and light, like an eggshell, but maybe not strong enough.

"Take the corners," she ordered. Sunna had just arrived to lend her strength to the effort, along with Iola, Raina, and Vigda. Geta clucked and smoothed a bed for Darna in the second sleeping nook, which was under a thick arch, much stronger-looking than the dome. The nook was big enough to hold them all if they hunched together shoulder to shoulder, where they would feel each other's heartbeats and shallow, frightened breathing. As soon as the shaking stopped, Myril checked Darna's pulse.

"She's all right for now, I think," Myril said. "I have to go see what happened outside."

"I'll look out for her," Sunna promised. Vigda gave her a nod, and Geta shooed her out.

"Bring the news back to us," Iola said. She had a pleading note in her voice, as if she suddenly cared what was happening outside her chamber. She seemed to really want to know.

"I will, as soon as I can," Myril promised.

The peresi's courtyard was silent in except for the drip of water from a broken pitcher that had rolled to its side on a bench beside the fountain. A tile slid off the roof, shattering on the marble walk below. The spell of the temple, the oppressive sense of being pushed into a haze of trance, remained unbroken. She wanted to escape. She was still wearing the plain tunic of a healer, not priestess robes, but she went out through the front to join the procession back from the shore. Fog rolled up from the harbor. She could hardly see across the street, but she could hear voices coming from all directions.

"I can't see a thing!"

"Where are the priestesses?"

Someone began a chant.

Myril looked up. Above the street, the fog was thin, so thin that she could see the blue sky above and a distant spiral of smoke. A flame shot across the narrow arc of sky. Someone screamed. She stood as still as she could, closed her eyes, and trained her attention on the harbor. She heard the splash of oars, moaning, and worried whispers from the same direction. The raft was still close to the dragon's island. Myril decided not to wait, in case Anara was going to rain down fire again.

She heard and felt her way through the fog, doing her best to ignore the people around her and avoiding the occasional flashes of fire. The normally short walk took a long time, and by the time she got to the base of her street, Anara had flown. Crossing the bridge, she saw that the water had risen again, but only very slightly. She couldn't even describe how much it had risen; it was only that she had the feeling of sinking into that cold winter water, salty like the sea, the wells going bad, the water taking them all back to itself while fire came from the hills.

Myril found her doorway blocked by her downstairs neighbor and a sodden-looking person pushing a wounded man in a wheelbarrow.

"I told them they couldn't go up," her neighbor said as she approached. "Where have you been? I didn't see you in the procession."

"I was in the temple," Myril said. The sodden-looking person was Eppie, looking very tired. "Who's that?" she asked, but then she realized who it was. "Both of you, help me get him upstairs, carefully."

Thorat groaned and thrashed as they lifted him, but he didn't have any strength to shake them off. "Be still," Myril told him, and he seemed to hear her, or maybe he had only fainted again.

As soon as they got him inside and laid him on his belly, Myril's neighbor hurried away to take care of the person pounding at her door below. A glance out the window made Myril glad that she'd taken her sign down. People were already lining up at her neighbors' doors. Most of them had only small burns or bruises from where they'd run into things in the fog, but she saw one man on a stretcher, apparently with a broken leg. She glanced out of the window. The fog was lifting, but it was leaving a deep chill in its wake that seemed to come from the bones of the city itself.

"Uh, Myril?" Eppie said. "Do you think he'll live?"

"I don't know," Myril said. "Let's see."

The burns on Thorat's back looked like they'd eaten away half his skin, but he was strong and in his prime, and if the dragon had wanted to kill him outright, she was sure that he would be dead already. Slowly, as she pulled the charred and salty-wet cloth away, Eppie told her the story through chattering teeth, how Thorat had been on the island, in the tower. Through the last wisps of fog, she could see that the island now looked like a small mountain. Away in the distance, smoke rose from the larger mountains, too, as if the whole land was splitting at its seams.

"I think he was thrown into the water," Eppie said.

"Amazing he survived that," Myril mused. She turned away from her patient to find the herbs she'd want for the poultice. She fumbled a bit because she was already so tired from the night's labor, even though her body hadn't been the one split open. She hoped Darna was still breathing well, that she was still alive. She'd had the pulse of someone who would live, but Myril was too tired to know if it was real or only wishful thinking. Geta and Vigda were with her, though, and Raina, and Iola, and Sunna. She hoped that Gallia would stay out of the way.

"What are you muttering about?" Eppie asked.

"Sorry, nothing. You're shivering. Get yourself some dry clothes. There are some in the chest under the other bed."

"All right," Eppie said. She sighed. They were all tired. The Midwinter vigil was the longest, and it was looking like they wouldn't sleep that day, either.

Thorat's pulse steadied a little as the morning wore on. He didn't wake up at all. Around midday, Eppie ran out, returning a little while later with a jar of stew, courtesy of Garren's wife.

"Did you go back to the training hall?" Myril asked.

Eppie shook her head. "Garren said that the Aralel and the other priestess were wounded, but that they got back to the temple all right."

They ate, then took turns keeping watch or napping. Myril had barely fallen asleep when the bells woke her, the same bells that had rung out for the death of the governor so many years before.

"Did the governor die?" she asked as she came back to waking consciousness.

Eppie snorted. She looked exhausted. "I don't think so; it started from the temple."

"Not Iola; I was just with her. Who, then?"

Myril wracked her brain, but she was too tired to think.

"Could it be the Aralel?" Eppie said.

That had to be it. Not the Aralel. She wasn't young, but... Eppie was talking.

"They just loaded her and that other young priestess onto the raft. She looked even worse than Thorat, from where I was."

Myril held up her hand. "I'm going back to sleep," she said. "Don't wake me until they come for me. You should stay here. Change the poultice at dusk and again at dawn and get help from downstairs if you need it."

"Sure," Eppie said.

Myril closed her eyes and was asleep instantly.

It seemed that only moments passed before she heard the messenger's feet on her stair. "Lord Chronicler says to go to the temple, take down what's said."

"For who?" Myril asked.

"For the Chronicles, what else? You need more parchment? He sent parchment."

Myril took the bundle, put her sandals back on, and set out for the temple again, leaving Eppie to care for Thorat. The girl had nursed him through an injury in the wilderness; she could manage this one with a fully stocked apothecary on hand, even if it was worse. It was going to be another long night for everyone, and the city was sinking.

§

Chapter 17

Mist gathered in patches along the street and in the alleys, making dense clouds here and there. The ground did not move perceptibly under Myril's feet, but she didn't trust it to stay where it was. There were plenty of people on the streets, but there was an eerie quiet as they spoke in whispers, if at all. The loudest sounds she heard were water bubbling, air blowing, and the distant bubble of lava at the place in the harbor where Anara's tower had stood.

To judge by the smell of the air, any fires that Anara had lit that morning had been put out, and the damp would suppress any but the worst of them. A gentle, ordinary winter rain began to fall, and Myril hurried the rest of the way despite her reluctance to go back to the temple. The silence of the streets felt ominous.

The Grandmother was not in her chair at the side house. Instead, she was standing, leaning on her cane. She pointed it at Myril. "You there! Hurry!"

"Where to?" Myril asked. If someone had died, she would have to go to the sanctuary, though her first thought was for Darna stitched up like a broken bag in the fragile shelter of Iola's quarters.

"The infirmary, you dolt." The Grandmother sat back down in her chair with a thud and a cloud of dust.

"Of course," Myril said, hoping that she sounded as confused as she felt. The Aralel was already dead, wasn't she? If not, why would they have rung the bells? She changed into the only dry robes she could find in the upper room and hurried back out, keeping to the covered walkways as the rain intensified.

The elders' courtyard was nearly deserted. She could hear some of the elders and refugee priestesses in the sanctuary, not praying yet but only conferring in whispers.

"She can't go; she hadn't named a successor."

"Most of the old ambassadresses are older than Nalani was, and they're all in the hills except –"

"It'll need a young woman."

"There's no one who can replace her!"

"They're all in the hills, hermits."

Myril blocked out the chatter as well as she could and paused to train her attention on the ambassadress's quarters. It was quiet there except for a whispered exchange between familiar-sounding voices, probably Rania and Sunna, Darna's shallow but steady breath, and the sound of slippered feet, pacing. They didn't need her there, not right away.

At the infirmary, she found Geta waiting for her. "How's Darna?" Myril asked.

"Sleeping, no fever yet," Geta reported. She looked even older than usual.

"You should rest," Myril said to her.

"No need for rest at my age," Geta grumbled. "We shouldn't have let her go." Geta led Myril on into the infirmary before she could ask who Geta was talking about. "I don't know if she'll live," Geta was saying.

"The Aralel?"

Geta shook her head. "Gone already. You heard the bells. Come see for yourself."

A crowd stood around one cot at the corner. If Myril hadn't overheard some of the whispers, she would never have recognized the young priestess from Getedun, the one who'd barely survived when Calar's Cerean followers had raped her and left her for dead.

"She was only beginning to be better, to want to live again," Geta said. "She wanted to see Anara up close. The Aralel, someone has to take poor Nalani's place, but now..."

Myril turned away, another question worrying her. "Will they say that the ambassadress died?" she whispered.

Geta shook her head. "Iola has to live. She might have to become the Aralel."

A cold shiver ran over Myril's arms and shoulders. "Not Iola. Surely there must be someone else, someone who knows something of the human world."

"The others have all left the temple, this temple at least. There can't be much more than a dozen of them. Now mind this girl and I'll go find Sunna to see about taking poor old Nalani to the hills."

Thorat must have been closer to the flames, but the young woman before her was smaller, thinner, and half of her skin was gone, not only on her back. "I can't." Myril whispered it to herself, but they all turned to listen. "I can't do anything for her. I'm sorry. Even if I'd come earlier, I don't think I could have."

"If only she'd been stronger, if we'd been stronger and told her not to go," someone said quietly.

"There are worse deaths," Myril said, as if it made any difference. "She could have gone not knowing if any of it was real, abandoned in Getedun."

Geta hadn't left yet. She made a noise which sounded like the beginning of a chuckle but turned quickly into a wracking cough.

"Sit," Myril said. "You need rest. I'll help you back to your room."

As she took the elder's arm, the young priestess breathed her last, rattling breath. A sonorous chant rose up to ease her soul's passing as Myril and Geta left the infirmary. The sound of the chant filled the temple, filled all the space it could in the world.

The chanting went on through the rest of the day, both for the young priestess and for the Aralel. It went on through the washing, the mending, and all the funeral preparations. The elders gathered to wrap the Aralel's body in a shroud, chant prayers, and stand guard, then everyone went down to the sanctuary at dusk. *So many vigils,* Myril thought, *and so few to keep them.* The young priestess from Getedun was wrapped in her shroud and lay beside the Aralel. Priestesses took turns dozing on mats at the back of the sanctuary as they took turns keeping the songs and chants and prayers in the air.

Myril wondered how many others knew about the secret hiding box in the Aralel's chamber, and if it would still be safe. She would have to tell the new Aralel about it, if there was a new Aralel.

Toward dawn, she slipped away to see Iola and Darna. Both were sleeping, with Vigda keeping watch and insisting, like Geta, that she didn't need to sleep. Raina was in the baths, washing out some linens.

"Do you think she's going to live?" Sunna asked as she came in from the garden.

Myril checked Darna's pulse. It was steady. "If she doesn't take a bad fever, she should be all right," she said eventually.

"Well, we'll have to make sure she doesn't," Vigda said.

"Where's Gallia?" Myril asked.

"Gone back to Tiadun," Vigda said. "I hope she stops to kill Calar on the way. If she doesn't, the pleasure will be mine, but I'd rather not go down into those lowlands again."

"This is the lowest of lowlands, though, isn't it?" Sunna said.

"And getting lower," Myril agreed.

Vigda sighed and patted Darna's hand. "I'll go back to the hills with the Aralel. You two, keep this one safe."

"We will," Myril promised. "As much as anyone can." She took Vigda's place at Darna's bedside for a little while, leaned against the wall, and slept.

§

Eppie was barely awake when Myril staggered back home the next morning. She'd dozed on and off through the night, waking from time to time to see that Thorat was still breathing, then sleeping again. Outside, the street grew quiet apart from occasional cries from some injured person who'd been prodded too hard by a healer. Eppie stayed wrapped up in blankets, waiting but only barely listening. When she did listen, she heard fire and the eruption of Anara's island. The image of the dragon exploding out of the tower, breaking her land, filled her vision every time she closed her eyes.

Myril checked Thorat briefly and fell onto the other bed, dismissing Eppie with a brief message for the Enatel, relaying what had happened at the temple. "Come back later if you can," she said. The Enatel had said that she and Thorat should go to look in on the dragons' gates in Coradun and Lemirun. There was no way that Thorat would be able to go, not any time soon, so she would have to go to both places. She wondered if the Enatel would even still be at the training hall, or if she would have gone to the hills already.

Mist rolled down the streets like smoke and ashes from the volcano fell down like snowflakes. Everything was still except for the sound of waves rolling up the harbor shore, up into the city streets, and gulls crying as they circled over the mist. Someone chimed a bell at a street-corner shrine. The ground felt uneasy beneath Eppie's feet, but unlike the morning before, she couldn't detect any movement in it.

Most buildings still stood as they had been, but one she passed on a corner at the top of the hill leaned precariously out into the square, its boards shaking loose in the chilly wind.

She hurried through the passage into the hidden courtyard. As she emerged on the other side, she felt relief washing over her like a warm bath. The passage held. She didn't realize that she'd been worried about it until she got through it. That must be a sign of hope. Anara hadn't destroyed the Defenders, not yet. She ran up the stairs and into the not-quite-silent hall.

The familiar smell of old sweat hung about the place, underlying the cold smell of too much incense from the vigil two nights before. A smaller, fresh handful of incense burned on top of its pile of ashes. Sovara knelt in front of the altar with her eyes closed and hands folded on her lap.

"Where have you been?" she asked Eppie.

"Tending Thorat."

Sovara nodded slightly. "Garren saw him out there and thought that he'd died. You brought him in to the shore?"

Eppie nodded. "I didn't know what to do, so I took him to Myril's place."

"She's a good healer. I was worried that he'd died too, but I didn't sense his absence, so I had hope."

"I'm sorry I didn't send word earlier." Eppie's stomach had grumbled at the mention of Garren, and she wished she'd gone by his place first.

"Garren should be here soon," Sovara said, as if reading her thoughts. "You young ones will be hungry." She took a deep breath, bowed her head toward the altar, then cracked her neck and rose to her feet. Resting her hands on her hips, she looked at Eppie.

"Come," she said. "Let's go outside and see what we can of the city before I go to see Nalani off."

Sovara led the way out onto the balcony, but instead of going down, she turned around and hoisted herself up onto the roof, muttering about being too old for climbing as she scaled the tiles.

Eppie had climbed many roofs in her scrappling days, but it had never occurred to her to climb this one, not even with the railing so close to the edge. She wondered that Sovara tried it at all, old and frail as she looked, but she was almost at the ridge already before Eppie scrambled up after her.

"A few years before you came along, we had to come up here and replace some tiles," Sovara said casually. She surveyed her old handiwork. "They seem to have held. Ink Pounders is sinking."

She pointed down to the bank of the East Canal, which had gotten considerably wider since Midwinter Eve.

"It shouldn't even be near high tide now," Eppie said as she looked down. The walls of the tavern showed a high-water mark higher than the windowsills. The taproom must be completely flooded. The thatch roof was burned at one corner, revealing part of the low-lying tavern's upper story, its bright tapestries now dulled by smoke and fire. Someone was there, cutting down the drapes and bundling them, looking furtively over his shoulder. The building was said to have been there from the time of the first settlers in Anamat, and followed the older style.

Next, they looked toward the palace, another place they couldn't see from the stair landing. Its gate lay askew on its hinges, but other than that, it seemed to have escaped the crossing time unscathed. "I wonder what foreign charms kept them safe," Sovara mused.

Finally, they both looked down toward the harbor. Where Anara's Island had been, a cone of lava grew. It was still smoking, still growing, still on fire.

Far away at the borders of the valley, some of the mountains were on fire too. The winter fields around the villages were half-flooded, and it looked as if people were erecting makeshift boat frames in their gardens.

Sovara looked at it all with a wry expression, then she smiled. "The dragons won't go quietly," she said. "They won't go quietly at all."

§

Iola told her, later, that Darna had woken up just long enough to say goodbye to her bandit mother before the Aralel's funeral procession set out for Na's Eye. They left Raina keeping watch, and Iola went up to the tower in a futile and foolish search for Anara, while Myril went to change Thorat's bandages. Sunna told them all about her walk around the rest of Theranis, how in the waning year, things had seemed not too different from before except for the rising waters along the coast in the northern provinces and the hostility of the villages.

For most of the moon-round, Myril trudged back and forth between the temple and her room, tending Thorat's wounds and Darna's. She scarcely had time to visit her old guild hall, and no more messengers came from it. The waters did not breach the temple walls except to fill the baths beneath the gardens, not to mention the laundries and half of the treasuries. No one knew what had happened to the mysterious launderers. They'd disappeared, as if they'd risen with the smoke, leaving nothing behind except for a few baskets floating on the tide and a vat of soap by the temple gates, as if to tell the priestesses to wash their own linens, which they did but not very well. Whether the launderers went to the hills or took to the sea, Myril never knew.

The harbor was quiet. It usually was, just after Midwinter. It took the fleets some time to reach Anamat from foreign shores, especially when the weather was as unpredictable as it was that year. They might have hung back, too, wary of the rising smoke. Still, some boats went out. Fishing boats made for a single day's sail went over the horizon, bound to the four quarters of the sea and all the ends of the earth.

There was a semblance of normal life on the streets of Anamat, but people were leaving when they would normally have been arriving to prepare for the trading season. People had left the city before, of course, even priestesses, who went to the hills. Those included some of the old ambassadresses, who were being summoned back for the choosing of the new Aralel.

Thorat lay on his front for most of a quarter-moon, and by the half-moon, he was ready to go back to his training hall, though not well enough to travel. He came back to Myril's place every day for a fresh slathering of salve. His back still looked red, but he could move and he was regaining his strength.

Darna was getting better too, though not as quickly. Her Midwinter had been a long night of labor and she had bled a great deal. She fell into fever at the new moon, but after a few days, the fever broke, leaving her only slightly weaker. She was restless, but she was still too tired to walk farther than the bounds of the ambassadress's garden. Sometimes, she stood in the middle of the chamber for a long while, staring at the egg in its corner. It was smooth, cold, and hard like marble. Only Darna dared to touch it, but it remained inert. On other days, she avoided looking at it at all, as if she could wish its existence away. No one really considered moving it elsewhere.

A full moon-round after Midwinter, a message came from the Chronicler, telling Myril to go record what happened at the choosing of the new Aralel. She didn't want to go, but she had to look in on Darna and Iola and the streets weren't much worse. They were undeniably wetter, though.

If anything, the closed-in feeling of the temple had grown worse. They'd barred the gates to petitioners because there was no Aralel, and the priestesses' pent-up energy threatened to explode in an imitation of Anara's tower, spewing forth frightened, desperate women instead of lava. Myril went to the ambassadress's quarters first, where she found Iola sitting in her sleeping nook, jabbing a needle into a piece of embroidery and staring sullenly at the egg, which was as big as a tea urn. Darna was sleeping. She'd had another fever but a mild one that had passed quickly. Her forehead was cool again and Myril didn't want to disturb her.

"Shouldn't you be at the sanctuary?" Myril asked Iola. "I have to go for the Chroniclers, to record what's said."

"I don't have to go," Iola said.

"All of the old ambassadresses must be there; you told me that yourself only yesterday. The rest of them have come in from the hills and the provinces."

"I'm not an ambassadress anymore. I've ended it. I didn't do what I needed to do. Being the ambassadress means nothing now, is nothing. I'm nothing."

"You've been under the earth more times than any of them, and more recently. They've walked days to get here. You only need to walk across the peresi's courtyard. You don't even have to leave the temple," Myril said. She didn't want to go either, and it should not have been her task to persuade Iola, who was not being reasonable. No one should have had to tell Iola that she needed to go.

"I'd go, if I were strong enough," Darna said from her sickbed. "You go for me. Tell me what happens."

To Myril's surprise, Iola relented. "All right, then," she said. "But only if you help me to look my station."

"The Most Blessed One?" Darna said, getting up with a groan.

Iola jutted her chin out, making her neck look even longer than usual. She looked strong and supple, as if she still had some of the dragons' powers. "No," she said. "I'm just an ordinary priestess."

There was nothing ordinary about her, Myril thought, but surely Iola knew that.

"I'll see what I can do," Darna said.

A little while later, Myril led Iola out of her quarters for the first time in over half a year. She was dressed in plain fashion, for the ambassadress, but there was no making her look like an ordinary priestess, much less an ordinary woman. She was still on fire with the beauty of the winged ones. It was as if she shared her pulse with the fire that was threatening to consume the city. Myril didn't touch her for fear of being burned.

Myril took Iola around the long way so that she could see the changes in the front courtyard. The water had come all the way up the processional way at the last high tide, leaving a line of washed-up seaweed just outside the gates. Two palace guardsmen stood outside the locked gates, looking bored.

Neither of the guards was Thorat. Myril wondered if he would go back to work at the palace or just stay in his sword hall, convalescing. He was healed enough to wear a loose tunic over his still-bandaged back and to walk a short distance without reopening his wounds, but not yet well enough to wield a sword.

"Where's Thorat?" Iola asked. "I thought he would come see me."

"You're not taking petitioners again, are you?"

Iola shuddered. "No, never again, only as a – as a friend."

"Or as a lover?" Myril said.

"I don't know," Iola said. "I don't know if I can." She looked out through the gates. "I'll have to leave the temple."

"You don't have to go today," Myril assured her.

Outside the gates, a man with a handcart was shouting at a scrappling running just fast enough to evade pursuit. Myril couldn't tell if it was a boy or a girl scrappling, not with the temple air like wads of wool in her ears.

It had taken a full moon-round to bring all of the old ambassadresses back to Anamat, but they were all there, a dozen of them, mostly old and clad in moth-eaten furs. They were an incongruous sight in the middle of the temple sanctuary with its polished floors and golden lamps, its silken tapestries and its perfect proportions. They looked as if they belonged more to Na's peaks more than to the silk-draped opulence of the ambassadress's chamber.

At the threshold of the sanctuary, Iola paused to take in the scene before her. She reached out to squeeze Myril's hand, her grasp too quick to evade. It burned Myril only a little.

"Thank you," Iola said. "I do need to be here." She set out to join the others at their round council table on the dais at the far end of the hall. A path opened up before her as she went across the crowded sanctuary, everyone spellbound by the grace of her movements. The last journey had aged her, but now, a year later, she looked like a younger woman again – at least, younger than the other old ambassadresses.

Their fellow priestesses, young and old, stared at Iola and whispered to one another.

"How did she survive?"

"She looks well."

"I heard that she didn't fly."

"No, that's impossible."

"She must have."

Myril tried to block out the sounds of speculation. Even in the temple, it seemed that most priestesses didn't know that Iola had stayed on the surface through the waning year.

She didn't know most of the women at the council table, but one of them was the Grandmother from the side house. She also recognized two elders who had visited from temples around the valley, and Jasela, who had been ambassadress before Iola. Jasela had left the temple looking like an old woman, but she'd been young enough to recover from her journeys. The rest of the white- and gray-haired old ambassadresses were strangers to her.

She shivered at the thought of any of them taking Nalani's place as Aralel, but the temple could not go on much longer without a leader. Since Anara's island had exploded, the ever-present tension between the peresi and the treasurers had built up to a fever pitch, cold glares turning into theft and accusations of worse. It was far more than the disorganized elders could diffuse. Iola wouldn't be much use at soothing those nerves, either. Understanding other women, even if they were priestesses, had never been her strength, and she was not very persuasive except with the dragons and with those who yearned to touch her flesh.

Myril shook away that thought. There was nothing there for her, she told herself sternly. Beyond the circular council table, Taira the temple librarian sat at a long table before a supply of ink, parchment, and sharpened styluses. She waved Myril over to sit beside her. There was no need to explain herself or to stand among the visitors milling quietly around, waiting for the whispered council to begin.

Iola approached the table, facing the combined gazes of those who had gone before her into the living heart of the earth, the heart which was now breaking open.

The Grandmother, who was one of the eldest among them, greeted her with an order.

"As you are the last to have journeyed beyond our realm, you will begin the invocation."

The cords of Iola's neck stood out for a moment as she gasped anxiously, looking for a moment like a hare caught in the path of a fox. Then the moment passed and she nodded. Iola did know how to chant an invocation. She stood shoulder to shoulder with the only people in the world who could hope to understand her, facing her fellow priestesses. For the first time, Myril wished that she had flown to the dragons' realm, but, like having Iola for a lover again, that was not a fate she could choose, even if it might have been possible once.

"Open yourselves, o winged ones. Open your hearts and your eyes to our council. Come, Anara, with your wings of crimson and gold, come, Galara and Getera, come, Tiada –" Her voice caught there, but she carried on. "Tiada, hear us if you can, and Kirala and Helana and Salara, wherever you may be. Come, Narama, Seigana, Tegana and Onara, Corala and Lemira and the great one of the hills, Na, who sends us fire. Hear us and guide our council."

She bowed her head. All of the women at the table hummed together, a tune Myril was sure she'd never heard before. Only the ambassadresses knew it. Every breath in the rest of the room stilled to listen. It was a song of the dragons, a song for this occasion only. It would never be sung again, not like this.

As the last note fioated free, riding on the wind to whatever ears the dragons had for them, the former ambassadresses looked at one another, assessing, waiting for someone to speak. Again, the Grandmother took the lead.

"After I came back to the surface of the earth, I stayed a little while in a provincial temple, where no one knew me. Then I went to the hills until last year, when Nalani called me back to watch at the side house. I know little of the city."

Each of them spoke in turn, most telling a story that was much the same at the beginning, a journey to a provincial temple, then into hermitage in the hills. Some had left their hermitages and lived a time as farm wives. None had borne children.

Finally, they came to Jasela. She looked much better than she had eight years before, when Anara had spat her up from the other realm, wrinkled and emaciated, drained almost to nothing. There were gray strands in her hair and she had circles under her eyes, but her skin was mostly smooth and her wrists looked strong as she worried her fingers together. "I fiew to the dragon's realm only twice, before the last and greatest of the Most Blessed Ones lay on that altar."

Iola stiffened but she did not interrupt.

"Eight years have passed since then, and though I have not lived as long in the outer world as many of you, I have seen more of it. I went first to Naramun, where I served as an elder in a small temple by the sea. From there, a seafaring man persuaded me to go with him, and since then, I have seen the city of Calandria, Ganat, and the wild lands to the north, where sacred bears roam. I am no longer a creature of the dragons."

Iola shook her head. "You –" she began, but the Grandmother gave her a warning look.

They all turned to Iola expectantly. "I have flown with the dragons seven times," Iola said, "but this last time, I did not fly. I am no longer ambassadress. There is none and will never be again. I have walked from the ambassadress's quarters to this sanctuary, and gone out to the harbor island. I have not ventured beyond that except for a few council meetings at the palace, which the Aralel made me attend." She looked down at her hands. She wore the expression of a young girl embarrassed by her own ignorance.

There was a long silence again, so long that some of the younger priestesses began to whisper among themselves. Myril and Taira scratched their notes as quickly as they could, recording the histories of the former ambassadresses.

"Who among us will take Nalani's place?" the Grandmother said at last.

All of them seemed to lean back from the table, but some of the old fur-clad hermit priestesses turned to look at Iola and Jasela. After a while, they spoke.

"I know nothing of the world beyond these walls," Iola said.

"And I know nothing of the temple, or of the dragons," Jasela said.

"That's not true." Iola said.

"Neither is what you said," Jasela countered.

"I only know what petitioners tell me, and that's worse than useless most of the time," Iola said. No one disagreed with that.

"You both have the strength of body to lead us," said one of the older former ambassadresses. "None of the rest of us do."

"Neither of them has the wisdom," said another.

"Good, then you take the Aralel's robes," said one of the more ragged hermits.

"I will not. I am old and dislike my fellow priestesses."

Another silence. They all looked at each other. It seemed that none of them liked their fellow priestesses.

"You must at least have some sympathy for them," Jasela protested. "I can have sympathy for the veiled women of Calandria, and the hidden ones of Cerea who are like cattle to their men. You must be able to at least understand our sisters' fears."

The Grandmother stood. She looked around the circle, as if silently questioning each of them in turn. Each of them nodded.

"Jasela," she said, speaking with a voice that belonged to all of them. "We name you Aralel, heir of Ara, who will lead the priestesses of Theranis in these dying days."

"But –" Jasela said.

"You will lead the prayer and we will all join in."

"I don't think I remember it," Jasela said quietly.

"Of course you do," Iola whispered to her. She squeezed Jasela's hand, and Jasela nodded.

Her voice was not as strong as Nalani's had been, nor was it as clear as Iola's, but she had seen the world, and that outer world meant more to the priestesses now than the dragons ever would again. If anyone could lead them beyond Theranis's doomed shores, she would be the one.

Iola looked as relieved as Myril felt. The priestesses of the temple, young and old, seemed to exhale together. Perhaps they would survive as individuals, if not as a community. If anyone could help them, it would be this one of their own who had gone beyond, who had crossed the night-dark seas. Wherever her travels had taken her, she was a priestess first, a priestess always. Weren't they all?

The temple gates remained closed that night as priestesses conferred with the new Aralel, but they would open again at dawn. After a time, each of them slept, retreating into the private world of dreams, or at least some of them did. Myril never slept well in the temple, and especially not in the ambassadress's quarters, where she went to stay with Darna while the former ambassadresses kept vigil in the sanctuary.

At dawn, they sounded the gong to announce that the new Aralel had been chosen. The treasurers opened the front gates to petitioners for the first time since Midwinter morning, and a messenger ran to the palace to carry the news to the governor. Myril escaped the temple, longing for the comfort of her own room.

§

Chapter 18

Even before she got home, Myril realized that she would not be able to rest so easily. The water had risen again and the streets were unsettled. Oars splashed on what had once been streets, and people were whispering of saltwater in the wells. There was another foreign ship on the horizon. Myril blocked out as much as she could and sat down to copy her record from the night before, but she was too tired to copy neatly, and she had a growing feeling that she needed to speak with the new Aralel as soon as possible.

She walked back to the temple. At least, her walk along the ordinary streets had cleared her head some. She discovered that Tiagasa had gotten there before her again. She must have woken up early and come as soon as the messenger announced that the gates were open. Her complaints sounded all the way to the attic of the side house, and they got louder as Myril approached the Aralel's study.

"You should have brought us in for the council. The old Aralel would have asked our advice before naming a successor."

"Begging your pardon, mistress of our Governor, but you might have come yourself, as an ordinary priestess, and I *did* know my predecessor. She was the Aralel before I became

295

ambassadress. As you know, only one who has flown with the dragons can lead the priestesses of Theranis. I was chosen. You would not have been considered or consulted."

"She would not have chosen you."

"Possibly not," Jasela said, "but the others did."

"We can refuse to recognize you. We can recall our guards from your gates," Tiagasa said.

Myril reached the Aralel's porch, and this time, Tiagasa's attendant knew that she should warn her mistress. She darted to the door. "Your Ladyship. That priestess who was here before has come. You asked me to tell you if she came."

"I have nothing to say that she isn't welcome to hear," Tiagasa said. "Think on it," she told the new Aralel. "I take my leave."

"I have not given you permission," Jasela said.

"Then give it now."

"You would not have survived the journey to the other realm," Jasela said. "You know that. Now go."

Tiagasa left, knocking over a stool and leaving it where it fell. She did not spare Myril a glance, but she did stop at the doorway to give Jasela a parting word.

"One half-moon. You have one half-moon to meet my terms, and then the guards go, and whoever likes can come into your sacred court." She spoke slowly, as if it pained her to have to explain things. She'd worn old robes again to show her disrespect for the new Aralel, but they were still fine robes, cut to make her look taller and handsomer than she was. Tiagasa's once-pretty face had hardened into a deep scowl. She probably didn't mind as long as she held the reins of power in her hands.

"Come in," Jasela said.

Myril turned away from the sight of Tiagasa parading through the elders' garden as if she were the most important person there. The Aralel's study felt dusty after its moon-round of disuse, and strange without the old Aralel in it.

"Greetings, Your Holiness," Myril said, making her obeisance.

"I trust you do not come in enmity?" Jasela said.

"Not at all. I come to share some things which the old Aralel entrusted to me, and tell you some other things which may be of use."

Jasela smiled. "Good," she said. "I am pleased to invite you to try some the wine she left. It is quite good, but you must pour."

"Of course," Myril said. It was too early to drink, but as she hadn't really slept, she didn't mind.

"I think I do remember you," Jasela said, leaning back as if trying to get comfortable in her new seat. "You are a friend to the ambassadress Iola, and you were briefly among my attendants after that last journey. Now you wear a guild's robes. You've left the temple?"

Myril nodded. "As soon as the old Aralel let me go, after my first season here, I was gone. I went too deeply into trance."

"That's a rare fault these days," Jasela commented. "No one trances much any more."

"It's dangerous," Myril said, "and it *is* a fault, even if ordinary trance is a rare gift. I can't do the work of a priestess, so I became a Chronicler and a healer. The most I'll predict is the health of a farmer's crops, and that's more reading the skies than trance divination."

"Interesting. Now tell me what you came to say. I won't have long to listen."

Myril told her about Lerat first, how she'd sent Lenasa with him to find what sanctuary they could for the priestesses.

"The wilds beyond Ganat are cold, but it's not a bad place in other ways," Jasela said, consideringly. "I've heard of Lerat. He's said to be a good man and quite infiuential. You must send him to me when he returns."

"I will," Myril promised.

A treasurer appeared at the door just then. "We need to give you an accounting. Nalani would want that," she said. She did not make the proper obeisance to the new Aralel, but Jasela made no comment on the snub. She was better at managing that kind of thing than Iola would have been, at least.

"Thank you, Myril. You may go," Jasela said.

Myril bowed. "I will return when I have further news, Your Holiness."

"I hope it comes soon. Those ships will reach port by evening, if I'm not mistaken."

"What ships?" Myril said. She'd heard more boats than usual, but she'd been too tired and preoccupied to pay much attention to them, and the path to and from the side house didn't give her a clear view of the harbor, much less the sea beyond.

Jasela sighed and motioned for the treasurer to wait, then drew Myril back into the inner chamber. "Iola and I went to the tower at dawn to see if the dragons would bless us. We saw no sign of Anara except for her volcano, there in the harbor, but what we did see were the ships. There are a dozen or more of them on the horizon. If the winds hold, they'll be here by sundown. My eyes aren't very sharp, but I thought that I saw a glint of gold. Only the Cerean king has a gold-prowed ship. His emissary must be returning."

"Girizit?" Myril said. "He's still here. He's been with Tiagasa at the palace all through the waning year."

Jasela clenched her eyes shut. "I wish I'd known that. I would have told her more firmly to mind her own house." She let out a frustrated huff. "Well, thank you for telling me that. You must keep me informed if you learn anything more of interest, and especially if you have word from your merchant friend. We won't have long."

"I will," Myril said.

The treasurer pushed her way in, carrying a thick ledger book and wearing what appeared to be her best robes. At least she did not plan to disrespect the new Aralel. Myril listened to the first words of their conversation as she walked away, and noticed that Jasela did not offer the treasurer wine. Myril hadn't had time to tell the new Aralelabout the hidden box and she wasn't sure how far she trusted her. She would have to come back to tell her, or else to take the box's contents away for safekeeping.

She wasn't sure what the Chronicler was doing now, either, but she did have a record of the night's proceedings to deliver, so she made her way across the side canal.

The Chroniclers' guild hall sat on a hillock that had kept it clear of the rising waters after Midsummer. That morning, it looked as if the damp had finally begun to creep into the almost-empty hall.

"Is anyone here?" Myril called as she came in.

An apprentice carrying a lumpy sack was the lone occupant of the main hall. He was splashing through puddles, apparently engaged in an effort to move things higher up. The shelves along the wall looked crooked, and half of their usual contents were missing.

He peered at her for a moment before he smiled. He recognized her. "You're Darna's friend, aren't you?" he said.

Myril nodded.

"Kinner, from Slaradun," he said, introducing himself again. Myril knew that she'd seen him almost every day that Midsummer, when Darna was at the palace, but he'd grown a little beard since then and looked really rather different. She was so sleepy. She should have recognized him.

"Eppie told me you'd been helping the regent, there in the temple, but..." Kinner looked worriedly over his shoulder. "Have you seen her lately, or Eppie?"

"I saw Darna this morning, but I haven't seen Eppie since just after Midwinter," Myril said.

"She said that she was going somewhere at the first quarter-moon, but that she'd be back soon. I just thought maybe you'd heard something."

Myril shook her head. She'd heard nothing. "I think she must still be outside the valley, but I'm sure she'll find her way back."

"And how is Darna?" he asked quietly.

"Recovering," Myril said. "She was sick for a while."

"Did she have a baby?"

Myril shook her head, not wanting to speak about that. "I came to see the guildmaster," she said. "He'll want the news from the temple."

"Oh, of course," Kinner said. "Do you want me to show you in?"

"That's all right; I know the way," Myril assured him. Kinner still seemed rather nervous, but he wasn't as jumpy as he'd been when she'd first seen him, back before the fall of Slaradun.

"I'll just run ahead and tell him you're here," Kinner said. He deposited his scrolls on the table and sprinted ahead of her, up the stair. Myril listened after him. The guildmaster was in an upstairs room. Perhaps he'd moved there to escape the rising water, but then she heard his heavier, slower footsteps following Kinner back down to his customary study.

The study itself was still mostly dry. The Chronicler was just sitting down when Myril arrived.

"You bring news?" he said. "Come, warm your feet. I have a brazier and dry slippers, though they may be too large for you."

"Thank you, I think I'm all right," Myril said. "The water isn't too cold today, though it is higher." She hesitated, trying to pinpoint what it was that made the room feel so different from the last time she'd been there. It wasn't only that so many of her fellow Chroniclers were gone. She noticed a new stool by the shelves just inside the window, and a crate made of freshly-split pine on the desk, about half full. The Chronicler smelled faintly of horses. Myril walked over to the desk and looked into the crate. The scrolls in it were old and included some of the ones she'd seen on the study's shelves in the past.

"Where are you taking these?" she asked.

"To a place that I know will be safe for now," the Chronicler said.

"I don't think they should go to the palace," Myril said. She wasn't sure that he'd meant the palace, but it was on the highest ground in the city. Raiding foreign merchants or none, the threat of the rising water became more urgent every day.

"They're not in Parnet's hands, or with the Cereans," the Chronicler assured her.

"The Ganateans are no better."

"Please, trust me."

"We had an arrangement to take them to a safe place. Did you stop sending them there?"

The Chronicler nodded. "The man who was receiving them from us has gone away," he said. "I didn't wish to leave them with anyone else. That mysterious order may have failed us, but if we scatter the texts to the winds, then perhaps some of them will survive."

"I can understand that, I suppose," Myril said.

"Even in the palace, some places are mysterious to the governor and his mistress. But I have no interest in the palace today. Tell me instead about the temple."

Myril handed the Chronicler what she'd written the night before. "I didn't have time to stitch them together."

"Or to copy them?"

Myril shook her head. "I went to speak with the new Aralel instead. I remember her from when I was an apprentice. She was ambassadress then, before Iola. You might be interested to know that Iola no longer considers herself ambassadress."

"She will not pretend to fiy at Midsummer again?"

"Even many of the priestesses in the temple believed that she did fiy, this past season, until she announced last night that she hadn't." Myril wasn't sure whether or not she was surprised that the Chronicler seemed to know more than some priestesses did. He had been on very friendly terms with the old Aralel.

"The more fools they are, then," he said. "I would have hoped that the dragons' ladies would be more perceptive."

"Maybe they were clinging to the hope that their world will go on," Myril said. "I can't blame them. As for whether she'll make a show of fiying again, I don't know. Maybe none of us will live to see Midsummer. It will be up to the new Aralel to decide if anyone tries to fiy, but I don't think it will come to that."

"Hmm. What wisdom does this new Aralel bring?" the Chronicler asked. "I can't think of that office without thinking of Nalani, even though I knew her before anyone ever thought she would be Ara's heir. Once, she was just a common scrappling."

"So was Jasela, I think," Myril said. "She says that she's traveled beyond Theranis since she left the temple."

"Really? That surprises me. I wouldn't have thought that a priestess would choose to surround herself with foreigners."

"We don't have much choice about it anymore," Myril said. "Just look at the water, the fire in the mountains. It hasn't slowed. The earth is unsteady, and now the new Aralel says that from the dragon towers she's seen –"

"Dragons?" the Chronicler asked hopefully.

"No, only their molten fire. Jasela and Iola went up to the tower at dawn today. There are masts on the horizon, Cerean ships, she thinks. They could reach us before the day is out."

The Chronicler pushed himself up from his desk. "How did I not hear of this already? Surely, they're close enough for anyone to see now."

"Has anyone come and gone from the hall today?" Myril asked.

The Chronicler shook his head. "They all went to the palace to wait for news of the new Aralel, and they haven't returned. Tiagasa is in fits that she and the governor weren't consulted about the choice."

"She said so, and she's not pleased about it being Jasela, either. She's granted the new Aralel a half moon-round until the governor takes his guardsmen from the temple gates and lets the foreigners run amok, unless Jasela lets Tiagasa lead her." When Myril closed her eyes, livid images crossed her vision, images of a flood of mud and fire and boots desecrating the temple yard, plundering its chambers.

"Myril."

She looked up.

"Worrying won't help. Besides, I don't believe that Tiagasa would tell the guards to leave the temple open, not while she has any chance of claiming its treasures for herself."

"There is that," Myril said. "Still, Jasela and Tiagasa were never on good terms. Tiagasa was one of her attendants after she came back from the heart of the earth. As Jasela recovered, she started to test her attendants. Tiagasa didn't do well."

The Chronicler shook his head. "Anyone is a fool to want to be ambassadress, especially someone like Tiagasa. She's much better suited to her current position, leading the governor and the Cerean merchant around by their penises."

Myril stammered. The Chronicler was not usually someone who spoke so crudely, even about people he didn't like.

"You think she doesn't?" he asked, eyes twinkling.

"The governor, she does," Myril said, "but I don't think the Cerean is taken in by her charms. She seems more smitten with him than he is with her."

"Interesting," the Chronicler said. He picked up the sheaf of paper and looked over what Myril had written.

"She's traveled far," he said. "I hope that she hasn't gained any new allegiance that is stronger than her bond with the sisterhood of priestesses. She and Tiagasa may find that they have something in common after all."

§

Myril walked back home past the blackened and soggy remains of Ink Pounders. It had burned at Midwinter, one of the few buildings that had been utterly destroyed that day. The business of the tavern had moved into the upper story of the neighboring building, and from the sound and smell of it, business had not slowed, even though the city streets felt deserted. It was getting toward midday.

She still didn't know where Thorat and the other followers of Enat had their hiding place. It had to be somewhere on the long hill leading up to the palace; she just didn't know where. Kinner's question about Eppie troubled her. She hadn't seen Thorat for a quarter-moon. He couldn't be wholly cured yet. She resolved to ask Garren at the sweet shop in the West Gate market and detoured there on her way home.

The square inside the West Gate was still above the rising waters, though half of the market outside the gates was flooded and the rest was a maze of puddles. Shopkeepers were putting their wares away in preparation for the midday rest, and Myril had to run across the square to reach Garren's sweet shop before the shutters banged closed.

"Wait!" Myril said, catching the edge of the shutter and holding it.

"I'm closed," said a woman's voice from inside. "Even if I wasn't, I don't have much to sell."

"I don't need much," Myril said. She felt like a scrappling, hearing that begging tone in her voice.

"I've got nothing for you." The woman pushed at the shutter, but Myril was stronger, strong enough to force it open a handspan more.

"I need to talk to Garren."

"You, the city watch, and me, too," the woman said, her voice softening a little. She released the shutter enough that she and Myril could see each other. "What do you want with him?"

"He and his friends were keeping something for me and my guild," Myril said. "I'm just asking after it."

"He never told me anything about his comings and goings. Now I don't know where he's gone. I didn't see any of the rest of them, either, not since last half-moon."

"None of them?"

"Only that farmer woman. I saw her pass by a few days ago, but she didn't stop. I'm not even sure if she's one of them, whatever they are, but I saw him talking to her, and she's not a priestess, or what the foreign fools think we all are."

Garren had lived with this woman half his life, and she still didn't know? "I'm sorry," Myril said instead. "I'll just hope that they're all right."

"I'll hope so too," the woman said. "Now off with you; I have baking to do."

"Do you want help?" Myril asked. "I've worked in the temple kitchens."

"I can manage on my own, and I've got a scrappling helping me. Besides, we might all be drowned tomorrow."

As if the woman had spoken prophecy, the ground sank a little beneath Myril's feet, or maybe it was just that she was very, very tired. She was tired of the temple, tired of the Chronicler's evasiveness. She didn't want to see the pain of the refugee priestesses. She staggered home and fell into her bed, not waking until halfway through the night. When she woke, she could hear the Cereans on their ships, out past where the breakwater used to be. They hadn't landed yet. They were waiting for something. She wondered if her dreams would tell her what, rolled over, and slept again until dawn.

§

Myril reached the temple long before decent visiting hours, when the kitchen priestesses were just starting the fires for the morning tea. The peresi's courtyard stank of petitioners, though most of them had left. So had some of the priestesses, to judge by the empty feeling of some of the rooms she passed. The garden looked sad and dilapidated, but then, it always did turn brown in winter. The girl keeping watch at the ambassadress's gate was dozing and let Myril in again.

She found Darna sitting up, scowling at her sandals.

"It's no good being well if I can't leave this place," she said. "I should go back to Tiadun or at least up to the palace to tell Giri where to stick his stupid head."

"Good morning to you, too," Myril said.

"It's not a good morning, and you know it."

Myril shrugged and looked over to Iola's nook. She was still sleeping. Myril sat down next to Darna and gestured that they should be quiet.

"What's happening out there?" Darna asked. "I heard that the Cerean fleet was in the harbor, but no one seems to know anything else."

"They're outside the breakwater, or that's what it sounds like. They haven't landed."

"They will soon, and then what are we going to do?"

"Maybe they're just merchants," Myril said, without conviction. She checked Darna's pulse, finding it strong and steady. "Lie down," she ordered. Darna's belly felt all right too, with no hot spots. She didn't wince at Myril's poking and prodding, either. "Does it hurt?"

"Not as much as not knowing what's happening outside of this room."

Myril sighed. "Sit up, then. Can you walk?"

"I can pace a little, but the garden's tiny. It's beautiful, but it's too small."

"Iola doesn't think so. Then again, you're not Iola."

"I'm not sure even she can take it anymore. She keeps going up to the tower."

"I heard some things this morning, on my way here," Myril said. "The palace has sent men out to the foreigners' ships. They want to know if the harbor is safe, but it clearly isn't, not with the island still spitting fire. With the submerged docks, it's dangerous for big ships, so they're staying out there for now. Farmers are bringing them fresh water and food and probably bargaining for passage across the seas while they're there."

"Don't they have small boats to come ashore in?"

"They do, but they're waiting. I don't know what for."

Darna stood up and paced across the room. She went over to look at the egg in its alcove.

"There's another thing I'd like to know," she said. "Where's Sunna? I haven't seen her in over a quarter-moon."

"I don't know where she is, and I haven't seen Eppie or Thorat, either. Garren's gone from the sweetshop. I'd like to know where they've gone, but it's also that they were hiding scrolls for me, for the guild. I want to be able to get those away from Anamat if it's going to be overrun by that fleet out there. They want to use them to try to chain the dragons or something like that."

Darna nodded. "I don't want to see that. They have to know that they're fools to think they can control the dragons. Not even Iola could do that."

"Do you think you could find the Defenders' place again when you're better?" Myril asked.

"We don't have that much time if Giri's people are here already," Darna said. "I'll take you there."

"You're not well enough," Myril said.

"I'm too well to sit here and wait for them to break down the temple gates. We're going."

Myril smiled. Darna really was feeling better. "All right, then, let's get out of this henhouse."

"I'm not sure if I should leave the egg," Darna said.

"Iola will take care of it," Myril said. She went over to the egg and moved it to where Iola slept, tucking it snugly in behind her.

They made their way to the side house. On the way, Myril heard Jasela give the order to shut the front gate, to let no one come or go that way, and to double the watch on the back gate.

By the time they reached the Pentangle, the city was waking up and the Cereans who'd been in Anamat all along were out in force. A procession of them marched down the hill to the harbor, led by Girizit. Behind them walked two dozen Theranian guardsmen surrounding the governor and his mistress, Tiagasa.

Myril and Darna ducked into a shaded doorway, but Tiagasa glimpsed them there. She whispered to the governor.

"I'm just stopping here to speak with a woman. I'll meet you at the boats."

Parnet frowned and gestured for a few guardsmen to stay with Tiagasa. Darna leaned against the wall behind her, feeling it for cracks. The door at their backs was barred. Servants began to troop by, carrying chests.

"Stay back," Tiagasa told the guardsmen. She approached Darna and Myril, speaking softly. "What brings you out on such a day, Regent?"

"Nothing that concerns you," Darna said. "Are you leaving?"

"Not at all," Tiagasa said, "but the king of Cerea does not travel from his shores, and we would like to lend some of our armsmen to his cause."

"Against the upstart Duke? I'm surprised you don't just invite him to take Tiadun from the whores ruling there now."

Tiagasa's lip twitched. "I think that we can do better, don't you?"

"You could have done much better," Darna said.

"Well, I must go. They will wait for me, but the tide won't." Tiagasa left without even addressing Myril.

"May the sea dragons take her," Myril said.

Darna nodded. They waited for Tiagasa and her servants to go on by, then Darna scurried up to the next side street and through a gate. Myril didn't even see the hidden way until they were walking down its steps, and when they walked back up on the far side, she looked behind her and saw only the fiat wall of the house behind them.

"It's getting more hidden," Darna commented. She stopped to gather her strength at the bottom of the stair, then began to climb up into the courtyard. Myril worried at her tiredness, but it was better not to be trapped in the temple. Darna led the way to a rickety stair. At its top landing, she fiddled with something on the wall for a little while until the door slid open.

"Who goes there?" said a voice from inside.

"It's me, Darna, and Myril, too."

"Huh." Myril recognized Raina's voice. "It's only me here now, and I should be going too." Raina had a lamp lit at the back of the room and had warm tea on the brazier.

"Where are the others?" Myril asked.

"Come have a cup of tea and I'll tell you," Raina said. "Then I'll be off to the temples to skewer anyone who tries to steal Anara's last treasures."

§

Chapter 19

Raina told them how Sovara had sent the Defenders to the gates and told them to leave the priestesses to fend for themselves. "I couldn't leave, though, and I told her so. She didn't seem to mind," Raina said. "Now that you've found your way here, I think I'll go back out to the farm, to make sure that the children have gone."

"Where will they go?" Darna asked.

Raina sighed. "Away from the valley. Some of them went to the hills with Ferrent – they're going looking for Harron among the bandits and I'll go after them as soon as I know that the other young ones are away. They're going with Ganie to a place in Calandria. Where they'll go from there, I don't know. If there's any place to come back to after this, I should be able to get word to them, but I don't think there will be. The tide is rising, and this is a tide that won't turn."

Myril heard the clash of metal on metal and a shout from the streets outside. "Some more of the Cereans are going up to the palace now," she said. "I wish that Lerat had come. I never would have thought that I'd wish to see him so much."

Raina stood and dusted herself off. "I'll just go, then. You two can stay here if you like. It's probably safer than anywhere else, even without the Defenders."

"Are you sure the others won't come back?" Darna asked.

Raina shrugged. "The only things I'm sure of are that the city is sinking and there are too many foreigners for me to fight off. I climbed up to the roof and I saw them coming. I don't want to be in their path," Raina said. "May the winged ones guard your journeys."

"And yours," Myril said.

As Raina disappeared into the hidden passage out of the courtyard, Myril tried to imagine how the priestesses would leave their temple.

"I'm going to climb up on the roof to see what I can see," Darna announced.

"You can't! You're not well enough. You'll undo all the healing in your stitches. Stay down here." Myril took a deep breath. "I'll go up myself. Then we'll go back to my room, get what we need, and hope that Lerat comes."

The fact that Darna did not insist on climbing up with her told Myril that she was, indeed, still a bit weak. She could learn a great deal from the sounds coming up through the walls of the neighboring houses, but she needed to see, too, to scan the horizon for ships, whether they were hostile or friendly. She didn't like heights, but if she could keep her balance, she would manage. She focused on the tiles under her hands and feet. Her limbs were shaking, but they were strong enough. She climbed until she got her leg over the ridge of the roof, and only then did she look up.

What struck her first was that she could see so much of the sky. It was blue and clear. Pretty wisps of light clouds drifted over the mountains, promising a sunny day. A little smoke spiraled up from Na's peaks, whether from a fire or from lava erupting, she wasn't sure. Some of the forest there was burnt black already. The fire had reached into the valley's high pastures before being put out.

Anara's island was a smoking cone in the wide bay that had once been a harbor. Its delicate thread of a tower was long gone and the dragon nowhere to be seen. The temple looked much the same as it always had except for the water lapping at its gates and the red-robed priestesses scurrying to and fro, keeping out of sight as if the clear sky might fall on them behind their locked gates. Across the harbor, the new temple the foreigners had built was already half-submerged, as was their brothel. Myril hoped that the women there had left it before they were taken to Cerea as sham priestesses.

There were ten Cerean ships in the harbor, each carrying between thirty and fifty men, and a handful of Ganatean ships about the same size. About a hundred foreigners were marching up to the governor's palace. Its gates stood open. Out on the harbor, Parnet and Tiagasa were boarding the Cerean king's ship. Girizit was with Parnet. He was wearing so much gold that it hurt to look at him, even from so far away. He handed Tiagasa onto the ship, then, over her protests, headed back to the shore while the sailors on the king's ship raised their sails.

Giri was rowed back to shore. The few remaining palace guards surrendered to the Cereans and fled. Myril steadied herself and looked away.

The horizon shimmered with pale, jagged shapes where there should have been only the bright line of the sky meeting the sea. More ships were coming. Myril raised one hand to shade her eyes, but they were too far away to make out. The sound of the wind and the waves masked whatever voices were there, and the sounds of the city, hushed and afraid, drowned out the rest.

"What do you see?" Darna asked.

Myril looked down and almost lost her balance. "Wait," she said. She slid awkwardly down and let Darna guide her feet onto the railing, then onto the landing. Once she had solid footing, she shook with delayed terror.

"I think I'd better go see the Aralel," Myril said. "More are coming."

"I'm not going back down there," Darna said. "Can you get back here on your own?"

"I don't know," Myril said, "but I'll find a way."

§

She went to her room first to gather up a supply of food and medicines, and while she was there, she thought she might close her eyes for a few breaths, but she was more tired than she'd thought. By the time she opened her eyes, the sky was already growing dark. She shook herself awake and listened. Leaning out of her window, she could hear the ships in the harbor. Two more of the Cerean vessels had gone. The women on her street were crowding into fishing boats. The waters were choppy and rising more quickly. She put on her sandals and hurried to the temple. The side house door was barred from the inside, so she had to go around to the back, where the priestess at the gate recognized her and let her in.

"Do you go to the infirmary, healer?" she asked.

Myril nodded. She didn't like to lie, but the truth was that apart from going to see the Aralel, she might be going anywhere. Crossing the elders' courtyard, she could hear that someone else was already with the Aralel, a man. They were in the inner room, as if Jasela were taking a petitioner there.

"Nakedness suits you, slave," Jasela said.

"My shame is covered," said the voice, still with a bit of an accent, speaking carefully. Was it Girizit? It had to be. No one else had that voice.

Jasela tsked. "Really, now. A year of tutoring and you still will not use the proper name of your male parts."

"You'll learn what proper is when you're back in Cerea. Now give me the things you promised."

"I'm not going back to Cerea, and I promised you nothing."

"You promised me the texts showing how to use the dragons' stones to bring the life back to a land, or to a man's... manhood, and I think you will come. You're too practical to let yourself drown."

"There are other options. Also, I only told you that I would see what I could find here in the temple. I did not in any way promise to give it to you."

"You implied it," Girizit said.

"You imagined that. I tell you now – and heed me – I tell you now that I did not find what you seek, and if I had, I wouldn't give it to you. Do you understand?"

"Her Highness will not be pleased. I'll tell her to call off the guards."

"Tiagasa? She's gone. Give me credit for at least knowing who has sailed out already. If she comes back, she'll share the fate of her fellow priestesses. She knows that, and she would do the same for me."

"We do like to see a woman who is too proud brought down, but not by you, by a man."

"Is that what you're going to do? Bring her down?"

Myril couldn't see Giri's face, but she could hear him breathing faster. "She and the governor have an arrangement with the king. They will take command of the Southern Reaches if they can defeat the duke. The king will control them better than him, ignorant as they are."

"He controls you, too. You're a nation of timid fools and traitors."

"Not as foolish as you, who worship worms with obscene acts."

Jasela snorted. "You'd better go now."

Girizit responded by going to the door. Myril slipped around to the corner so that he wouldn't see her.

"May the fates keep us apart," he said in parting.

"May I never see your face again," Jasela replied.

She peeked out as Girizit passed. He looked much less imposing in a loincloth, without his cloth-of-gold coat. Two treasurer priestesses, the biggest and strongest of them, met him at the base of the stairs and hurried him away. Myril went to Jasela's doorway.

"Who goes there?" Jasela said. "I can see your shadow. Announce yourself."

Myril stepped in.

"You heard us, then," Jasela said. "So, now you know my secret. I was in the court of the Cerean king for a year, teaching that fool our ways."

"No wonder he's so much better-spoken than he was as a scrappling."

"I heard about that too, but not from him." Jasela led the way back into her inner room.

"The ships that were on the horizon this morning, did you see them?"

Jasela nodded. "They're still too far away to tell their intent, but Girizit is nervous. He didn't expect them. He wouldn't have come here in such a hurry if they were friendly to him."

"From what I could hear, I think they may be Lerat's ships or allied with him. None of them looked or sounded like Cerean ships. Some of them are Enomaean, too."

"I hope you're right, but just because they're enemies of Cerea doesn't mean they're friends of ours. They could be raiders from the far coasts of Enomae or more Ganateans. In any case, we'll know in the morning."

The Aralel's private chamber was in some disarray. Papers were down from their shelves, boxes lay open with their contents spilling onto the floor.

"Were you really looking for it?" Myril asked.

"I suppose I was, though I'm not convinced that it exists."

"It does," Myril said, "but it would be no use to them without a living dragon. It's just a very old text which says what we all know, that the stones have power only by grace of the dragon, and the way to cultivate their power is to become kin to the dragons or to do homage to them. Here, I'll show you."

Myril went to the corner of the room and lifted up the carpet. She pushed on the corner of the flagstone and it swung up heavily. She propped it up and took one small packet from inside, handing it to Jasela. She put another packet under her arm and closed the lid again.

"Take this with you if you escape this land, and take it to wherever the priestesses go," she told Jasela. "The guild stored some of the old texts at another place in the city. I'll go get them. I may not have time to come back for these in the morning."

"So, you have a plan to save the Chronicles of Anamat as well as our priestesses?" Jasela chuckled. "That is good work, for one who was so quiet as a novice."

"I only did what came my way."

"You should go now before I ask you to stay and help us instead of rescuing your dry scrolls." With that, Jasela shooed her out. "And may the winged ones know who assaults them, and who would lift their wings."

§

It took Thorat many days to reach Tegana's gate, walking and climbing along rough roads that were sometimes almost impassable because of new rockfalls. He met very few other travelers along the way, and those that he did see were headed for the coasts or far up into the hills. It was a lonely, rainy walk. If Iola no longer flew to the dragons, if there was no ambassadress any more, then what use could the Defenders be? He didn't know. Sovara had abandoned them, gone on her last quest without naming a successor. With no Aralel and no Enatel, the orders of the dragons were gone.

Tegana's gate was on the border, well into the mountains and only a little way off the main road to Anamat. The temple that had once guarded it stood abandoned, its empty towers looking out over a sweeping plain. He hadn't seen a dragonlet since Anamat valley, and there he'd seen only one on the road near the mountains, as if even the dragonlets were abandoning the lowlands.

Tegana had been Iola's home dragon, the first dragon she had seen and touched, the first dragon that had carried her on her back. Her colors were reflected in the hills, but all he could see was the pale luminosity of Iola's skin and the raven-black fall of her hair reflected in the sullen light, in the misty rain, in the wet branches of the winter-bare trees against pale marble polished by time.

The gate was open and empty. He sat in front of it as night fell, an angry streak of orange sunset showing through the clouds. He sat through the darkness of midnight and all the way to the gray cold light of dawn, and he felt nothing from the gate. Tegana was gone, into the hills or to the depths of the earth. He couldn't reach her, except that in his half-sleep he thought he'd glimpsed a dragonlet running around a bend in the path, back to the Anamat road, back to Iola.

Tegana might be gone, but for all he knew, Iola still lived. He shook out his stiff legs and scratched what he could reach on his healing back. He would forget the dragons' gates. Sovara could guard them; they could guard themselves. He was going back to Iola.

He thought that the gate flickered for a moment and he almost changed his mind, but then he imagined a ship's mast far out on the horizon, bronze gleaming in the sun. To stay in the hills would be to betray Iola, and that he could not do.

§

Thorat reached the valley's edge late in the afternoon on the fourth day. His return journey had been swifter than the way out, either because he was getting stronger again or because he knew what waited for him at the end. He had a good view out over the valley as he crested a small rise. He could also see the foreign ships ranged along the sea's horizon, closing in to take whatever they could of the last of the treasures of Anamat. The priestesses would not be safe, especially not the ambassadress. Thorat pressed on across the valley through the darkening night.

Reaching Anamat's walls after dark meant that the gates would be closed, a custom that had held firm as the city watch thinned, a last bastion of control over the increasingly chaotic comings and goings. Thorat thought of trying to go through one of the old secret ways, but the rising water had flooded most of them, and he'd never been very good at finding them to begin with. He knew the one by the West Gate best, having come and gone that way to Raina's farm, but that gate was ringed with campfires, probably foreigners'. The palace gate was no better, so he made his way to the low-lying East

Market, which had become too soggy to provide much of a place to camp.

He was footsore and road-weary, but he was almost there. The road leading up to the gate was a mess of planks and stepping-stones on mud. Moonlight glinted on puddles. He passed by the cave-like overhang where he'd once gathered around a campfire with the other East Market boys in between bouts of mischief. It was cold and dark, not even a scrappling in sight. He hoped the scrapplings were all out raiding the Cereans' ships, or else that they'd gone back to their villages, or found some other, better place to live, a place that wasn't sinking.

He crept along the wall to the place where the gap had been, feeling for it as he went. He was almost upon it when a voice called out.

"Halt, there!" A watchman. Thorat cursed himself. If he'd had his eyes open instead of concentrating so much on the feeling, if he'd been listening at all, he would have seen the watchman coming or at least heard his boots splashing through the mud.

Thorat squinted into the torchlight and held his hands out, away from his sword belt.

"What's your business, man, creeping in the dark?"

"I'm sorry. I just got back to the valley. I'm looking for a place to camp."

"Awful late for that. Come on those ships, did you?"

"The Cerean ships? I think not!"

"No, the other ones. Rumor says they're making landfall up the coast toward the Lemirun hills. Are you scouting for them?"

"No. What ships are those?"

"I don't know, just that they're there. I'll take you in to the guard house, just in case. The watch master might want to question you. Give me your sword."

Under other circumstances, Thorat could have taken the man in a fight. The watchman was bulky and muscular, but he hadn't had Sovara as a sword master. Thorat was tired and it was dark, the ground muddy, and he didn't want to waste his strength fighting an ordinary watchman who could well be an ally.

"You'll give it back, won't you?" Thorat asked as he unbuckled the sword.

"This is a good piece. Enough to pay for passage to Calandria, I'd think."

Thorat almost wished he'd fought to keep it. Another watchman was coming.

"What's this?" the newcomer said.

"Taking him in to Pannen."

Thorat laughed. "Pannen. That's right; he's watch master here now, isn't he?"

"He is. You know him?"

"I do," Thorat said. "He might even do me a favor."

§

At first, Pannen was not inclined to give Thorat his sword back. "I still don't see why you're creeping around our old haunts tonight. There's foreigners afoot, lots of them. I don't like it, and half the men are over in the Cerean camp, trying to buy their way out. That farm out there, first one past the market? You remember it. Their spring went to saltwater. Another week like this, there'll be no freshwater in all Anamat except what the rain brings."

Thorat took another sip of the very good ale that Pannen had poured for him. "I was on a journey up to the north. Coastline looks like it's changed there, too," he said.

"Were you in the mountains?"

"Lots are going there these days, I was just... Listen," Thorat said. "I came back for a woman. You remember that girl, from when we were scrapplings?"

"That quiet, pretty one? Didn't she go into the temple?"

Thorat nodded. "I want to get her out before the Cereans go in. I can't do much else for anyone, I don't think."

"You might be able to help us somehow. I have hopes that the new fleet that's landing east of here will take passengers to some place other than slavery in Cerea. The women, they might survive if the Cereans take them. They've got no use for us men except as oar-slaves." He shuddered at the thought.

"If you call that surviving."

"They call it worse than death," Pannen said. "You remember I had a friend at the harbor temple, too? She left a long time ago, went to a village. I'd like to go look for her, but I don't know where to start."

"You could go to the village where she went."

Pannen shook his head. "It's abandoned." He leaned out of his guardhouse door and stood there for a while.

"It's getting light," he said. "Maybe you should go. Take your sword, I suppose. I hate to let it go, it's a good piece, but I can find another way to buy passage."

"Thank you," Thorat said. "May we live to see another day."

"I'll drink to that," Pannen said.

They both emptied their jars and Thorat set out for the temple.

The morning was misty and rain clouds blocked the light of the rising sun. Thorat went to the front of the temple first and found one of the palace guardsmen there, watching the gate.

"Don't bother," he told Thorat. "They're not letting anyone in, and on the off chance they do, they'll want half the governor's treasury just for a fuck."

Thorat eyed the locked gate. There wasn't even a priestess at the gatehouse. "I'll take that advice, then," he said, and hurried away before the guard recognized him. He couldn't think of any reason they'd let him in at the back gate, either. His old secret way into Iola's chamber was flooded, he knew that, but it was the only thing he could think of. He took off his sandals and waded down the alley to the canal, near where the entrance had been. It was all but completely covered, with only its hidden capstone showing. He tucked his bedroll and sword under the eaves of a house overhanging the canal and hoped they would be there when he returned. He dove under the water. The gap between the stones was closed, inpenetrable.

He came up for air. He had learned to swim as a boy but hadn't practiced much in years, and the water was cold enough to take his breath away. He looked again at the little gap between the capstone and the water and decided to try again. On the second try, he slipped into something...and it immediately closed behind him. Water. No air. He blinked into the pitch-dark water. The phosphorescence was gone, too. He tried to go back but couldn't.

He would die trying to reach Iola and no one would ever know. Except Pannen, maybe, but that hardly counted. He kicked toward the temple, upstream; it was the only possible way. He opened his eyes once or twice just in case there was a light. Then, finally, he touched a pocket of air along the ceiling of the passage. He gulped it in and dove again. He reached another pocket, and after that, the ceiling rose. There was a whole long stretch where he could get his face out and pull himself along with his hands. His fingers and toes were going numb. He almost missed the opening. He'd passed it. Something was different, unfamiliar. He pulled his way back, then dove again.

Three strokes up the side passage and he could get his whole head out of the water. Another three, and his feet could touch the steps below. By the time he got to the entrance of Iola's bath chamber, he was out of the water except for his feet. Dripping with muck but wading and alive. He reached the grille. It was locked.

He cried out with every bit breath he could summon. "Iola!"

§

Chapter 20

Darna stayed at the Defenders' hall all day while Myril went out. She came back just after dark, carrying a satchel of bread from the temple kitchens and a jar of stew. They ate and slept. In the morning, Darna woke to the sound of someone on the stair. Myril coming back? But no, Myril was sleeping beside her. She tried to sit up and every muscle in her body protested, especially the ones around her womb.

"Who's there?" Her voice caught from lack of use.

The steps on the stair stopped.

"What do you mean, 'Who's there?' Who are you?"

"It's Darna."

"Oh!" It was Eppie. She bounded in, carrying a bulging bag of bread and a jar of tea. "I thought some of the others might have come back too, so I brought these. Also in case I got stuck in here. I saw that fleet coming and I just... I just couldn't stand there in the mountains while they looted Anamat."

"I'm glad you're back," Myril said. "Have you seen Thorat?"

"No. Why?"

"I dreamed that he was near," Myril said.

"Wouldn't surprise me if he came back," Eppie said.

"What did you see out there?" Myril asked.

Eppie sat down and poured herself some tea, then passed the jar to Myril and Darna. "I went to Coradun, that was where Sovara sent me, and then looked over the mountains into Lemirun. There was no life at Corana's gate except for an apple tree full of fruit, still ripe."

"Even in winter?"

Eppie nodded. "It was no different at Lemira's gate except that there was only a lot of fresh, green grass. Every night that I slept by her gate, I dreamed of dragons until the last, and then I dreamed that all of Anamat was falling like Anara's island did, so I came back."

"What's happening here now, this morning?" Darna asked.

"That new fleet is landing," Eppie said. "I saw a messenger from there go to the harbor temple, and then a priestess ran to the other shrines. We should go."

"Are they Lerat's ships?" Myril asked.

"Who's Lerat?" Eppie asked.

"Wait, I'll go see." Myril went out onto the landing while Darna got herself dressed and finished her cup of tea. She came back quickly.

"They are Lerat's. It's our only hope of getting these texts to some place safe," Myril said. The boxes at the back of the training hall weren't large, and there were sacks at the back of the room, which would make them easy to carry.

"Half the harbor temple is on their way out already," Eppie said. "There might not be room for us."

"There'll have to be," Myril said.

The building shook, sending a roof tile to the courtyard below. Darna felt it in her bones. "I think we'd better hurry."

§

Because so many Cereans were on the horizon, Jasela had closed the gates to petitioners again almost as soon as they'd been opened. The other priestesses weren't happy about it – a full moon-round without petitioners already meant that they had only what they'd gathered before Midwinter, and many of them needed more, and they were hungry for direct contact with the world outside temple walls. Iola was allowed to stay on in the ambassadress's quarters, but with Darna gone, it seemed too quiet.

Iola sat looking at Anara's statue for the first half of the day after Darna had disappeared. No one came at midday to bring her dinner, as if they'd forgotten about her. She didn't mind – she wasn't hungry. She didn't know where Darna had gone, but she'd left the egg, so she couldn't have gone too far.

After midday, Iola went up to the tower and looked at the bright, empty sky. Some clouds moved into a shape that suggested one of the lesser dragons. She stared at the East Canal for a long time, as if staring at it could make its dragonlet materialize. All that she saw was a sea dragon, far away, and only for an instant. The ships that had been on the horizon were at the mouth of the bay, and she could see another fleet coming in from the east. They looked like Theranian ships, but she wasn't sure.

It got cold after dark, so she went back down and crawled into bed. She drank a little wine and found some old bread that Darna had stashed away. She slept.

And then someone was calling her name. Not "Most Blessed One," not even "ambassadress" or "priestess," but "Iola." Instantly, she was awake, feeling all the hungers of her body, and thirst. She took a drink from the jar by her bed to loosen her sleep-thick voice and called back. "I'm coming!"

She found the grille, and Thorat on the other side, stinking of sewage and stumbling with cold.

"Get into the baths," she said. He was chilled to the bone and the bath was steaming. She put a hand in. Hot, too hot. "Don't," she said. "It's gone too hot. The dragons are coming closer again; they're too close for it to be safe in there."

He began to shiver violently. She found a cold bucket and mixed it with hot from the bath and sluiced it over him, washing him until he smelled like a human again and until the shaking had eased enough that he could talk.

"Lie with me" was all he said, and so they did, making no pretense that it was for the dragons. At last, they could be themselves with each other.

§

She woke up in Thorat's arms. Bright midday light streamed in through the clerestories. The chamber shook. Far away, a wall of stone fell noisily.

"Thorat?" she said.

He grunted and rolled over. He looked wretched with exhaustion, but he was there in the flesh, touching her. She wished that she could let him go on sleeping, just so she could keep looking at him. They'd rinsed the muck from his clothes and laid them on the side table. They were damp but no longer dripping wet. Someone was at her gate. What if they found him, she worried, but who would find him? The other priestesses? They wouldn't condemn her for doing what they wanted to do themselves, and it didn't matter anymore.

Over their heads, the roof was falling, not quickly, but it was definitely falling. She'd seen it shaking in the quakes before, but this time, the trusses were shaking loose. The golden statue of Anara tilted, its eyes dull and lifeless. The spirit of the dragon had gone out of it as all of Anara's energy plunged into the stones below, to make something new of them or to take them down into the other realm.

She shook Thorat's shoulder. "You have to wake up," she said, but he only mumbled and burrowed under the covers. It reminded her of trying to wake Myril when she'd spent all night reading, back when they were novices. Where was Myril now?

Thorat's eyes blinked open. "I think you'd better get up," Iola said again. "Someone's here." She handed him his mostly dried clothes and went to the door. It was one of the novices.

"Most Blessed One!" she said breathlessly. "The Aralel says to gather whatever you can carry. Practical clothes for outside, and something to sell in case you need to. They're sending whatever provisions they can from the kitchen to the ships. Hurry. We'll all have to go at once!"

"Go where?"

"To the ships. To the wilds beyond Ganat, they say. Haven't you seen?" She gestured to the sky to the west. "The mountains are on fire, and the hill temple and the palace too. The Cereans are landing and Lerat's boats are waiting. We must bring whatever we can."

"Bring it where?"

"I don't know, but we need to go. They all say so."

"Tell Jasela I'll come soon. Tell her not to wait for me."

Someone in the peresi's garden shouted at the novice to hurry. Beyond Iola's gate, the peresi's courtyard looked like a market square at closing time as blankets and tapestries were turned into bundles, hastily shouldered.

When Iola turned around again, Thorat was standing behind her.

"I'll go with you," he said. "I need to get my sword and to go to the training hall before we leave."

"Don't leave me. They won't let you back in."

"They'll all be gone. There'll be no one to stop me or to stop anyone else. You have to come with me."

"I will," Iola said. "I'll go with you wherever you go."

"Really?"

Iola smiled. "What else is there?"

Thorat took her hands in his for a slow moment, then they broke apart to gather a few things from Iola's chamber, a handful of jewels and some of the more practical clothes. Iola didn't know what she'd need. Thorat arranged them into a pack on her back and found a plain, dark cloak that she could wear over everything. They couldn't go out the way Thorat had come in – Iola couldn't swim, it would ruin the clothes, and the end was most likely shut – so she led him out to the back courtyard.

A throng of priestesses had gathered there, young and old, carrying everything they could. They could all hear the sound of metal on metal coming from the front gates. Iola went straight to the priestess at the gatehouse. "I'm leaving, with him. Tell the Aralel if she asks."

The priestess's eyes went wide when she recognized the ambassadress. "But – but it will be safer if we all go together."

"I'll protect her," Thorat said.

The priestess looked worried, but she let them out. "The winged ones go with you," Iola said.

"I'm not sure I wish for that anymore," the gate priestess muttered in response. The mountains were spewing smoke and ash. The ground shook again.

Iola trailed Thorat through the rattling streets, keeping her hood up. She could hear the high-heeled boots of the Cereans everywhere. Thorat retrieved his sword from under the eaves where he'd hidden it, and led the way up through a bewildering series of alleys, splashing through a low street and across what had once been a bridge. Iola tried to take everything in, to see and to remember in case she needed to get back to the temple, or anywhere else.

He turned down a side street and then into an alley. "Na's blood," he cursed. "It's blocked, gone."

"Hey, you there!" A woman called from the house beside them. "If you need to get in, you can come through my house. I've seen you in the yard plenty."

Thorat thanked her.

"Some women left a while ago, that young one and two others," the neighborly woman said. "They were carrying boxes."

"Did one of them have red hair? The other tall and dark?" Iola asked.

The neighbor nodded. "They've gone to the ships."

"I think we should go after them," Iola said. "There isn't much time."

"Is anyone left inside?" Thorat asked the neighbor.

"Just that man from the West Market, the baker."

As if responding to a summons, Garren's voice let out a yell from inside. The woman darted into her house, and a moment later, Garren emerged the way she'd come. He'd been running, but he skidded to a halt at the sight of Thorat.

"You're back!" he said. "I just got back to the city and..." His voice trailed off as he looked at Iola. "Your companion," he said slowly. "You'd better get her to the ships. The shrine exploded; there's nothing left inside, or won't be, soon. The last I saw of Sovara was at Lemira's gate, and she said that she would stay there until the end, her end or the dragons'. I came back for Anara."

The woman pushed past them, a bundle slung over her shoulder. "The roof is on fire! Run!" she shouted as she ran toward the harbor.

"Why?" Iola asked Garren as she saw the smoke rising from behind him.

"The Cereans will never have Anara's shrines. Come on. I have more work to do. Get yourselves to safety."

"Should I come with you?" Thorat asked.

"Go with her!" Garren said. "Hurry!"

"I guess we'll go, then," Iola said, still unsure of her direction.

Thorat nodded, looking grim. "If only we could see Anara."

"I'd stay for that," Iola said. They started to walk. "She'll be down at the harbor if she's anywhere."

"I'd like to say goodbye to the others," Thorat said.

"Let's go, then, and find out what the priestesses are running to," Iola said. She wasn't a priestess anymore. Her world was ending. She realized that she had never truly been happy until that moment. "We'll stay, though, won't we?" She smiled at Thorat and ran, laughing, to say goodbye to everyone else she'd ever cared for.

§

The sea was a mass of sailing boats tossed on the waves, as if every trading ship and fishing boat in the known world had converged on Anamat. Eppie and Myril carried as much as they could between them, texts and swords, while Darna limped behind, carrying only a small bundle of the Defenders' long knives. Apart from those, she was barely able to carry herself. She didn't even have her tools, not that she was likely to get much chance to use them again.

It seemed to take them half the day to get across the city, and they had to wade most of the way. The wind had picked up, and despite the sun, the air was cold. A plume of ash drifted up from the volcano in the harbor. They went past the walls to a place where a new inlet had formed, out beyond the East Market, or what had once been the East Market. People were getting into small boats and tenders and going out to the fleet of ships just at the edge of the deep water, all their movements chaotic. Darna took the lead and cut a swath through the crowd to a likely-looking small boat.

"We're looking for Lerat," Myril told one of the sailors there.

"You and everyone else. He's over in the middle of that crowd." The sailor pointed to a mass of shouting people grouped around a low rise in the land.

Myril shivered.

"You can do it," Darna said. "I'll watch your side."

"And I'm on your other side," Eppie said.

They elbowed their way forward to where Lerat sat on a high pile of crates in front of a long line of people waiting to speak to him. He kept his eyes moving, scanning the crowd. When he saw Myril, he nodded to her. He said something to the man next to him, who nodded and then made his way toward them.

"Captain says to bring you to his ship. He'll be along later."

"How much later?" Darna wondered.

"With the tide? I don't know. It's going to take all day and maybe the night to load everyone up, and some will get left behind. We'll be the last to leave, but it's the best ship. Come on, what did you pay him?"

Myril seemed at a loss for words, so Darna jumped in. "We have an arrangement," she said.

"That's lucky for you," the sailor said. They jostled their way down to the water's edge, where he helped them into a small boat. The moment Darna's feet left the shore, everything felt wrong all of a sudden.

"I have to go back."

"That's madness," the sailor said. "Sit down."

"What for?" Myril asked, but then she realized too. "Don't you think it would be better off here, with them?"

"No, I had a sign, a prophecy. Anara never tells me anything, but she said to take it far from these shores. I'm going back to get it." Darna climbed back out of the boat.

"Get what?" Eppie said. "Never mind; I'll come with you."

"You might not get out," the sailor warned. "The boats are filling fast."

"I'll take my chances," Darna said.

"Where are we going?" Eppie asked her as she trotted to catch up.

"Temple." Darna walked as fast as she was able. She looked around for something to use as a cane, and eventually she found a stout stick leaning against the wall.

They met the priestesses halfway back to the temple, fiooding toward the shore and the boats. Darna fiattened herself against the wall, looking down at her feet, hoping that none of them would recognize her. No one did, not until the very end.

"You there!" The woman was wearing the Aralel's robes. It was the new Aralel, Jasela. "Come with us, for your own safety."

Darna shook her head, then decided to approach the new Aralel. "Did anyone get the egg?" she asked.

Jasela looked puzzled. "What egg? What?"

"No one told you about it? It's in the ambassadress's quarters. If she's there –"

"The Most Blessed One left, with a man," said a nearby priestess.

The Aralel frowned.

"She wasn't carrying much," the priestess supplied.

"I'm going back in," Darna said.

"They'll rape and kill you," Jasela warned. "I've seen them. The gates at the front broke."

"I'll kill them first," Eppie said.

"You shouldn't go either," the Aralel said. "You're young. They won't care that you don't think you're a priestess."

"We'll hurry," Eppie said. "Besides, I know the back way."

It was clear from the expression on Jasela's face that she had no idea what Eppie was talking about, but she let them go. "May the dragons fly with you," she said.

"And with you, Your Holiness," Darna replied.

Moments later, they were in the back courtyard. The invaders hadn't reached it yet, though they were noisily crashing through the front part of the temple. Eppie led the way past the kitchens and into a corridor near the old sanctuary, then into the closet and down a long, dark passage hidden behind some storage shelves. They could hear the sound of breaking wood through the walls, war whoops, the clatter of things being stuffed into bags, looting. At the end of the passage, Eppie pushed the hidden door open. She paused before they stepped out into the garden.

There were two Cerean armsmen standing just inside the ambassadress's gate.

"Take your sandals off and sneak in quietly," Eppie said. "I'll guard your back."

Darna nodded. She left her sandals just inside the passage and dashed from there to the cover of a tree beside the bath's outer wall. She edged along the wall toward the porch.

"Boss is in there," one of the Cerean guards said to someone outside, in Cerean. "This is his claim."

Whoever it was grunted and went away.

"Did you hear something?" the other guard said.

Darna ducked down, stilled her breath, and listened. She could hear whoever it was inside. The Cereans' boss. Well, she'd have to take her chances with him, and she did have a very good knife in her belt. She wondered if Eppie had heard, but she was out of sight, and besides, Eppie didn't understand Cerean. She looked back. Eppie was nowhere to be seen. Darna darted in through the door to the gilded marble chamber that had been her prison since Midsummer.

He didn't hear her at first. He was looking at the egg and looking at his pack. He had a ledger in his hand and was making notes of some kind. A large crate stood at the center of the room, half full with ornaments gleaned from around the room. The statue of Anara slumped sideways over the offering place and was littered with shards of marble and dust, but he still made a warding gesture as he turned to it.

"Melted down," he muttered to himself. "Melted down, it could buy my freedom even now."

Then he saw Darna. He took a step back and drew a long, curved dagger from his belt. It was an elegant piece of work but not Theranian. In reply, Darna drew her own dagger. It was hot in her hand. It had a dragon stone in it. She hoped Giri wouldn't be able to tell or, if he did notice, that it would frighten him.

"If you'd wanted your freedom, you could have had it a long time ago," she said.

"Not what you call freedom. That's only slavery to these... things." He waved dismissively at the statue of Anara. "Did my men let you in as some kind of joke?"

"They don't know that I'm here."

"Are you a ghost, then, to drift past them unseen?"

"Maybe so," Darna said. "Or maybe the dragons are playing tricks with you."

Giri's lip twitched. He fumbled with his dagger. "If you're a ghost, you won't bleed," he said, edging closer.

"That's right," Darna said. She sidestepped, moving closer to the egg, still brandishing her own dagger.

"I'll get you," Giri said.

One of the men called from outside. "Hey, boss! You need a hand in there?"

"Not yet," he said. He turned back to Darna. "I'd like to show you that I'm not your enemy."

"Really? What else could you be? You betrayed me and all of us."

"That betrayal, much as it may have hurt you at the time, pained me, but it got me much further toward this position than I could have otherwise. If you don't curse me – and I know that you can – then I'll give you your choice of the things here."

"They belong more to me than they do to you."

"But you, ghost-girl, have no armed men to carry them for you. I'll see you down to your ship with it and make sure that the men don't touch you. Then you may go where you like."

Darna didn't believe him, but she didn't want to have him test her ghostliness with his dagger and wasn't confident enough that she'd be able to get him with hers.

"Step outside for a moment," Darna said. "Speak with your men. Ask for two more to come. I may wish to take something heavy."

"Very well, ghost-girl."

The moment his back was turned, she swept the egg into a blanket from the sleeping nook. The blanket smelled of sex. Who had come? Then she remembered that the priestess had said that Iola had been with a man. It had to be Thorat. There was no other man she would have left with. Darna threw the egg in its blanket over her shoulder and went into the bath chamber just as Giri returned, with four armed men at his back.

"There's no girl here," one of them said.

Giri looked around. She hoped he felt foolish. She went over to the wall where once or twice a way had opened into the garden for her, out to the back of the temple. Yes, it was still there, but the magic in the walls was gone, but there was still power in the egg on her back and in the stone of her dagger. She set the stone against the wall and pushed. She fell through into the garden as the world shook again. She heard the eruption of a volcano somewhere far away.

Eppie was still waiting at the end of the passage. "Hurry!" Darna said. "Lock it!"

"I can't," Eppie said. "It's broken."

Darna handed her the sacked egg. "We'll have to jam it, then." She found a loose rock and pried it free, then used it to smash the gate.

"Out there!" Giri shouted. His voice echoed strangely. Rocks fell.

"We'd better run," Eppie said. She sprinted back along the passageway as it crumbled. They wove past the foreigners looting the back courtyard and out into the streets. Darna kept her long knife in one hand and struggled to keep up with Eppie. Along the way, splashing and staggering past the remains of the East Gate, they met a gang of men so foreign that Darna couldn't even guess where they came from. Eppie passed Darna the egg, drew her sword, and neatly sliced the leader across the chest. That dissuaded the others and they ran off, in search of less well-armed loot.

At the shore, the crowds had thinned. On the sea, the ships lay heavy in the water, but there were still people waiting at Lerat's feet. They shouldered their way back toward him.

"Eppie!" someone called. Darna turned to see Kinner pushing his way through the crowd. "Where have you been?! I was afraid you were gone or dead!"

It was as if he didn't even see Darna. She smirked. Perhaps he'd forgotten her when she'd gone into the temple, but he clearly hadn't forgotten Eppie, who was red-faced from running and fighting but now also quite clearly blushing.

"Will you come with us?" Kinner said. "We're going to Calandria, the Chronicler and Nolerin. I said I'd go with them."

"Nolerin's there?"

"Your Highness! Pardon me," Kinner stammered. "I didn't see you."

Darna would have told him that she didn't mind, but just then, someone else called her name. She turned to see Iola sailing through the crowd. Her voice was clear as a bell, and even with a pack on her back and a plain, dark cloak, something about her commanded attention.

"We need to talk to Lerat and get on the ship," Eppie said.

"They won't be able to carry everyone," Thorat said.

"All the more reason to hurry," Kinner said.

Thorat and Iola followed them through the dwindling crowd to Lerat, who recognized Darna and waved her forward.

"We're low in the water," he said. "I thought that you were aboard my ship already, Regent of Tiadun."

"I had to go back to the temple for something important. Along the way back, I met these two. May they sail with us?"

"Who are they that I should take them when there are others still fleeing?"

"One is among the last of the Defenders of the Dragons, and the other the last living woman to have flown with the dragons."

Lerat nodded. "Row them out to my ship," he said to one of the sailors. "You go to the Chronicler?" he asked Kinner.

Kinner nodded but looked hesitatingly at Eppie. "I'll go with Darna," Eppie said. "But I'll meet you in Calandria."

"If we survive," Kinner said. He looked at the sea with dread in his eyes, and Darna remembered how he'd been declared useless for fishing in his home village because of his seasickness. She squeezed his hand.

"You'll survive," she assured him, "and you'll see Eppie again; I'm sure of it."

Darna climbed into the boat first and Eppie handed her the egg. With the egg in her lap, she felt steady again, even though the boat tipped crazily.

Iola and Thorat hung back, not wading out to the boat at all.

"Come on," Eppie urged. Clouds had come up and rain was starting to fall. The earth shook again.

"We're staying," Iola said.

"We'll see Anara one last time," Thorat said. "We can go to the hills. Let someone else go beyond the seas in our place."

"But..." Eppie reached out to Thorat. He shook his head. She let her hand drop.

Kinner climbed into the boat too. There were people were trying to get on, but the oarsmen shooed them away. There simply wasn't room for everyone.

"Send Myril my love," Iola said. "Thorat and I might not live, but she will, and I'll see the winged ones again."

"May they go with you," Darna said. She turned away. They had what they wanted, which was each other, but she hated to leave them so soon.

"Go with each other, then, like Ara and Enat. You are Ara and Enat, you know," Eppie said.

"I'll let two more on, then?" a sailor said. Eppie nodded and two more climbed onto the boat, then they rowed away from the sinking shore of Anamat forever.

§

Lenasa met Myril as she reached the ship and embraced her. "Thank you for sending me with Lerat," she said. "You may wait in our cabin if you like. If I'm not going to be a priestess anymore, or a princess, I might as well be a merchant's wife and scribe."

Myril waited in the cabin, trying not to hear all of the chaos outside. The gentle rocking of the boat kept increasing until it made her feel ill. She went out onto the deck and found a quiet corner behind some barrels, where she sat down to listen and to watch Lenasa commanding the newcomers to the ship, telling them where they might rest and where they could and could not go. She wore her authority easily.

The hills were smoking and the sky was darkening with rainclouds. The wind blew cold; the waves grew longer, larger. The city's roofs ran up the hill in waves, much like the sea. Dragonlets had lived there. That city had contained Myril's whole life since she was very young, but now it was falling as the earth shook it down and looters ran through its streets. Many boats had set sail already, trying to get out ahead of the storm. From the deck of one of them, a priestess with a sword on her sash waved. It was Sunna.

"On to the wilds beyond Ganat!" she called out.

Myril waved back. She could see Jasela on that boat too, and some of the elders. Part of her heart went with them, but she could not sense Iola among them. She listened. She thought that she heard Iola, running through the streets with

Thorat by her side. They were together. Iola would not want her anymore, if she ever had, no more than she would want anything beyond the dragons' shores.

Later on, a familiar voice drew her attention to a nearby ship, an Enomaean one. She stood and ran to the rail. It seemed to be the Chronicler, of all people.

"Lord Chronicler," she called. "Where do you go?"

He looked too surprised to answer. A turbaned head came up beside him. "You are Darna's friend, the healer?" he said. "I am Nolerin, who guided her horse across the mountains. I will guide your guildmaster to a place where it is safe."

"But the priestesses are going somewhere safe too, I think," Myril said.

The Chronicler cleared his throat and found his voice. "No, last of our guild-priestesses. The place they go to is safe for women, not so much so for texts. They carry some with them, but my friend here says he knows another place. If one place is better than another, some of our tales will survive. We scatter them over the earth, and where the soil is gentle, they will take root."

His friend, he'd said. Of course. Myril felt foolish for never having seen it before. The Chronicler was old, but he wasn't a celibate by choice; it was only that there were few men he desired, and fewer still who felt the same for him.

"May they wing you on your way," she said.

Nolerin and the Chronicler whispered to one another in a language she did not understand. "Come with us," Nolerin invited her. "You can meet us in Calandria, at the temple there. We will wait for you."

Myril promised to ask for passage to Calandria, then she went back belowdecks to wait for whoever else would come.

§

Lerat's ship sailed out into a thunderstorm that evening. Behind them, the city fell in a rain of thunder. When they looked back, all they could see above the waves was a single gold-roofed tower falling, and Anara's wings sketched on the clouds, or maybe it was only spines of lightning.

That was the last anyone saw of Anamat, as far as the histories go.

"I wonder where they are now," Darna said as they sailed away.

"Thorat and Iola?" Eppie said.

"They're together, and with the dragons," Myril said. "That's all either of them has ever wanted. They're blessed. They always were, even though it's also a curse."

Darna nodded. "So it is."

Water lapped past the prow, and the night sky shone bright with milky stars overhead.

§

In the morning, they found themselves on an empty sea with no other ships in sight. The sea was still murky but the sky had cleared. A ragged strip of land ran along the horizon.

"What land is that?" Eppie asked.

Lerat shook his head. "I can't say for sure, but we can't have sailed further than the end of Theranis."

Darna went to the rail and squinted, trying to pick out familiar shapes in the dark landform. "Could it be Tiadun?" she asked, so quietly that she thought no one but Myril would hear her.

"Could be." Lerat's voice boomed. "Let's go have a look."

With one wave of his arm, he had the ship turning toward the sunset, the sailors also eager to find out what this place was, even if it was treacherous ground hollowed out by the dragons' retreat.

Myril came to her side. "Do you want to go?" she asked.

Darna nodded. "I see smoke from the hills, campfire smoke. It could be Vigda or some of the villagers I once knew." She turned to Lerat. "Take me to that shore. It's time for me to claim my throne."

§

Darna landed on the shore of what had been Tiadun and followed the trails of smoke to her mother's moving hearthside. In the lowlands, she traced the dragon's dormant currents and built the shells of temples where those streams surfaced. The stones would call them back when they rose, and would call her hatchling home when it spread its wings. The beacons are there still, waiting.

Myril and Eppie passed through Calandria like a wisp, invisible in the city's vastness. Kinner joined them there and they journeyed to a desert temple far from the green valley of Anamat. There, the dragon's egg waits for a distant time, far beyond its homeland's final sunrise.

As for Thorat and Iola, no one knows, except that they were together at the end.

§

Author's Note

Writing this series has been an epic journey in itself, complete with delays and side-quests. Along the way, I've been helped along by teachers, critique partners, editors, beta readers, and other writing buddies who've become too numerous to list. In more than a decade of writing, I've built and explored an island world, a place you could walk the length of in a couple of weeks, with one principal city, inspired by a patchwork of real and imagined places. Its magic was fading, and now Theranis has slipped away into a long hibernation. This concludes the story of the dragons and their priestesses.

Today, I bid a long farewell to Anara and all the dragons that live in the chambered earth, not knowing where or whether we will meet again.

--Amelia Smith

www.ameliasmith.net